M.R. Forbes

BOUND

The Divine, Book Four

Published by Quirky Algorithms, Inc.
Seattle, WA

CHAPTER ONE

Landon

IT STARTED IN A WAY I could never have expected it to. It started with, of all things, an alarm clock.

To be more specific, it was a clock radio; one of those kinds with the big blue LEDs that plugged into the wall. What year was this anyway? The song was 'Man in the Box' by Alice in Chains. I felt like that should have meant something to me, but it didn't.

I kept my eyes closed. Something told me I shouldn't open them. Something in me made me afraid. Of what? The truth? That couldn't be right. It fled as soon as I heard the soft groan of contentment on my left.

"Landon, are you going to shut that thing up?"

I twisted my head in the direction of the voice and willed my eyelids to lift. I was greeted with a vision of beauty; long, silken black hair framing a heart-shaped face. Violet eyes still half-closed, looking at me, filled with a gentle mirth. A perfect, white smile behind soft, full lips.

"Yeah," I said, returning her smile. I bent back the other way and hunted for the snooze button with my hand, smacking it down at random in the general vicinity of the sound. It took me a few tries, but I turned it off.

I blinked a few times, and tried to remember whatever it was that

I had been feeling only a few moments before. It was like that was real and this was the dream, but I knew that couldn't be true.

"Are you okay?" she asked me. She sat up, holding the sheets to her chest more out of habit than modesty, and ran her fingers through my hair.

"You don't feel... I don't know... strange?" I asked her. "Like you're dreaming?"

"I always feel like I'm dreaming lately." She leaned over and kissed my cheek. "Snap out of it, love. We have a plane to catch."

She threw the covers off of her and onto me, hiding my view of her perfection beneath the down. Normally, I would have rushed to get the blankets off so I could catch one last glimpse before she vanished into the bathroom. Today, I hesitated. Why did everything feel so wrong?

I heard the usual morning sounds; using the bathroom, brushing the teeth. Then the tinkle of the shower. It was the sound of the falling water that broke me from the trance. I threw the covers aside and slipped out of bed, taking only a few seconds to stare out the window at the crystal blue ocean outside. A white sand beach preceded it, empty but for a few gulls standing lookout.

Tahiti, I remembered. We were in Tahiti. We had come for vacation, two weeks of bliss away from the day-to-day. Some time to be alone, to reconnect and recharge. Time for just the two of us.

"Landon, are you coming?" she asked.

I stopped looking at the beach and at the blue ocean beyond. As I turned to head towards the bathroom, I could swear one of the gulls was looking at me.

It was a stupid thought. I laughed at myself and entered the bathroom, emptying my bladder before joining my wife in the double-stalled shower. Not that we used half of it anyway, but it had come with the hut. As usual, I caught my breath on the sight of her.

"Anxious to go home?" she asked, leaning in and kissing me.

"Good morning."

I didn't know. For an instant, I forgot where home was and that there was anything waiting for me there that would have made it worth going back to. My hesitation drew attention.

"You aren't okay, are you? What's up?"

I tried to sputter out something, anything. I shook my head and shrugged. "Just a dream," I said. "The strangest dream. I guess I'm not awake yet."

She took my shower puff, squeezed some soap out onto it, lathered it up, and threw a perfect beanball. It made a solid squishing noise when it smacked into my forehead. Eyes closed in defense, I caught the puff on the way down.

"Wake up," she said, laughing.

I laughed with her and tried to get myself together.

Excited. I should be excited. We'd spent the last two weeks alone, which meant two weeks without Clara. She could be a handful sometimes, but what would anyone expect from a six year-old? She was also a ball of loving energy, and the second most important woman in my life. Two weeks without her had been relaxing, but Charis was right. I was anxious to go home.

"Yeah," I said. "Not as anxious as you are, I bet."

"You know I love you, but part of me has missed her since we got here."

I couldn't, and didn't blame her. "It's been a lot of fun though," I said.

She looked me in the eyes, a sly smile on her face. "It's been ten years since our honeymoon. I think we earned it. Now hurry up."

Ten years, and yet she didn't look a day older to me. We finished the shower and I stepped out onto the marble floor and caught a peep of myself in the mirror. I looked pretty good, too.

"What time is the flight?" I asked, heading into the bedroom to grab my clothes.

"Twelve-thirty. We have half an hour to get dressed and check out. The cab should be on its way."

I nodded even though she couldn't see it, and pulled open the top drawer to the dresser. One outfit for each of us rested there. A pair of underwear, socks, designer jeans and a dark blue polo shirt for me. A white sun-dress for her.

"You're going to freeze when we get back to New York," I said. I had already questioned her choice of return dress a few times, so I was sure I was going to hear it.

"Shut up," she replied. "I'm a big girl. Between the airport, the car, and the apartment, we're only going to be outside for a few minutes anyway. Besides, it isn't that cold in October."

I smiled and slipped on my clothes, and then went back to the window to get one more good look at the ocean before Charis finished drying her hair and dressing. The gulls were still standing along the sand, though a pair had found something to fight over. They squawked and chased one another, leaving an empty gap for a third bird to swoop in and steal the prize. I couldn't see what it was, but did it matter anyway?

"Do you think Clara had fun with your mom?" Charis asked, stepping up behind and wrapping her arms around me. I took them from the front and held them to my chest.

"I'm sure she's had loads of fun," I replied. My mother had been difficult for me to deal with as a son. She was a doting grandparent.

She pulled her arms away and went over to the dresser to grab her clothes. I didn't take my eyes off the beach. There was something about the waves that was hypnotizing. The way they lapped in at the shore, the last remnants running up the sand and forcing some of the gulls to either get their feet wet or step out of the way. Peering further out, the water looked strange - as if it were moving backwards. I blinked a few times and was going to point it out to Charis when a gull swooped down and landed on the sill right in front of me, squawking loudly and looking up with red eyes.

"What the…" I stumbled backwards, and the bird made a noise, almost like laughter, and took off again, vanishing into the sky.

"It's just a bird," Charis said, laughing. "You've never been afraid of birds before."

"Did you see its eyes?" I asked.

"No."

There was something about those eyes. Bird eyes were black, not red. Part of me knew there was a reason for it, but it was an idea I couldn't catch onto.

She finished dressing and we grabbed our bags and headed out of the hut, along a paved walkway to the hotel. It was all open-air, with a simple thatch roof to keep the rain off and plenty of ceiling fans to cool the visitors. An attendant greeted us there. He took our bags and brought them around front where the taxi would pick us up while we checked out at the front desk.

By the time we were done paying the cab had arrived and the attendant had loaded our two suitcases into the trunk. We didn't say much, and he didn't say much, because the language barrier was too thick. He smiled and bobbed his head when I handed him some cash. That was a universal language.

A forty minute drive to the small airport, another two hours to sit together while we waited for our flight - a sixteen hour red-eye that would see Clara in our arms sometime tomorrow afternoon. We passed the time playing games on our tablet and looking at the photos we had taken. We would both have fun telling Clara all about our adventures.

The plane ride was uneventful. We flew through a couple of heavy thunderstorms that bounced us around a bit, but I had zero fear of flying and the turbulence was more like an amusement park ride. Charis got a little nauseous, but she held it together pretty well, even finding a few hours of sleep between the chaos and the calm. Still, when we finally touched down in JFK, she was ready to kiss the dirt.

I called my mother the moment the pilot said it was safe to do so. Clara picked up.

"Hello," she said, in her little chipmunk voice.

"Hello," I said, making my voice deeper and more raspy.

She laughed, not falling for it. "Daddy!" the shout hurt my ear, in the best way possible. "Are you coming to Nana's?"

"Of course, sweetie. We're at the airport. We'll be there before you can blink."

"I blinked," she said. "You're not here."

I chuckled and gave Charis the phone. There had been no service on the resort in Tahiti, so she hadn't heard Clara's voice since we'd taken off in the opposite direction. She had tears in her eyes while she talked to her.

They let us off and we were surprised to find a limo waiting to pick us up, courtesy of Nana. I expected her to dote on Clara. Treating us to something was a surprise.

My mother lived in Harlem, in a fairly decent mid-rise where crime was lower than average, and the schools were pretty good. We'd moved there right before puberty, and it was there that I had started the life of electronic crime that had brought Charis and I together, an act of carelessness that I still considered the best mistake I had ever made. I took her hand and squeezed it, thinking about the day we had met at the Museum of Natural History, when she had come to lay eyes on the chalices I had been assigned to watch over. She had been amazing then, and she was amazing now.

"I know what you're thinking," she said. The inside of the car was nearly silent, outside of the messages pouring through the radio to the driver up front.

I smiled and looked at her. "You do?"

"You always get all sappy when we visit your mom. I've never seen anyone else so happy to have been incarcerated."

Of course, it hadn't made things easy for us. I couldn't get a job in anything that remotely touched computers, which had left my greatest asset wallowing. Instead, we survived on the salary of a Senior Security Officer for Macy's. The pay wasn't that bad, but we liked living in the hustle and bustle of the city.

"I wouldn't have met you otherwise," I replied.

She laughed. "Yup. Sappy."

The car glided to a stop outside of the apartment and we exited while the kids outside stared at us, mouths hanging open. They hadn't seen too many limos in their neighborhood and the fact that it didn't drop us off and leave made it an even bigger spectacle.

We took the stairs up to the sixth floor. My mom lived in apartment sixty-six. 'Route Sixty-six' she always called it. She'd gone as far as to decorate with lots of relevant Americana - road signs, license plates, photos of the Grand Canyon, that kind of stuff. My mom was a little wacky.

"Anybody home," I called out, raising my voice a few octaves. I rapped on the door and we waited, expecting to hear the pounding of small footsteps racing to greet us.

Silence.

"Hello," I said, knocking again. "Mom?"

More silence.

I turned to Charis, the worry on her face sure to be echoing my own. I had left my key to her place in our bags. "I'll go get the key," I said. I felt my heart beginning to race. "Keep knocking."

"Mom, it's Charis," she shouted while knocking, the desperation leaking into her voice. "Are you okay in there?"

I ran down the steps and out to the car where the driver was waiting. He had his head down, looking at his hands. He was holding my keys in them.

"How did you-" I started to ask, but then he lifted his head. A faint spark of recognition passed through my anxious mind and it tried to put him in a specific place, at a specific time.

"Nobody is going to answer, kid," he said. The corner of his mouth curled into a grin, or a snarl. It could have been either.

"What do you mean?" My heart started racing faster, and my mind churned like a hurricane, trying to figure out how I knew this guy.

He tossed me the keys. "Go on up. See for yourself."

I stood there and stared at him for a few seconds, trying in vain to make the connection, and then I turned and sprinted into the building and up the stairs. I was out of breath by the time I reached the sixth floor.

Charis was gone.

The door was open.

"Charis," I said, rushing ahead.

As I neared the apartment a smell caught me and raised my concern to full-blown panic. I nearly tripped trying to make the turn into the the doorway.

I slipped on the blood.

I fell backwards onto my rear, my brain trying to process the grisly scene in front of me and failing. I tried to cry, to express the sudden, intense pain that lurched into my soul, but nothing came. Instead, I vomited into the dark red mess below me.

Somewhere in my mind, in some small piece that was still able to function in the face of grotesque catastrophe, I finally figured out where I knew that face, that smile from. In near perfect sync, a thick laugh rose through the atmosphere, pummeling me with its familiarity.

The dream. Forgotten no more.

I almost had enough time to scream when he grabbed me from behind and tugged me over to a nearby window.

"This is just the start, kid," he said through clenched teeth. "I have an eternity to make you feel every kind of pain I can imagine. Being a god, I can imagine quite a lot."

The Beast, I realized, as I felt my body lurch forward and then crash through the window. I watched the ground rising up to meet me, and everything began flooding back.

This was for you, Sarah, and for all the rest of creation.

I hope it was worth it.

CHAPTER TWO

Rebecca

IT STARTED IN JAPAN.

IT had taken me almost two months to get here, no longer able to tag-along with Landon and his friends through demonic transport rifts or on the wings of angels. It had taken a number of bodies, three dozen or more, each scared when I took their consciousness from them, and confused when I released it again. I was getting good at being a spirit, but to be honest, I didn't care for it. Whatever benefits came from being able to slip from shell to shell were lost in the flood of memories I was forced to endure whenever I claimed a new form.

I just wanted to be me. As me as I could be, in this state.

I just wanted to be Rebecca.

Not Reyka, and certainly not Solen. Just Rebecca, the once-upon-a-time child of a vampire and a succubus, who thought she knew the path to true power and with it true happiness. Rebecca, who had needed one of God's own swords to pull the curtains of darkness aside and teach her the real meaning of happiness.

It hadn't been easy getting here. After they had trapped the Beast, I had used the body I had taken - the one that had thrown aside the fiend Izak and saved everything, but had been forgotten in the shock of the aftermath - to try to catch up to Sarah and the

Were. It was a futile effort. So many people, suddenly having their consciousness returned. So many others, already dead, their bodies tumbling to the earth as soon as the Beast's power fled them. In the mortal body, I couldn't make them move away from me. I couldn't make them forget I was there.

I considered abandoning the body to follow, but as a spirit I was slow unless I had something to hold onto, a purpose that propelled me forward. Landon was gone, and while the purpose remained, I had lost my beacon.

So I stayed. I tried to get through the armies of terrified humanity, but it was a waste of energy. The Beast had left Mumbai a ruin, the psyche of the people destroyed as only he could manage. It would take years to fix this place, if anything ever could. I wondered how the news would report it. An earthquake. That was my bet. There was enough rubble to justify the excuse, enough fire and destruction and death. Nobody would ever know what had really happened. The dead would stay dead. The Sleeping would continue to sleep.

Two months, but at least I was finally here. I'd been wrong about the earthquake. They'd called it an outbreak of some made up disease and quarantined *everything*. Nobody in or out. A wall of military kept it that way. I had to abandon my shell then and make my way through the vast expanse of space, little more than the thought of him trapped in there with the Beast to keep me going. I'd never believed in anything beyond myself before, but now I saw God's hand arch across the all of everything. He'd saved me from that dark demise. He put me on the path to salvation.

I just had to walk it.

I hailed a cab outside the airport, still a little awkward in the body of a short, round, Korean businessman with an odd taste for animated pornography. I preferred women because they were more familiar; a better fit, and less jarring to re-live the lives of. I would have chosen a woman, but I was afraid it would make me easier to spot. It was one thing to wander humanity as a ghost. It was another to walk right up to the Nicht Creidim.

I had no idea if they had an artifact that would allow them to see through the shell to the soul behind the wheel. There was no way to be sure they didn't have something that could destroy me for good. I had taken Elyse by surprise, right before she had opened the door to let Landon in. Her possession had felt different from the others, like she had the ability to resist, but didn't. As though she were allowing me to control her rather than being subjugated by my power.

She was strong, that one. I knew that's why I wanted her back. Between her strength and her access to the Nicht Creidim's collection of relics, she was the only mortal on Earth who could survive through what I knew would come next.

What was that, exactly? I'd spent more than enough time trying to answer that question. The top layer was simple enough: find a way to get Landon out of the Box without allowing the Beast to escape with him. Or, find a way to destroy the Beast while he was still inside the Box. I knew he had gone in with another, Charis. I knew he loved her, and would want her to be saved too. I would try for his sake, but she wasn't my goal, he was.

How to do either of those things? I didn't know. I didn't even know where to start. I had seen Landon in Egypt. I had seen him vanish, and I had seen when he returned that he had been given something, a bracelet. Maybe whoever had given it to him could help?

First, I needed a shell. A permanent, mortal shell that could fight the Divine and make it through. That was why I had come to Japan. That was why I wanted Elyse. One step at a time.

The cab dropped me off near the front of the dock. Most mortals didn't know about the Nicht Creidim, or if they did they called them by other names that were incorrect, but close enough. This driver knew what awaited at the other end of the pier. He didn't want any part of it.

"Good luck to you, sir," he said. He was speaking Japanese, but fortunately so did my host. I had the part of his mind that allowed me to do the translation.

"Keep the change," I said, handing him a large bill from the man's wallet. Of course he would have Japanese currency, he was headed here before I took him over.

I shoved the body over across the back seat of the cab, and grabbed the handle with meaty fingers. A soft shove, the door swung open, and I waddled out. The driver didn't waste much time getting out of there, making a tight three point turn and revving away. I stood at the mouth of the dragon and stared down its throat.

I took a deep breath and starting walking forward, retracing the steps that Landon had taken when he'd come for the sword. The Deliverer, sister to the Redeemer, which had pierced my heart and made me whole. Staring ahead into the deepening twilight with mortal eyes, I felt a weakness and vulnerability that I could barely describe. Did humans feel like this all the time? I wondered that often.

The smallest splash behind me alerted me to an attacker. Before, I would have heard or smelled him from a dozen yards out or more. Now, I had just enough time to squat beneath his attempted grapple, and then sweep his legs out with an awkward twist. The motion took him off his feet, but it also brought me off mine.

"Christ!" I shifted, trying to bring the weight under control and put myself back to my feet. I flopped onto my side and shoved with a pudgy arm, feeling the muscles complain. I had only gotten halfway up when a sneaker planted itself in my gut.

"Stay down," he said.

I stumbled to my hands and knees, lifting my head to get a look at him. A younger man, with a ring in his nose and a tattoo on the side of his face. He had short, spiked hair and big ears. "Take what you want," I said, staying still. He was a few yards away. I wanted him to come closer.

"I don't want your money," he replied.

"What do you want?"

He smiled, his teeth extending into sharp points. A vampire. It figured.

"Your blood," he said.

If he were human, I could have just dumped the Korean and taken him. He would have been a better ride. He wasn't, so I couldn't. Jettisoning the body and floating in the aether wasn't an appealing thought just yet.

He started walking towards me, but he looked confused. "This is the part where you're supposed to be afraid," he said.

"This is the part where you're going to be afraid," a voice said from somewhere in the darkness.

The vampire and I both turned our heads, seeking it out. She jumped down from the warehouse next to us, landing softly despite the twenty foot drop. Elyse.

"You're a fool to come around here," she said.

I didn't know if she was talking to me, or to him. Probably him. I waited.

"Who are you?" he asked. He did look a little bit afraid.

"I'm security." She started walking towards us. She was decked out in black, her head covered by a scarf so that only her eyes were visible. They turned my way for only a moment, but I got the feeling she knew who I was.

The vampire's grin widened. "You're hot, so I'm not going to kill you," he said. "I'm going to make you my bitch."

He really had no idea who he was dealing with. I didn't understand how that could be? Even if his family didn't know this was Nicht Creidim territory, they would have known to stay away.

Elyse didn't answer. She pulled an ornate dagger from her hip and threw it at him. He didn't even move, his eyes following the trajectory of the missile while it planted itself in his stomach. I expected the wound to begin steaming immediately, but it didn't. Blood began running out like a river and he screamed from the pain.

"Please," he screamed. "Please help me." He looked down at the dagger in disbelief, and then dropped to his knees. What kind of vampire was this?

Elyse finished her approach, took hold of the dagger, and pulled it from his gut. Intestines trailed behind it and he fell over onto his stomach, dead. He didn't turn to ash.

"What?" The word escaped me without thought.

Elyse knelt and wiped the blade off on his back, and then turned to me.

"Rebecca," she said. "I'm glad you've come. We need to talk."

I stayed on my hands and knees, looking at her. I didn't know what to say.

"How did you know it was me?" I asked at last.

She lifted her scarf back from her head, revealing a bald scalp, her forehead carrying a fork-shaped scar that had been inlaid with gold. A small amount of blood still oozed from the wound around it.

"The secret to seeing spirits," she said. "You aren't the only one."

I stared at it, my eyes wide. "Where did you learn that?"

"As you know, we have quite a collection of ancient scrolls. If Landon had known how many, I'm sure I would have met him sooner." She held out her hand, and helped me to my feet. "If you were trying to look inconspicuous, you failed. If you were trying to look helpless, you succeeded."

I pointed at the body of the vampire. "I don't understand that."

She looked back at him and sighed. "The world is changing, Rebecca. I don't think in a good way. He's the second I've put down this week."

"Shouldn't vampires know to stay away from here?"

"The vampires do. He isn't a vampire. Not a true blood-drinker, anyway."

I was more confused. "I don't understand."

"Come," she said, taking my hand. "I'll tell you everything I know. I think perhaps we can help one another."

CHAPTER THREE

Rebecca

SHE BROUGHT ME INTO THE warehouse, down into the hardened subterranean estate where she lived. The others looked at me curiously, wondering what she was doing with a mortal in tow, but they knew well enough not to question Joe's daughter.

She led me to her apartment, an open space with a huge fish tank ringing the outer walls. She made us some tea, and we sat on a soft mat in the center of the floor, sipping chamomile while we talked.

"You were going to tell me what's going on," I said, lifting the porcelain cup to my shell's mouth. The fingers barely managed to get a passable grip on the handle, and I nearly poured the drink into my lap. "Vampires that aren't vampires."

She took a delicate sip from her own cup, and then put it down next to her. "Yes. It started about two months ago. The same time as the so-called outbreak in Mumbai that made people start killing one another."

"It was the Beast."

She nodded. "I wasn't sure, but I suspected. As did father. His exact words were, 'I wonder if we'll ever see the Deliverer again'. He can be a little… single-tracked… at times. The riots ended. At first I believed Landon had defeated him, but then we started hearing rumors."

I had been single-tracked myself. All of my energy had been poured into arriving here. "Rumors?"

"That the diuscrucis were gone. Both of them. That there was a new Demon Queen, who also happened to be the daughter of Baal himself. That the Parisian archfiend was back in play, more powerful than he had ever been before, and with the demon Izak under his heel. That Hell was back on top, and defeat was inevitable without Landon to put things right." She caught my eyes in hers, and held them in a steel gaze. "That they had broken the world."

So much power had been funneled into the Box. A universe of energy in a Rubik's Cube. Had our universe not been able to withstand it? "Landon trapped the Beast inside Avriel's Box. He had to join him there to keep him contained."

"You want to free him," Elyse said.

I couldn't hide it from her. She had seen into me, when I had taken her. I don't know how, but she had. "Yes."

"So do I."

I didn't understand. "Why? Why do you care about him?"

She laughed. "I don't care about him. I care about us. Humanity. The world is broken."

"You keep saying that. I don't know what you mean."

She picked up her cup, and took another soft sip of the tea. "That... thing... I just killed. Where do you think it came from?"

"I would have said the same place all vampires come from, but you've already said he wasn't one."

She shrugged. "Technically, he was, I suppose. He wasn't always. He changed."

"What do you mean, changed? As in, from human to vampire?"

"Yes. It isn't just vampires. People are changing into other things too. Some of them, I don't know what they are. I've never seen it before."

I still didn't believe it. "You're telling me that humans are turning into demons?"

"Yes and no. They're taking on the characteristics of the Divine, we think according to their genetics, though there may be some other factors that we haven't considered yet. For the most part they're still human, but they have power. Divine power."

"I would think you'd be in favor," I said. "The whole goal of the Nicht Creidim is to use Divine power against them."

"To save humanity. Not to have it become the very thing we fight. These people are abominations. To kill them is to free them."

"So, that's why you're glad I came? Because you think Landon can stop this somehow?"

"I know how you feel about him. When you took over my body, I could feel it too. A strange devotion. I knew from the rumors he had gone missing, which meant you would be searching for a way to help him. You understand some of the things our family has collected, and in your current state, it made sense that you would seek me out again. I'd seen the writings about spirits, and so I made an Eye of Third Sight and waited for you.

"The changelings started appearing soon after the Beast was trapped inside the Box. We think there's too much power concentrated into too little space, and it's having massive side effects on our world. We need to release the energy."

"If you release Landon, you release the Beast," I said.

""Of course, which is why we can't just take the Box and open it up. Releasing the Beast would be worse than dealing with changelings, which is why I was waiting for you."

"What do you need me to do?"

"Sarah."

I almost choked on my laughter. "Sarah hates me," I said. "How in the world can I help you with her?"

"I don't need you to make friends with her", Elyse replied. "I need you to get through her. I can't get near her, you know. All of the things we've collected, and we have nothing to protect us.

There aren't supposed to be any true diuscrucis, so neither side has created anything to fight them. I may have the genetics to make me resistant to the Divine, but as you are aware, I'm not impervious."

"I was never sure if I took you by force, or by invitation," I said.

She smiled, but didn't offer me a clue. "She can Command me, if she sees me as a threat. These days, she sees everything as a threat, but I don't blame her for that. Both sides are after the Box, because they believe they are best suited to protect it. The fact is that they would prefer if Landon remains in there with the Beast for all of eternity."

"What about the Nicht Creidim?"

She took another sip of tea, finishing the small cup and placing it off to the side of the mat. "Joe wants the Box. He believes he can use the power to destroy all of the Divine. An ethereal EMP. Considering the energy he could unleash, I think he can do it. He doesn't realize that it will be more like a nuclear blast than a magnetic pulse. The power will go everywhere, and expose us even more. He'll destroy the Divine, only to turn us into them."

I was beginning to understand my place on the board. I was the Queen to Landon's King, able to traverse the field while he was pinned down. Sarah couldn't Command me, because I had been transformed. God still held dominion over all things, and He had put me on this mission, I knew. He wanted me to save him.

"Okay. Let's say I agree, and we work together to find Sarah. Let's say we get close to her. Then what?"

"Simple. We steal the Box."

I wasn't expecting that. "Steal it? Why? Sarah has more reason to want to free Landon than anyone. We should work with her."

Elyse laughed. "Does she? How do you know? She is a true diuscrucis. Her ultimate loyalty will be to herself. Think of what she can do, if she finds a way to harness the power of the Box to her own ends. Power that no one can have without tearing the world apart, even if by accident. No, we need to take the Box."

"And bring it where?"

"Wherever the Beast came from in the first place."

I closed my eyes, catching the memories. I had followed his instructions to bring Sarah through the rift. A special rift that was the only link between this world and the one he had been trapped in. You didn't go to it, you called it and it came to collect you. "I can't open the rift anymore, and even if I could, it's a one-way trip."

"Not so. The archfiend Gervais has created a permanent connection to the Beast's original prison. He's been seeking a means to steal the power that remains there in hopes that it will lead him to a method of taking what is trapped in the Box itself. He doesn't just want to be the minion of a god. He wants to be a god."

Gervais. He had been granted a gift of power from the Beast, which was the only reason he was still standing. Of course, like any good demon he had been given a taste, and now he wanted it all.

"I can't get past Gervais, especially now that he has Izak back under his control. Besides, you didn't say anything about how this is going to help Landon? Even if you could put the power of the Box back into the Beast's prison, Landon will still be trapped with him."

"Do you take me for a fool, Rebecca? All the information I've shared with you has come from a single source. One who has proven their reliability, and whose goals are similar to ours. He's given me assurances that there is a way to free the object of your infatuation, and to remove the Beast's power from play."

There was silence for a few minutes, while I considered her words. Assurances? There were no assurances among demons, not in anything. Still, I had been guided to this place by something so much bigger than me. How could I have been brought back, only to be led astray?

"Fine. What's your offer?"

Elyse smiled. Was I making a mistake even considering this? "A partnership. You get to use my body to help save the diuscrucis. I get to return the power of the Beast to where it belongs and make things right again. We both get to stop Joe from polluting the world with creatures that shouldn't be, and Gervais from claiming power that isn't his."

Stopping Joe was one thing. Gervais was a different monster altogether. One that came with an equally powerful slave. "Do you have a plan to defeat the archfiend?"

"Not defeat, no. A different plan."

CHAPTER FOUR

Landon

"Do you see him?" Charis asked.

We were hunkered down behind an ambulance, peering around the corner in search of the gunman that had opened fire on us.

"No. Maybe he gave up?" I stuck my head out a little more, and a bullet bounced off the hood of the van, nearly ricocheting into my face. I ducked my head back in. "Wishful thinking."

The Beast. I knew it was him, though it had taken a little while to realize. It seemed as if every time we played this game the memories returned faster. That I knew who I really was, and Charis knew who she really was.

Not that it had helped.

Our power had been his power, and when we poured it all into the Box, we had lost control of it. He was the closest thing to a god here, for real. We were little more than mortals. The only difference was that we couldn't die, not permanently anyway. He could catch us, have his way with us, destroy us in infinite ways, and we'd always come back.

There was no way to measure time here. No way to know how long it had been going on. The one thing we'd learned - maybe the only thing we'd learned - was that the longer we stayed alive, the more we remembered. It would take a lot to convince me that was a good thing.

"We should just let him hit us, and get on with it," I said. I didn't really favor the thought of recalling the other countless deaths we had suffered at his hands. Calculated, measured deaths. He was building up the pain the way any good torturer would. The only consolation I could find was that he would run out of ways to slaughter us once a few thousand years had gone by. At least, I hoped he would.

"Come on," Charis said. She grabbed my hand and pulled me away, towards a dark alley.

I tugged against her. "We did that last time," I said. The memory came back to me, and I shivered. He had eviscerated Charis, and splattered me in her blood before decapitating me. I looked around the street, and led her to the next parked car, bullets pinging off the sidewalk behind us.

My mind went back to Avriel, the archangel who had spent thousands of years in this place with the demon Abaddon. Time had no real meaning here, but the pain and the memories were real enough to make it meaningful. I could only imagine what he had endured, both while he was in the Box, and after he had been released. All of that torture and suffering, and not only had I extended it for him, but once he was finally freed, I had gotten him killed.

Of course, Avriel had power of his own. He had said they battled, the demon and him. He hadn't always lost. We weren't so lucky.

"Where to?" she asked. We stayed crouched behind an old Camaro, and I searched the buildings across the street for his position.

"It doesn't matter," I said. "He's going to come for us soon."

"What do you mean?"

She hadn't seen it yet, which surprised me. "How much do you remember?" I asked.

Tears sprung to her eyes in an instant. "Don't ask me that," she said.

I didn't blame her reaction. "Each time, I remember a little more. Each time, he lets us live just a fraction longer. He wants us to remember. He wants us to relive the pain, over and over again. I remember the last time. It will be over soon."

She laughed. A heavy, defeated laugh. "Over? This is never going to be over. You and I both know that. He'll kill us, and we'll start again."

I peeked out at the buildings across from us again. The longer we lived, the fewer times he could end us. It wasn't much, but at least it would hurt less.

"Dante will find a way to get us out," I said, trying to convince both of us. "Sarah won't give up either."

"Sarah? Don't try to make me feel better by pinning our hopes on her. You know what she is, and what will happen."

I grabbed her arm and pulled her down two more cars, oblivious to the bullets. "It doesn't have to be that way. She held up when Josette died. She kept it together when Gervais took Izak. She saved everything."

Charis turned me around so she could look me in the eye. "I'm not saying she didn't do a good job, but that was then. This is now. Who's going to keep her grounded? I don't have much faith in her being on her own. I'm sorry, love, but that's the truth."

A glint of steel was the only warning. I threw Charis to the side, getting her away from the sword that sliced down towards her head. It wasn't Ross, but one of his creations, a grotesque clone of Charis, with a twisted and mangled face, covered in bleeding sores. She hissed when the blow came up empty, and jumped at me.

I was only mortal here, but I still knew how to fight. I sidestepped her punch, grabbed her arm, and brought a knee up into her stomach. I smelled the fetid stench of the air bursting from her lungs, and nearly paused to vomit. Instead, I twisted the arm until it snapped, and shoved her so she was between me and the car. I heard the gunfire, and the body shook while it caught the bullets that had been fired at me. I found Charis on her knees, and pointed to a storefront. We inched towards it, using the creature as a shield.

It had to be time, I knew. He would be here any second, the pissed-off smile on his face, his anger at being stuck here unable to be contained. He would kill us again, after some kind of torture. He liked to kill Charis first, to make me watch her die. Sometimes he would add my mother, or a child for the two of us. That had been his first effort, and little did he know, it had been the most painful.

We reached the store, and Charis opened the door and held it for me. Once we were in I dropped the corpse and we scrambled deep enough inside so that the shooter couldn't get an angle. We would have a few seconds of quiet.

"There has to be something we can do," Charis said. "How can our power hold him, contain him, if we don't have any?"

That was a new idea. One we hadn't had before. Was the Beast making a mistake by letting us live for longer periods, or was it intentional?

"Hold that thought," I said, as if that could bring it to us sooner.

"Good morning, children," the Beast said. He appeared from nowhere in his pinstriped suit and sunglasses, wearing his crap-eating grin and holding his pocket watch. "I'm sorry I'm late. Honestly, I thought my Charis would get you, or at least slow you down. Either you're getting more resourceful, or I'm getting lax."

"Go to hell," Charis said, spitting on him.

He was deliberate, reaching into a pocket and pulling out a monogramed handkerchief to wipe the spittle away. "I tried to go to Hell. You stuck me in here instead." He lifted a hand and clenched his fingers together while twisting his wrist.

I heard her spine break.

Charis cried out in pain, and fell to the ground, paralyzed.

The Beast looked at me, the anger obvious. "You and your bitches." He drew a line in the air, and her skin spread apart down her arms. She screamed louder, but kept her eyes on him, defiant.

"You can kill us as often as you want," I said. "You aren't getting out of here."

He laughed. I hated it. "You've said that four times now, and you still don't remember my answer."

I tried to remember that part. "Why don't you tell me again?"

He opened up more cuts on Charis' body, leaving her panting, with tears in her eyes. She refused to look away from him, fighting the pain with her own anger.

"Do you really think I didn't make arrangements, kid? As small as your odds of getting me in here were, I'm not stupid enough to chance getting stuck forever. I know how to get out of here. It'll take me some time, but I have plenty to keep me entertained."

He laughed again, while I tried to think through what he had just said. The words were familiar, and now I remembered that he had said them before.

"Ah, now it comes back to you," he said. He looked over at Charis, writhing on the ground, a pool of blood below her, and then he looked at his watch. "I'm afraid I'll have to cut this short."

He turned his wrist again, and her stomach erupted in a geyser of blood and guts. I tried to close my eyes, but he didn't let me.

"Oh no, kid. You're going to watch. Every time. I hope it hurts."

It did. Every time. I would have thought the repetition would make me numb, but it only made it worse. It was hard enough to watch someone you loved die once. Try doing it again and again, stuck in a twisted Groundhog Day.

I felt a small sense of relief that she was out of it for another round. "How are you going to do it?" I asked.

"Do what?"

"Get out of here. How can you do it? I think you're lying." I remembered now. He'd told me he was confident he would get out. He may have even told me how.

He smiled. "I'm not going to tell you this time. You're getting the hang of this a little too easily."

He broke my neck.

CHAPTER FIVE

Rebecca

"ARE YOU READY?" I ASKED.

We were still in her apartment, but we had cleared the tea set, and now we sat on our knees facing one another. She looked comfortable in the position, but my shell's body was straining from the weight pressed down on it.

"I'm ready," she replied.

We had spent another hour going over ground rules. The most important one was that she needed to lead the way through the warehouse. She had some things she thought might come in handy, so the so-called 'armory' was going to be our first stop. Of course, there were things in there that even she wasn't technically allowed to take, so it was going to be a fun exercise getting out with the stuff. It didn't help that Joe was already ticked at her for suggesting his plan was foolish. She was certain that if she were caught going rogue, her father wouldn't have too many qualms about either killing her, or imprisoning her. Fighting the Divine meant having the steel will needed to make those kinds of sacrifices.

I closed my shell's eyes and took a deep breath, nervous and unconvinced that Elyse was dealing from a straight deck. There was no better choice though, so I detached myself from him. As always, it was an experience with a measure of pain attached;

every part of my soul catching fire at once for just an instant. I felt my complexities fall away from me, and my motivation reduced to only a single directive. Help Landon.

Elyse was still, the Eye of Third Sight glimmering on her forehead. She was looking at me.

"Amazing," she said. "I haven't seen one outside of a body." She reached her hand up towards me. "Do you feel that?"

I didn't feel anything. Was she touching me? I floated in her direction, a gossamer thread on a puff of air, drawing closer and closer. Her eyes followed me, until I was under her nose, and flowing down her mouth.

I could have taken her then. I could have settled my soul over hers, and gained her body and mind, but I didn't. For this first part, she needed to be the driver. Instead, I settled for tapping into her, so I could at least see what she saw. I don't really know how I did it, or how I knew to do it. In that state it was more instinct than understanding.

The Korean was still kneeling in front of her, and his eyes began to flutter as he regained himself. I felt Elyse moving. She got to her feet and went over to a wall with a pair of katana mounted to it. She lifted one from the rack, eased it from its scabbard, and returned to the man. She knelt down in front of him, positioning the sword angled up from the ground. Before he could open his eyes, she reached out and pulled him onto it, impaling him through the heart. He died without a sound.

"He was impure."

That was all she said. She didn't have to explain to me, or make an excuse. He was a means to a more important end; his death was a trifle compared to our needs. On the other hand, was she suggesting that I had made him impure by controlling him? Didn't that make her impure? Would she commit seppuku once our work was done, or was she as hypocritical as I had found most humans to be?

She took the body and lifted it, showing a surprising amount of strength in her lithe frame. She held him over her shoulder, careful to keep his blood from getting onto her clothes, and carried him into her bedroom. It was an interesting place, with a foam mattress on the floor and random artwork covering nearly every inch of the walls that the fish tank didn't occupy; a menagerie of artistic renditions of the naked form, in every style and medium I could think of.

The north wall had a fireplace, and it was there that she dropped the body with a slight grunt. Only then did she remove the sword. "Less blood this way," she said, talking me through her actions.

"The artwork," I said. I had never spoken to my host before. It felt strange, the words more of a vibration than sound.

"The human body is an amazing thing. Look around at these works, and consider the years of observation it took to create such masterpieces. The study of every muscle, every movement." She pointed at one that was little more than a few thick brush strokes on a white canvas. Still, it was undeniably human. "It is easy to explain something in a thousand strokes, but what about in three? I look at these, I study them, and I learn. My strengths and weaknesses, my successes and failures. It is very important to know yourself. The better you do, the more powerful you become."

"God created humans," I said. *"You want to destroy God."*

She laughed, and then walked back out into her living room. She opened a closet and reached up onto a shelf, bringing down a small wooden box. "God didn't create man," she said. "Not originally. The science makes that plain as day, for anyone who chooses not to be ignorant. No, God came here. He discovered us. He made the angels in *our* likeness. In their jealousy, they destroyed us. He punished those who did it, and gave us new life. That is the true story of creation. That is why He is the enemy."

I knew her words were untrue. I had been touched by Him, and I had felt His goodness. He had changed me, in every way my soul could be changed. *"That isn't how the Divine understand it to be,"* I said.

She opened the box, and took a small ruby from it. It was etched with demonic runes. "I wouldn't expect that your masters would want you to know the truth. That is why we fight, Rebecca. We are the rightful owners of this world, not you or your kind." She couldn't disguise her anger and hatred. "It doesn't matter now. We need to stop the poison first, and then we can move on."

"I didn't ask to be what I am," I said. I don't know why, but I felt like I needed to defend myself.

"Few enough of us ask to be what we are. That doesn't change it. Your guilt lies in your progenitors."

She took the stone and brought it back into the bedroom. She held the crystal, rubbed it between her thumb and forefinger so that the runes began to glow, and then threw it into the fire on top of the dead man. The crystal erupted in a geyser of hellfire that reduced the body to ash within the few seconds that it burned.

"Only the most powerful demons can control hellfire," she said. "But did you know that they make these for their loyal servants, to give them a taste of that power?"

She turned away from it and went out and over one doorway, into her bathroom. It was a massive room, with a large closet, a shower, and a jacuzzi. The fish tank wound its way through here as well. Small sharks combed the bottom of the tank, while a ray skated the top.

Elyse pulled off the ninja clothes she had been wearing. Passing a full-length mirror, I could see all of the kit she wore in rings and necklaces and hip chains that she kept hidden from sight. She was also covered in tattoos and scars, some that had been carved and filled like the Eye, others that were inked in demonic runes or seraphim scripture. Naked, I could almost feel the stolen power radiating from her.

"What does it all do?" I asked.

"Protection," she said. "I don't have anything of my own but the natural strength of my muscle, and the understanding of physics to turn my body into a weapon. Against a vampire, that is usually enough. Against an archfiend or a seraph, I wouldn't last a blink."

She grabbed a thong, a lacy bra, a pair of skinny jeans, a black cami, a leather jacket and calf-high black boots. She left the knife she had used on the vampire in the closet. "We've got better tools than that."

On her way out, she picked a pair of sunglasses from a nearby shelf, and wrapped a bandana around her bald head to hide the Eye. Passing the mirror again, I could see that nearly all of the tats, scars, and jewelry was hidden from view.

"You've done this before," I said.

"I'm Joe's favorite retriever," she replied.

We left the bathroom and her apartment, stepping out into the carpeted hallway and turning right. Elyse walked with confidence, her head up and her jaw out, challenging anyone who might happen by to question her activity. As we reached the corner of the hallway, Joe came around it, leaving her to spin out of his way, grab his arm, and pin it tight against his back before he could react.

"Ahh, nice move, darling," he said with a laugh. "I should have been more careful."

Elyse leaned up and kissed the back of his neck. "You should father. You never know what might be wandering these halls."

She let him go, and he turned around, looking at her with intense brown eyes. "In here? Not likely. The diuscrucis might have been able to pull it off, but they're gone. Why are you headed for the armory, anyway? Shouldn't you be in bed?"

She didn't hesitate. "There was another changeling outside, a vampire. I was going to get the stone and make sure the area was clear."

Joe waved his arm. "Don't worry about it. I'll tell Reza to have

Yu do a sweep before he comes in. Get some rest. I have a lead on that girl, Sarah, I want you to check out in the morning."

Elyse cocked her head. "Sarah? What kind of lead?" I could tell she was faking. She already knew something about it. But how much?

"I'll tell you in the morning, sweetheart. It can wait until then."

"Tell me now. Maybe I can do some research ahead of time. It will help me fall asleep."

Joe pursed his lips in consideration, and then shook his head. "I know you. You'll be up all night instead. I need you rested for this one. None of this stuff makes you impervious to fatigue."

I could feel her getting angry, her heart beating faster. "Father, I'll be fine. You know I don't need much rest."

He turned and started walking away. "In the morning. Good night, Elle."

"Stubborn pain in the ass," she said under her breath. "Good night, father."

She stood there seething until he had gone, and then made a beeline to the armory. It was around the corner and down a quiet hall, behind a huge steel door that required both fingerprint and retina scans for access. She stuck her finger in the hole and bent her face to the level of the eyeball scanner, and the door clanked and swung inward. She ducked inside and pushed it back closed.

When she turned around, all of the lights blinked on, revealing a long square room. It was sterile and barren, an empty room with a cold steel floor, ringed with hundreds of cabinets built into the walls. It looked more like a morgue than an armory.

"Do you know what you came for?" I asked.

She answered by walking to the back of the room, and reaching up to pull open a higher shelf. Inside was a Roman spatha. She lifted it from the black velvet pad it rested on and showed it to me.

"What is it made of?"

Both the hilt and the blade were the same dull, plain, matte black, though the hilt also had black leather wrapped around it for grip. Etched lines ran across the blade itself, a smooth rhythm of letters from opposing alphabets.

"I don't know," she said. "It is believed to have been forged from the ore of a meteorite, by a Roman blacksmith who then went on to gift it to Augustus Caesar. The runes and scripture were added later, when the blade was gifted by Tiberius Caesar to one of his greatest generals, who also happened to be Awake. He convinced an archfiend and a seraph to etch the blade, using another Divine artifact to glamour the weapon, and keep the truth of the work from being known to either side."

"*I take it he was a Nicht Creidim?*"

"Of course. This blade is one of our most prized possessions, for obvious reasons."

A sword that could kill both angels and demons. I could imagine how thankful Landon would be for a weapon like that.

She turned it over in her hand, showing me a dark stone that was resting in the pommel. She held the blade up and let her pinkie brush against it. Everything but the stone vanished. She put it in her pocket.

"*Where did it go?*"

"Heaven and Hell aren't the only places out there," Elyse said. "There are many places close to this one. There are many places to hide things. This particular bauble came from a djinn."

She put her hand up into the same shelf one more time. It was above her head, but she seemed to know exactly where everything was placed. She took down a brown leather glove that looked too big for her tiny hands. Stitching of demonic runes twisted and turned all around it. She slipped it on, and it looked as if it shrunk to fit her. "It can glamour anything it touches."

She made her way over to another drawer on the south wall, bending down to pull it open. It was filled with all kinds of throwing blades. There were two distinct rows, one for seraph and one for demons. She took a half dozen knives from each side, and tucked them into pockets sewn inside her boots.

Then she went to a third drawer and removed three more of the red crystals that had exploded into hellfire. "Father is going to be pissed at me for taking these," she said.

"*More pissed than for taking the sword?*"

She laughed. "Not a chance. Just one more thing to collect."

She made her way back to the front, and opened a shelf near the door.

"One of our newest additions. Landon destroyed most of them, so they are incredibly rare."

She reached into the back and lifted a silver chain. As it became taut, it pulled its attachment out and left it swaying in front of her. A crystal amulet filled with a red, viscous smoke. I had seen it before, when Merov had put it around my neck as a birthday present.

"*Why do you have this?*" I asked. The amulet was made for demons, not humans.

"It's an insurance policy. When a human breaks the crystal and drinks the blood, they're able to regenerate for a short time. A few hours. At least, that's what my brother Kelvin said. He's our top researcher."

"You haven't tried it?"

She put the chain over her head, and tucked the amulet below her cami. "Like I said, it's very rare. We can't go wasting it just to see if we're right. Kelvin has a lot of experience. I trust his opinion."

Seeing one of them again made me uneasy. It was a reminder of a different place, a different time, when I had betrayed Landon after he had been so kind to me, all in my lust for power.

Elyse checked her other gear one more time, making sure she wasn't missing anything, and then went back to the door. She had to run her finger and eyes through it to get out too. She backed away as the door swung in.

Joe was standing behind it.

"Didn't I tell you to go to bed?" he asked.

I could feel Elyse's heart rate increase, and she lunged forward and threw a heavy punch into her father's face. He was caught off-guard, and he stumbled backwards, giving her time to pull an ordinary knife I didn't even know she had and press it to his neck.

"Elle?" Joe was confused, but not afraid.

"I'm sorry, father," she said. "Your way is going to ruin this world. I'm going on my own. Now, tell me what you know about Sarah."

Joe shook his head. "You always were stubborn," he said. "Fine. I'll tell you." He let his body relax, and Elyse started to relax with him.

"*No*," I said, all too familiar with this trick.

Elyse was strong, but she was young. Joe's shove sent her backwards, where she hit hard against the wall, the knife clattering to the floor. He was on her in an instant, his own fists pummeling her body with sharp blows that threatened to break her ribs.

"I won't kill you," he said, "but you need to learn a little more respect."

I didn't ask her for control. I took it. All at once I became flooded with her memories. It was my second time through them, and so they didn't cause much pain. Within an instant I could feel my heart beating, and the blood flowing through living veins.

Joe's next punch came in, and I angled my forearm to push it aside, into the solid wall. I had always been fast, and in a body like Elyse's, I was even faster. I caught the blow from the other side and turned my arms, wrapping his up and twisting it at the elbow until it threatened to break. He grunted and wrinkled his forehead in pain and anger.

"I don't know what's gotten into you," he said. He backed up a step and threw a foot. I let go of his arm and sidestepped, and then moving in and smacking him hard in the chest, knocking the wind out of him.

"Sarah," I said. I could feel Elyse observing, but there was nothing she could do. She could see spirits, but she could only protect herself from the outside.

"Elle, the Box has the power to destroy all of the Divine. We can put an end to them, a total end." He coughed and choked between the words, slumping down against the wall, accepting his defeat. He held his arm across his chest, keeping weight off it.

"We'll become the Divine," I said, knowing what she would say. "It's already started happening. That isn't why we're here."

"We'll have the power of the Divine," he replied. "Isn't that what we've always been after? Isn't that why we collect all of their artifacts? You can't deny that they are superior to us in every way."

I stopped and stood there, not sure how to respond.

"The vampire changelings, they don't need to drink human blood to survive. They feel the compulsion because of the way their genes change, but it can be controlled. In exchange they get increased stamina, strength, longevity, intellect. Who wouldn't want that?"

"They aren't human," I said, my voice little more than a whisper. "Isn't that enough?" Humans were inferior, but there was something to that inferiority that was appealing. So few resources to work with, and yet they still managed to thrive.

"No," he said. "It isn't."

I bent down and picked up the knife. "Tell me what you know about Sarah," I said. In the past it would have been a Command, but my Commands didn't work anymore.

"Fine," he said. "I'll tell you because I think you can get to her, but keep an eye on your back Elle. Once you have the Box, I'll do whatever it takes to get it back from you."

"You're welcome to try," I said. I stood over him, holding the knife and waiting.

"New York. She's in New York. Montauk. She's living like a mortal, and keeping her signature disguised. The only reason we found her is because she slipped up in her web browsing, of all things. Our sister in the NSA caught an encoded and encrypted message on a Tor message forum. She's been in communication with Ulnyx, the Great Were that the diuscrucis befriended."

That was an interesting development. I had assumed the Were would catch up to her. What I hadn't considered is that they would work together. "You're sure it's her?"

He nodded. "We don't have a precise location, but the IP address block was Montauk. You want to find her, be my guest. I'll deal with your insolence after I get the Box."

For just a moment, the idea to kill him crossed my mind. Reyka would have done it and not cared. Reyka was dead, lost in the power of God's Blade. Joe was defenseless, unarmed, and not threatening. Besides, he was Elyse's problem.

"I'll deal with you after I get the Box," I said. I leaned in and kissed his cheek. I figured it was what Elyse would have done. Then I turned and walked away.

He didn't try to stop me.

CHAPTER SIX

Rebecca

IT WAS A LONG FLIGHT from Kyoto to New York. We touched down nearly twenty eight hours after the confrontation with Joe. I had given Elyse control back for some of the trip, so that we could discuss all of the various tools, markings, and scars she was wearing. I had her memories, but trying to sift through them for details was a dull waste of time. It was easier to just have her explain what she was capable of.

Quite a lot, it seemed. She wasn't invincible, and she certainly couldn't withstand damage the way a Divine could, but she had a laundry list of tricks up her sleeve that would come in handy more than once, I was sure. She had one trick that was naturally born into her, because she was fully mortal; Divine couldn't See her.

It made it a lot easier to get into and out of the airports, where there were always Divine stationed to keep an eye on one another. It was true I could have managed it on my own in my ghost form, but Elyse's body fit me like a tailored glove, her lithe strength and balance superior to any of the forms I had taken before. She was the best shell I could have wanted, and I was grateful to have succeeded on that front.

We traveled light, carrying a single backpack filled with the items that wouldn't make it through security, most of which were sharp. I had used the glove on them before we'd gone through, so while the machines had shown the truth of our cargo, the humans watching them had no idea. All they'd seen were a bunch of metal figurines. I was a collector, after all.

Once we landed, I wandered through the parking garage for a while, until I spotted a valet parking a red Porsche that looked like it wanted to be driven. I asked Him for forgiveness as I approached the attendant, a young man with an acne scarred face and straw hair.

"Excuse me," I said, trying to sound sexy instead of threatening. I could see him shake, clearly startled, before he turned around.

"Can I help you?" he asked. His face turned red, and his eyes made their way up and down Elyse's body. I couldn't blame him, even the most pious seraph would have trouble ignoring it.

"Yes. I think I locked my keys in my car. Can you help me?" I pointed down the row towards a random car.

"Uh… Yeah, okay." He looked down at the fob for the Porsche, searching for the button to lock the doors.

That was when I hit him in the temple. Hard, but not too hard. He crumpled to the ground like a bag of meat. I lifted him under the shoulders and leaned him up against the car next to us.

"My apologies," I said, taking the keys from his hand and giving him a quick kiss on the lips. He was out cold, but maybe he could feel it in his subconscious.

Sliding behind the wheel, I felt a sense of exhilaration to be able to drive again. It hadn't been that long in terms of time, but it felt like forever. I started the car and whipped it backwards, then peeled out through the parking lot. I almost careened right into an oncoming Mercedes, having to slam on the brakes and twist the wheel to avoid it. I had forgotten that I was as mortal, and nobody was going to move out of the way for me.

The other thing I had forgotten, because I had never kept a shell too long, was that my body was human, and needed to rest. I couldn't keep going indefinitely without breaking down, and after an hour on the road that found me still on the west end of Long Island, I knew I needed to stop to sleep.

I pulled the car off the highway and rode along the side streets until I happened upon a Holiday Inn. My eyes were feeling heavy, and my concentration was fading; both feelings I hadn't experienced in a long time. As a vampire, I would tire when I was hungry, or if I had to be out in the sun. Otherwise, I didn't waste time asleep.

Getting out of the car, I had another sensation that I wasn't used to. I was hungry, and not for blood. There was a McDonald's across the street from the hotel, and I decided I would grab a bite to eat there right after I checked in.

The woman at the desk was friendly enough, though she did give me a look because I had taken off the jacket. Swirls and scars ran down both arms to the cuff, in intricate patterns that any artist would have been amazed by. She just seemed disgusted.

"Room 203," she said, handing back my credit card and the room key. One more crooked glance, and I was off to the room to drop off the jacket, and then head across the street. I checked a wall clock as I passed by. Eleven o'clock.

I found the stairs, and then the room, using the card to get in. Once I had entered, I put the backpack down on the bed and unzipped it, returning the knives to their spots in the boots and putting the knife Elyse had used on Joe back into its compartment in the sleeve of the leather. That had been a great trick. Once I was re-armed, I went back out of the hotel and across to the burger place.

I was a vampire. I had never eaten fast food before, though I knew about it from television. My most intimate knowledge of the place was to avoid the blood of humans who were regular patrons, because it would taste of their poor diet. Elyse's stomach was grumbling though, and there was nowhere else nearby to sate its hunger. At least I could cede control to her if I was that disgusted by the meal.

It was quiet inside, the only patron another traveler who looked like he was resigned to the choice as well. He stared down at his burger, taking a bite, grabbing a few fries, and taking another bite. It was almost enough to make me turn around and walk out.

I stayed because I needed Elyse, and more importantly I needed her body, even more than she needed my possession. I stepped up to the counter, set to order a meal large enough to keep us going for another twenty-four hours if needed. The cashier was talking to someone else in the back, and pointing to a spill on the floor. He turned to face me, and froze.

The look was too frightened to be one of admiration. Could he see me? Did he know what I was? I didn't have much time to wonder, because I felt a wave of hot breath wash over the back of my neck.

"You'll do," the voice said from behind me. A clawed hand grabbed my left wrist from behind.

I took a deep breath and shook my head. "I recommend you let me go, dog. I'm hungry, and not in the mood to deal with a mongrel like you."

Another huff of fetid air, followed by a soft growl. "Not scared of me, eh? Come on then sweetheart. Give it your best shot."

The machismo was familiar. Another changeling? Or the real thing? There was an easy way to find out. I stepped backward, stomping the heavy riding boot down on the were's foot and being rewarded with the crunch of bone. He started to howl, but I used his grip on my wrist as leverage to turn myself around and slam him in the head with my elbow. The blow made him let go, and knocked him backwards. He fell to all fours and looked up at me, his damage already healing.

"Not bad," he said. "You'll be a fun one."

He didn't back down, so I was going to assume he was the real thing. Even so, he was being incredibly brazen. I reached into the pocket of the jeans, finding the black stone and taking it out. It grew warm in my hand, and when I thought about the spatha, it materialized in place. The were was on his way, claws aiming to take me apart, leaving me almost no time to react. I ducked and twisted, using the weapon to smack his hands away. He crashed into the counter and over, sending the cashier running.

I had the blade ready by the time he came again, and he lost his left hand on the way by. He shrieked in pain, and watched it begin to steam.

"What the hell?" he asked. "You aren't a seraph. That isn't a seraph's sword." His eyes were wide. He knew what would happen. It was inevitable.

"It's better than that," I replied. "Well, worse for you. Better for me." I walked up to him and kicked him in the head. He tumbled over, howled one last time, and turned to dust. I was right, he had been the real thing.

I turned back to the counter, rendered into nothing but splinters after the were had gone through it. The employees had fled, so I returned the sword to wherever, and then grabbed a few burgers and some fries from the rack. I had my eye on the door when I remembered I would need some hydration, so I took a cup and filled it with soda. I walked out without looking back, giving a small wave to the other diner when I passed him. He was crouched under the table, a puddle of urine pooling around his leg.

"You're safe now," I said.

I was going to get a good night's sleep.

CHAPTER SEVEN

Landon

WE WERE IN A JUNGLE. At least, I think it was a jungle. Dense vegetation surrounded us, thick canopies of trees hid us from the sunlight, and it was raining. Even if it wasn't a jungle, it sure felt like one.

"Do you think we lost him?" Charis asked.

We were sitting together behind the massive trunk of some tree or other, trying to catch our breath. We had managed to slip the wolves he had sent after us when we had fallen into a river and let it wash us downstream. I could still hear them howling in the night. I could hear him whistling.

"For a minute, maybe," I said. "But this is all part of the game. He's been toying with us for how long now?" I had lost track of how many times we had died. It had to be in the hundreds. At first, I had thought I would remember each one, but now I only remembered the pain, and the fear.

"I don't know. I've lost track." She sighed. "I don't want him to catch us again."

It didn't matter. We both knew he would. Maybe that was the point of this. Keep chasing us, keep catching us, keep killing us until we were nothing but broken souls. He wasn't just out for revenge, he wanted to destroy us - in heart, soul, body, and spirit.

"What do you remember?" I asked. We had done this every time, recapping what we could capture from our previous go-rounds in the Box. The memories had been coming faster for a while, but just when I thought we had them, they would ricochet away like a rubber band.

"I remember Clara," she said. "He gave us a daughter to torture us with."

That was the first memory. Somehow, he had discovered how much it had hurt me, and so Clara had been coming back, subjected to more suffering and agony, tortured in front of both of us. Watching someone torture a child was beyond disturbing. When it was your own, even if it wasn't real, it was the truest form of anguish I could imagine.

Charis was crying, her body shaking from her sobs. "I underestimated everything about this," she said. I could feel my own tears welling up, mirroring hers. We were both trying to be strong for the other, but the truth was that his efforts were succeeding.

We *were* breaking.

"What else? Think Charis. We put him in here. We're holding him in here. How? How can he have all of the control, if we're keeping him trapped?"

Those were the questions we tried to commit to our minds, to ask one another every time we came back. I knew there had to be an answer, that we should be able to do something against him. It didn't make sense that his power could be absolute, because if it was he would be able to escape.

She wiped her eyes and set her jaw. "Our power was his power. We don't have anything on our own."

"That can't be true. We're Divine. Diuscrucis. We have the blood of angels, demons, and humans in our veins. That has to count for something."

I heard barking echoes through the growth. They were getting closer.

"We were the only ones who could absorb his power," she said. "We were the only ones who could use it."

I nodded, my mind racing along that path. "So we should be able to use it, shouldn't we? It's the same power. We're just in a different place."

She smiled. "Yes, I think that's it. We need to remember that. Come on." She got to her feet and grabbed my arm. We ran through the greenery, pushing past thick, heavy plants and through brush and bushes. The snarling and barking of the wolves was getting louder.

"Why should we run?" I asked.

"We need to last as long as we can," she replied. "We need to remember."

His power was our power. We could take his power. We could use his power. I kept repeating the words like a mantra, committing it not only to my mind, but to my soul. An ingrained message, an instinct. We needed to do better than to run. We needed to be able to fight.

We pressed on, dodging trees, seeking another escape. The wolves couldn't be far back, and now I could hear the laughter carried on the wind. He knew we were running. He was amused.

"There," Charis shouted, pointing at a climbable tree. "It won't keep us alive forever, but it will buy us some time."

I followed her to it and we scrambled up, finding a resting spot in a branch thirty or forty feet off the ground. A minute later the wolves arrived, barking and growling, claws scraping against the trunk of the tree, six in all.

"The power," I said. My breathing was heavy from the run and climb. I closed my eyes and focused, trying to find that river of energy I had grown to depend on. It wasn't there.

"It isn't in Purgatory," Charis said. "It's here. It has to be. It's all around us."

I looked up, trying to find the sky behind the trees. Was there a sky here, inside the Box? Or was it all a trick, a lie? I kept my eyes focused on it, refusing to blink though they became dry and scratchy. Was it like those posters that seemed to be just a pattern of color, but turned out to be the Statue of Liberty, or a sailboat? Was the power out there?

"Oh, Lannnnndddooooonnnn!" His voice echoed loudly, and he appeared at the base of the tree.

I didn't look down at him, but I knew he was there. I kept my eyes on the sky.

"Hellllloooo?" He put a hand to the tree, and it began to shake. It took immense effort, but I didn't let it break my concentration. I could see a spot of blue through the canopy, and as I stared, it began to fade away, turning towards a dark purple.

"I've almost got it," I whispered, hoping Charis would hear me, and the Beast wouldn't.

"Hey, kid! What gives?" He kicked the tree, shaking it wildly.

I grabbed onto the branch I was sitting on for balance, but I didn't shift my eyes. They burned and teared, but I refused to break again.

"I'm going down," Charis said. "I'll see you soon."

We both knew he was going to kill us again. The only question was how much we would remember. The further we got, the better we might do. I felt the tree shift as she jumped down.

"Hey, asshole," she said.

"You're starting to like the pain, aren't you?" he said. "Have you ever been eaten alive before?"

The wolves snarled, and a moment later she was screaming, I could hear teeth smacking against bone.

"Landon, you really need to see this."

I felt his power, beckoning me to look. The sky had turned a deep hue of blue and red, and I could make out lines of power dancing along it. I focused there, like casting out a fishing line. I hooked one of the lines, and pulled.

I didn't look at him. I didn't have to. I brought my own power to bear, pressing it against his, and refusing him. Only then did I look down.

His smile was gone.

Charis was dead, her body a meal. It fueled my anger. I jumped down, landing lightly on my feet in front of him.

"That was faster than I expected," he said. He might not have been smiling, but he still didn't seem impressed. "Since you think you've got some balls now, let's see what you can do."

He stood there, hands at his sides. He eyed me calmly, waiting.

I felt the anger building, and his power with it. I felt it pouring into me, filling every cell of whatever I was in this place. I gathered it in, bringing it all to my hands. I held them out in front of me, and a ball of blue lightning began forming there, a bright ball of energy. His energy.

Ross waited, watching me with curiosity, but not fear. If I hadn't been so angry, I might have known better. If my heart hadn't been in control, I might not have made the mistake of throwing the lightning at him.

It launched forward, a solid stream of blue energy, arcing at him in a wide, round beam. It smacked into him, and vanished.

The laughter returned, deep and rich. He shooed a wolf away from Charis' head and lifted it up, showing it off to me. "It's still my power, kid. You can't hurt me with it."

He threw it at me. As it approached, the eyes and mouth opened, and a scream came out. I closed my eyes then, knowing it was over. The head exploded an inch away, converted to the lightning ball.

It washed over me.

CHAPTER EIGHT

Rebecca

I WOKE UP AROUND NOON the next day with a terrible stomach ache. It was a new experience for me, to go through the weakness of human digestion, and I didn't enjoy it. I kneeled over the toilet, waiting for a sign that the burger and fries would be rejected, but in the end I was stuck with the discomfort.

It took almost ten minutes for me to shed all of Elyse's charms in order to shower. If I was going to get close to Sarah, I couldn't go in smelling like blood and fast-food. I washed the smells out, enjoying the feel of hands through long hair, and the sensation of the warm water on the body. I checked her over for cuts and bruises, finding only a small bit of discoloration on the wrist the were had grabbed. I shook my head, still not accustomed to the frailty of mortal flesh, and then shut off the water. Once I was dry, I let Elyse take over. I had taken the trinkets off, but I didn't know how to put them all back on in the right places.

"Nice work with that were," she said, once her voice was returned. She was fast putting her stuff back on. I assumed that was why she started talking. She wasn't ready to be an observer again quite yet.

"*He was as agile as a rock,*" I said. The were really had been no match for anyone with skill. "*You would have handled him just as easily."*

"Maybe. I think the more important question is - what was he doing in a McDonald's looking for a toy? It's brazen, even for a were."

The thought had crossed my mind last night, before I had fallen asleep. What had he been thinking, stepping out into public like that? Weres could avoid humans all day, but attract too much attention and the angels would come looking for you. Attacking a mortal in a restaurant was the definition of attracting attention, and unless you were Great an angel versus a single were was always a win for the angel. Always.

"Something's happened to the angels," I said. *"At least around here."*

"That was my thought."

"Okay, but what?"

She wandered out into the bedroom and pulled a fresh pair of undies from the backpack. She slipped them on and then put yesterday's outfit on top. Traveling light meant wearing dirty clothes.

"The changelings?"

"Can't be. You saw the vampire back in Japan. He wouldn't hold his piss against a seraph."

"True. Hey, do you mind if I drive for awhile. It's a little boring, being-"

I shut her up by taking control. We weren't friends, we were business partners, and I wasn't interested in any efforts to change that.

There were police cars outside the McDonald's when I left, and they were talking to the cashier from the night before. I started towards the Porsche, until I saw they had recognized the stolen car too. An officer was standing next to it, on his radio while another man prepped it for towing. I cursed under my breath and headed back the other way. The parking attendant was sure to have described my appearance to them, because I hadn't thought to glamour myself.

Out of view, I pressed the glove to my cheek and pictured a different face taking the place of Elyse's. Then I went one step further and put myself in uniform, peeking around the corner to make sure I got the details right.

There was no way to be sure it had worked, so I took a deep breath and stepped out from my hiding spot, trying to make it look like I had walked around from the other side of the building. In this form, the police made me more nervous than any were could. The Divine didn't care that much about bullets. I wished I could have said the same.

"What's the situation?" I asked, approaching the officer by the Porsche.

He looked at me, his head traveling up and down. "Are you one of the new recruits? I don't think I've seen you on this beat before?"

I smiled and nodded. "Officer Smith," I said. "I just got switched to days."

He rubbed his chin with his hand. "I'm surprised they let that go through. There's been a lot of crazy crap happening lately. Like that asshole that tried to rob the Mickey Dee's over there. He must have been on something, messing up the place and then taking off. I think he had an accomplice who stole this car from the airport too, but then they just leave it here? And then there was the guy who was eating there. He says some ninja chick was fighting with a werewolf, and that's how everything got trashed. We checked him for drugs, but he came up clean."

"Wow," I said. "That is crazy."

He laughed. "So, why did they send you over here? I think we've got everything under control."

I hesitated, but not long enough to make him suspicious. "They didn't send me. I was just on routine patrol, and I saw the action."

"Heh, yeah, I used to do that a lot when I was young. A few years, you'll realize that you're better off not knowing as often as you can get away with it."

I laughed along with him, and laid eyes on his squad car, trying to judge how far I could get before the other cops noticed. There was only one way out of this.

I let go of Elyse, feeling myself becoming immaterial again. With a final lucent thought, I aimed myself at the officer and pushed. We were so close, I was in him before he could take another breath. I clamped down on his soul, and shuddered as his memories flew through me. It was the emotions that always caused the most pain, and this guy had some pretty nasty ones. It gave me new respect and understanding for his earlier statement.

"Rebecca?" Elyse asked, looking at me. I knew she could See me through her Eye.

"Hey buddy," I said to the tow truck driver. He stood up to look at me. "You good?"

He gave me a thumbs up. "Yessir."

"Then I'm gonna take off. It's almost the end of my shift." I started walking towards the policeman's car, Elyse trailing behind. We got in and I drove us out of there, through the back so the other officers wouldn't see.

"That was fantastic," she said while we exited the parking lot and made our way back to the Long Island Expressway.

"It was necessary," I replied. My voice was thick and deep. "I didn't want them all chasing after us." I looked over at her. "When I let him go, you let him go. Got it?" I didn't want her killing a policeman. Talk about trouble.

"But-"

I slammed on the brakes, stopping the car in the middle of the road. Tires squealed behind us, but nobody raised a fuss. "The guy in the parking garage knows what you look like. You kill a cop, and we'll never get off this island."

She held up the hand with the glove, and waved at me. "Do you want to bet? This is war, Rebecca, and there's no room for compassion."

"How can you be such a hypocrite?" I asked. "You're as dirty as he is, if not more. You let me in on purpose. He has no choice."

She started to say something and then stopped, shrinking back into the seat. I accelerated gently, satisfied that I had won that round.

We were in Montauk three hours later. I'd lived in New York for all of my vampiric life, before going to Hell. The only two things I knew about the place was that there was a lighthouse at the end of it, and a lot of wealthy people lived nearby. I had been there once when I had been little. Merov had brought me to a large mansion on the oceanfront to meet with a lesser fiend. I didn't know what kind of business they had done that day, but we'd never gone back. I don't think Merov liked the sand that much.

We drove slowly down Main Street, watching the people walking past the rows of quaint shops and restaurants, as though Sarah was going to just appear out of thin air, maybe doing some antiquing or finishing up at one of the diners. I didn't see her, and I didn't see anything out of the ordinary. Everyone here was human, as far as I could tell.

"No idea where she's staying?" I asked.

"You heard Joe. The triangulation wasn't precise. She has to be in the area. The fact that there aren't any other Divine around only convinces me more."

"You think they're staying away?"

She nodded. "I wouldn't get to close to her, if I was Divine."

We pulled over into an empty spot on the side of the road. "It's time to ditch the car," I said. "I can put him to sleep for a little while. Plenty of time for us to disappear."

"Yeah, you're probably right." She closed her eyes and waited.

I sent a message to the officer that he was really tired, and needed to sleep for a while, and then I let him go. I floated away, back to Elyse. This time when we joined, it didn't hurt at all.

I left him sleeping there and started walking along the main strip, peering into the windows of the shops just in case Sarah was in one of them. She wasn't, but I hadn't expected it to be that easy.

"Where are you, Sarah?" I whispered under my breath. It had been two months. If the Divine were staying away right now, they wouldn't be forever. Maybe that was why she had reached out to Ulnyx?

I walked east along the strip once, not wanting to double back because I didn't want the officer to find me. He would wake up with a headache and no memory of what had happened to him, and probably just drive himself back home to deal with the consequences of vanishing like that. It was better than the Korean man had gotten.

Finding nothing in town, I headed south until I reached the beach. Seeing the pale sand brought back memories of that single trip I had made with Merov. I had never actually gone out onto it, because water and vampires didn't mix very well. That didn't matter now, and I walked forward, leather boots sinking into the sand. I bent down and picked some up, letting it slip through my fingers and feeling a sense of amazement at the stuff. For all of our strength, there were some places the humans did have us beat.

I continued east along the ocean, finding an almost instinctive enjoyment in the sound of the water crashing onto the sand. It was too cool for swimmers, but a lot of others were just walking, finding the same base comfort in the majesty of it.

I should have known He would bring me to Sarah, as soon as I forgot that I was looking for her.

CHAPTER NINE

Rebecca

SHE WAS STANDING ON THE beach, staring out at the ocean. She looked different from the last time I had seen her - older, heavier, more filled out. She was wearing a tight black turtleneck sweater and a pair of jeans, sunglasses over her empty eyes, her feet bare in the sand. She had cut her hair short, into a simple bob that really brought out the planes of her face.

I saw her head flick over towards me for just an instant, but she dismissed me as anything but another passer-by. Right now, I was. I kept my eyes forward, looking at her from the edge of my peripheral vision. The last thing I needed was for her to suspect me of anything.

She didn't move, or turn to watch me once I had gone by. She was looking out at the ocean, just another human contemplating their position in the universe, except her position was of more importance than any of theirs. I walked another fifty feet or so along the sand and then turned and sat cross-legged, keeping my own vision on the water and waves. I couldn't see her from here unless I brought my eyes all the way to the edge of the socket, but that meant I could get a glance over from time to time.

I'd have to keep track of where she went, and follow behind. There was no way she had the Box on her, since her clothes were too fitted to disguise its size and shape.

The wind was cool on my face, and it raised so many emotions in me. Sorrow, regret, loneliness, anger. Regret was foremost. Hindsight was always twenty-twenty, but I never should have betrayed Landon in the first place. Looking back on it, I felt like I was someone else, trying to understand a person that I couldn't recognize. I only realized I was crying when I felt the sting of the air on the tears, and had to blink them away.

"Are you okay?"

I was surprised to have had someone sneak up on me. I had to resist the urge to reach for a weapon, and instead just slowly turned my head. Sarah was kneeling down next to me.

"Uh. Yeah. I'm okay." The words were quiet and forced. I felt my heart race. I was terrified.

"Do you mind some company?"

I swallowed the lump in my throat. "You want to sit with me?"

She shrugged. "You look like you could use it."

I didn't know what to do. If I turned her down, she might leave and I would have trouble following without raising suspicion. If I accepted, she might figure out there was something off about me.

"Uh. Okay. Sure. My name is Elyse, but you can call me Elle." I put out my hand.

"It's nice to meet you, Elle. I'm Sarah." She sat down on the sand next to me, leaving a few inches of space between us. "What are you doing out here?"

I had to close my eyes to catch myself. I felt the power of the Command even though it couldn't compel me. Elyse had been right about her not trusting anyone.

"I just came to think. I did something I wish I hadn't and now I have to deal with the consequences."

She smiled. "I know what you mean."

Of course she did. "You do?"

"I thought I knew what I wanted, but a good friend showed me how selfish I was being." She looked out at the ocean. "But not before they got hurt because of it."

"Are you sure you aren't talking about me?"

"I've come to discover that making mistakes is pretty normal. The difference is in how hard you try to be different, and to make up for them. It's really hard sometimes, but I wake up every day and try to do the right thing. To make the people who love me proud."

I could sense the sadness in her voice. I had expected Sarah to have suffered beneath the weight of the Box and what Landon was going through. I expected that it would have broken her. It seemed she was holding up fine. Maybe Elyse had been wrong.

"That's what I want," I said. "I'm not always sure I'm doing the right thing."

"Just do your best. That's all anybody can expect."

I nodded, staring out at the waves. Was taking the Box from her the right thing to do? What if she was trying to get Landon out, too? Had Elyse misjudged her, or was she just having a moment of lucidity that would crumble as soon as the real pressure was on?

"Do you... see things, Elle?"

The question brought me out of my head. "Excuse me?"

"I'm sorry. I know it's a weird question, it's just that... well... I have this perception, like a sixth sense about people. The ones that are different, anyway."

I could have kicked myself. Of course she would be able to tell that Elyse was Awake. That was why she had tested me.

"You're saying I'm different?"

"Are you?"

I wasn't sure what to say. "I..." I sat in silence for a moment. "I have delusions."

"Where do you live?"

It was a strange question, and she didn't Command the answer. "I don't have a home."

"Do you want one?"

She had taken in the Awake before. I decided to play along. "Of course… I mean… why wouldn't I? My family thinks I'm crazy. They don't understand… the monsters. I've seen them."

"I know you aren't crazy, Elle. I've seen them too." She lifted her head, and then turned around. "I have to go now. If you need somewhere to stay tonight, there's a small house about half a mile down. It has white shingles on it. That's where I live, but I'm going out of town for a few days."

Going out of town? I was only going to have one shot at the Box. "Why would you let me stay there? How do you know you can trust me?"

She smiled. "Can I trust you?"

The question was a Command.

"Yes."

"There you go. That's good enough for me." She pushed herself back to her feet. "I'm meeting someone now. If you want to stay at the house, just come by after nine. I'll leave it unlocked for you."

She reached out and patted me on the shoulder, and then turned and headed up the beach. I risked a quick glance back, and then whipped my head towards the ocean.

She was meeting Ulnyx.

I closed my eyes, praying that he wouldn't recognize Elyse, or her scent. He had been part of Landon when he had seen her, but I knew weres well enough to know he wouldn't forget a face, body, or smell like hers. Were the dirty clothes and salty sea air enough to disguise me?

I held my breath and waited. When half a minute passed and I hadn't been confronted, I turned my head again. They were gone. It had been four o'clock when I had abandoned the squad car. That gave me about three hours to get into the house, find the Box, and get out of there. Depending on what her plans were, maybe less. It meant I had no time to waste.

There was no sign of them along the beach as I meandered in the direction Sarah had indicated. Every once in a while I would stop, stare at the ocean for a minute, and then continue on. Each time, I couldn't help but find myself drawn back to the same contemplative thoughts. I wanted so much to do the right thing, to do right by Landon, and to honor the grace that I had been granted.

It took me about half an hour to reach the house. It was easy enough to spot, both due to its more diminutive size, and the white shutters flanking each of the windows. Not for the first time, I wished that I could See.

Instead, I approached the house slowly, crawling up the side of a nearby sand dune that peaked about twenty feet from the foundation. I could see into one of the rooms from there, a living room with an old television, a leather couch, a coffee table and two end tables. There was also a rocking chair in the corner.

I slid back down the dune and circled to the front of the house. There was a long gravel driveway that headed out to a cross street and ended in a circle there. I didn't see any cars and it still looked deserted, so I ran across to the other side behind an outcropping of brush.

Fairly certain that nobody was home, I walked up to the front door, keeping every cell of my eyes and ears attuned to signs of life. I had seen Sarah leave the beach with Ulnyx. I didn't know where they had gone, but I did know they would be here eventually and I didn't want to still be nearby when they returned. I guess I could have passed myself off as too stupid to know the difference between five and nine, but the last thing I wanted was to make Sarah more suspicious than she already was.

I twisted the handle on the door. Locked, as expected. Elyse had come prepared. I turned my hand so that one of the rings pressed against the handle. From the outer edge it was a simple wooden ring, made of teak and stained a deep maroon. The runes were all on the inner edge, and I felt the warmth of them against my finger while I activated the ring's power. The lock clicked. I turned the knob and entered.

I was in the living room I had seen from the window, and now I could see a set of stairs against the back wall before an archway that led into the kitchen. The was no one else here. I closed the door behind me and locked it again. I was in. Now I just needed to find the Box.

It had to be upstairs in one of the bedrooms. I ascended slowly, staying alert to anything that would signal the arrival of anyone. At the top was a tiny hallway with a bathroom over the kitchen and the two bedrooms splitting the rest of the space.

The doors to the bedrooms were open. The one on the left looked lived in: an unmade bed, some clothes on the ground, books littering the floor. The other was neatly organized, and had a musty smell to it that told me it was rarely if ever visited. Not that I had expected Sarah to be shacking up with anybody, but I had no way to know if I was the first wayward Awake she had extended herself to.

I entered Sarah's room. I didn't know how I was going to find it. I only knew that I was as sure as I could be that it was here somewhere. I went over to the closet, which was nothing more than a curtain hung over a cut-out in the room. I pushed the curtain aside and was greeted with neatly stacked piles of clothing, but no Box.

It was at that moment that I wondered how she could leave the Box here, unguarded, and be sure that no one would try to grab it while she was out. I hadn't seen any demonic runes or angelic scripture etched into the walls or the door frame. I hadn't noticed anything that would indicate the house was defended at all.

My heart began to race. The fact that I hadn't seen anything made me suddenly sure that I had missed something. I moved the curtain back into position and closed my eyes, listening.

A minute passed. I didn't hear anything. Maybe I was

overreacting, being too jumpy. I knelt on the floor and looked under the bed. It was clean. I pulled back the pillows, opened her dresser, and rifled through her underwear. She left the house unguarded because the Box wasn't here.

I knew that had to be the reason. This was going to be harder than I expected. I needed to be here, or nearby when Sarah returned. I needed to find out where the Box was. I closed Elyse's eyes, letting go of control and allowing her back in.

"*You need to get out of here,*" I said. "*I'll stay behind. They're bound to show up sooner or later. Hopefully they'll say or do something to help us find it. Come and get me when they leave.*"

I wasn't sure I could maintain myself in one place, separated from a body. I had been able to do it when Landon was nearby, but his energy was the energy I was bound to. There was no other way.

"*You need to get far enough away that Ulnyx won't smell you.*"

"I'll go for a swim. The salt and damp should disguise me well enough."

"*The water is freezing.*"

"I'll survive. If I have a shot at the Box, I'm going to take it. Be ready."

"*Okay. Good luck.*"

"You as well, Rebecca."

I focused my desire on finding Landon and then let go completely, feeling myself evaporate through her, my mind reduced to little more than a whisper. I needed to know where the Box was. I needed to stay in the house, because that was the way to find out.

Elyse could see me with the Eye. She waved at me, and then made her way out.

CHAPTER TEN

Landon

WE WERE IN A HOUSE. I couldn't say where, or even when, because the house had no windows, and none of the doors led anywhere but to another part of the house, or in some cases, to a part of the house we had already seen before but couldn't connect under any string of architectural logic.

There was nothing new about it. Nothing fresh. The house was a cliche, a tired idea it seemed that Ross had caught onto somewhere and fallen in love with. He used it in unoriginal ways, sending things out of the woodwork to try to attack us, while his laughter reverberated through the rafters.

Ross. I'd stopped calling him the Beast. I'd stopped thinking of him as the Beast. It made him sound more powerful than he deserved. True, he was still destroying us with near impunity, and sure it still hurt in every way imaginable, but from the hopelessness of it had sprung a new kind of strength that I hadn't even known existed.

"No attacks for a couple of minutes," Charis said.

We had settled into a pair of high-backed, winged chairs angled in front of a roaring fireplace. I stared into the fire, waiting for it to spring out at us, or for something to spring out from within it.

"Stay focused," I said.

It was the realization that had brought that hidden strength into play. Our fight wasn't against Ross. Our fight was against ourselves. Each time he killed us, we lost what had happened before, all the memory and none of the emotion. Each time we came back, we remembered a little bit more. Each time, he made sure to start the cycle again before we could put all the pieces together.

We had to stay focused to remember the parts that were important. We had to repeat them in our minds, over and over and over, until it was so committed that it became a part of the bare threads of who or what we were in this place. It had taken time to figure that much out, and in that time we had lost important information.

Other things, we brought back, some almost as soon as we re-spawned. It was funny to think of it that way, like we were trapped in a video game, but having passed through a door just to wind up on the opposite side of the same room, it felt like one.

"Our power is his power," I said. " We can use his power."

"Not against him," she replied. "It doesn't work."

"Not directly. What if there was another way?"

We were both silent for a minute, each of us repeating the mantra. 'What if there was another way? What if there was another way?'

"He created this place," Charis said. "What if we created something? Made our own monster?"

"It's still his power that is making it. He can unmake it."

She gave an exasperated sigh. "How does that not put us back to square one?"

I heard the creak of the door behind us swinging open, and got to my feet. "Where is our power, Charis? It can't all be his. It just can't. Sarah had to pour some of her energy into the Box. We're almost the same as she is. It has to be available to us."

I looked up at the creature that had stepped into the room. A young woman in a long white Victorian style dress. She looked back at me with cold black eyes.

"This is really unoriginal," I shouted. I knew Ross would hear me.

"You don't like the ruffles?" he asked, through the mouth of the woman. "I mean, I know you tend to go for the ones in the skintight denim, but look, she has black hair." She reached up and twirled a strand of it between her fingers.

"Just get on with it," Charis said, stepping up next to me.

"Now, what fun would that be?" She shook her head. "First, let's see what you can do with my little abomination here. She took me a long time to make, relatively speaking." The eyes flashed from black to white, and then she attacked.

She went right for Charis, moving so fast it was more like she flashed from one spot to another. Her hand snapped forward and caught her under the chin. The force broke her jaw and threw her back against the wall over the fireplace. She bounced off and landed face down.

I set myself while the abomination turned my direction. She had a twisted smile on her face, so similar to his.

"Come on," I said.

She hissed, one moment six feet away, the next right in my face. I tried to punch her, but she blinked to the side, and then raked my cheek with eight-inch claws. I could hear them sliding along the bone, and I felt the warmth of my blood spilling out of the wound.

Not that she could kill me. Maybe I should have let her finish the job so we could reset again, but there was something in me that told me it would be a mistake to give up. To ever give up. I stumbled from the blow, but I straightened up to face her.

"You can do better than that."

She smiled again, and her teeth grew out into fangs. Blink! She was back in my face, her teeth coming down on my neck.

It hurt. A lot. I cried out, planting my arms against her, trying to shove her away. I couldn't get any kind of grip on her through all of the fabric, which was fast becoming soaked in my blood.

"Hey Virginia," Charis said. I found her back on her feet, a steel poker in her hand.

The creature turned towards her at the same time the poker was angling in at her head. Blink! She was on the other side of the room, out of the path of the weapon. Blink! She grabbed Charis by the throat, and threw her across the room. Blink! The abomination followed, flashing from one spot to the other, bending down and raking her across the chest.

I focused, finding the Beast's power and pulling it in. The poker rose from the ground and shot towards the creature like a bullet.

Blink! She vanished before it hit her, appearing in front of me again, smashing me in the gut with sharp fingers. I felt them tear through my stomach and into my intestines, threatening to pull them out.

"Daddy!"

The door to the room swung open, and Clara stepped in.

She was wearing a blue and pink dress, her brown hair pulled back into pig tails, her face angry and afraid.

"Clara?" Charis said. Clara wasn't real. We didn't have a daughter.

"Let my daddy go," she said.

She was walking towards me, her eyes sparkling in a swirling mixture of light and fire. The abomination held my insides in her hand, but she turned her head towards the girl.

"What is this?" Ross asked. "I made you."

"Shhh!" Clara put her finger up to her lips. "It's a secret."

"What are you talking ab..."

Clara raised her hand, and the abomination vanished, Ross with it. I felt wetness at my stomach, the blood running freely now that the claw wasn't plugging the hole.

"Fix it," Clara said, looking at the wound.

Bound

"What?"

"Fix it."

She came to me and put her small hand in mine. I felt something then. Not the touch of a child, but the touch of something else. I focused, taking in the Beast's power, and mixing it with the thread of energy I felt running through her palm. The hole in my stomach vanished.

"Clara?" Charis was back on her feet, coming over to us. Her chest was just as torn as mine.

"Fix it," Clara said. She held out her other hand.

Charis took it, and her eyes changed the way I imagine mine had. A moment later her wounds were gone. She looked at me. "Landon?"

I smiled. "The connection," I said. "Our power is here."

In a child. A little girl. She was our daughter, but she wasn't our daughter. It was a complicated metaphor, courtesy of the Box. She had been there all along, through so many of the cycles of pain and torture Ross had forced us to endure. He had destroyed her so many times, dissipated the power before it could consolidate and before we could recognize it for what it was. He hadn't made her. He couldn't make anything.

"Come with me," she said. She started tugging both of us towards the door.

"Do you think it will be that easy?"

The abomination appeared in front of us, blocking the path. It had changed. The hair was gone. The dress was gone. It was a humanoid shape devoid of feature or detail. Claws, small eyes, sharp teeth, a head, two arms, two legs, and a torso. That was it.

"Go," Clara said, gesturing at it.

Ross laughed.

I yanked on our power, bringing it into me, and then let go of Clara's hand. I leaped forward at the creature, my own hand elongating into a set of claws. Blink! It tried to escape, but I reached out to it and held it with Divine power. I brought the claws up and around, severing its head.

"Easier then before," I said.

The room started shaking.

"This way," Clara cried.

She started tugging Charis towards a new door, one that hadn't existed a minute ago. Her little legs were too slow, so Charis scooped her up as we ran.

I looked back over my shoulder, at Ross making an appearance of his own. He had his watch in hand, and he'd lifted his sunglasses aside to look at it.

"Not bad, kid. You might make a sport of this yet."

He motioned with his hand and the doorway became a wall. Charis staggered to a stop.

Fifty weres burst through the double doors, charging into the room. They parted around Ross, and a stream of them headed for Charis.

"No," she said. She kicked one in the head, sending it backwards and knocking over two more. She spun and punched another with a free hand, then leapt over a fourth. One of the weres tried to intercept her in mid-air, and she let go of Clara just long enough to smash it aside before catching her again.

Ross watched, and then shrugged. "I guess I need a few more."

"You'll need an army," I said. I found the poker, still laying on the floor. I focused, superheating it, melting into hundreds of white-hot balls of iron. I swept them around the room, pelting the weres, burning through their hearts. I didn't know if they would heal or not. They didn't.

Ross looked around at the dead mess. "Fine. I'll do it myself."

He pulled a gun from a shoulder holster tucked under his suit jacket, and shot Clara in the head.

My heart jumped as her head slumped into Charis' shoulder. She wasn't our child. She wasn't a child at all, not in truth. It didn't make the act any less disgusting. "Clara!" I ran towards them, Ross forgotten.

"Too far," Charis whispered. She reached up and stroked the little girl's hair. "Landon, we have to remember."

I reached them in time to put my hand on top of hers, so that both of us were caressing her head. "You're right." I swallowed every emotion, and pushed a single thought towards my soul, one that I hoped would carry over to the next regeneration.

"Clara." I whispered.

The gun fired two more times.

CHAPTER ELEVEN

Rebecca

I HAD NO CONCEPT OF time in my ghostly form. I had no concept of much of anything. The only thought that kept repeating was to find out where the Box was, where Landon was, so that I could set him free. The only emotion I felt was eagerness.

Sarah showed up with Ulnyx at some point. She went to get him a beer while he spread his massive bulk out on the sofa.

"He never got back to you?" the Were asked.

"No," Sarah said. "I tried calling, e-mail, text message. I even posted to that damn internet channel he likes so much." She came back in and handed him the bottle.

Ulnyx huffed. "I never thought Obi would take himself out of the game while Landon was still twisting in the wind. Hell, I'm still in." He used his teeth to break off the end of the longneck, and swallowed the drink in a few large gulps.

"You aren't the one who…" She didn't finish the sentence.

Ulnyx did. "Lost their girlfriend? He needs to man up and grow a pair. We've all lost something or someone. We'd have lost even more if Landon hadn't sacrificed himself."

"You can shift into a monster. Obi has what? The smallest slice of power making him a little tougher? He's more human than human, but he's still human. Help me roll this back."

I watched Ulnyx get up and lift the coffee table, pulling it off the rug. Then he helped Sarah roll it up to the couch, just enough to reveal a small metal handle attached to a block of stone, covered with a thousand sigils and marks. Sarah grabbed the handle and lifted the stone away from the floor. All of the sides were enclosed except one. That was why I couldn't find it, and why no angel or demon would have found it either. It wasn't just hidden from sight, but also from Sight.

Avriel's Box. It was a mottled black, with blue lines of energy coursing along the Templar script on the outside, pulsing and pounding in a strange rhythm. Landon was in there. So was the Beast. I had let Avriel and Abaddon out of the Box. I knew what had occurred in there. If I had a form, I would have shuddered.

"It keeps me awake at night sometimes," Sarah said. "I can't stop thinking about the fact that Landon and Charis are in there with him. I wonder what he's doing to them. How it feels."

She'd seemed so strong when she talked to me on the beach, but now I could hear the cracks when she started talking. Underneath that exterior was a soul struggling to stay sane in a time that was beyond crazy.

"How do you know they aren't kicking his ass?" Ulnyx asked. "Why does it have to be the Beast that's winning?"

"Sometimes, they may be." She kicked the rug, rolling it back out, and then sat down on the couch. Ulnyx regained his position there. "The Box is a universe inside of itself. It has its own rules, and its own laws, but there is one that must be maintained. It was Avriel's mistake, and Alichino's mistake. They thought it was just about the power, the energy. I only realized while I lay there staring at the ceiling. They had missed the most important piece."

I felt the answer, as much as I heard it.

Balance.

"Even the Box demands balance. Avriel balanced Abaddon. Landon and Charis balance the Beast."

"What does it mean if they're balanced in there?" the Were asked.

"It means that they can never lose," a new voice said. Dante. "It means they can never win either."

He appeared between them on the couch. He was wearing a simple navy blue suit with a red tie, his hair slicked back. He looked old, but energized.

"That isn't completely true," Sarah said.

Dante shrugged. "We've discussed this, dear. I even went to Alichino with the idea, and he ran some computer models. The odds are astronomical."

"What are you talking about, old man?" Ulnyx asked.

"Don't get your fur all bunched, signore. I assume since you were inside Landon for a time you have a solid understanding of the balance?"

A short growl served as the Were's response.

"Yes, well, just as the balance can be tipped here, it can be tipped there. The trouble is, it is much easier to do here, and the effects are much easier to understand. If you think of it in terms of a mathematical equation, the-"

"Forget it," Ulnyx said. "Get to the point."

"There's a one in a million probability that Landon and Charis can sufficiently overpower the Beast to break the balance. After which, there is a one in a million probability that doing so won't destroy this realm, and perhaps all of them."

"You can't know that," Sarah said.

Dante glared at her. "No, and neither can you. Nobody knows what would happen if the balance was lost inside the Box."

"The Beast could bust it too," Ulnyx said.

"Yes, which is why I asked you two to meet me here." He paused and looked around the room. "Where is Obi-wan?"

Sarah sighed. "He wouldn't come."

Dante didn't look happy. He stared at the ground and rubbed his chin with a frail hand. "There is strength in numbers, but if we must, we must."

"Must what?"

"As you are aware, I can't stay here for long, which means my usefulness is limited. We need to get the Box to Switzerland, to the CERN laboratory. Alichino will meet us there, and together we will destroy it."

What? Every particle of my being cried out, my whole existence feeling the threat of his words. How could he?

"Dante, no," Sarah said. "You're going to kill Landon."

The Outcast didn't seem fazed by the idea. Had my form been capable, I would have killed him.

"I'm sorry, signora. Was that not what Landon asked of us before we lost him?"

"Sarah told me to come here to help you get Landon out," Ulnyx said. "Not to finish burying him."

"He deserves for us to try," Sarah said.

"At what cost?" Dante replied, his voice rising. "We already know that your father is plotting to use the Box to gain the Beast's power for himself. Do we wait for Gervais to send Izak to come and take it from us? Or do we wait for Lucifer or the seraph to throw an army at us so that they can take control? There are only three of us, and I cannot even stay here long to help you. How do you propose we keep the Box away from everyone who knows anything about the Divine indefinitely? It's going to be risky enough trying to get it to Switzerland. I have given you two months to find an answer, and you have none."

None? How could there be no hope? I didn't believe it. Where was Elyse? She needed to make a try for the Box, before he could convince Sarah to help him.

"I've lost everything else," Sarah said, her meek reply little more than a whisper.

Dante's face softened. "I know, signora, but I promised Landon I would find a way to destroy the Box for all time. The longer we leave it in this world, the more the risk it poses to all of everything. I'm sorry, but Landon would want the Box out of reach of everyone who would want to use it for their own aims. We must destroy it."

I could feel the pain of the words, even in my ghostly state. There was little chance that Elyse could get the Box away from Sarah, Ulnyx, and Dante. She couldn't even stand up to Sarah without being under my control. Landon was as good as dead unless I did something, but I was powerless. I had so little self, so little substance, but I had enough to pray. Please, help him.

There was a knock at the door.

"Expecting someone?" Dante asked.

Ulnyx raised his nose. "Whoever it is, they smell like sweat and seawater."

Sarah turned to the door. "It's okay. I'll take care of this."

That was when I knew it was Elyse. It took every bit of effort I could manage, but I propelled myself towards the door. If Sarah tried to Command her again, she wouldn't stand a chance.

Sarah put the Box down on the coffee table and headed in the same direction. She walked right through me, leaving me with a strange feeling of lightness that I hadn't expected. I fought to keep myself from becoming disoriented. Landon needed me to reach Elyse. We needed to take the Box before they could destroy it.

She reached the door and put her hand on the knob. I was a few feet behind, struggling to keep up. As soon as she started turning, the door slammed open, the force of it smashing into her arm and sending her flailing backwards. Elyse stood there, knife in hand. Her head was bare, and the Eye glowed at my presence.

"Hurry," she said, running towards me.

"Elyse?" Sarah was stunned, but recovering. "St-"

I was inside of her, my vaporous soul clamping down on hers and taking the wheel. She stumbled once while she ran, the transfer completing, but I regained my balance and shoved Sarah aside before she could react.

"I'm sorry, Sarah. I won't let you kill him."

Three more strides, and I was in the living room with Dante and the Were. It was too small in here for Ulnyx to shift completely, but his hands grew out into large claws. I stuck my free hand in the pocket of the leather jacket, finding a small brick there. I broke it and threw it at him.

The dust spread across his face, and he cursed and howled while his body shifted back to human form and he began to choke. The Box was sitting there, beckoning to me, only a few feet away.

"Stop." Dante moved in front of me, holding his hand out.

I knew he expected something to happen, but he had no more power over me than Sarah did. I didn't stop. I jabbed the knife into his gut and shoved him out of the way, knowing he could flee to heal. I reached down and took the Box, careful to keep it in its protective enclosure. In front of me, I could see the back door that led out to the beach. That was my escape route.

"No." I felt Sarah's power wash over me, harmless.

"You can't Command me," I said. "I'm going to find a way to save him. I have to." I jumped over the couch and sprinted to the back door. I had opened it halfway when the first bullets started raining in.

CHAPTER TWELVE

Rebecca

I STOPPED MOVING FORWARD AND dove to the ground behind the kitchen counter. I couldn't hear anything but the sound of rapid gunfire, the shattering of glass, and the thuds and clinks of bullets hitting different surfaces. I didn't need special powers to know what was going on. The Nicht Creidim had followed me, or Sarah. They had seen me take the Box, and now they were making their move.

I stayed low, waiting for the initial round to wear out. I hadn't heard Sarah scream, so I could only assume she'd avoided getting hit.

The pace slowed when magazines were emptied, and almost in unison the attackers had to stop to reload. I pushed myself to my feet, staying crouched so I wouldn't be visible in the window, and started slinking back towards the door. I had only taken two steps when a huge claw landed on my shoulder.

"Going somewhere?" Ulnyx asked. The dust I had thrown at him had worn off.

"They're going to kill us all," I said. "We have about three seconds while they reload, and you may be tough, but a hundred silver bullets will leave you paralyzed on the floor."

I felt his breath hot on my neck, and then the weight of his claw vanished and he shot past me out the door. A few seconds later I heard the first scream.

I could have left him then, made my escape and let them deal with the Nicht Creidim. I could have, but I didn't. Something in me told me not to, that Landon wouldn't abandon him to die. Instead, I followed him out the door. It was dark, with the only light coming from the house, but I could see the blurry form of a man face down near the water and the dark mass of the Were headed for his next victim.

I dropped down when the bullets started coming again, and I heard the Were roar. I knew he was being peppered by silver, but based on the screams he was getting even for it. I stayed low and ran along the side of the house behind him.

It was the second roar that scared me. The one that I heard when I neared the front of the house. Three mangled bodies had already slid down the side of the sand dune where I had perched earlier, their throats ripped away. Ulnyx had been making short work of them to that point.

The dagger, I knew. Elyse called it Wolfsbane, and she had wanted to bring it with us, but it had already been out. Now I knew why. I took a deep breath and rushed towards the source of the Were's complaint, daring the bullets to find me and praying that they didn't. I could hear them whistling past my ears, still targeting the house even though I was coming towards them. Were they so preoccupied with their target that they hadn't noticed me?

I didn't see the butt of the assault rifle until it had slammed into the side of my head, sending me sprawling and threatening to rip me from Elyse. It was a blow that would have knocked anyone else unconscious, and I was sure that had been the plan. From my position on the ground, I could see the Were on his knees in human form, blood running from a dozen wounds. He glared at me, his face twisted in anger.

The gunfire started again, aimed at the house. I realized they were happy to kill Sarah, but just as happy to keep her pinned down, their attack loud enough to prevent her voice from reaching them. A pair of black boots stopped just in front of my head.

"Elyse. Joe told me if I wanted the Box, all I had to do was follow you. You've always been the best retriever." I recognized the voice through her. Cousin Ken. He bent down and pulled the Box from my outstretched hand. "Thanks for retrieving it for me."

I lifted my head so I could see him. Long, thick black hair, a handsome face, big muscles. An amazing martial artist, and a talented musician. That was what Elyse's memories told me. I smiled. "Did you think it would be that easy?"

He laughed. "The Were is contained, the bitch is pinned down, and you've got a concussion. I think everything has gone perfectly."

Not everything. I released Elyse and shoved myself forward. We were so close, the trip only took a few seconds, seconds that he wasted waiting on my reply.

I took him then, screaming inwardly at the pain of his memories. His childhood, the abuse he had suffered under his father and had to endure because of their family's code. The anger and pain he teased out in motion and song and violence. His secret lust for Joe's favorite daughter.

It flowed through me, and then he was mine.

Elyse laid there, groggy, her own consciousness not as able to deal with the blow she had taken. She stared up at me. "Rebecca?"

I nodded and put the Box back on the ground. I had the assault rifle in my other hand, and I brought it up to my shoulder. Divine didn't have much need for firearms, but that didn't mean I'd never trained to use them.

Three shots, and each of the Nicht Creidim closest to Ulnyx fell to the sand. I dropped the gun and walked over to the Were. My motions were shaky while I fought to get the balance of the new body right, but I made it across the sand and pulled the Wolfsbane from his stomach. He cursed at the pain, and then it all began to heal. I was sure he didn't know why they hadn't just killed him, but I did. There was a market for pieces of Lucifer's dark creations, and the Nicht Creidim had no problem cutting those pieces out. After all, they would grow back anyway.

"Who the hell are you?" he asked. "Or maybe, what the hell are you?"

"There are six more of them, Were. Do you want to help Sarah, or do you want to chat about my lineage?"

He got to his feet, shifting once more.

"Maybe I should just rip your head off."

I held up the knife. "They only have one of these. I can use it on you, or you can go take care of the rest of the assault team."

He laughed. "Whoever you are, I like your style. I'll be back for you in a minute." He bounded off towards the other side of the house.

I didn't plan on being there when he came back. I returned to Elyse, who had only managed to get into a sitting position. "We need to get out of here."

There was a set of keys in my pocket, and I knew from Ken's memories which dune he had left the car behind.

She nodded, but she was groggy and slow. I swapped the Wolfsbane for the hidden jacket knife, using the plain steel to stab myself in the heart before I abandoned my host and retook Elyse.

I could feel the throbbing in my head, but I ignored it and got to my feet. I took the Box and the keys from Ken while he knelt on the ground dying.

"I told you it wouldn't be that easy."

He looked up at me with tears in his eyes, and I stumbled forward in a moment of panic and remorse. It wasn't that I had killed him, but I had done so with no emotion, and no hesitation. It was an action I was sure He wouldn't have approved of.

"I'm sorry," I said. Then I started running over the sand towards the waiting vehicle. A few seconds later I heard the gunfire stop, as Ulnyx caught up to the last of them. He would be back for me, but he wouldn't know which way I went. I crested a larger dune and slid down the side, right to the door of a Nissan Leaf. It seemed like a ridiculous car to launch an assault in, but the electric engine kept it stealthy. I opened the door, jumped in, and started it up.

I could see the Were bounding towards me in the rearview as I drove away. He gained at first, but I pegged the pedal to the floor and watched him fade.

CHAPTER THIRTEEN

Landon

"WELL, I GUESS WE'VE COME full circle," I said. We were standing on the observation deck of the Empire State Building. Manhattan spread out below us, glass windows and steel reflecting the sunlight from above.

"Maybe he ran out of fresh ideas?" Charis asked.

How many times had we died now? How many times had we watched Clara be killed? Since we had uncovered her secret, she had returned over and over again, bringing our power with her, and trying to help us escape from Ross.

"I don't see Clara," I said, spinning around. The deck was empty except for us.

"We're getting better at this, Landon, but this can't be all there is. We're still losing."

"I know." I leaned in and kissed her forehead. "We're getting stronger. Did you see his face the last time, when Clara bit him? He didn't expect us to get this far."

"We have eternity."

"Not if I can help it."

I'd been committing a lot of those thoughts to memory, too. In the beginning, it had seemed the only hope for us lay in Sarah and Dante to find a way to destroy the Box, and us with it. But without any way to understand the passage of time out of this place, I was more resigned than ever to be locked in this eternal spawn, die, repeat. It helped that we were slowly getting stronger, and living longer between resets, but the emotional scars remained. The torment, the anguish. It didn't fade. It never faded.

Still, there had been signs that we might not need outside help to overcome him. The fact that we were remembering more and more, and faster. The fact that Clara was getting stronger with each regeneration. Charis' realization that the Box would never have held him long without us. The balance, she said, and I knew it was true. I wasted a whole cycle of this charade railing about how Malize screwed us, because he knew what would have to be done and didn't say so. Complaining about it was a waste now, but if I ever got some more face time with him, I would be sure to speak with my fist.

"The balance can be tipped," I said. "The same as it can in the real world. We can overcome it, and destroy Ross here."

"Except we don't know what the consequences will be, or if they can reach beyond this prison."

"As in destroy the whole world?"

"Yes. Or worse."

Like, destroy everything. That was the fear, but there was a wrench in that consideration. "Do you think he's going to hesitate to tip things his way if he has the chance? That's what he wants after all. The results will be the same."

Charis smiled. "Better us than him, right?"

I returned her grin. "As far as I'm concerned it is. Maybe if we break him, break this place, we can get out?"

The elevator announced its arrival, and we turned to see who would be joining us. The doors slid aside. Clara.

"It took you long enough," I said to her.

She rolled her eyes at me and stepped out onto the floor. Before, she was a child of four or five. Now she was at least nine.

"That's your fault, daddy," she replied.

"Where is he?"

She looked back toward the elevator, and then ran to the windows. "Not in here. Not out there. I've hidden us from his eyes."

"You can do that?" Charis asked.

She giggled. "No, of course not. You can."

That was a new development. It wasn't like Clara was a conscious thing for us. She was our connection, which was only getting stronger the longer we were trapped in here. My opinion was that she grew at the same rate as our trust, understanding, and love. That she seemed to be able to sense Ross… I wasn't sure what that meant yet.

"Don't be so surprised," Clara said. "These are the things that he knows nothing about. Things he doesn't understand." She was part of me, of course she knew my mind. "He's stronger than you. His power is ninety percent of what's in here. Still, what you share is lost to him. Even one percent of that can hold its own against one hundred percent destruction."

Lost to him? Was she suggesting…

"No time, daddy," Clara said. She took my hand, and then Charis'. "Let's go."

"Where are we going?" Charis asked.

"Away. We're hiding right now, but we can't stay. He'll find us if we stand still."

"I don't want to run from him," I said.

She sighed like I was the dumbest person in the world. "We aren't running from him, daddy. We're leading him."

Leading him? "Where?"

"Circles," she replied.

Charis laughed. "The longer we survive, the stronger we get. We just need to evade him until we're too powerful for him to stop."

"You get a cookie," Clara said.

"Okay, so how do we keep moving? Where do we go?"

Clara smiled, the way only a precocious nine year old could. "Memories, mommy."

"What memories?"

"Yours."

The elevator doors dinged, and Clara twisted her head to look at them. "He's fast." She grabbed our hands, and pulled us towards the glass windows.

I pulled back. "Clara? There's nowhere to go."

The doors opened. I was expecting Ross. I got Abaddon.

"Diuscrucis," he said in his cold voice. Black tendrils of despair crept out away from him, slipping along the floor and ceiling towards us.

I felt the fear. I could tell Charis did too. "This can't be real," I said. Abaddon had fled to Hell.

I couldn't see his body through the cloak of black power. The center of him was a swirling mass of impenetrable emptiness.

"This can't be real," I repeated.

Clara pinched my hand, and I looked down at her. "Time to go," she said. She turned back to the window, and the glass shattered outward, letting in the heavy gusts of air that owned these heights. "What are you afraid of?" she asked me. "You've done this before."

Abaddon was coming closer, moving out of the elevator towards us. His darkness spread, wrapping around the rest of the windows and threatening to choke us off. "He isn't real," I said again. Maybe it was time to go, but I wasn't going to run away until I proved myself right.

I found Ross' power so much more easily now. I pulled it into me, and then squeezed Clara's hand and took only a single thread of energy from her. I wrapped it around the energy, and threw it forward at Abaddon, pushing with my will for the glamour to be lifted.

The entire facade fell away, leaving Ross standing right in front of the elevator in his pinstriped suit and sunglasses, an old-fashioned Tommy gun pressed against his hip.

"The game's starting to get interesting," he said.

We couldn't survive getting shot here. It was a good thing Charis had already made the decision to jump for me. I felt Clara's hand give a hard tug, and I gripped it tighter in response. I could almost see the bullets go flying overhead as I tumbled backwards out of the window.

If we couldn't survive getting shot, how were we going to survive a thousand foot fall? I kept my grip on Clara's hand and tried not to scream. The sky rushed away from me, and a few seconds later I saw Ross stick his head out of the broken window.

"Oyster, sir?"

What? I blinked my eyes a few times, trying to get my brain back up to speed. The tower was gone, the sky was gone, Ross was gone. I was on my feet... somewhere. A tuxedoed server was holding a silver tray of oysters a little too close to my face.

"Uh... no, thank you," I said, taking a step back The waiter was expressionless as he moved on. "Where the hell am I?" I whispered.

"Maine," Charis said, appearing behind me. "Seventeen-seventy-five. Nice tux, by the way."

She looked strangely gorgeous in a period proper gold hued dress with a modest hoop and lots of embroidery. Her hair was pinned up on her head, and she had an ease about the whole thing that made me a little uncomfortable. I looked down at myself, noting the black wool tuxedo coat and pants. It made me even more uncomfortable.

"General Montgomery?" I asked. I had all of her memories. I had a guess where we were.

"Yes."

Charis would spend the night in the arms of one of

Montgomery's top officers. Two days later, the good General would lead a militia north into Canada to try to take Quebec. He would fail, in no small part to her sending advance warning to the Canadian and British troops stationed there.

"You were wearing a red dress," I said. I looked out past her, to where uniformed officers of the American militia were kibitzing with their patrons. We were in a small mansion belonging to a local businessman. It had a nice big downstairs for entertaining, and six bedrooms upstairs, which according to my memories were also being used for entertaining. Red dress Charis was likely in one of those rooms, without her red dress.

"Don't get jealous," she said. "This stuff happened two centuries ago, when I was still alive."

"I'm a little torn," I replied. "You were aiding the enemy, after all."

She laughed. "Your enemy, not mine."

"Not really mine either. I wouldn't be born for a long time after this. It's kind of crazy to be here now."

I looked around the room again. "Where's Clara?"

It was as if she was just waiting for us to look for her. She stepped out from the midst of the gathering, in a frilly white dress, her hairstyle matching Charis'. She came up to us and took my hand.

I squatted down so we were at eye level. Charis joined me. "Now what?" I asked.

"He'll try to change things, to undo what we've made," she said. "It will be hard for him, because the memories bind us and give us strength. They're more real to us than anything he can conjure up, and true creation is hard to destroy. He doesn't really know how to make, he just fakes it. The cracks are everywhere if you know where to look."

"He found us pretty fast in New York," Charis said.

"He knows New York well. It will be harder for him to find us here."

I didn't completely understand the rules of the game of hide and seek we were playing, at least not on the surface. Clara was an extension of us, so there had to be some base part of ourselves that knew what was going on.

"So we just hang out here until he catches up?"

She nodded. "Yes, daddy. Then we have to run again, and we have to be quick. Leave too soon and he'll be able to follow right behind. There is no leaving too late."

I knew what she meant. I could still hear the cracking of the Tommy gun ringing in my ears. "How do we know if it's the right time?"

"Things will change," she said. "That's the clue. It's the right time when we see him. We have to all be together, not touching but close by. Think of a memory. Any memory to get us away, but detailed is better. It makes us harder to find."

"Okay, let's just concentrate on staying together then," I said. "What happens if he kills us?"

She rolled her eyes at me again. It was super cute, but I hated when she did that. "He didn't know you could do this. Now that he does…"

She didn't need to finish. I got it. He wouldn't let us live long enough to remember again. Maybe he wouldn't let us live at all. I could picture an endless cycle of rebirth and murder, from now until never.

"So the longer we survive the more powerful we get, right?" I asked. "The more powerful we get, the easier it will become to defeat him."

"Yes, and no. Remember the balance, daddy. Always remember the balance."

The answer gave me a chill. I leaned forward and kissed her on the cheek. "Thanks, Clara." She was so real sometimes.

I stood back up and looked out at the assembly of soldiers and citizens. There was nothing to do but wait for Ross to show his face. When he did, we would leave.

"Any particular memory you'd like to visit?" I asked Charis. I was trying not to think too much about this one.

She laughed. "How about the time you made out with Tammy Robinson?"

I could feel my face turning red. "I was sixteen," I said.

"It was very cute. Your first chance to get to first base."

She was patronizing me. "I've learned a lot since then."

"You guys," Clara said, tugging on my pants. "Let's get something to eat."

Charis laughed again. Could it be possible that we might actually be able to enjoy ourselves in this place, even if only for a few fleeting minutes at a time? It was nice to not have Ross right on our tails for once.

The three of us wandered through the house, drawing curious glances from the others because our kid was the only kid around. She didn't seem to notice, using her nose to track us to a table of American classics. Pie, turkey, potatoes; it was like the original Thanksgiving. It smelled great.

"You don't really need to eat," I said.

She looked up at me and stuck out her tongue. "Daddy, think in metaphor." She grabbed a loaf of bread and took a bite from the end. "I don't want to have to spell everything out to you." Her words were mumbled with a mouth full of food, but I heard them all the same.

"Quite a little darling," I said to Charis.

"I think she's perfect," she replied, her eyes holding mine.

"I never thought of you as the motherly type." Not that I ever thought of myself as a father either.

"Me neither, but I see you and I together when I look at her. I like that."

Together, but not quite. Being in the Box hadn't exactly left us any time to do anything even close to what I had shared with Tammy Robinson. Still, I knew what she meant. Watching her die so many times had been pure agony.

A murmur started to rise from the living room, and before I knew what was happening Charis... Red Dress Charis came running into the room, holding her dress wrapped around her and looking back over her shoulder. She slammed right into me, her face snapping up to look into mine, her eyes wide with fear.

"Get out of my way," she said, looking backwards again.

"Landon, this never happened," the real Charis said.

Ross was here already? I pushed fake Charis out to arm's length.

"Let me go," she demanded. Her foot whipped out into my leg. I felt the pain of my kneecap shattering beneath the force, and I fell to the ground. Fake Charis' eyes narrowed and flared an angry red.

"Not so fast," Charis said. She had grabbed a serving fork from the table, and she jammed it into her counterpart's neck, and then threw her across the spread.

I couldn't heal here, not like I had outside the Box. Charis lifted me up and put her shoulder beneath mine so I could stay off my leg.

"Excuse me, sir?" The waiter was back. Charis didn't wait for him to do anything surprising. She slammed the flat of her hand into his nose, and he flopped backwards with a groan.

"Is it time?" she asked Clara.

She was still chewing on the bread, taking smaller bites and looking around. "Not yet."

"Why don't you heal your father, like you did in the house?"

"Sorry, mommy. I can't. It isn't safe."

What did that mean? "Let me go," I said. "I can manage." She slipped out from under me, and I brought my weight down gently. It hurt, but I had a lot of experience with pain. "We need to get out of here."

I heard the sound of a musket hammer drawing back. There was a pop, and a ball of iron whizzed by my head. I found the shooter across the room, a soldier with a wide grin.

"Really? Not yet?"

She smiled up at me. I noticed a couple of her front teeth were missing. "Okay, we can go now," she said. "We need to get out that door." She pointed back at it, only ten feet away.

Ten feet was nothing unless your leg was broken. He pulled the hammer back again and took aim.

The waiter's silver platter was resting a few feet away. With a thought, I brought it up in front of us, just in time to catch the second bullet. I started limping backwards, until Charis scooped me up and tossed me over her shoulder like a sack of potatoes. The entire house burst into flames around us.

"Going somewhere?" Ross asked. I felt him tug on the platter, and I countered it, showing him that I could.

"See you around," I said. I felt Charis shift as she kicked open the burning door. A wash of frigid air flowed in around us.

"Enjoy it while it lasts, kid," he said. He let go of the platter, ducking under it as it sped by. He crouched there while the flames engulfed him, his face framed by the fire.

CHAPTER FOURTEEN

Rebecca

I SAT ON THE EDGE of the bed in a small room at the Hilton Hotel, right outside of JFK airport. I cradled the scripted stone that held the Box on my lap, running my finger along it, tracing the lines of pulsing blue power that proved that Landon and the Beast were still in there. I tried not to think about what he might be going through, or how much pain he might be in. I tried to concentrate on what would happen next.

The Leaf was quiet, but its range was limited. Ken had left a more conventional motorcade in Amagansett, three Cadillac Escalades to transport the Nicht Creidim back to base with their prize. I took the one that Ken held the keys to. It was too bad none of them would be coming back to claim the others.

The alone time while driving had led me back to considering how easily I had killed Elyse's cousin. He had redeemed me, had He not? I was doing His will, and His work. So why did I feel like there was a part of me that was still a demon, and a monster? The thoughts almost brought me to tears, and to questions I could only resolve with faith in place of understanding. I believed in my goal. I believed in my purpose. It had to be enough.

They would miss Ken's return, of course. They would send people out to discover what had gone wrong. They would find

Elyse's knife in his chest, assuming Ulnyx and Sarah didn't hide or destroy the bodies. They'd miss the Escalade too, which is why I'd driven it to La Guardia, set it on fire, and then taken a cab to the other airport. They'd figure that out eventually, but not before I was on my way to… where?

I hadn't known, so I checked into the hotel and sat in the room there, holding the Box like it was a baby. I'd taken a little more time for myself, to be alone with it and think. To allow a minor calm before the major storm I knew was soon to come. Every party who knew anything about the Divine or the Beast wanted their hands on the Box, and now the only thing between it and them was me. And while I was almost indestructible, I was still dependent on mortals to be able to do much of anything.

One last deep breath, and I put the Box across the room, out of my own easy reach. I returned to the bed and reduced my grip on Elyse, allowing her to regain her body while I clung to her like a parasite.

"You did it," she said. She started to get up, but I clamped down on her again, and made her sit.

"*Leave it over there. We need to talk.*"

"You want to know what to do now, correct?" She sounded amused.

"*It would be helpful. I'm not convinced this isn't the part where you betray me. You don't really need me anymore.*"

"Don't sell yourself so short, Rebecca. I'm not going to betray you, and I do still need you quite a bit. You're crazy if you don't believe Sarah will catch up to us, or at least has the potential to. Besides, he's insisted that if I'm to get what I want, we can't do it without you."

"*Who has insisted?*" I had searched her memories and there was nothing in there about her supposed clandestine meetings with an anonymous tipster. Or maybe it was in there, but she was somehow blocking it from me. I was never completely sure if I was taking control or if she was giving it.

"You'll find out soon enough. For now, I'd appreciate a shower, a new pair of panties, a meal, and a little sleep. My head is killing me. Four hours, no more, and then we need to be on the next flight out to Peru."

"*Peru?*"

"Cusco, to be specific. That is where I was supposed to meet him once we'd recovered the Box."

"*This contact of yours, how do you know you can trust him?*"

"I have no choice. Neither do you, and neither does Landon."

"*You do have a choice. Dante said they had a way to destroy to Box. You could let him do it. It would solve your problem.*"

She shook her head. "Dante is relying on a demon who was banished from Hell. Do you think I'm about to trust that over the person who has been right about everything so far?"

I couldn't argue. We had the Box, which meant I had control over Landon's fate. All I had to do was hang onto it. "Fine. I'll do it your way."

I wrapped myself around her again, taking away her control and relegating her to the subconscious. Controlling her was becoming so easy, it was almost as if I were alive again, and her body was my body. I stripped off my clothes, grabbed a fresh pair of undies from the pack, and went into the bathroom. Elyse might have had a headache, but I shut that part of her down, closing off the nerves so that I didn't feel a thing. I washed off the salt and sand and blood under a hot torrent of water, and afterwards wrapped a towel around me and ordered room service. I was nodding off when it arrived.

The sound of the knocking surprised me, and I jumped to my feet ready for a fight. The aggression turned to embarrassment as I went over to the door and opened it for the porter. He was an older man with a thick mustache and a pot belly. He stared at me, his face flushing, before pushing the food into the room.

"Bacon cheeseburger, fries, and a soda," he said. "Where do you want it?"

I motioned to the center of the room, and he pushed the cart in. His eyes lingered on my bare legs.

"I have some clothes that need to be laundered immediately," I said. "Can you take them, or do I need to call for someone else?"

He arranged the meal on his cart. "Hey, cool lamp. Where'd you get it?"

I saw he was looking at the Box, which I had been either tired or stupid enough to leave on the table. I was surprised he could see it at all.

"An antique store in Montauk. Can you take the clothes?"

He turned his head back to me, his eyes tracking top to bottom again. "I don't think we have launder services on site. We can't get anything back in less than twenty four hours. Did you say Montauk? I have a nephew who lives out there. Which store? He loves antiques, he'll be pissed he missed this one."

He could see the Box, and he was showing a little too much interest in it. "You left the food. If you can't help me with the clothes, please see yourself out." I leaned down and back, my hand searching for a knife. He was making me uneasy.

He put out his hands. "What, no tip?"

I couldn't find a weapon, so I stepped towards him and put my hand on his throat instead, shoving him up against the wall. "Are you going to leave, or do I need to kill you to get rid of you?"

His face turned white, and his body fell limp. "No… no… I'm so… sorry. I just wanted… you know… a tip. I'll go… please… please just let me go."

I released my grip and backed away. He started running for the door. Once he was gone I slumped down on the bed, my appetite lost.

I'd only had the Box for a number of hours, and already I was paranoid. Just because he was Awake didn't mean he was dangerous. He might not have even known he could See the Divine. Not everyone did. Besides, how could anybody possibly have found me so fast? I cursed myself for my foolishness. I had spent five years in Hell, and here I was falling apart at the first sign of trouble. Maybe instead of rejecting that part of me, I should embrace it? It might be the only thing that could help me in the hours and days to come.

There was one thing I was sure of. The sooner I got to Peru, the better.

I put the dirty, salty clothes back on, shoved the Box into my pack, and headed for the door. I should have just gone to the airport in the first place, and spoken to Elyse there, instead of wasting my time in the hotel room. I would't make that mistake again. I could eat and sleep on the plane.

There was no point in checking out. I put the glove to my face, glamouring myself into a fat old woman before I fled the room, taking my time heading through the hallway and down into the lobby. When the elevator doors opened at the bottom, I passed by the still-scared porter, who had wrangled up a security guard. I had no doubt the front desk was on the phone with the local police, and depending on what was said, I was sure the Nicht Creidim would be back on the scent in a matter of minutes.

I exited the hotel and grabbed the first cab I could, sliding into the back seat and slamming the door closed. I needed to get out of New York by land. The airports would be crawling with too many teams from too many sides before I could sneak a flight out. Which direction would they not expect me to go?

"Penn Station," I said. I could get a train from there to anywhere, and the crowds would be thick enough to keep me obfuscated.

A grin in the rearview mirror was my reply. The driver's head dipped, and I saw a flash of red behind his brown eyes. "My lucky day."

He didn't know who I was. He couldn't have known what Elyse

was. I'd made sure to cover the Eye, and he shouldn't have been able to see through the glamour anyway.

"Excuse me?"

I saw his smile again. "Penn Station. It's a good fare." He turned his head to look at me, his smile widening even more, revealing a set of sharp incisors. A vampire.

"Hungry?" I asked, catching his eye.

He returned his gaze to the road. "You don't smell like a Divine. I don't See a Divine, and you don't look like a Divine. Glamoured?"

"Two pieces of advice. Mind your business, and keep driving. I'm not an angel."

He laughed, but didn't turn around again. He was silent for a couple of minutes, but I guess he couldn't help himself. "You aren't a demon either. Not a were, not a vamp... hell, you aren't even one of those newbie pricks that have been popping up recently, screwing everything up for the rest of us."

"Didn't I tell you to shut up?"

"Not directly. Hey, I'm not trying to butt into your business. I'm just making some small talk with a fellow tortured soul, or whatever kind of soul you have. I'm not going to get to feed on you, I might as well chat. My name's Randolph, by the way."

Randolph. I searched my memories. "Not Randolph Hurst?"

That made him turn his head again. "Do I know you?"

I tried to keep my face from betraying me. Randolph had been one of Merov's associates, in charge of the blood trade inside city limits. He'd always been a cordial vamp, a thinker instead of a fighter. Give him a sword, he'd just as soon prick himself with it. Give him a dollar, he'd turn it into a million within a week.

I'd killed Merov and Landon had shut down the exchange, and then some. It seemed now Randolph was stuck working as a cabbie. Or at least he was posing as a cabbie to assist himself with some other scheme.

"No, but I know you."

For someone like Randolph, that was the best way to break any thoughts he may have had about finding a way to profit from me.

"Demon, then," he said, "and not a minor creature like myself. There haven't been too many of your type around New York since the assault on that church. It's been great for business, but you know how some of our kind can be. Take away the leadership, and they resort to all kinds of bull. The angels being busy with the bigger fish hasn't helped on that front. They used to be great for keeping the less subtle fiends out of the way. Anyway, you come to set up a new hierarchy? If you have the guts and the power to do it, and you know who I am, then you know how I can help you."

He would be able to help me if that was my goal. He had connections to the entire global network of vampire families, and could swing me anything I needed. Except the one thing I did need. "I'm just passing through right now, but I may take you up on that offer later. If you want to get in good with me, tell me more about the angels and the 'newbie pricks', as you put it."

"Promises don't mean anything to us, you know that. You'll have to give me something of value. Information?"

I wouldn't have expected Randolph to be that easy. "The true diuscrucis is holed up in Montauk," I said. "I've seen her."

His face appeared in the mirror again, and I could see the dollar signs in his eyes. "How do I know you aren't lying to me?"

"I'll swear it on blood, if you pull over."

He didn't pull over. "We can work it out when we get to Penn. The angels have been gone since the church thing. Not a single seraph has stepped foot in New York, not one. Demons are going nuts, taking humans at will, and getting more bold every day. I don't know where the hell they are, I mean, one seraph can do a pretty damn good job here, considering the mess the other diuscrucis left us in, before he got trapped."

I wasn't sure if he had known about that. "You don't know

where they went?"

"I've been asking around, just out of curiosity. I've heard things are worse in other places where there are still archfiends lording over the rabble, and that the ranks of angels have gotten thin enough they can't be everywhere at once. The diuscrucis took care of Reyzl and Merov, so there's a huge power vacuum in these parts."

Not enough angels to cover a city like New York? They were in worse shape than I had thought.

"Crazy times," I said. "What about the newbies?"

"You think the stuff about the seraphim is crazy? This is crazier. Ever since the diuscrucis got trapped, we've been getting more and more mortals turning up with pointy teeth, calling themselves vampires and trying to enlist in the families. Most of them we kill, but there have been a few who were strong enough to get in. It's not just vampires either. I've even seen a nightstalker wandering around the streets. Anyway, they're a problem. The weak ones are still strong enough to kill their own kind, and they aren't smart enough to do it without drawing the wrong kind of attention from the rest of us. Some of the strongest have worked their way into a few of the families, but they're still not the real deal. Who knows what will happen if they start reproducing, assuming they can. The whole freaking gene pool is being poisoned."

I couldn't stop myself from laughing that time. Elyse was concerned the changelings were screwing up humans, and Randolph was afraid they were messing up demons. It seemed nobody wanted them around.

"Only demons are appearing?" I asked.

"Yup, but that's not all. There are the ones that change, the ones that don't change, and then there are the ones that die."

"Die?" Elyse hadn't told me about that.

"It's a mortal epidemic, and if you ask me it's just getting started. Five hundred reported cases on the East Coast alone, fifty just in the last week. It seems they develop some kind of nasty black rash, run a fever for a few days, and then drop dead. Even worse, if we drink any tainted blood, we get it too."

Vampires getting a human disease? If there had been any doubt left that the Beast's power was at the root of this, it evaporated in that instant. "So how do you know who to bleed?"

"We don't. Not completely. It's a new game of chance, but the elderly have been pretty safe so far. If you had been an actual person, I would have taken you somewhere and drained you, had my fill, and then sold the rest. With the diuscrucis gone, the exchange is back in business, only now we're trading for clean plasma."

I didn't say anything else. I just sat and tried to absorb what he had told me while he finished the drive to Penn Station. Dante was right that just having the Beast in the Box wouldn't be enough. If his power was leaking out and infecting the world, it was only a matter of time before it either killed off or completely transformed humanity. Whatever we had to do to get Landon out, we had to do it fast.

"Penn Station," Randolph said, about twenty minutes later.

The cab rolled to a stop outside the entrance. I held my hand out so he could cut it and we could seal the deal.

"Ah, no thanks. I believe you well enough, and I'm a little blood shy these days."

"Suit yourself." I pulled back my hand and pushed open the back door.

"Don't forget what I said about being able to help you, when you're ready." He flashed me his toothy grin one last time.

"I won't forget. Oh, and Randolph?"

"Yes?"

"There is one more thing you can do to help me. I need a credit card that isn't connected to me."

He shifted around in his seat, took out a wallet, and handed me a fancy card. "You have twenty-four hours, and then I'm going to report it lost. Don't forget I did this for you."

I smiled. "I'll be back after I finish my current business. You're the first vampire I'll come to see."

I pushed the door closed at the same time another older woman approached the cab. I considered warning her to the next one, but instead watched her get in and close the door.

CHAPTER FIFTEEN

Rebecca

TWO HOURS LATER I WAS on my way to Kansas in the sleeper car of an Amtrak train. The waiting in Penn Station had been tense, but we'd gotten underway without incident and made it out of New York unscathed. I'd spent most of the time standing on the platform, keeping an eye on the stairs, and reconciling what Randolph had told me.

The angels were dealing with archfiends, but the lesser demons were getting wild. It was an interesting approach, and it made sense. With the main power base gone in a given region, the other fiends would be spending more of their energy jockeying for position and fighting amongst themselves. It was a little more problematic for humanity, because there were some truly stupid Divine out there, but not as much of a problem as a concerted effort by a higher ranking demon could cause. As a side benefit, it would also allow me more breathing room to deal with the Box. The angels were stretched thin, leaving them mostly out of the picture. The demons were busy fighting amongst themselves. There were plenty of other players left, but every little bit helped.

I also spent some time considering the longer term picture of the changed mortals. If they were integrating into the societies of their new species, eventually they would begin to reproduce. Once that happened, would they become stronger, or weaker? Would there be vampires that could stay outside during the day unaffected, who didn't need to drink blood, but maintained the enhanced stamina and intelligence? Or would they lose traits that made them superior, the strength and longevity? There was no way to know, but it was certain this was just the first push on a domino.

My eyes glazed over from looking out the window at the landscape passing by. The trip was supposed to take a little more than a day to complete, with a couple of exchanges along the way, but I wasn't planning on going the full route. We'd be in DC in about an hour, and I would catch a flight there. It wasn't as far as I'd prefer to have gone, but I was navigating a delicate balance between time and distance. It wouldn't take the Nicht Creidim forever to figure out where I had gone, and if by some chance Sarah managed to get to Obi, the former marine could certainly hack into any transportation system he needed to help track me down.

I took the pack and pulled it up onto my lap, opening the zipper just enough to see the blue glow from the Box. It comforted me to look at it, and to know I was in control. With any luck, I'd be meeting with Elyse's contact before the sun had set again.

The power pulsed along the surface, running through intricate channels, brightening and dimming in tune to whatever logic the prison followed. I knew so little about it, beyond how its creator and the demon Abaddon had become trapped in it. The Beast had told me where to find it, once he had deemed me ready to make my return from Hell. I had been powerful then, in many ways much more so than I was now. I only had one weakness, that the Redeemer had turned into a strength.

I took a deep breath and put a finger on the box, feeling the warmth of the energy it fought to contain, the energy that was leaking into this world. I looked around at the people on the train. Would they change faster or die sooner because they had been so close to me? If the Box's power was like radiation, these mortals didn't stand a chance.

Returning my eyes to the Box, I wondered what he was going through in there. The Beast had tortured me once when I had questioned the need to bring Sarah into his game. I could remember the pain of being torn apart and put back together, so slowly and purposefully that it made the agony more intense and immeasurable than any other kind of wound could. Torturing souls in Hell had been part of my training.

None had screamed the way I had.

"Final stop, Union Station," the voice said over the loudspeaker. "If you're transferring, please hold onto your ticket and check the board for track information. Thank you for riding Amtrak."

I didn't stand until everyone else had disembarked. Only then did I sling the pack over my shoulder and make my way out, the hidden dagger in my jacket ready to be used. Nobody stared, nobody approached. I was still in the clear.

A quick walk through the station, and I would grab a taxi to Dulles International. I had never been in D.C. before, and I was amazed by the construction of the station; a magnificence in marble and light that stood in stark contrast to the old dinginess that Penn Station brought to mind. The beauty of it distracted me, and that distraction almost caused me to lose the Box.

A gloved hand dug into my shoulder, stopping my brisk pace. I tried to turn around, to face my assailant, but a second hand wrapped up under my other arm and pinned me, shoving me towards the wall and an access door nearby. I could tell by the size of the hand and the feel of the person behind me that they were taller than me, and well-muscled. At first, I wriggled in their grasp, trying to kick at the feet or twist from the grip without drawing too much attention. For every movement I made, my attacker countered it with equal and opposite force, leaving me stuck in their grasp and moving to a more private location. I needed to get out of this now, because I didn't know what was waiting on the other side of the door. Had they been expecting me?

There was only one thing left to do, and so I let go of my control of Elyse and pushed myself towards my captor. I was too close to understand who they were, and I never got to find out. No sooner had I let go of Elyse than a blazing heat greeted my ghostly form, propelling me away. I only barely managed to latch back onto her before I was sent off into the distance.

"Damn. Will you cool it, Rebecca?"

I knew that voice, but how did he know it was me? I stopped struggling.

"I'll walk myself, Obi-wan."

His hands left my shoulders. As soon as they did, I spun around and struck out at him with the knife.

He was expecting the move, and he caught my wrist and pinched the nerve, making me drop the weapon. "Hold on a sec, will you? I know what happened, but I'm not here for Sarah."

I looked up at him. His face was damp with perspiration and his breath smelled like alcohol. A rough Eye was painted on his forehead in... mascara?

"Then what are you doing here?"

He waved towards the access door. "Can we just get out of sight? It isn't safe out here."

I nodded. It was obvious he had come running from some drunken stupor somewhere, and I wanted to know why. I walked to the door and opened it. It was nothing but a small janitorial supply room. He pushed me in and closed the door behind us, stopping to pick up the dagger.

"I can't believe he was telling me the truth," he said, as soon as the door had shut. He used his hand to wipe some of the sweat away.

"Who?"

He grinned. "So, I'm at home, sitting on my couch, downing

another shot of tequila when my phone rings. I pick it up, and there's this guy on the phone. He tells me I need to track down an Elyse Everness, and to check transportation databases."

He was talking fast, and the words were coming out a little stilted. I put up my hand. "Wait, slow down. I was at Sarah's. I heard her say you don't answer your phone."

"I do when the battery is dead and it still rings. Anyway, he texts me a photo of this thing on my forehead, tells me to draw it with whatever I have, find out where Elyse is going, and get there. He tells me she's really you, and you've either got the Box, or you will soon enough. I know Sarah, and she's a sweet kid. I love her like a niece, but destroying the Box? Hell, no. I wasn't helping her with that, I don't care what Landon wanted. I lost enough already." He put his hand on the wall to steady himself.

"Who?" I asked again.

"I'm getting to that. He tells me you have the Box, and you're going to get Landon out. That there's a way." His eyes started tearing. "Too much dying, too much destruction. I can feel the balance you know. I know its in the crapper, and it's going to get worse without Landon. The angels have the Deliverer, but they can't be everywhere at once, and the demons will figure out they're being played sooner or later. Either that or Gervais will get them organized. He can't kill Gervais with it you know, because he's not a demon anymore. He's something else."

His voice sped up as he spoke, until I could barely make out what he was saying.

"Obi, get to the point. Who told you to find me?"

"Yeah, right. He's an odd one. British accent, kind of soft, like a trannie or something. Laughs at himself a lot. Said his name was... Matt?"

I remembered the demon Templar. "Max?"

He pointed at me and grinned. "Yeah, that's it. Told me he was waiting for us in Peru, but you weren't going to make it without help. So I tracked you down."

That's who was feeding Elyse her information? Why hadn't she wanted to tell me? I knew Landon trusted the demon, and that made me feel better about this whole thing. Elyse might have her own selfish goals, but it seemed we really did want the same thing. "I didn't use the name Elyse Everness to book the ticket."

"Of course you didn't, that would be stupid. You used an anagram of Reyka Solen, and you paid with a credit card you got from one Randolph Hurst, who happens to be a vampire. I put two and two together."

"You did all that drunk?" I was impressed.

He shrugged. "It wasn't that hard. I've already got the algorithms set up to track the known Divine in town. The bigger problem is that you were spotted the minute you got off the train. I was waiting right outside the gate, you just didn't notice me. They went to get some backup, but they'll be poking around here soon enough. We need to get on a plane to Peru."

"So you're going to help me?"

He waved the dagger in front of him. "I want to stick this thing into your heart for all the crap you've done, but first things first. Yeah, I'm going to help you."

"Fair enough. I deserve whatever you want to dish out. You have a car?"

"I can do better than a car. I pulled some strings." He flipped the knife in his hand and held it out to me. "We just need to get outside in one piece. Let's move." He pushed open the door to the closet and peeked out. "You go first. I'll hang back so if anyone tries to grab you, I can hit them from behind."

I stepped in front of him, slipping out the door during a break in traffic and moving into the crowd. I was nearing the Center Cafe when I heard the first scream.

I took the hint, diving to the side as a round of gunfire echoed through the Station. Chips of marble scattered from the spot where

I had been standing, and I came up from my roll facing the shooter. It was just in time to hear the extra loud boom of Obi's Desert Eagle, and watch him drop.

I knew right away he wasn't alone. The shooting had caused most of the mortals to run, to scatter in every direction that wasn't near the now fallen Nicht Creidim. The decision hadn't been unanimous. A half dozen or so stayed back, and even as the other humans shouted, cried, screamed, and fought their way past, they drew their own guns.

Obi was running towards me, and I raised my hand, holding up all of my fingers and then pointing behind him. He rolled his eyes, and then dropped to his knees, sliding along the floor to where the shooter's body lay. He flopped over and levered it, using it as a shield against a sudden barrage. Some of the bullets skipped off the floor around him, creating more divots in the marble. Others found the dead man's flesh. Obi's arm reached out, firing off two quick rounds and dropping two of our attackers.

"Get outside," he shouted back at me, leaving me to make a run for it while he hid beneath a corpse. I wanted to help him, but I only had the knives, and our enemies were too far away. "Go!"

I didn't have a choice. I stayed low while I ran for the doors, where the rest of the people were fighting to get out. More gunshots rang out behind me, and I heard another shout and thud in the background. I joined the crowd, pushing through them and getting outside, finding myself face to face with a policeman.

There was no hesitation when I let go of Elyse and floated into this one, wrapping around his soul and taking control. I felt the hurt of his memories: the demanding parents, the disappointed ex-wife, the rebellious son. He was a good cop though, a straight-shooter with the best intentions.

"Get out of the way!" I started shoving the frightened mortals aside. "Keep it safe," I said to Elyse, who nodded and kept going towards the street.

I hurried back inside as the whole scene fell quiet. Obi had emptied his clip, and apparently so had the Nicht Creidim. There was a frantic rush by both parties to reload, and Obi had to get out from under cover to do it. I took the policeman's gun from its holster and started firing, the bullets missing the target in my still clumsy hands, but doing the job of keeping them distracted. Obi saw me and jumped to his feet, running towards me and using my cover fire to escape and reload. I kept shooting while I rushed the three remaining attackers, my bullets still off the mark but managing to hit one in the shoulder. The other two finished replacing their clips, and I found myself in a hailstorm of metal.

Bullets ate into me, piercing my shoulder, my leg, my chest. My shell was wearing a vest, and so nothing vital got destroyed. I continued the charge, pulling the baton from my belt as I neared them, ignoring the pain of the wounds I was taking. I was out of bullets, but I could still fight.

They didn't bother with knives at this range. I was right in their face, and their guns rose, the muzzle flashes blinding me while the bullets found a better target in my face. I could feel the life draining from my host, but he had done his job. I let him go, giving him a few final breaths before he fell over and died, finding my way to the Nicht Creidim closest to me - a woman in business attire. I was angry enough that I barely noticed the pain of her memories while I wrested control of her body.

The next part was simple. I was too close to miss. I turned to the two men standing next to me and shot them both in the head. Once they were face down, I dropped the gun and started walking towards the exit.

Obi stood there, his mouth gaping. "Rebecca?"

I winked at him.

"Holy crap."

"Elyse is waiting outside. Go get her for me?"

"Yeah, sure."

He turned to leave, but I took hold of his arm.

"You need to shoot me first."

He looked at me, then down at his gun. "I can't…"

"You have to."

He shook his head. "No way. I know you're cold blooded, but I'm not going to shoot someone in cold blood."

I slid my hand forward and pulled the gun from his grip. There was no ceremony to my suicide, and it left him visibly shaken. He stood there for a few seconds, looking at my ghost form.

"Max said you'd changed. I was hoping maybe he meant in a good way."

CHAPTER SIXTEEN

Landon

IT WAS ONE OF THE last places I wanted to be. It was one of those things that a person would never want to have to relive, or remember, and one of the worst experiences of my short mortal life. Not a total loss type of experience, but an embarrassing one.

"Awww, you look so cute," Charis said.

We were standing in the gymnasium of Philip Randolph High School. We were surrounded by teenagers decked out in their youthful finest. Other than the athletes, the boys looked awkward in their rented suits that didn't fit quite right, and the girls looked overdone in bright, frilly gowns that were too tight, or too short, or too revealing. Some random pop song was playing over the strategically placed speakers, and directly in front of us, swaying like a robot with his hands on the hips of Carly Lane, was one of P.R. High's biggest geeks.

Me.

"Daddy, you suck at dancing." Clara had been giggling at me since we had arrived in the memory, stepping out of the door of the eighteenth century mansion and into the door of the gym.

"What did I do to deserve this?" I watched my younger self shift from side to side, the anxiety obvious from a mile away, and flexed my leg.

The wound had healed when we had time-warped, thanks to what Clara called the 'carryover effect'. We were using our connected power to change the Box, to recreate its world in the image of these memories, and make it as real as could be expected here. The creation countered Ross' destruction, and so it had carried over to the damage done to my knee. It was still a little stiff, but it was good to know I could still recover from a hit if needed, even if Clara said it wasn't safe to do a full regeneration.

"I think you're adorable." Charis had watched little me with a smile on her face from the minute we'd arrived. "Just think, in two years you'd be under arrest."

"I wasn't always this nervous. Just with girls." I turned to her. "You're like a whole different world."

"A bad one?"

"I wouldn't say that. Now."

We'd been here for at least an hour; a long time considering how fast Ross had discovered us the first time. I wasn't convinced his delay wasn't intentional. Maybe he was hoping to catch us off-guard? We had passed the time standing there, trying to look like a pair of chaperones, though Clara had drawn a lot of confused glances.

I scanned the room, taking in all of the familiar faces. The captain of the football team, the cheerleaders, the glee club and the nerds. Everything had seemed so contained when I had been in school. Life had seemed so simple... and now? So much was happening behind the scenes. So much that most people would never have a clue about, and I was sure it was better that way.

Harold Nash wasn't looking where he was going, and his shoulder bumped my arm as he stumbled by, trying not to let anyone see the tears in his eyes because his girlfriend had chosen a very poor and public moment to dump him. He muttered an 'excuse me' below his breath without slowing, and I looked back to where Tanisha Peck was watching him go with a sad satisfaction. It was hard to believe that the re-creation of my memories could be so lifelike. In fact, now that we had a few minutes away from Ross, it was amazing to me that we had made all of this inside a cube that would fit in the palm of my hand.

"Bigger on the inside," I said.

Charis' eyes told me she had caught the reference.

"Shouldn't we stand closer to the door?" I asked Clara. She had moved us away from it when we arrived.

"The door doesn't mean anything, dad," she said.

"What do you mean?"

She rolled her eyes. Again. "When we run, we don't need to go through a door. Anything will do."

I pointed to the other side of the gym. "Like a basketball hoop?"

"If you want to think of it that way."

I didn't think I would fit through the hoop. "So we just stand here and wait?"

"I wouldn't recommend it."

I had been expecting Clara's voice. The speaker wasn't her. I looked past her to where one of the kids was standing. Tim. I had known him from the computer class we had been in together. He was tall, thin, brown hair and blue eyes, and smart, very smart. His idols were Aristotle, Copernicus, Tesla, and da Vinci. He had taught me everything I knew about hacking, and I guess in a way was indirectly responsible for me being here. Which is why it also made some kind of twisted sense that he was talking to me, as if he knew what he was talking about.

"What do you mean?"

He looked at Clara, and then Charis before putting his eyes back on me. "It's all about positioning," he said. "Think of it like the sun. All the planets revolve around the sun, and they have orbits that bring them in alignment once in a while, in a period of time that can be calculated based on velocity, gravitational forces, et. cetera. You're like Earth, and he's like Jupiter. If you never move, he'll know exactly when you'll be aligned, and you won't have time to get out of the way."

"Clara?" Charis asked, looking for confirmation.

"You're cute," she said. "It isn't that simple."

Tim looked offended. "Why not?"

"You haven't accounted for interference. Variable gravitational force."

"It's minimal. You're over-emphasizing the effect."

"I am not."

Tim smiled. "You are."

"I am not."

"Yes, you are. Don't believe me? Just keep standing there. He already knows exactly where you are, he's just waiting for the right moment."

I had no idea what they were arguing about, but those were all the words I needed to hear. "There's no harm in moving," I said, reaching out and taking Clara by the hand. For a minute, I thought she would resist, but she followed along, with Charis bringing up the rear.

"Where are we going?" she asked.

"Does it matter?" I replied, pulling them towards the doors on the opposite side of the gym. We'd have to cut through the middle of the dance floor, and maybe I'd even have to come face to face with myself, but it was better than the thousand ton anvil that was Ross falling on our heads.

"See, I was right," Tim said, watching us run. "You gained a few seconds."

I still had no idea how he knew what was going on, but I would work that one out later. We reached the crowd of teenagers at the center of the room, and I very unceremoniously shoved geek-me aside. "Excuse me."

The activity drew the attention of the real chaperones, who starting shouting to one another. A moment later the music vanished, and a couple of unarmed security guards moved into our path. I didn't remember any guards at my prom.

"Not that way," Clara said when she saw them. Both guards began to grow, gaining height, fur, and claws, until a pair of Great Weres were blocking the doors instead.

"Where then?" I turned around, searching for another way out. The kids were all backing away, leaving us standing alone in the middle of the room. I heard a scream, and one of the teachers arced up over the kids, coming to land in front of us, her head nearly severed from her neck.

"You remember Mrs. Trainor, don't you?" Ross asked. I couldn't see him yet, but the sight sent the others into a scattered panic. They rushed in every direction, trying to escape him, or the Weres, or both.

I looked down at the body of my science teacher. She had always been one of my favorites. "Clara?" We needed a way out. Any way out.

"Climb," she said.

"Climb wh-" A rope was hanging from the rafters. A rope that hadn't been there a second ago. "Charis, take Clara. I'll slow him down."

"How are you going to do that?" she asked.

"Just climb."

She didn't question, because she knew it would only be a waste of time. She picked Clara up and positioned her to cling from her back. Then she started to climb.

I heard snarls and I turned to face the Weres. They were both coming at me, their huge forms covering the distance in a half-dozen strides. I realized as I watched them gather that I wasn't the target at all.

I focused and pushed, sending a shockwave through the ground and shattering the wood floor with the force of my launch. I got there before they could lift off, using my momentum to grab the arm of one and swing him into the other, and letting it pull us all back to the end of the room. I felt my heart catch in fear as the wall of the gym came rocketing towards us. There was no healing here, and I was about to splatter myself.

Only, I didn't. Somehow, I found enough of something to get myself turned so that one of the Weres was between the wall and me. He hit it first, with enough force to break every bone in his body, and to smash through the cinderblocks to expose the outside. I felt my body compress against his, his ribs breaking, and my own stretching to their limit. Then I tumbled to the floor, the wind knocked out of me.

"Your artistry was decent, but your technical was crap, kid," Ross said.

I was on my hands and knees, trying to regain myself. He was standing a few feet away, and I could see Clara and Charis dangling from the top of the rope behind him. He noticed me looking back, so he turned too.

"Don't worry about them. They can't go anywhere without you, and you can't go anywhere without going through me. Which, I don't think I need to tell you, doesn't look promising."

I shoved myself to my feet, prepared to take my chances.

"You had me there for a minute, kid. It's a weird feeling, not being able to find someone in a finite space. Then, I remembered something."

"What's that?" I shouldn't have given him the satisfaction, but I needed every second I could get to regain my strength.

He smiled.

"I'm the god here."

He turned and waved his hand. The rope snapped, sending Charis and Clara into a hundred foot free-fall. In the same motion, he turned back to me and I felt my breath get choked off.

It's a strange thing, when you think you have a chance, and then discover that you don't. Thousands of thoughts race through your head at once, but in front of them all is the pain of failure, and the terror of knowing the consequences. We had been on the run for an hour out of an eternity. It might as well have been a millisecond for all the good we had done. Clara was going to die and this time she wouldn't be back. Ross would cage us, and keep us, to flog and flay until the end of time, or until he sprung himself from the Box, and our torture continued back in the 'real'. I would have hung my head had there been time. I would have at least felt that first drop of remorse.

It was all interrupted by the twist, the change in expectations that brought everything full-circle. My eyes were blurring, my throat was on fire, and Ross was standing over me, the satisfied, arrogant grin painted across his face. I could see myself in the reflection of his shades, on my knees, my face white. I could feel the life draining from me, the death that when added to Charis' would reset this squared universe back into his design.

Then his face changed. The grin morphed into a scream, and a burst of light exploded from the corner of his neck, growing in intensity as the line moved from right to left until it severed his head from his body.

I had seen them fall, but I hadn't seen Charis catch them. I hadn't seen her use her own control of Ross' power to rip a claw from the other Great Were's hand, or come up behind him to use the improvised weapon.

"Some god," she said, while the corpse tumbled to the floor. My ability to breathe returned, and everything around us began to crumble.

"Take my hand," Clara said, holding it out to me.

I fell forward in order to latch on, and the world around us reorganized.

CHAPTER SEVENTEEN

Rebecca

WE WERE SUPPOSED TO HAVE a police escort to Dulles, the arrangement that Obi had told me about. It didn't work out that way, due to the war zone the Nicht Creidim had created around the train station. Instead, we had been forced to steal another car and hope that in the aftermath it wouldn't be noticed until we were well away.

The ride was tense, and Obi refused to speak to me. I tried to explain to him about the sword, about His redemption, and about my desire to save Landon. He told me to shut up because I was making his head hurt more than it already did. He didn't want to know about redemption or the notion that I had been saved by God.

"If God saved you," he said, " it was an accident."

The words hurt, but I understood. Dealing with the Divine took a toll on everyone, and mortals most of all. It was more than the things he had lost himself. It was also the things he had to see and endure. The hundreds of dead they had left in their wake, innocent mortals caught up as pawns in the Beast's game, the violence and chaos of an undying war. He had a right to be angry, and in my soul I forgave him for it.

We made it to the airport, found a flight to Peru, and were thirty thousand feet up only four hours after arriving in D.C. I felt relieved to be skyward, though there was a part of me that feared we had been spotted. It would be trivial for a fire demon to rip the plane right out of the air, and we couldn't count on the seraphim to protect us.

Maybe we hadn't been spotted, or maybe they had chosen to let us alone. In either case, the plane landed in Cusco with no interruptions. I spent the entire flight sleeping, waking to find my head on an also-sleeping Obi-wan's shoulder. I picked it up and shifted in the seat, and then shoved his arm to wake him. His eyes shot open and he reached for his gun, which had been glamoured as a laptop and put into my pack with everything else.

"We're here," I told him, pointing out the window at the cement and grass rolling by. "Did he say where to meet him?"

"No." He brought his hand up and wiped away a bit of drool from his lip. "Did you manage to make it through the flight without killing anybody?"

I glared at him for a second, and then looked away. Maybe I was being heavy-handed with my approach, but what choice did I have? It was the way I knew how to fight, and how to survive.

We were off the plane and walking through the terminal when Obi's phone began to ring. He pulled it from the pocket of his jeans and stared at it for a second before answering.

"We're here," he said. There was a pause while the caller spoke. "Crap. Okay. Be there in five." He hung up.

"Well?"

"Max has a lead on our first target, but he said they're getting antsy. We need to rendezvous with him at the terminal entrance. He's got a car." He started walking faster, his size forcing me to jog to keep up with him.

"Target? Obi, I don't know what the hell we're supposed to be doing here."

He shrugged. "Neither do I, but I've run out of things to trust, so

I'm just going with my gut. If we've got a target, I'm going to hit it."

His fast walk turned into a run, and I sped up to keep pace behind him. We dashed through the airport, winding our way around the other patrons, who turned and watched us like we were crazy. We reached a set of stairs and Obi jumped, falling from the first platform to the second fifteen feet below, and landing like it was no trouble at all. I couldn't duplicate the move, but my smaller feet took the steps faster, and I hit the ground floor only a dozen feet behind him. I could see the exit up ahead, a wall of glass and sliding doors with cars parked out behind it.

Obi barely slowed when he reached it, almost crashing through the glass instead of waiting for the doors to slide open. He shoved himself through the crack and then stopped, his head flailing in each direction. He saw something, and started towards it at a run.

I followed behind, trying to see past his body to whatever had clued him in. A limo driver in a black suit and cap, holding up a placard that said 'Solen'.

"A pleasure," Max said when we reached him. He threw open the door to a dusty stretch and helped shove us into the back. Then he ran around to the driver's side and got behind the wheel. He tore away from the gate, the momentum throwing me into Obi's lap.

"Get off me," Obi said, his hands finding all the wrong spots as he tried to shove me away.

"Are you sure?" I asked. "Your paws seem to have a different idea."

He scowled while I pushed myself to the bench seat immediately behind Max. "Max, are you sure we need her?"

His laughter was musical. "I'm afraid so, old chap. Afraid so. Hold on."

The wheels screamed and the car shifted. I braced myself against the roof to keep from being thrown around again.

"Would you mind telling us what the hell we're doing?" I spun around and watched the forward view. Max was careening around the rest of the traffic, driving the long limo like it was a Lotus.

He turned his head to look at me. "Of course, of course. I've got a line on the djinn who has the Damned."

"The damned what?"

He laughed and turned the wheel, sending us around a guy on a scooter. He wasn't even looking at the road.

"No, no. Just the Damned. It's one of the Swords of Gehenna, the counterpart to the Redeemer, actually. We need to retrieve it."

Obi threw himself to the space next to me. "What do we need it for?"

"I told you already, lug nut. I want to get Landon out of the Box." He finally put his eyes back on the road, slowing behind an old van before accelerating around it. "That's not accurate. I want to help Landon get himself out of the Box. I think he can do it, but he'll need a little outside intervention."

"What kind of intervention? What are you talking about?"

"Balance, sweet cakes. In case you still haven't wrapped your mind around it, everything that has happened was meant to happen. In fact, it's all going rather swimmingly."

Obi's face began to flush, and he looked like he wanted to strangle the Templar. "Swimmingly? Are you kidding me?"

"It's a long story, but for now I think it's enough to say that even if Landon had known he was part of the bigger plan, he would have been more eager to go along with it, not less. I'm driving this limo a hundred kilometers per hour for a reason."

"So you're saying there's a way out?" I asked.

He looked back at me and nodded vigorously. "Of course there's a way out. There's always been a way out, it just... well... let us find the djinn and the Damned first, and then I'll tell you everything I know. If we don't recover the swords, my words are wind."

He blew around a Toyota and sped up even more. Within

minutes, we had entered the main city of Cusco, and were captured by the downtown traffic.

"How did you hear about this djinn?" I asked, looking out the window to the mountains surrounding us.

"I've always known about this djinn, and I've always known he has the Damned. I also know who gave it to him."

"How?" Obi asked. His eyes darted back and forth, taking in the sights of the city, right now a line of cars traveling in both directions down the main square, with pedestrians walking on either side.

Max's laughter was loud and deep. "I'll give you a hint. He's driving this car."

I was confused before. I was more confused now. "You gave it to him? So why don't you just ask for it back?"

"I wish I could, my sweet. I'm afraid he's grown quite partial to my gift, and is less than willing to return it. I'm hoping to convince him, but if not..."

He didn't need to finish the statement, but I wasn't sure how we were supposed to help him handle a djinn. I didn't even know what kind of power they held beyond Kafrit's ability to extract absorbed souls.

The car came to a sudden stop, pushing Obi and I into the back of the seat.

"Time to run," Max said, opening his door. Our doors opened at the same time, and we poured out of the limo while the cars behind us began to honk and their drivers started to scream. "Too-da-loo!" Max waved to them.

We followed him at a run, across the thoroughfare and down a smaller street. Left, then right, two blocks, and then left again at a full sprint. Nobody seemed to notice the demon, but Obi and I were mortal, and we didn't get any such invisibility. Every eye followed us when we passed.

One more right turn, and we were standing in a small alley

where a woman was sitting against a stone wall, a large white dog laying at her side, its head in her lap. She looked up as we came to a stop in front of her.

"Abaz?" Max asked, his deep voice echoing down the alley. "Come on, my furry friend. I know it's you."

The dog lifted its head lazily, turned and licked the woman's face. She stood up.

"A strange congregation. Who are you?"

She was wearing a long gypsy skirt, a white linen blouse, and sandals. Her skin was a dark olive, her hair brown and sun drenched. Every finger wore a different ring, and her neck was submerged in chains. If the dog was a djinn, this woman had to be a witch, a servant to the Divine lounging next to her.

"My name is Max-"

"No, not you." She put up her hand, one of the rings flashed, and Max froze in place. "You." She pointed at me. "You wear the Eye. Who are you?"

"Let him go, and I'll answer your question," I said.

"Answer my question anyway." Another ring flashed, and I felt some kind of power roll through. I was reminded of Sarah's attempt to Command me.

"Maybe I won't," I replied, moving towards her.

She wasn't afraid, but she shifted her head, curious. "Immune?" She looked over at the dog.

I heard a click next to me, and saw that Obi had pulled his gun. He was aiming it at the dog. "We don't have a lot of time for games. Are you Abaz, or not?"

I didn't see it happen, but one moment the Desert Eagle was in the former marine's hand, and the next it wasn't. He was left standing there, pantomiming.

"Not," the smooth voice said. The dog was gone, replaced with a small man with a thin mustache and flat nose, dressed in a white linen suit and holding Obi's gun.

"I can get a message to him, for a price," the witch said.

"We need to see him in person," I said. "What's the price for that?"

"Tell me who you are, and then I'll name my price."

I looked back and forth between the djinn and the witch. Who was a slave to who?

"My name is Elyse, I'm-"

I didn't get to finish before the djinn was behind me with a knife to my throat.

"I didn't ask for the name of your shell," she said. "I asked for your name."

I saw it now, the Eye etched into the ring she wore on her right pinkie. It was an otherwise plain, tin thing that looked loose on her finger.

"You can see me?"

Her head dipped and raised.

"My name is Rebecca."

The knife pressed against my neck, and I felt the bite of the blade and the warm stickiness of the blood it was drawing.

"No. Your real name. I won't ask again."

"Reyka. Reyka Solen."

The djinn was gone. The knife was gone. He was standing at her side again.

"See, that wasn't so hard. I've heard the name Solen before. Vampires, from New York. You're Merov's girl. Ah, yes, I see it now. The betrayer." She laughed. "No, I won't bring you to Abaz. You can't be trusted."

I had to hold my breath to contain my anger. We needed to see Abaz, to get the Damned back. I wasn't going to let some petulant witch stand in the way of that.

"Whoa, wait a second," Obi said. "What if we go without her?"

The witch's laughter got louder, and the djinn joined her. "You don't understand, Jedi. I know who you are. I know why you're here. I know what you want from Abaz. I won't give it to you. Like these djinn, the sword is ours. Go back to whoever sent you, and tell them that the creator Himself can't pry the blade from our hands."

"That's not an option," Obi said.

She shrugged. "You prefer to fight over it? Very well."

There was no time. The djinn appeared behind me again, his arm wrapping around my neck and bringing the blade in to cut it open. I tried to squirm away, but his grip was ridiculous.

The next thing I knew, I was laying in the middle of the street, the leather jacket the only thing that saved me from some serious road burn. The djinn had stayed airborne until he smashed into the wall of the building on the opposite side of where we started. What the hell had hit me?

"You aren't playing fair," I heard Max say. Had he thrown me?

My confusion was lost when the ground started shaking. I propped myself up on my elbows to see the demon standing between the witch and us. His back had sprouted a row of spiked bone along his spine, and a pair of black leathery wings hung from his shoulder blades. He turned an enlarged, bony head back towards me.

"Uh... run?"

He turned around and grabbed Obi, his wings launching them towards the sky. A moment later, the walls on both sides of the alley collapsed inwards, putting a pile of rubble where we had been standing.

I got to my feet and turned around, looking for the djinn. His jacket was laying in the street, but he was gone. Max landed beside me, clutching an almost white Obi.

"What the hell, Max?" I asked.

"It's a long story, lollipop, with a lot of deceit and trickery involved." He looked almost embarrassed.

"Save the chit-chat," Obi said. "They're getting away."

"I'll get her," Max said. "Rebecca, can I give you a lift?" He looked at Obi. "I nearly broke my back getting you away from the collapse."

Before I could prepare myself, Max grabbed my arm and swung me around, and then wrapped his arms under my shoulders and carried us into the sky. We circled the city while the demon searched for the witch.

"There. That car."

I didn't see the car he was talking about. We launched from the sky at a ridiculous speed. I could feel my hair whipping out behind me, and my face being pressed back against the bone. It was exhilarating.

We slowed when we neared the car, an old green Land Rover. I could see the djinn behind the wheel, the witch riding in the back. She didn't turn her head to look back at us. She tossed a small bag out of the side window.

We passed it by, and I turned my head to watch it tumble to a stop. A moment later, it began to grow.

"Golem!" The stone around the bag pulled in and gathered, rising up into the shape of a man. It started running behind us, chasing us. It was fueled by the power of the djinn, and it moved faster than Max could fly.

Max looked back at it. "I'm going to drop you on the car, okay?"

I didn't like the sound of it, but what other choice did we have? "Do it."

His wings shifted, and we shot forward. The moment we were over the Land Rover, he spread them wide and we were caught like a parasail, standing us upright and giving me one moment in time to drop onto the car at the same speed. He let go, and I fell onto the roof.

I only looked back once to see him land behind me, a black sword appearing in his hand. Had he picked my pocket? The golem slowed to fight him, leaving me to deal with the witch and her servant.

I took a deep breath and pulled a cursed dagger from my boot while I clung precariously to the small seam between the roof and one of the back windows. I felt the motion of the car, and I guessed what was going to happen. I swung my legs out of the way, letting them dangle from the side of the car as a stiletto punched through the sheet metal. It looked more like a syringe than a sword, and I could only imagine what it would do if it punctured me. Gathering my strength I pushed back and swung in, my legs going through the open window. I let go of the roof and fell inside, getting a lucky boot into the witch's face as a reward.

"Solen," the witch said.

She stabbed at my ankle with the blade. I could see it more clearly now, a cylinder of crystal with a greenish liquid inside. Poison? I pulled my left foot back and crossed over with the right, kicking her hand away. She reached out with the other and one of the rings flared. Her touch on my skin itched, but she seemed confused by the lack of effect.

"You think a Nicht Creidim would go anywhere without protection from fire?" I threw my body forward and smothered her, knocking her against the side of the car.

"What about from ice?" I couldn't see her hand, but the next time she touched me, it burned as much as fire. I brought the dagger around towards her face, but her other hand came up and blocked it.

The pain of the cold was spreading. I had to get her hand off me. I gathered my weight and shoved myself back away, breaking the contact but winding up on the opposite side of the car. She smiled, and the door opened.

I should have fallen out, but somehow I managed to dig the dagger into the upholstery and hang onto it while I fought to keep my legs from dragging onto the pavement and pulling me away from my grip. I could hear the witch laughing.

"You have no power, Rebecca. There is nothing you can do."

I hung there. I had thought taking Elyse's body and having the power of the artifacts the Nicht Creidim had collected would give back what I was lacking, but I was being trounced by the first real demon I had squared up against. And she wasn't even a demon. Just a mortal who had somehow gained more power than she should have been able to. If we hadn't been in a speeding car I could have tried to possess her, but there was no guarantee that would work either, especially when she had an Eye.

"Sacerdos ab Ordinario delegatus, rite confessus, aut saltem corde peccata sua detestans, peracto, si…"

I felt a tug at my soul. The bitch was trying to exorcise me!

That was when I remembered the red crystals. I reached into the pocket of the jacket with my gloved hand, grabbing one of them, but then I hesitated. If I killed her, she wouldn't be able to take us to Abaz and the sword. If I didn't kill her, she was going to blast me to who knows where, and probably kill Elyse.

I glanced over at the djinn, still driving the car and ignoring everything that was happening behind him.

"…obsessum ligatum, si sit periculum, eum, se et astantes communiat…"

The pull was growing, a pressure that wanted to steal me away from Elyse. I made up my mind, taking the crystal and rubbing it between my fingers.

"…genibus flexis, aliis respondentibus, dicat…"

I strained against the pull, feeling so much tension in every movement. The runes on the crystal began to glow, and it took all of my energy just to drop it at her feet. The crystal threw up a gout of hellfire, catching the witch off-guard and reducing her to ash in the space of a breath.

It also made the car explode.

CHAPTER EIGHTEEN

Rebecca

I FELT THE HEAT OF it wash against me, and then I was in the air, surrounded by metal. The ground moved perpendicular to me, changing from gravel to grass. I curled up, hoping to minimize the number of bones that would break on impact.

Elyse was stronger than she looked, or at least the runes on her body held true. I hit the ground and half-rolled, half-slid along it, feeling the force of the impact, but not shattering beneath it. Finally, I came to a stop.

I looked up at the road. The car was gone, reduced to nothing but fragments. I had been lucky none of them had hit me. The witch was gone, dead for sure. The Damned? She'd had it stashed somewhere, and now we'd have to find it the old-fashioned way.

What about the djinn? Had he died in the explosion, or whisked himself away? I didn't know enough about their power to know if that was even possible.

I turned back the way we had come. We had joined a road headed up into the mountains, and behind me was a bit of pavement and a turn. There was no sign or sound of the demon Templar despite the fact that killing the witch would have destroyed the golem. Where had he gone off to? I stared at the turn for a few minutes, watching for his appearance. When he didn't show, I took a seat in the road and waited.

An hour passed before they came around the corner, riding an old rusted motorcycle with an equally dilapidated sidecar attached. Max was driving, his form returned to its more normal visage and his head bedecked in a pith helmet and thick riding goggles. Obi rested in the car, his hand balanced across the front of it, Desert Eagle aimed forward.

"What took you so long?" I asked as the bike stopped alongside me.

"My apologies, pumpkin pie. After you killed the witch, I returned to Cusco to pick up our feisty friend here. It took me a bit of time to find transportation that wouldn't clue them in to our arrival from a mile away." He patted the worn seat behind him. "Shall we get going?"

"The djinn who was driving the car got away. I have a feeling subtlety is off the table. Anyway, I'm not going anywhere with you. First, give me back the stone." I held out my hand.

"A pity, that. I was hoping for a frictionless encounter." Max's face split in half from the length of his grin. He reached under the helmet and let the stone roll into his hand, then tossed it to me. "I was just borrowing it."

"How did you even know I had it?"

The question just made him laugh harder.

He patted the seat again. "We need to get moving, dearie."

I didn't expect Obi to pipe up for me, but he did. "Wait a second, man. Enough of this crap. First, what the hell are you? Second, what the hell are we doing here? You said you would explain when you had time. Ding, dong, the witch is dead. You have time." He jumped out of the sidecar for emphasis, coming to stand next to me with his arms crossed.

Max sighed, took off the helmet and goggles, and dismounted the bike. His normally mirthful appearance turned sullen. "You're right of course, General. I should explain myself to you. First, I'm sure Rebecca can tell you what I am."

I nodded. "In part, I can." I looked at Obi. "Max is a Templar, a Divine sworn to fight the Beast. He's also a demon, which I think makes him unique among all of the Templars. It also turns out, he's more powerful than he's let on, and not at all what he's sold himself as." I turned my gaze to Max, angry curiosity gathering. "How a reaper has managed to survive outside of the depths of the pit for this long? I can't answer that."

"A reaper?" Obi asked. "As in Blue Oyster Cult?"

"Not quite," Max said. "That would be my boss. Or at least, the boss of all of the other reapers. As I said, sugar plum, it involves quite a bit of deceit and trickery, which happen to be my forte. Suffice it to say, Death is not very pleased with me right now."

Obi put up his hands. "Back the bus up, man. First, Death is a real... umm... I don't know... thing? Second, how are we supposed to believe anything you say, when you just said you're the God of Lies."

Max sighed again. "Obi, Obi, Obi... Death is not death. That is a process that is typically rather natural in mortals, and while there is a chaotic logic to it, it's self-managed. My Death is the Lord of Death, a demon whose main purpose it to torture murderers. People who have caused the death of others. The reapers are his helpers, and because they're assigned to deal with the souls of the violent, they're gifted more of Satan's power, via Death, than is typical. I'm not a god. Not even close. But I am a liar, a cheat, a thief, and an accomplished actor. You'll believe me, because you have no choice. You'll also believe me because above all things I'm a Templar, and my number one purpose is to rid this universe of the Beast."

I looked from the demon to Obi and back. I hadn't seen the former marine look happy yet, and he looked even less happy now. His shoulders slumped, and he stayed silent.

"What are we doing here, Max?" I asked.

"The Box," he said, "is a prison. A prison has a door. A door has a key. Or in this case, six keys. Three went to the demons, three to the angels."

I unslung the pack from my back and held it up in front of us. "This isn't a prison. I can let everything out any time I want to."

Max shrugged. "That is one way of looking at it, I suppose."

He knelt down in the road, taking a narrow dagger from somewhere on his person and scratching a square with a straight line through it. He drew two 'D's on one side, and a 'B' on the other. "This is the inside of the Box." He waved his hand, and the letters all moved onto the line. "This is what is happening now." The letters started moving across one another, but always stayed on the line. "Landon and Charis fight the Beast, but the Box is a universe of its own, and as a result it maintains its balance. The Beast will win some, the disucrucises will win some, but neither will gain a strong upper hand."

He smiled again. "As you know, the balance can shift and teeter before it topples. Like this universe, it can be toppled, but it won't be easy." He reached out and took my pack, unzipping it and removing the Box. "When the flow of energy changes color, that means the balance is shifting one way or another. Which way? I don't know."

The flow was steady right now, an even, pulsing blue. He put it back in the pack and handed the whole thing back to me.

"It's no accident that Landon and Charis are in the Box with the Beast. It had to be so to contain him. Of course, I couldn't tell him that ahead of time, because he might have altered his plans in an effort to find a more final solution, a solution that doesn't exist. This is no trivial situation. It took Malize a millennia of meditation and thought, and two millennia of preparation to build the tree whose branches we now flutter upon like sick sparrows. Even so, our success is anything but assured. There are still so many factors and so many things that can go wrong - the future isn't preordained after all. Malize tried to guide the pieces into the right spot, but the game still has to be played to its final move."

It was a lot to take in. A lot to consider. "My redemption?" I asked.

"Why do you think Malize gave Landon the sword? It wasn't to stab you with it, per se, but it was one of the futures he predicted and arranged for out of many possible futures. It just happened to be the one that came to pass."

"You're saying we have no control?" Obi asked. "That our fate is some logic tree?"

The Templar shook his head. "Quite the opposite. Malize postulated what *could* happen. He didn't see into some kind of threads of potential of what *would* happen. It's an algorithm of possibilities."

"Fine. Where do the swords fit in? You said that they're keys?"

"Exactly. Keys to a prison. The power of the swords will hold the Beast inside, and give Landon and Charis the opportunity to get out."

"And then what?"

Max looked confused. "What do you mean?"

"The Beast's power can't be contained in the Box on its own. That's the whole reason they had to go inside in the first place. If you let them out, then what?"

Max raised his finger. "Ah... the confusion. No, my candy corn, Landon and Charis will come out, but the power that binds them to one another, and together to the Beast, will be left inside. He'll still be trapped as he always was, like a fly to a glue trap."

I felt my breath hang. "But, Landon and Charis... You mean they'll be..."

"Mortal?" he replied. "Maybe, but I don't think so. To be honest, I'm not sure what they'll be, other than out of the Box and back in this universe. Will they move on to Purgatory? It's possible. I don't know."

It wasn't a comforting thought. Landon would be free, but as what? A mortal? A spirit like me? Neither were fates I would wish on him or his loved one.

"I know you thought this would be easy... but there are some... complications." Max chuckled at his sarcasm. "First, we can only open the door inside the Beast's original prison. It will allow us to capture his remaining power and get it all in one place. More importantly, the creature Gervais also has set his sights on the power of the Box, and since he has possession of the Redeemer and the only path back to said prison, we'll have no choice but to bring everything he needs right to him. Third, we'll need to keep an eye out for Baal's daughter, Vilya."

"What about her?" Obi asked, finally speaking up again. "She's on our side."

Max's face darkened.

"She's not on our side?"

"No."

"But... she saved Charis from Hell," Obi said. "She said she... crap."

"How do you know?" I asked.

"Consider it for yourself. She rescues a Templar from Hell by allowing her soul to be absorbed, thereby insuring that she will have a direct line to the Beast when it all comes down. Not only that, she knows that she'll have to be released from captivity in order for the diuscrusises to put the Beast in the Box."

I did consider it for myself. "It sounds a little too convenient," I said. "How could the Beast have known what it would take for them to trap him?"

"His true age is almost beyond measure. You don't believe he understands the rules of higher existence? In any case, I was masquerading as one of his servants while I was in Hell myself. Believe me, she's a servant of the Beast. Sarah was smart not to trust her and tell her where she was hiding, but she doesn't need to find Sarah. Gervais has the best chance of getting the Box back, and so she's waiting for him to retrieve it. That's when she'll make her move."

Obi shook his head. "If she's a servant, why didn't she try to help the Beast *before* he went into the Box?"

"Contingencies, my good man. Malize isn't the only one who has them."

"That's great. Just great. So… Vilya and Izak have a death match. Who wins?"

"Do you want the bad news now, or later?"

Now it was the former marine's turn to laugh. "Oh, now you're going to tell us the bad news?"

"When the two most powerful demons in the world have a death match, what kind of collateral damage do you think that will create? The whole thing is a super typhoon that we're not only going to have to walk right into the middle of, but we're going to be forced to create in order to succeed."

I shivered with a sudden chill that went right through Elyse's body and into my soul. "Is there any good news?"

His eyes brightened, and he smiled. "Yes, my cookie. You can't be killed. Plus, we'll have the swords. It should balance things out a bit."

I was really starting to hate that word.

CHAPTER NINETEEN

Landon

"GOOD EVENING. MY NAME IS Walter, and I'll be your server. Can I get you started with a glass of water? Do you prefer sparkling or flat?"

I blinked a couple of times and looked at Walter. He was decked out in a fancy tux and bow tie, a picture of classic servitude. Charis was sitting across from me, a smile on her face and a glow in the air around her. She was vision of splendor and beauty in a deep red velvet dress. I returned her smile, but I wasn't feeling comfortable. Where was Clara? Where were we?

"Flat is perfect. Can we also see a wine list?" Charis asked. Walter bowed and headed off to fulfill the request.

"Where are we?"

She moved her head in a slow arc. "You've never been here? New York City. The Oak Room. I came here once before, with Joseph." She pointed to a table in a dark corner. "Back there."

I shifted so I could see where she was pointing. I couldn't make her out from here. All I saw was a slender leg that ended in a red pump. I could see Joseph though, his brown hair and stubble framing his strong jaw and bringing out his blue eyes.

"Are you okay?" I asked. This memory couldn't have been easy.

"You're sweet for asking. I'm fine. I thought of this memory on purpose. I wanted to share this place, this time with you. I loved Joseph, but that was as far as it went. I know that sounds trite. You... you're more than love. I know you, inside and out. We've already been through so much together."

I knew what she was saying, because I felt it, too. Not that I had too much experience with love, or how it felt to be in it. I just knew what I would sacrifice, what I would do in her name. I knew I wanted her around, and I wished we could have a normal life, a house and a real Clara. Maybe it was simplistic, but it would do.

Walter returned with the wine list and the water. He filled our glasses. "How are we doing over here?"

"We're fine, Walter."

"Very good. Please, browse the wine list. If you have any questions, don't hesitate to ask. I'll be back in a few minutes." He headed off again to wait on another table.

Charis flipped through the wine list. This was way too normal and it made me uncomfortable.

"Where's Clara?" I asked.

"I sent her away," she replied, as if that was a perfectly normal answer.

"What do you mean... sent her away?"

"She's waiting in a limo outside, keeping an eye out for the Beast. Just relax, Landon, and you'll be able to feel her, too. I just wanted some alone time with you, while he's busy being regenerated. We won one, and we deserve a chance to celebrate."

I took a deep breath and tried to calm myself. When I did, I could sense Clara as Charis had said, in a car in the street outside the restaurant, watching YouTube.

My next smile was authentic.

"I still can't believe it. You were amazing."

She shook her head, causing her hair to fall in front of an eye and framing her face in the most beautiful way possible. "I was desperate."

"Not that much of a difference."

Walter wandered back over and Charis ordered a bottle of champagne. I imagined it was expensive, but this was our construction - we didn't need to think about money.

"So," I said, pausing. "I think this is the first minute we've had to rest since we met. Even that was… how long ago? It feels like a week and a lifetime both."

"Yeah, everything's been pretty rushed. Then again, time has little enough meaning here."

"Or out there." I remembered my battle with Abaddon, and what he had said. Ten thousand years, and for what? Looking at Charis, at least there was something to be grateful to have eternity for. "It's just… I don't know… if this were a normal relationship I'd be asking you about your childhood, and your folks, and your hopes and dreams. I already know all of that stuff."

"Maybe, but I think some of my opinions of those memories are going to be changing. This place is changing us. How could it not? I remember what he did." Her voice trailed off, and she looked down at her plate.

Walter saved the day, returning with the champagne. She snapped out of her pain and watched him pop the cork and pour.

"Are you ready to order?" he asked.

"We're good with the champagne for now," she said.

"As you wish." He left again.

She raised her glass to me. "To you, and to Clara. Two bright points of light in the darkness of this hell."

I had raised my glass with hers, but I flinched at her toast. "We'll get out of here. I promise."

Her smile was hopeful but unconvinced. We tapped glasses and took a long pull on the bubbly, and then poured some more. I lifted it to drink, but she put her hand on my wrist to stop me.

"Not too fast," she said. "I want you to remember this moment, this setting. Commit it, just in case. One speck of normalcy in our lives."

I nodded and took in the picture of the restaurant, the vision of her, the breaths I was taking without being on the run. I'd been dead for five years, and only now did I feel any sense of peace at all.

It was interrupted when the other Charis went storming past, Joseph following behind her. She looked angry, and he looked remorseful. I knew what he had done, what he had said. I knew what had happened after, in the heat of the apology and the tide of the emotions. Everything was always so urgent. Despite our shared affection and the fact that here we had a child, we'd had no time for that.

Her look was mischievous. "You have a look in your eye," she said.

I could feel my face flushing. "Just a thought. Maybe a regret. There's something about you that Joseph knew, that I don't. Not personally, anyway."

"I could say the same about you."

I laughed. "No you can't, and you know it." Nobody knew me that way. I'd never had the chance.

She licked her lips, and then pushed her chair back and stood up. "We should do something about that."

My heart began to pound, the heat in my face intensifying. "What about Clara?"

She came over and took my hand. "She's fine in the car. She'll let us know if the Beast shows up. Come on, love."

I stood up, and her lips met me there, soft and warm and filled with passion. We stayed that way for too long to be appropriate, and when she broke the kiss I was a puddle of goo. I reached into a pocket and found a wad of cash, which I dropped onto the table.

"That should cover it," I said. Charis started dragging me towards the door.

We were out of the restaurant and passing through the bar. It was a stroke of luck, bad or good I'm not sure, that I noticed anything at all other than Charis, and even better or worse luck that I saw the smoke.

"Charis, wait," I said.

I stopped and stared at the wisp of white air rising from the bar. It curled up into the sky and then spread apart into perfectly formed angel wings. I followed it back down to a slender cigarette, and the cigarette to dry lips mixed into a white beard. The head shifted just a little, just enough so that I could see that the smoker knew I was there, and knew I was looking at him.

"It can't be."

I looked back at Charis, who seemed just as shocked. I had a sudden feeling our consummation of the relationship would be waiting a bit longer.

I walked over to the bar. Charis and I found a space on either side of the man, and leaned in. We were nice and close, and when I made eye contact I was sure.

"Avriel. How are you here?"

"Who are you?" he asked, suspicious. "How do you know my name?"

I stared at him without answering. Avriel wasn't supposed to be in the Box. Avriel had been set free. What the hell was going on?

"Well?" he asked again. "Who are you, and how do you know my name?"

Something had changed. Was Avriel himself, or was he Ross? Had he recovered that quickly? "Are you Avriel? Avriel the Just?"

He was deliberate, taking the cigarette from his mouth and stamping it out in a nearby ashtray. "Who wants to know?"

"My name is L-"

Before I could finish, he'd pushed his bench out of the way, and a wrinkled hand was headed for my face. I ducked under it just in time, but didn't avoid the knee that caught me in the gut and bent me over.

"Get away from me," he shouted. "Both of you. Get away from me." He pushed his way past us and ran out the door.

"Just when you thought it was safe to go back in the water," I said.

Charis kissed my cheek. "I guess you still owe me."

We ran after him.

Clara was waiting for us outside, leaning up against the side of the limo. I did a double-take when I saw her, because she had grown up again. She was barely a child anymore, now a teenager with all of Charis' looks.

"Which way?" I asked her, skidding to a stop. She tilted her head behind her, and I saw his back vanish over the wall and into Central Park. "You could have stopped him."

She smiled. "I didn't know he was running away from you."

"Ross?" This wasn't part of the original memory, I was sure.

"No. He's not strong enough. Not yet."

"Come on." I hit the gas again, and the three of us ran across the road, playing Frogger with the cars and vaulting the wall behind Avriel. We raced along the path, dodging pedestrians and keeping an eye out for a suit with long white hair, but he was gone.

"Lost him," Charis said, pulling to a stop and looking around.

"Clara, you can't find him?" I asked.

"Sorry, Pops. I've got nothing."

I spun around, searching the trees. There was nothing but shadows. I walked over to Charis and put my forehead against hers. "Whatever he is, he's gone. We might as well go back to plan 'A'."

"Guys... gross." Clara joined us, her eyes sparkling in the starlight. In the moment, I wished more than anything that we were normal, and she were real. Was it crazy to love a figment of your imagination?

"How long until Ross levels up?" I asked.

"You know time is meaningless, but if you want some kind of

measure... three hours? Maybe four or five? Until he catches up anyway."

Time wasn't as meaningless when you could never get enough of it. I took Charis' hand and started walking back the way we'd come. If plan 'A' was out, we could at least relax at the restaurant for a while, instead of standing around outside.

"Are you coming?" I asked Clara. She was standing behind us, just watching.

"Wait," she said. I stopped and turned around. A dark shape was passing behind her.

"Clara!" Charis tried to warn her.

She must have known what would happen. That was the only thing to explain why she didn't move. The creature pounced towards her, dark and slick and formless. A wraith, I knew. I had fought one before.

It was only inches away when Avriel burst from the trees, sword in hand, and slammed into it. Caught by surprise, it howled and stabbed out wildly with a dozen spears of sharp oil that the seraph avoided with seeming ease, twisting and hopping to the side, then charging back in with his blade.

Its face snapped out at him, sharp teeth in a huge jaw trying to wrench his head from his body, but he planted a fist into it and forced it to retreat. The sword came around in a wide arc and smashed through the blackness, sizzling in the night air and bringing an intense smell of frankincense with it. The demon howled and tried to run, but it didn't make it very far. Avriel pounced on it and stabbed it a dozen times or more, until it finally lay still, and then vanished.

"Wraiths," he said, probably the closest thing to a curse the angel could manage. He looked over at Clara. "Okay, fine." He walked to where she was standing, unfazed by the whole sequence of events. The seraph fell to his knees and held out his sword. "I've been waiting for you."

CHAPTER TWENTY

Rebecca

THE RIDE WAS SHORTER THAN I expected, and it didn't make me happy to learn I could have jogged there in the time I had waited for Max to show up. According to the demon, the name of the ruins was Tambomachay. At least, the mortals who were there saw only ruins. He insisted that it was much more than that, and had been for nearly four thousand years.

Unless you were into archaeology or history, it didn't look like much; a few stone walls sticking out of the side of a hill, with a picturesque landscape surrounding it. At the top was a row of four square arches that had been filled in with stone to keep people from trying to get inside, and two more of these arches rested near the bottom right, looking like they should have been going somewhere.

According to Max, they were. What we were looking at was the newest version of an ancient home to the djinn, a complex that had been built by the Inca in order to both worship and serve the Divine. He couldn't say what had happened in its history to put it in its current state, but he was pretty sure somebody had done something to piss the djinn off.

"Glamoured?" Obi asked.

We were standing right in front of one of the arches, looking at the cement.

"Not a glamour you're used to," Max said. "Djinn are a little... different."

Obi knocked on the cement. It sounded solid enough. "'Ha-ha' different, or 'oh crap' different?"

"Just... different. It isn't the glamour that makes it, it's the power that keeps anyone out that the djinn don't want in, both mortal and Divine alike."

"We can't get in?" I asked.

Max laughed "Oh, we can get in." He reached into a pocket and withdrew a simple wooden ring. It wasn't one of mine. "I took this from that djinn the witch was controlling. Possessing something of the djinn's should be enough to bypass security."

When had he taken it, while the djinn had his knife to my throat? I found the stone in my pocket, and gripped it tight. It was easy enough to picture needing to call on the sword, and finding that Max had stolen it again.

He walked up to the cement and pushed the ring against it. There was no sound, no fancy glowing lights, or anything that would suggest the ring had done anything.

"Perfect," he said. He handed the ring back to Obi. "You can't see it until you touch it."

"Kind of lousy security," Obi said, taking the ring and pushing it against the cement. "A retina scanner would be more effective." He handed the ring to me.

"Trust me, muscles, only a fool walks into the home of a djinn uninvited."

I put the ring against the cement, and it vanished in front of my eyes, revealing a long corridor lined in marble and gold, with flaming sconces providing illumination.

"I guess that makes us fools," I said.

Max nodded. "Quite right. Let's go."

We walked in. There were no djinn here that we could see, but I was sure they couldn't be far away. They had to know we were coming, so I expected we were walking right into a trap.

On purpose.

Again.

The corridor split at the end. To the left, the floor sloped downwards, deeper into the earth. To the right, it stayed flat, but ended soon after at an ornately carved wooden door. From here, the carving seemed to depict two of the djinn's favorite things - alcohol, and sex.

"Not there," Max said. "This way."

We took the downward slope. It continued for a few hundred yards before evening out and branching to four corridors. These hallways were lined with simpler doors that gave no indication of their purpose. Somehow, Max knew where we were supposed to go.

"The gathering room should be riiiiggght... here." He stopped and made a right hook, leaving us staring at a smooth wall. "Of course, they don't want just anyone to get into their most important places. The ring?"

I pushed the ring against the wall, and passed it on. The smooth wall became a simple archway into a much grander room.

It explained the reason the floor had sloped, because the ceiling was a good two hundred feet away. The walls were mosaic, a menagerie of rainbow colored glass with an ethereal light behind it, casting bright shadows everywhere as though the room was encased in faceted gems. At the distant rear was a collection of fur carpets, large round beds, huge pillows, and a single golden throne, which sat empty. The Damned was clearly visible, hanging from the wall above the throne, a mottled and chipped chunk of iron with a midnight black hilt laced with gold.

Resting on one of the giant pillows was a woman, short and petite with long golden hair, dressed in a billowy purple velvet gown and covered in enough rings, chains, and bracelets to fill the display cases at Tiffany's.

"Hmm... this is unexpected," Max said.

I didn't have to ask him what he meant. In two rows running off-center of the room were cages, glass cages. Inside every single one of the cages was a djinn. They stood, sat, and floated, and looked generally unhappy with their predicament. A collective gasp rose up at the sight of us.

"Not a witch. A coven." It made sense. A single witch couldn't control a djinn, but a coven could combine power to do some pretty heavy lifting. "I take it the bitch on the bed is their leader?"

"I heard that," she said. She leaned forward onto her elbows and regarded us. She looked young, but I doubted she was. "You're fools to come here."

"That's what I said," Max replied.

The witch stared at us, amused. "You've come for the Damned. I'm sorry Samael, but you can't have it."

I looked over at Max. Was he Samael? Was that name supposed to mean something?

The djinn in the white suit stepped out from between the rows of other djinn. He had shed his top clothes, leaving himself bare chested, with two swords strapped to his back.

"Abaz," Max said under his breath, ignoring my questioning glance. He motioned with his head to the cage closest to the witch. Inside was a diminutive djinn in a green vest and black pants. His head hung against his chest, defeated.

She looked at Max. "Come, Samael. Don't pretend that you don't know me."

"You may know that name, but I don't know you." He didn't sound convinced.

She slid to her feet and put her hands together. "I wonder... You don't know me, you don't remember me, or you don't want to remember me? I was just a child when you brought the sword to Abaz, and asked him to keep it for your master. I was hiding in the shadows, watching. My name is Abalita."

"Abalita?" Max's eyes shifted back to Abaz, who had lifted his head to look at the woman. "I didn't think it was possible."

"For a djinn to have a child with a mortal? Neither did he, or my mother, but here I am."

"You threw your own dad in a cell?" Obi asked. "That is messed up."

Her eyes burned in green and gold. "Do you know how the djinn live, Obi-Wan Sampson? The alcohol, the gambling, the sexual gratification? They take on young girls like my mother, force them into a life of service in exchange for a thimble's worth of power, and don't even notice when they've died. They believe the world is for their pleasure, that all of life is for their pleasure. Did you know there are no female djinn? Not anymore. Where did they go, I wonder?" She looked over at Abaz. "I imagine they just got tired of it and left, and none of them even noticed."

"I loved your mother," Abaz said, getting to his feet and putting his hands to the glass bars.

"You did? How long ago did she die? Do you even know how old I am?"

Abalita seemed to forget about us, storming to the cage and pushing her hand against Abaz's chest. He cried out in pain and fell back.

"You can understand though, can't you Reyka?" She turned back to us, and approached me. She didn't seem at all afraid that we could harm her, and I doubted she was counting on the one free djinn to be her sole protection. "You killed your father for the things he did to your mother, and to you."

And would have done to Landon. "What's your point?"

"You understand the need to take care of yourself. To look out for yourself. To count on no one. You did what you had to do. You can't have the sword, because I need it. To protect myself, and to care for my family. The sword has more uses than to simply turn light to dark."

"Abalita, the sword is Cursed," Max said. "Whatever power you are pulling from it will darken your soul."

"More than growing up in this place, an afterthought to the whim of immortal children? I doubt that. The seraphim and the demons have a purpose for humanity, as despicable as it may be. The djinn use us as nothing more than toys, playthings easily forgotten and discarded. So I learned to harness the power of my birthright. I adopted the women brought in to worship them. I taught them how they were being deceived, and trained them to fight back. Now the djinn are our trophies. Samael, you know how strong the djinn are. The power of the Damned is the only thing that keeps them in their cages."

"We need the sword," I said. I understood her pain, and her desire to punish those who had caused it. In another time and place, I may have been more sympathetic. I may have even sided with her. Not today. Not when collecting the blades was the only way to get Landon out.

"I know."

She turned her back on us. I pulled the stone from my pocket and willed the obsidian spatha into my hand. The floor began to vibrate, and Abalita's sisters poured into the room. They were witches, all of them, their power that of the djinn. I didn't know if the blade could kill them without taking their heads. I didn't even know if I would get to find out.

Golems rose from between the cages, masses of stone pulled from the ground beneath the room.

"Rebecca, the sword," Max said. His face began to change, his body shifting into pure reaper.

The shirtless djinn appeared in front of me, sword in hand, ready to strike. I brought the blade around to block, and then heard the echo of a gunshot. He fell away from me as quickly as he had arrived, thrown to the ground by the force of the bullet pounding into his skull.

"Behind you," I shouted to Obi. He lowered the Eagle, a jagged Cursed blade appearing in his hand from somewhere on him. The golem threw a mountainous fist, but he jerked away and came back, the edge creating sparks along the stone shell.

"Man, why am I never prepared?" He slipped around another heavy punch.

"Rebecca!" Max had finished shifting, and his voice became deeper and more frightening. I put my eyes on the Damned, still hanging on the wall, though it looked like Abalita was going for it. I felt a wave of energy wash through me, a witch's power bouncing off Elyse's tattoos.

I started running at the same time I grabbed one of the knives from my boots. In one smooth motion I threw it at Abalita's back. I didn't know that much about djinn, and I knew even less about human-djinn hybrids, but I was sure she wouldn't have turned her back if it had left her defenseless. At the last moment, she ducked to the side, reached up and snatched the dagger from the air, then turned and fired it back. It was the move I'd anticipated, and I dove forward, rolling under it and back up. I'd forced her to slow, and gained a dozen feet.

I heard screaming behind me. I didn't know what Max was doing, but the witches weren't happy about it. Then I heard a grunt, and he tumbled past me, a golem wrapped up in his arms.

More gunfire echoed in the enormous room, and an unmistakeable cry rose from the back, proving bullets were effective after all. Two more shots, a thud, and then it stopped.

Abalita and I raced onto the pillows and beds, towards the back wall where the Damned sat. I almost caught up to her, lunging forward and getting a hand on the rear of her velvet dress, tearing it along the seam and finding myself with a handful of cloth. I almost caught up. She pulled the blade from the wall and leveled it at my face.

"You've lost, Reyka," she said. I didn't hear any fighting behind me, which wasn't a good sign. "Get up."

I took a deep breath and got to my feet. I dared a look to the back, to see Max being held by two of the stone golems, and Obi with the djinn's blade to his throat. Two of the witches lay in a growing pool of blood, and the others looked like they were ready to claw him apart.

"What about your sisters?" I asked. "The sword is darkening their souls, too. What did you save them from that the hatred and chaos of Hell is a better end?"

She looked back at them. "You have no idea."

"You know I do. They'll turn on you, and on each other in time. It may take hundreds of years, but it will happen. You've seen it happen already."

It was a guess, but the math added up. Abalita had to be nearly a thousand years old, if she had been alive when Max had brought the sword to Abaz.

"Only to those who are weak. Who don't truly believe."

"I'm not saying your father, or the djinn don't deserve to be punished, but at what cost to you? At what cost to these girls? How many have you had to bring in from the street to replenish your coven? How many lives have you ruined to continue your revenge?"

I understood it now. I understood why the witch had been out on the streets with the djinn. She hadn't been lounging, she'd been recruiting. It was the Damned, I knew. She had never been cut with it, but using its power had damned her all the same, only so slowly and subtly that she had never sensed the change. I also understood that once I would have done the same thing, and I wouldn't have needed the Damned to make it so. I had been born with that evil inside me.

Abalita looked past me, to the cage where her father sat watching the exchange. "It is my right."

"It is your undoing. Give me the sword, Abalita. Let it go, and there may be hope for you, and for your sisters."

She kept her eyes on Abaz. "They'll kill me. They'll kill us all as soon as they're free, and then they'll go right back to their misogynistic ways. You may be right that the sword has changed me, Reyka. Nothing will change them."

I followed her gaze back to Abaz and felt a cold shudder in my soul. His eyes weren't penitent, they were gleeful, anticipating that I would convince her to let the sword go.

"You see it," she said. "I can tell that you do. You know what it's like, because you have lived it the way I have."

I had, and I could. That didn't change what I had to do. My path was set, and God had put me on it. Wherever the djinn had come from, I wasn't going to let them stand in my way.

Abalita still held the Damned, the point aimed at my heart. I had the obsidian spatha in my hand. Who was faster?

I brought the blade up and lunged, feeling the pain of the flesh as the Damned bit into it, and the wrenching of my wrist as the spatha bit into her. My breath vanished with the piercing of Elyse's heart, and I felt the power of the weapon seeping towards her soul like a bottle of spilled ink. I pushed back against it, wrapping her up tight so it couldn't pierce me to reach her, at the same time I used my momentum to turn around and pull the blade from Abalita's grip.

I stumbled back towards the front of the room, impaled, gasping but lucent. The cages had been weakened by the death of the witches. They shattered at the loss of the sword.

Abaz's eyes were frightening joy. I used my free hand to pull the Damned from my chest, the skin on my hand ripped open by the blade.

It clattered on the ground.

"Daughter," Abaz said, practically dancing onto the pillows to stand in front of Abalita. The other djinn were free as well, and one grabbed the bare chested djinn from behind, taking his blade and running him through. The golems turned to sand beneath their power, and the other witches all fell prostrate to their will.

"Why?" Abalita whispered in accusation. I couldn't see her, but I knew the question was directed at me.

"She wants to die last," Abaz said. I heard the breaking of bones, and the soft drop of a body landing on a pillow.

I dropped the obsidian sword and fell to my knees, my hands grasping for the vial of blood around my neck. Elyse had said it would heal, and I could only hope she was right. I wasn't ready to lose her.

"Abaz." Max was at my side, and he picked up the Damned. "Heal her."

"And why should I?" he replied. "She just forced me to kill my own child."

Elyse was dying, her body faltering. I couldn't get her hands on the amulet.

Max snorted. "A child that you couldn't have cared less about. That much is plain. She saved your life, you owe her the same."

Abaz laughed, a childlike cackle. "I may be immature, but I'm not ungrateful."

I felt a hand on my head, a fountain of warmth, and my breath returned. I drank in gulps, refilling starved lungs.

"We're leaving with the Damned. Consider your debt to Malize paid."

"Of course. Now, Samael, take your toys and the sword, and hope we never meet again."

CHAPTER TWENTY-ONE
Rebecca

"How did you know Abaz wouldn't kill us all?" Max asked.

We hadn't wasted any time fleeing the underground palace of the djinn, taking the motorcycle from Tambomachay back through Cusco to the airport. Max had wrapped the Damned in a swath of Templar scripted cloth and rested it in the sidecar with Obi. We'd made the ride, and then he'd bought us all tickets on a red-eye flight to Seattle. So far, my efforts to get him to speak about his past, and the name Samael, had been fruitless.

"I didn't," I replied. "But I assumed that if you had left the sword with him, there would be an expectation that he would give it back one day. From what I know of djinn, that meant there had to be a bargain or a debt involved."

"You couldn't have known he would heal you... well, your host, though," Obi said.

We were already through security, the Damned safely glamoured to a walking stick, which Max was using to great affect, hobbling along on it as though he felt as old as he seemed to be.

"I know what you're thinking, Obi." His words at the train station echoed within me, and I knew he thought I was the same monster that had stabbed Landon in the back. "I was going to heal her myself." I'd zipped the leather jacket to hide the hole and blood stains, but now I unzipped it a little to lift the amulet out from under my shirt.

He took a few more steps away from me when he saw it. "Oh man, is that?"

"Yes. According to Elyse, Landon missed a few."

"And you're okay with hauling it around? Doesn't it remind you of anything, like the fact that you helped set the Beast loose?"

We stopped walking.

"I had nothing to do with the amulets."

"No?"

"No. Charis made the amulets to draw Landon in. I was only supposed to tail him until he got the…" I stopped talking, realizing this wasn't helping.

Max got between us before Obi could say anything else. "Children, please. Tit for tat, none of us are innocent. Let's focus."

"You're one to talk," Obi said.

"Yeah, Max. Who the hell are you, really? A demon Templar, who can turn into a reaper? Who goes by the name Max, but whose real name is Samael… oh, and you've been Malize's errand boy for how many hundreds of years?"

The demon looked at both of us and pursed his lips. Then he motioned to a row of seats in front of one of the gates. "I see the good will is running out. It's true I've deceived you and Landon. That is my forte, after all, so I will ask you this: how do you know you can believe whatever story I tell you? I can lie to the diuscrucis, and he can't tell. What hope do you think you have?"

Obi and I didn't sit, but we did look at one another, our animosity forgotten for the moment. "Damn it, Max," I said. "How am I supposed to help you save Landon, if I can't even trust that you *want* to save him? How can either of us believe a single thing you've said?"

He raised his index finger. "An excellent point. *Res ipsa loquitor*. You have witnessed my actions. You tell me which side of the balance they fall on."

We were silent for a minute.

"Neither side. You're fighting the Beast," Obi said.

Max clapped his hands together. "Yes! You have the Box, Rebecca. You have the Beast. I will help you rid this world of him, and return Landon to the place where he belongs. Whatever else I may do or say, that is the obvious truth."

"Fine, but the cat's out of the bag, Samael. Why not give us a little more context?"

"My name is Samael. I was human once, a mortal, many years ago in the time of Jesus. In my life, I was a singer, a womanizer, and a thief. I was handsome, and it made me good at all of these things, but most of all, I was a liar.

"Yet I followed the word of the son of God. I wrote ballads about Him, and worshipped Him while I lifted a purse or defiled a virgin. In some ways, I was the original diuscrucis, balanced in my deeds of good and evil.

"When I died and the tally was taken, the evil turned out to be greater. I should have gone to Hell, but Malize intervened. He spoke to Lucifer on my behalf, and I was brought to Heaven as an angel. Satan had Azrael to cultivate the souls of the damned. Malize made me his counterpart, the angel of death."

He closed his eyes and shifted, but not to the reaper form I had already seen. His face was light and delicate, his hair lustrous, his white robes flowing out around him, with tendrils of light trailing away and a massive pair of ivory wings spread out behind.

"Only Malize hadn't brought me up because he wanted death. He brought me up because he needed a liar. He told me about the Beast, and about his tree of possibilities. He asked me to serve him, and only him, even in the face of God himself, because of the threat the Beast posed to all that He had created. He convinced me of the need, and promised me an untold reward.

"In his name, I committed the ultimate sin and murdered a

fellow angel, for no better reason than to fall. And I did fall, right into the lap of Baal, who took pleasure in my failure and made me a servant of Azrael."

His form shifted to that of the dark reaper. "I used my position of power to spy on Hell, and to keep tabs on the Beast, becoming Malize's eyes where he could not go. Many years passed, until one night I discovered a message from Malize, asking me to meet him. That was when he told me of the swords and bade me to collect each one and pass it into safekeeping. All except the Redeemer. I brought that one to him.

"I served Malize, and through him God, with my gift for lies. I tricked Satan himself into trusting me, and it afforded me the freedom I needed to know everything I needed to know. I noted when the Beast appeared, and followed the words Malize had forced me to memorize. Thousands of branches, and I needed to be aware of every one in order to do my part. So far, I have."

Max returned to his human form, and regarded us with serious eyes.

"Let's just get this done so we can all get on with our lives, or afterlives, I guess," Obi said.

The demon's intensity vanished, and he clapped his hands together. "Right you are, my good man. Our flight leaves in forty-five minutes. Shall we?"

We followed along towards our gate.

"I know we're going to Seattle. What do we need to do once we get there?"

"Not us," Max replied over his shoulder. "You."

"Me, as in, just me, by myself?" I wasn't sure if that was a good thing or a bad thing. After our experience with the djinn, I was leaning towards bad thing.

Max stopped walking again so he could look at me. "Not all of the blades are being held by half-djinn with daddy issues. Getting the Deceiver back is going to be a bit more of a precarious proposition. I had originally given it to a Templar named Gavin St. Croix for safekeeping. It turned out his skill at deception was equal to my own."

"He double-crossed you?" Obi asked.

"More than that. I understand that the war between Heaven and Hell is just that. I accept there is a risk that anyone can change sides, at any time, for any reason." His eyes burned into me at that. "What I didn't expect or account for was that Gavin would not only renounce his position as a Templar, but that he would sell one of the Swords of Gehenna to a mortal, for no better reason than to live out the remainder of his days in material comfort." His voice had been rising as he spoke, and he nearly shouted the last few words.

"You're telling me a mortal has the sword? How come neither side has tried to get it back?"

His laughter was laced with his anger. "They have tried, but the sword isn't called the Deceiver for nothing. Whoever holds it can not only lie, but it casts a glamour on the soul that few Divine can see through."

"A glamour on the soul?"

"Everything changes. Your perception of what you hear, what you see, how you feel. The Deceiver is unlike the other blades, because you don't know it's been used on you until it's too late."

"I take it there's a Heavenly version?" Obi asked.

"Yes. It's called Truth. It counters the effects of the Deceiver."

Obi laughed. "So, dumb question, but why don't we go get that one first?"

"An excellent question, old chap. There is a time for everything, and everything in its own time."

"Translation?"

"I have a plan to bring Truth to us. Besides, as I've said, Rebecca should be immune to the blade's power."

"Should be?" I asked.

"Don't fret, my salted caramel cupcake. Thanks to your run-through with the Redeemer, you are uniquely situated to be able to see the glamours, but not fall victim to them. It's one of the reasons we worked so hard to bring you into the game."

A tree with a thousand branches, and one of them with my name on it. Max had said it was math, not fate. A potential, not a pre-determination. I hoped for his sake he hadn't been lying about that.

"What's the other reason?"

"Our target is a twenty-two year old, unattached millionaire. I think Elyse has the look, and I know you have the resume."

"Are you suggesting you want me to seduce him?"

"In so many words."

I closed my eyes, licked my lips, and tried to calm my suddenly pounding heart. It was a big ask, after what I had put Landon through. Except, that attraction had been real for both of us. This was just a game within the game.

"I'm not happy about it," I said.

"I didn't expect you would be, but our needs dictate our actions."

"Can you shut up with your turn of phrases?"

Max smiled. "His name is Brian Rutherford. He's the founder of Madalytics."

"No way!" Obi said.

"You've heard of it?" I asked.

"Called the next Google, worth a couple billion dollars. Heck, yeah."

The demon shrugged. "His father was Evan Rutherford, an entrepreneur in his own right. He was the one who bought the Deceiver from a collector in Belgium. I don't know about Brian, but Evan was Turned."

Obi deflated at the news. "Oh. You think he's cheating to win?"

"I think it's very likely."

We started walking again. The flight was already boarding by the time we reached the gate, and we waited our turn to be herded onto the aircraft. I shifted the pack from shoulder to shoulder, feeling the weight of it growing in my soul with every step forward. Science, I could do. Combat, I could do. Half-succubus or not, seduction had never been one of my strengths. At least, not intentionally. Now I wished I still had that Divine gift.

I settled in for the flight, thankful that Max had at least hooked us up with first class. The extra space was appreciated, and I stretched out and watched the take-off through the window. Obi had grabbed the aisle seat straight away, and offered the middle to the demon. Despite everything we were going through together, he hadn't thawed towards me at all. It might have bothered me, but I didn't need his approval.

"Elyse." I let go, giving my host a chance to have a body for a while. There wasn't much she could do on the plane, so I decided that was the best time to let her out.

"Hey, Max," she said. "Rebecca's given me a little playtime."

He'd had his eyes closed, but now they popped open and he smiled at her. "How's my favorite human holding up?"

Obi leaned his head forward. "Wait. I'm not your favorite?"

"You don't count. You may not be Divine, but you still have some of Landon's gift in you. Elyse has gathered the power she has on her own."

"So, you're saying I'm your favorite overall? I can live with that."

Max and Elyse both laughed. In the moment, I wished that I could sleep without taking her body back.

"How are you holding up, Obi?" Elyse asked. "Max gave me a summary of what happened in Mumbai."

Obi was black, but his face paled. I thought he would be angry, but he stared down at his feet while he answered.

"It's more than that. To learn there's so much more out there, and that it's even more ugly than mankind can be. To meet someone who wants to fight back against it, and learn that even he can't protect us without turning some shade of ugly himself. To still be a friend when half the time you want to punch the guy in the face, and the rest of the time you want to do everything you can to help him stay alive and sane. To fall in... I don't know. Not love, but there was something there. She died, and almost killed me. I still have nightmares.

"I spend my time always looking out of the corner of my eyes. Always ducking, always listening. Paranoid, traumatized, whatever you want to call it. I tried to go back to work as soon as I got a flight out. First call, a guy who was beating on his wife." He turned his head, to catch Elyse's eye. "I've never felt so angry before, as I do now. I barely have control of it on good days, and I have to drink myself to oblivion on the bad days, or else I know I'll kill someone. I'm not someone I ever wanted to be, and it hurts like hell."

"I'm sorry," Elyse said.

"You're sorry?" I asked. *"You'd have no problem killing anyone in your own family to get what you want."*

"That's hardly fair, Rebecca. In many ways I'm the same as Landon. I just want humankind in control of their own destiny. Anyway, I was born and raised to fight this war." She was speaking to me out loud. Now she reached across Max and put her hand on top of Obi's. "I am sorry. Rebecca thinks I'm nothing but a killer, because of the things I've had to do. She doesn't always see beneath the surface of things."

A tear rolled from Obi's eye, down his cheek to splash onto the seat. He split his mouth into a half-smile. "Thanks, Elyse. I'm sorry you got stuck carrying her around. I had to find out what she was about the hard way."

I didn't say anything else after that. If I could have, I would have let go of Elyse completely, and let the plane fly off without me. Vampires were superior in strength, intelligence, everything. But now I saw that I was an idiot. All the years I'd chased after the demonic dream, to be at the top of the food chain and look down on everyone from above. It had left me a novice at truly understanding anyone beyond what I needed from them. For as sure as I was that it was my mission from God to save Landon from the Beast, I had to admit the truth to myself.

I wanted to be redeemed. I wanted to go to Heaven. It was as much about what saving Landon could do for me as it was about what it would mean for him.

If I could have cried, I would have done that too.

CHAPTER TWENTY-TWO

Landon

"Waiting for her?" I asked, still trying to wrap my brain around what had just happened, and what was happening now. How could he be waiting for something that only existed because of Charis and I?

The seraph didn't move. He just looked up at Clara.

"I accept," she said, taking the sword from his offered hands.

"What's going on?" Charis asked.

Avriel got to his feet, and Clara leaned in and kissed his cheek, then handed back the blade. "He's here to help us," she said.

"Avriel isn't in the Box anymore." It seemed an obvious statement, but now I wasn't so sure.

"No, he isn't," Clara replied. "He's only a piece, a small piece. A shade of the angel you knew, the one whose life you forfeit, and whose death haunts you."

She knew because she was half me. "How can that be?"

"It is in the construct of the Box. When he escaped the piece was held behind."

"I need to take you somewhere," Avriel said. "There is something for you. A gift."

I had a thought. A frightening thought. "Clara, if a piece of Avriel was left behind, couldn't a piece of Abaddon have been left behind too?"

"It's possible. I don't know. If the binding was intentional there has to be a reason for it."

"I have something to show you," Avriel repeated. "A gift."

"Show me," Clara said.

Avriel bowed. "Follow me. We must be careful. I can feel their power building."

"Whose power?" I asked.

"The Beast," Clara said. "He can't find us yet, but his energy is re-forming. He'll try to slow us as much as he can."

"Come," Avriel said. "A gift."

We had no choice. We followed behind Avriel, back out of the park and into the street. He stuck his fingers in his mouth and whistled, hailing a cab like a lifelong resident. We piled in, with Avriel taking shotgun.

"Where to?" the driver asked.

"City Hall," Avriel said.

"You said a gift. What kind of gift?" I said.

"I don't know. All I know is that I must remain to bestow a gift, and protect you until it is bestowed."

Not very helpful. "How come you didn't show up before now? We could have used your protection a few ugly deaths ago."

"I couldn't find you. Your energy was too weak. The longer you survive, the stronger it grows."

And the older Clara became. It made as much sense as anything else did in here. "Strong enough to defeat Ross?" Why not? He was still in the process of re-forming, while we were getting more powerful.

"No," Clara said. "Remember the balance. You can try to find him now, while he's weak, but his power grows faster than yours, because your power is his. He has a natural affinity to it that you don't."

Like a fish versus a dolphin in a deep dive. We'd need to come up for air. "Do you think this gift will help?"

"It can't hurt."

It was scary how much she sounded like me when she said that.

We rode in silence. I watched the city streets go by, trying to find things I recognized from before I'd died. The world was a little different here. We were in Charis' memory, a New York from before I had even been born. So much was identifiable in a vague understanding of the past, and yet now it was the real present.

I was just beginning to ease into the thought when something hit the side of the cab and sent us careening towards a parked car to our left. I reached out to put my arm around Clara, to protect her from the force of the crash, while the driver screamed and Avriel threw open his door.

The windshield shattered and something grabbed the driver and ripped him out, still screaming. A large, twisted face peered in, a broken monster I'd never seen before.

It howled when the angel powered into it, throwing his shoulder against it and sending it flying off the car.

"Ross?" I asked Clara.

"No." She looked scared.

If it wasn't him, it had to be something else. I focused, throwing open the door from the back of the cab and climbing out, with Charis and Clara right behind me. Avriel was on the sidewalk to our left, standing opposite the creature, sword in hand. Almost twenty feet tall, with tree-trunk limbs and massive claws, it put Ulnyx to shame. The seraph looked outmatched against it.

"No time to spectate," Charis said, pointing. Three more of them were crowding us in, racing down the street from both directions.

I focused, feeling the power come pouring in, feeding my energy and strength. I pulled air towards me, condensing it, crushing it into a tiny space, and then tossing it out at the oncoming monster like a transparent bullet. It slammed into the creature, forcing it to the ground while half its torso vanished beneath the pressure. The results caused me to smile. For once, this was going to be easy.

Maybe I spoke too soon. I heard shattering glass, and a fourth monster exploded from a window above, coming down at me like a twisted knife. I focused, bunching my legs and springing up towards it, breaking its expectation of my fear and taking it by surprise. I wrapped my hands around its head and twisted, snapping its neck and leaving it dead before it hit the ground.

Still airborne, I could see we were in more trouble than I'd thought. Every side street had more of the creatures running down it, headed towards us like a hill of angry ants, and the first one I had downed had recovered and found its legs. I focused to soften my landing and hurried to Charis and Clara's side.

"You're sure this isn't Ross?"

"Yes," Avriel said. He was splattered in black blood, but was unharmed.

"So Abaddon is here." As if things weren't bad enough. "He might want you, but we need you, so I guess we're your protector." I turned to Clara. "Can we leave the memory?"

"Avriel has been established here. You'll lose the gift."

It wasn't what I wanted to hear. The first round of reinforcements turned the corner and came into view. I looked around, desperate for a street sign. Greenwich and Warren. We weren't that far away.

"Come on," I said, running east down Warren. There were monsters coming at us westbound, which meant a collision was unavoidable.

"Right into them?" Charis asked.

"We don't have a choice."

We were in New York City. There was stuff everywhere. Trash cans, parked cars, street lights, windows. I didn't need to tell Charis what to do. Together we used our energy to pull everything in and throw it forward, peppering the oncoming creatures with whatever we could find. The front lines fell, coated in glass or smashed with sheet metal and steel. It reminded me of Mumbai, only here we had the power to break through the enemy. Here, we were the Beasts.

The realization was sobering. Destruction, chaos… was that all we were capable of, when it came down to it? What else had I done in the last five years? Every time I tried to take a break, to relax and create something - a relationship, a friendship, a life of my own - it all fell apart in another wave of bad mojo. Was that all there was to me? All that I existed for? Maybe Abaddon had been spot on. Ross had tortured Charis and me with visions of the life we could have had, or should have had. Would we ever get the chance to try that afterlife on for size?

Not today.

I could hear the hissing and howling behind us, and when I looked back there was nothing but a sea of monsters, tongues lolling, fangs bared. They chased us down the street, towards City Hall and whatever gift was waiting, their huge legs giving them greater gains than our own.

It wasn't much of a challenge to stop them. With a bit more focus and effort, I was able to start pulling blocks of cement and brick from the surrounding buildings and send them backwards into the onrush, knocking them over, dropping them back. Few of the blows could kill but most of them could slow, and all we needed right now was time. I reached further away, finding mailboxes and televisions, bottles and cans. I sucked them in and threw them back out, in a rhythm with Charis that we couldn't have managed without Clara beside us. It was the truest test of our connection, the purest form of our innate togetherness.

Then Avriel fell.

It seemed impossible, an angel tripping in the street. Did he catch a foot on a crack, or was he pushed by an unseen hand? What mattered was that he wasn't moving and so we weren't either. We'd been able to slow them. We needed something more dramatic to stop them.

"There's too many," Charis said.

I reached out and grabbed Avriel's hand, pulling him roughly to his feet.

"How can a shade do this?" I asked. "How can a piece have so much power?"

Clara stood next to us, looking a bit older than she had only a few minutes ago. "We found Avriel. He must have found Abaddon."

"Or Abaddon found him," the angel said.

We turned to run, but the monsters had gotten smarter. They held cars up as shields from our debris, and the ones we'd felled were back on their feet. They drew in closer, threatening to surround us. The memories of Mumbai flowed back in.

"Now what?" Charis asked. The four of us stood with our backs together. I scanned the environment in search of anything we could use.

A raindrop fell.

Had we created it, somewhere in our subconscious? This was our world after all. I looked up at the sky, a starless sky. There were no clouds either. There was just... nothing.

I closed my eyes, feeling Avriel's wing against my back from below his jacket. I remembered Josette, who had given me the gift of holy rain to defeat the demon Reyzl. We could make it rain. We had an angel.

I smiled. I was sure Charis was smiling too. So was Clara.

"Avriel, got any good prayers?" I asked.

The creatures were closing in. With the connection, I was able to do something I had never done before. In a single thought, a single command, we pulled the rain from a cloudless sky and at the same time threw a wall of debris between us and them. Avriel began to chant, holding his arms up to the nonexistent heavens, and sending an arc of blue energy from us into the air.

The rain continued to fall, but it was different now. It tasted of salt and hope, and all around us were deafening screams of pain and the sound of sizzling flesh. It was my first effort on a much grander scale, and it didn't disappoint.

We stopped the rain when the howling stopped. We dropped the wall a minute later. The monsters were gone. Every last one of them.

"It feels good to have a winning streak," I said, first hugging Charis, and then Clara. Even the seraph looked satisfied.

"The gift," he said. "This way."

We weren't far from City Hall. It seemed odd that the gift would have been left there, but it was as good a place as any. We walked empty streets for the final few blocks, and then made our way onto the grounds.

"There's an old subway station," Avriel said. He brought us onto the grass, over to where a line of metal grating rested. "The gift is down there."

"Where's the entrance?" I asked.

He shook his head. "Lost."

I looked down at the grating. It wasn't a problem to move it, or to make an entrance of our own. I focused on the metal, forcing it to corrode. It only took a light kick to make it crumble, and then I could see the blue glass of a skylight beneath it.

"Be careful," Clara said. "He can feel the power. He's getting closer."

We needed to get in before Ross found us. "I'm going down."

I didn't mess with the glass. I just jumped.

The skylight shattered as my feet smashed through it, leaving me tumbling towards the cement below surrounded by blue slivers that reminded me of Christmas ornaments. The fall would have broken my legs at least, but at the last moment I seized the air and used it to break my fall; a single dash of heavy power for just an instant.

Avriel fluttered down behind me carrying Clara. He launched

back up through the new opening and returned with Charis.

We were in a subway station. A beautiful, ornate subway station. I looked back up at the other skylights that remained and at the tiled walls and arches. A sign over one of them said 'City Hall'.

"There." Avriel pointed to a spot on the ground directly beneath a round skylight. A spectral light was filtering in through glass that had no access to the outside, its beam focused on a dark bulge on the ground.

"That's it?" I asked. I walked over and knelt before it. I don't know what I had been expecting. Something impressive, magical and ancient. An artifact, or maybe even the Box's version of the Holy Grail. Something with runes, at the very least. Templar script would have been even better.

I reached out and wrapped my hand around the grip, picking up the revolver and turning it in my hand, examining it. I knew it was old, because it was layered in dust, the exterior of the steel rusted and pitted. The grip wasn't much better - the wood dry, cracked, and separating. It didn't look like anything special, or anything that could harm Ross. It didn't even look like it could fire.

I opened it up, looking into the cylinder. There was a bullet. A single, ordinary bullet. I knew it was ordinary because I dumped it out into my hand, rolled it over, and checked it for runes. Nothing.

"I don't understand."

I said it softly, a whisper, more to myself than to the others in the station with me. A single bullet to shoot Ross? It was the most obvious answer, but I couldn't understand what made this weapon any different from any other gun we could conjure up or steal from a pawn shop. It didn't radiate any power. It didn't suggest any special capability.

I felt a hand on my shoulder and twisted my head. Clara was there.

"Maybe it isn't time for you to understand," she said.

I put the bullet back into the chamber, closed the cylinder and got to my feet. I turned to where Avriel and Charis were waiting. A shade of the angel had been held behind, to protect us and to lead us to the weapon. Clara was right. Maybe the power was there and I just couldn't feel it. Maybe we weren't strong enough. I looked the gun over one more time.

We just needed to stay alive long enough to use it.

CHAPTER TWENTY-THREE

Rebecca

THE FIRST THING WE DID when we got to Seattle was pay a visit to Staples and buy a laptop for Obi. I was in charge of getting through Brian Rutherford to the Deceiver, but he was in charge of getting me in front of the guy in the first place. He'd picked out something thin and light, muttering about installing a secure operating system on it while Max paid.

After that, we'd settled in at the Hotel Andra, a boutique hotel near the center of the city, offering us quick movement to wherever we needed to be. Max also preferred it because its small size would make it easier to monitor and defend if need be. It was his opinion that we were stupid if we didn't think Sarah and Ulnyx would catch up at some point, especially with Dante able to show up anywhere at a moments notice. One one hand, he didn't sound like he was too happy at the idea of their involvement. On the other, I had a feeling he wanted them back in the game before it was over.

The only thing I knew for sure was that Max himself had pretty much said he couldn't be trusted.

"Anything yet, Obi?" I asked. We had rented two adjoining rooms, and now I sat on the edge of his bed and watched his fingers fly along the laptop's keyboard. Every time I looked at him, I thought about what he had told Elyse. I tried to find sympathy for him, or empathy, or something that didn't feel selfish. So far that had been a failure.

"Getting there," he said. "I got a line into Madalytics, working on pulling up their calendar. Hopefully he's got something marked off that we can find you a way into."

"I have a feeling he won't be putting 'S and M session' on his corporate calendar," Max said with a laugh.

"Meeting with Mistress Pain?" Obi replied, grinning. "I could be wrong, man, but I'm guessing that's not the best outlet for Rebecca to do her thing."

"I don't have a 'thing'," I said.

Obi glanced up at me, but didn't say anything. He didn't need to. I bottled my angry retort and sat quiet instead.

"Here we go," he said a few minutes later. "I had to get into his Google account. He's got a meeting tonight with an investor. They're supposed to hit some restaurant called 'El Goucho' at eight."

"Business meeting? How is that going to help?"

Max put his hand on my shoulder. "Do you have any experience as a waitress?"

I looked up at him. "What do you think?"

Obi started laughing.

"What's your problem?" I asked.

"I think your definition of 'eating out' doesn't lend itself very well to this. Let me find something else."

"No," Max said. "We don't have time." He looked me over. "Waitress may not be the right part for you to play. No, I have another idea." He flipped his eyes to Obi. "Can you get into the restaurants reservation system and make sure Mr. Rutherford and his guest wind up sitting next to you two?"

"Yeah, sure man. I... Wait. What do you mean?"

"We can't have a gorgeous young thing like Elyse sitting in an upscale restaurant by herself. At least not at first. Here's what I want you to do."

Max explained the plan. Obi didn't like it, but he set to work on getting into the restaurant's booking system. At the same time, he ordered me to head out to Nordstrom to find something to wear. I was fine with the denim and leather, but I couldn't argue its appropriateness. I unloaded all of the hidden daggers, pulled off my glove, and left everything at Obi's side, taking only the black stone that would summon the spatha.

"I know you won't let anything happen to this," I said, opening the pack to take one last look at the pulsing blue runes before letting it leave my sight.

"You've got that right."

I zipped it up and headed for the door. "Be back in a few."

I made a straight line to the elevator, and then out the door onto the street. It was a cool day, with a bit of mist hanging in the moist air but otherwise fair enough. Not that I would have cared much if it were sunny or raining - I wasn't thrilled to leave the Box behind, but I was happy to break away from Obi and Max for a while. Max was a little eccentric and I was still on the fence about how well we could trust him, and Obi alternated between grating and impossible. I knew a lot of his pain was indirectly my fault, but he didn't need to keep taking advantage of every opportunity to salt the wound.

That was only one of the thoughts that ruled my mind while I made the short walk from the hotel to Nordstrom. My head wandered from one thing to another: Hell, Landon, Elyse. I even went back to an outing with Merov when I was seven and he had taken me to some fancy store in the garment district and let me pick out a ten-thousand dollar gown to wear for my birthday party.

I was so wrapped up in the memories that I nearly ran headlong into a changeling. I angled out of his path to avoid a total collision, settling for his shoulder clipping mine.

"Excuse me," he said, his voice soft and meek.

I know he couldn't see what I was, and at first I wasn't even sure what he was. His face was red, his eyes downcast. He looked like he was in a bit of pain, his hands curled under a draped wool coat. There was no sign of the sense of superiority or the aggression that had marked my other interactions with the altered humans. Instead, he only looked afraid. It was the eyes that had given him away, an odd tinge of red, and his fingers. He hadn't realized that his sharp claws had dug their way through the wool.

I turned to watch him as he hurried past, and then across the street. His head darted left and right, on the lookout for something. It was suspicious in a way that captured my attention and didn't want to let it go. I should have continued on to the department store, grabbed something short and tight that would attract lots of attention, and gotten Elyse's ass back to the hotel.

I had two hours, and I could find a suitable strip of cloth in a matter of minutes.

I followed him.

He walked for a while, east to the Pike Place Market, disappearing into the crowds of tourists there and making it hard for me to follow. I managed to keep the tail, flowing through the traffic and leaving an eye on his back. Watching him, I could tell by the way he maneuvered that he wasn't just hiding his clawed hands. He was holding something in them, and I wanted to know what.

He kept going, weaving through the foot traffic and jaywalking whenever he could. I stayed a few dozen feet behind, in the shadows when possible, and always with a few people between him and me. I stalked him like a cat, focused and intent, all the way to an alley between two old buildings.

I started running, eager to catch up before he could vanish.

I was too late.

The alley was empty - nothing but trash bins and leaky pipes. There were no doors he could have gone into, and no fire escapes he could have climbed. He had vanished into thin air. How?

I was trying to work out how he'd worked his Houdini magic when I felt a presence behind me. It wasn't the changeling, but the smell gave him away.

"Elyse."

I turned around.

"Father."

He was in a long overcoat and a fedora, the bulges beneath the coat unmistakeable. He was armed for both conventional and Divine warfare. Two more of the Nicht Creidim fanned out behind him. Elyse's sister Rae, and an uncle, Paul.

"How did you find me?" I asked.

He laughed. "That's the funny thing. I wasn't even looking for you. I was following the changeling. Now that I have you though... Messy business back in New York."

"You followed Ulnyx?"

He nodded. "It wasn't easy, but they weren't expecting we would know where to find them. I heard about what happened at the house. You attacked your own family? Really, Elle... I know you're stubborn, but don't you think you took it a little too far."

"Ken was going to kill me to get the Box. You would too, except you can see I don't have it."

"I also know you were traveling with the diuscrucis' boy toy, the marine. I'm assuming you left the Box with him, somewhere in the city."

There was no point in denying it, it was a big city. "True. Which leaves you with a decision. Do you try to kill me and find Obi on your own? Or do you try to capture me and get me to tell you where it is? Or do you let me walk away and tail me back to the Box?" Or do I let go of Elyse and take control of your meat? I wasn't sure I could.

"Considering you're out here unarmed, I'm leaning towards making you talk. Yet, I'm curious. Why were you tailing the changeling?"

"He intrigued me."

"That's my girl," he said. "Do you know what he was carrying?"

I shook my head.

"An artifact. A scrying stone. I was going to use it to find you, which is why I'm also considering letting you go. I don't want to harm you, daughter, despite your treacherous indiscretion. You're willing to do what it takes to hold to your beliefs, and considering I taught you that, I can't really blame you for it."

A scrying stone? I hadn't known something like that even existed. I could understand why Joe would want it. I also knew it could come in handy.

"Who is he bringing it to?" I asked.

"A seraph," he replied.

"An angel hanging out in an alley?"

"Not an angel. A seraph."

"There's a difference?"

He shrugged. "There is to me. This one hasn't died yet. He's a changeling. The first seraph I've heard of. It turns out he's been able to use his new situation to rally a lot of the other changelings in the city here, though I'm sure it doesn't hurt that he's rich."

Was the world really that small? "His name isn't Brian Rutherford, is it?"

"Bingo. How'd you know?"

I took a deep breath. So I was suppose to seduce a mortal seraph who was already at the top of Joe's hit-list, and who was about to have an artifact that could tell him the future? I needed to stop the chit-chat and find the were changeling.

I wasn't about to clue him in that I knew anything about the Deceiver. The question was, did he know? "I've heard he's been collecting a lot of artifacts. I wanted to find out exactly what, to see if he had anything that might help me deal with the Box."

"I can help you deal with the Box, Elle."

"No, father, you can't. Now if you'll excuse me, he's getting away." The only trouble was, I didn't know where to.

"Look around, sweetie. I think he's already gotten away." He unbuttoned his coat and spread it wide. He had a shotgun on one hip and a sword on the other. "Are you going to come quietly? I know your hand-to-hand has gotten better, but you're outnumbered three to one."

I started reaching for my pocket, to the stone nestled there against my leg. Was I being foolish? I wasn't sure.

Rae drew a pistol from a holster on her thigh. "Elyse, don't." She was older than Elyse, someone the girl had always looked up to. A beauty in her own right, with dark skin and almond eyes.

My hand stopped. I counted my heartbeats. One...two... I was calm, despite the situation. I dropped my hands to the side. "Okay," I said. I couldn't beat them like this. It was better to let them take me and then catch them by surprise.

"That's my girl," Joe said.

He started walking forward when I saw a dark shape falling towards him from the rooftop above.

"Joe!" I tried to warn him. I don't know why, because under different circumstances he would have killed me already.

He heard the vamp coming, and he twisted and raised the shotgun, falling on his back and firing up into it. The changeling cried out, thrown off-target by the force of the blast. He landed at Joe's prone feet. He wasn't alone.

The alley filled with changelings, jumping off the rooftops to land with us in the dark corridor. Weres and vamps mostly, but one of them was a nightstalker. He came down next to Uncle Paul and slammed him with a fist that sent him crashing into the wall, bouncing off and landing with a groan.

Rae started shooting, silver bullets tearing into the false demons and creating a din of pained cries. They hurt them, but they didn't stop them, and three of the changelings charged towards her.

I found the stone in my pocket, pulled it out and summoned the spatha. A vampire came at me, claws leading fangs, and lost his hand and then his head to the blade. I ducked under a swat from a were, pivoted on the balls of my feet, and shoved the sword backwards into his gut, ripping it forward and using the flat to block a second attack. Behind me, Joe tried to get to his feet, but the nightstalker had reached him, and he picked him up by the neck.

"Son of a..." he thew punches into the creature's chest, but it didn't seem to notice. He howled in Joe's face and squeezed tighter.

I looked back down the alley. There was nowhere the changeling could have gone. There was no way he could have escaped. Yet these altered mortals were here, and they had to have come from somewhere.

It was the Deceiver, I realized. A glamour. It had to be. Max had said I could see through it, but that clearly wasn't the case. At least, not like this.

Another were pounced at me, and I jerked to the left and punched him hard in the kidney. He landed and turned, twisted in pain and opening his mouth to huff for breath. I loosened my control of Elyse, holding onto her soul but letting her take her body back.

"Rebecca, what the f-"

I saw it, as nothing more than a suggestion in the simplicity of my raw spiritual consciousness. The building to the right had a door. I could see it as though it too were an apparition, a transparent overlay to the visible lie.

"*To the right. There's a door.*"

"I can't see it," Elyse said.

"*Just go.*"

She ran towards the wall.

"*Two feet to your left, the handle is in line with your ribs.*"

She reached out towards the wall, moving her hand until she found the knob that she couldn't see. She pulled the door open and stepped inside.

"Close it," I said. *"We don't want Joe to follow."*

She pulled the door closed, and then we looked around. I could see the truth over the glamour - the dirty, cracked mortar of the walls, and the set of old steps that led down, overlaid with a small storage room filled with boxes.

"There are stairs in the middle of the room. Old stone stairs. Climb down them."

Elyse walked forward more slowly, unsure of my instructions. "There's nothing there. Just boxes."

"There are stairs. Do it."

She put her hand up to her head. "Rebecca."

"Do it!" I screamed at her soul and she cried out in pain.

"I can't see it."

"You have to trust me, Elyse. If Rutherford gets the scrying stone we'll have no chance at getting close to him."

She growled and stepped forward into the boxes that should have prevented her forward motion. When they didn't stop her she started moving more confidently.

"Down the stairs, right in front of you."

The first step was timid, but then she ran the rest of the way down. We dove about twenty feet underground and spilled out into a long corridor of dirt and wooden planks. The glamour didn't extend down here.

"That was-"

I didn't let her finish. I took hold of her again, forcing her eyes to become my eyes, and her body to become my body. I continued the run down the tunnel.

It fed into an abandoned city, an underground world of wooden structures that would have been commonplace in the eighteen hundreds, but surprised me with their existence. They had been cleaned up, painted and patched, glassed and lit. I stumbled into it unseen, but now I could hear the voices of this secret world in hushed murmurs around me. What was this place?

I was on a wide street that looked recently swept. It continued a few hundred feet ahead, and I could see two more streets stretching off to either side. A neon sign over one of the larger structures read 'Brian's' next to a flashing beard and mustache. I could hear eighties rock music pumping from inside.

"You've got to be kidding me." I was here to get the Deceiver, and I had a feeling the sword was waiting for me in the old-time bar.

At least it looked like I might be able to skip the seduction after all.

CHAPTER TWENTY-FOUR

Rebecca

MY FIRST THOUGHT WAS TO walk right in, head held high and nothing but confidence oozing out of every one of Elyse's pores. It was a part I knew how to play, having perfected it as the laughing stock daughter of Merov Solen, the weirdo who didn't think vampires needed to drink human blood. I had poured millions of Merov's money into the research, and all the while it had been a front, a way to distance myself from my father, and a means to get the diuscrucis to trust me. The Beast had told me that was what I had to do, and I had done it. I had played that part well, and it had worked to convince Landon I wasn't like the others. It was heaped in with all of my other regrets.

The idea of making a grand entrance as Reyka Solen fell to the curb when one of the patrons made their way through the open doorway of the bar and hurried past my makeshift hiding place in the deeper shadows. She had a look of concern on her face, and tears in her eyes, and I could only guess she was going to find out what had happened to the group that had jumped us. I watched her back disappear down the tunnel, and tried to decide what to do. In two minutes she would discover their ambush party was dead, because I was sure Joe and family was too much for a bunch of new demons with zero fighting skill. She would come running

181

back with the news, and then what?

At the same time, I had to assume Brian Rutherford was in there, and that he had the scrying stone. If I gave him enough time to use it, would he be able to know what I was going to do even before I did?

Whatever I did, I needed to do it fast. I left my place in the shadows and dashed across the lit areas of the underground village, keeping my eyes out for anyone on the streets. I could hear things happening in the other buildings - clattering plates, laughter, conversation. It was as though the changelings had come down here to find the normalcy that the Beast's power had stolen from them. And maybe they had. Maybe that's what they had gone out into the alley to defend.

I reached the side of the bar and crouched beneath the flashing facial hair. I had an idea, and a violent and simplistic backup plan.

"*Wait here*," I said to Elyse, letting go of her and propelling my spirit form out of her body and into the void. I passed right through the wall of the structure, fighting to keep my energy focused on the motion. I needed to be fast to make it in time.

The place wasn't crowded. Eight changelings sat around a single old wooden table, directly in front of a bar where a nouveau-were poured drinks. The eighties hits were blasting out of an old jukebox hunched in the corner, and on the table sat a simple rough stone, covered in demonic runes.

My mark was there, sitting to the left of a young, bald man with a thick, trimmed beard and mustache and wearing blue jeans and a brown sweater. He had to be Brian Rutherford. There was nothing about him that would give him away as a seraph, but then again his back was covered.

"I don't like it," the mark said, digging his elongated claws into the table. "Whoever she was, she was good. I wouldn't have even noticed, except she smelled so sweet."

I'd underestimated him, thinking he wouldn't have picked up my scent. I pushed harder, feeling myself floating along the stale air, directly towards Brian.

"The question, Alex, is how did she know you were carrying the stone? I thought you said you picked it up at the terminal locker and nobody saw you."

"I didn't see or smell anybody," Alex replied. "I tucked it under my coat first thing and got the hell out of there. I brought it straight to you."

"What is it?" The question came from a young woman on his right, a cute little thing in a jean jacket and linen skirt.

"I bought it from a dealer in China," Brian said. "It's supposed to have belonged to Jacob, or Isaac, or one of those biblical guys. You recite the Hebrew on the face and it will glow red whenever someone nearby means you harm. Well, means me harm, anyway. It only works for one person at a time, but at least while I'm down here I'll know you guys are all safe."

Not a scrying stone? What was Joe trying to pull? I kept moving towards Brian, closing the distance as fast as I could. It was still taking too long for my comfort.

"I don't think you need a stone to know we're in danger, Brian," the girl said. "The others should have been back by now. It was what, twenty against one?"

I was only a few feet away from him now. I could feel the other people around me, their eyes all on or near the spot where I was floating, but I was invisible. I was taking a chance trying to possess a changeling. I didn't know if I could even do it, but my hope was that since they were still some kind of human, my grip would hold.

"I know. I'm worried about them too, but the entrances are hidden. There's no way anybody is going to be able to get in here."

Nobody, except me. It was my last thought as I plunged into his body, drawn to the warm throbbing of his soul. I reached out for it and wrapped myself around it.

Taking control normally meant pain, as the energy of a person's lifetime flowed through me, teaching me who they were in only seconds, and offering me the hooks I needed to latch on and become the driver of the mortal shell. I expected that when I joined with the false seraph I would either be met with this pain or cast out entirely, to find myself back in the emptiness of the strange space between all of God's places.

Neither of those things happened.

Instead, I found myself in an open field, laying on the grass, with way too much sunshine beaming down overhead. I squinted my eyes to ward it off and tried to bring myself up to my elbows to look around. A hand entered my field of view - large, strong, and young.

"Are you okay?"

That was the question from whoever owned the hand. I reached forward and took it, and was pulled to my feet.

"My name is Brian. How did you get here? Actually... how did I get here?" He let go of my hand and rotated all the way around. "Where am I?"

I knew where, but I didn't quite believe it. I mimicked his rotation, taking note of the lush grass, the strands of evergreens, and the mountains off in the distance. "This is your Source," I said. Except, he was a human. He shouldn't even have a Source.

"My Source? I don't understand. Two seconds ago I was in the Underground with my friends. Now I'm here with you, which I'm not ready to believe is a bad thing, because you're amazingly beautiful." He took a breath and calmed himself. "I've learned not to trust anything I see."

I didn't understand either, but I was sure that I didn't want to be here. I closed my eyes and tried to will myself away from him.

"Hello? Hey. Do you have a name?"

I opened my eyes. We were still in the field. I was stuck.

"Rebecca," I said.

"Rebecca. Your name is as pretty as you are. I would remember your face, if I had seen you before. You aren't a figment of my imagination. My father used to tell me there were demons who could possess souls... but you aren't possessing me either. If I didn't know any better I'd say you were lost."

Did I look lost? I sure felt it. "I shouldn't be here. Neither should you. I'm not a demon. I'm not lost. I'm trapped."

"Trapped?"

"Here, with you. I want to leave, but I can't. I'm a spirit, a ghost. You can't see me, back in the real world. I don't always have control, and I... fell... into you. Anyway, this is your Source. It's a place in your soul where your power comes from."

Brian laughed.

"What's so funny?"

"Just a strange way to meet someone, that's all."

I smiled. "God has a way of bringing people together."

"I guess He does."

I stared at him, trying to decide what to say. I needed to get out of his body and back to Elyse before things got any worse. "If you have a Source, that means you're Divine. You can push me out."

"I've heard of the Divine. My father... he was a... servant. He made a deal with a demon, in exchange for wealth and power. He was a cold man. A ruthless man. He tried to raise me in his image. He told me about the war between Heaven and Hell, but he only liked to talk about how we could profit. I didn't want anything to do with it, with him. I believe in good, and if there is a war, I want Heaven to win. Everything I have, I've earned by the grace of God. I didn't ask for this."

His voice was rising as he spoke. By the time he finished I could tell he was near tears. I decided the best thing I could do was to play dumb and see what else came out.

"Brian? I don't know what you're talking about."

He put up his hand, and then pulled off his shirt. He was lean and muscular, but it wasn't his pecs that interested me. Freed from the cloth, a pair of fresh golden wings swept out to either side of him.

"I was in the hospital six weeks ago because I was having pain in my back so intense that I couldn't stand up. The doctors couldn't do anything for me, and after three days they sent me home with nothing but a bottle of oxycodone. Two days after that, these things sprouted from my shoulder blades."

He turned so I could see them in full. The skin around the base of the wings was a mess of scar tissue.

"You're changing," I said. "It's happening to a lot of people. You're lucky, because others are dying from it."

"You mean the bacterial infection people have been getting?" he asked. "You're telling me that's what, a Divine disease?"

"In a sense, I guess it is."

"I don't want to be Divine," he shouted. "I was there, when the demon came for my father. I was there when he ripped him open from nose to toes and ate his still beating heart. 'The price agreed,' the demon had said. This isn't natural. This isn't right. I'm not even dead yet."

It wasn't uncommon for demons to ask for such things as part of the bargains they made with mortals. I wasn't going to tell Brian, but his father had made a good deal.

"The people with you. I saw them. They were changed too."

He licked his lips and nodded. "At first, I tried to just live my life. Go to work, stay focused on my company. Then one day, this guy shows up in my office, out of nowhere. He's covered in tattoos and jewelry. He tells me I'm not human anymore. That I'm impure. That I have something I don't deserve. He tried to kill me, but I have this sword... it's an heirloom... it lets me make people see things my way. I think that's what he wanted to take, and he didn't know I knew how to use it, or had the power to use it. I couldn't, before this." He flapped his wings a couple of times for emphasis.

"I don't know why you're telling me this," I said.

"The others. You mentioned the others. I realized it wasn't safe for me, and wouldn't be safe for anyone like me. Not human, not Divine - where would we fit in? I did my homework, went to shelters and paid to help spread the word. I can't believe how many people have come to me in so little time. I've being doing what I could to build a home for them, a place for them to be safe. There's just one thing I don't get."

"What's that?"

His wings swept back and forth again. "Why am I the only angel?"

I stared at him. I had been charged with seducing him, of lying and tricking my way into taking the Deceiver. Only now I had another way. A straighter path that I would never have dared taken in the past. The fact that he had become an angel was proof that he was a good man, a faithful believer, despite the sins of his father. God had turned me from the chaotic road to the benevolent one.

"Brian, I... I haven't been completely honest with you, and I'm sorry. I... I wasn't sure if I could trust you. If you know about the Divine, then you know how dangerous it is."

He stood and looked at me, his face turning hard. "Who are you? Did you bring me here?"

"No. Well, I might have brought you here by accident. I was trying to possess you. I'm sorry." Obi's words echoed in my mind. So did Elyse's. They all thought I was still a monster, less human than any of them. Even Max thought I was good for nothing but lies. "I was the one who followed Alex. I didn't know he was going to lead me to you."

I could see his jaw clenching, his doubts ebbing and flowing. He wanted to believe, but he needed more of a push.

"I wasn't the only one who's looking for you. There's a man, Joe, he's the leader of the Nicht Creidim. They're humans who want to destroy all of the Divine, including the changelings. The man who came to you in your office, he was one of theirs. Joe confronted me in the alley where your people attacked us." I stepped closer to him, so I could put my face right into his. I could tell he was still unsure. "You have no idea what you're dealing with. Your people didn't come back because they're dead. The girl you sent out, she won't be coming back either."

He paled at the words, and his strong resolve crumbled. "Why? What do they want?"

"The sword," I said. I knew that had to be why they were here, and why Joe had lied to me. I had Elyse's memories, and I was sure they wouldn't have gone to such lengths for a ward stone. The question was, did he know that he could use the blade in conjunction with the Box, or was he after the weapon for another purpose, like to trick Elyse into surrendering it? "Do you even know what you have?"

He shrugged, and took a step away from me. "It belonged to my father, and his father before that. He said that if I would make a deal with a demon, I could make people see things that weren't there... illusions. That I could make every dream I could ever have come true." His eyes were sad when he stared into mine. "My dream is to be normal. I wish I'd never heard of the Divine. I can see them, you know. The vampires, the weres, the fiends. They mix in with humanity, but I always know they're there. I've always known. I wish I didn't. Anyway, the sword can't give me that. I'm becoming less normal every day."

"I need the sword, Brian. It's called the Deceiver. It was forged by a powerful demon, and it's a weapon of Hell. I need to take it with me, to stop what's happening to you, to save all of us from what's going to happen if I don't. You have no reason to trust me, I know, but I'm begging you. In the name of God I swear I'm telling you the truth."

He surprised me then, reaching out with his hand and using it to cup my face. I felt a warmth, a strength that wasn't human at all. If I had to name it, I would have called it the Touch of God, and it flowed into me and brought me to a state of peace I could never have imagined. It was a taste of the Heaven I was seeking.

He held me like that for a few seconds, and then nodded.

"I believe you. How do I push you out?"

"I'm not sure. Just do whatever feels nat-"

The field vanished, and I felt a wave of dizziness and nausea overtake me. In an instant, I was back where I had started, floating in front of him, my mind a flood of emotion and desperation. It took me a few seconds to focus and regain enough understanding to capture the moment.

I didn't like what I saw.

Elyse was in the room, her arms pinned behind her back by Uncle Paul. Rae stood next to him, gun trained on Brian's forehead, while Joe sat at the end of the table, his feet up on the wood. Brian's head was resting against the table, where it had landed when he fell into his Source. The other changelings were immobile from fear.

"He's awake," Joe said. "Good morning, sunshine."

Brian lifted his head and eyed the man. He must have remembered our conversation, because he shot upright. "How did you get in here?"

I knew Elyse could see me, but she didn't give any indication. She sat still in her uncle's grip, submissive.

Joe laughed. "I knew your father. He was a real asshole, but he was smart. He knew how to stay under the radar. You, on the other hand. You've brought too much of the wrong kind of attention to yourself." He dropped his feet to the floor and slid his chair back, then stood and walked over to where Rae was waiting. He reached under her long coat, and pulled out a chipped and rusted blade.

"This is how," he said. "I know it doesn't look like much, but the truth is rarely pretty."

Truth? Max had said he was hoping the blade would come to us, and now I understood why. But Joe couldn't have had it all this time or Elyse would have said something. It was Uncle Paul. He must have been in possession of the sword from the start.

Joe walked back over to the table. "You don't look like you know what I'm talking about. If I hadn't gotten knocked down by your goons, I'd probably be in a better mood to explain it to you. Since I'm not... Give me the Deceiver, and I won't kill every single one of you."

He was lying. I knew it before he even said it. He was going to take the sword, one way or another. I needed to get to Elyse, to stop him before he killed Brian and everyone else in the room. I pushed myself forward, moving at what felt like a snail's pace.

"You're going to kill us either way," Brian said. "You can't lie to me."

Joe stopped smiling. "No, I guess I can't."

His arm twitched, and he had a gun in his hand, dropped from the sleeve of his coat. The changelings had overcome their fear, and they tried to rush towards him, but a single bullet to each of their foreheads shut them down before they could gather momentum. Within seconds, only Brian remained.

"You son of a bitch," he said.

I was still too far away from where Uncle Paul was holding Elyse, but I was close to Rae. I changed course and concentrated, my soul crying out in searing agony as I made myself go forward. If I didn't do something he was going to die, and both the swords, and Landon, would be lost.

"Give me the sword, and I'll make it painless," Joe said.

Brian might have been changing into a seraph, and he might have had a good heart, but he wasn't a warrior. None of them were. It was up to me.

I felt myself move into Rae's body, and I stretched myself around her soul, clamping down tight on her with the force of my desperation. Her memories flooded into me - her warrior upbringing, the pain of the tattooing and scarring, the nights she spent in the arms of her lovers. Her jealousy towards Elyse, who was younger and more favored.

I also felt her resist. There was heat, and pain like I had tried to step on the surface of the sun. I clenched my will and fought, pushing through it, screaming at the intensity of the memories and somehow finding my way to the other side. She was strong enough to fight back, but not strong enough to win.

Her eyes became my eyes, and I turned and aimed the gun at Joe's back. I pulled the trigger and he fell forward onto the floor.

I pivoted to Uncle Paul, who pulled his arm tight against Elyse's neck.

"Brian, get out of here," I said. I didn't know if he knew it was me. It didn't matter. He skirted the table and ran, rushing past us and out into the underground.

"Let her go," I said. I aimed the gun at him. I didn't know how accurate my shot would be.

Paul smiled. "Fine." He pushed her towards me, with enough force that I lost the target trying to catch her. As she stumbled into my arms, he began to chant. "Sacerdos ab Ordinario delegatus..."

I shoved Elyse aside, aiming to stop him, when I was thrown forward onto the ground from behind. Before I could recover, the cold steel of a blade was in my back.

"I don't know who you are," Joe said, "but I figured there must be a reason Elyse put that Eye on her head. Thanks for helping us find the Deceiver. It'll sure come in handy to have her lead me to wherever you stashed the Box."

I couldn't believe it. Not only had Joe somehow survived the gunshots, but he had killed his own child to get to me. Paul was still speaking in the background, finishing the exorcism, and I could feel my spirit being pulled away. There was nothing I could do, no way to stop it. They would find the Deceiver, and they would make Elyse bring them back to the hotel. They would use it on Max and Obi, and waltz out of there with the Box, and with

Landon. I felt the wetness of my tears in the eyes of my host.

I had failed.

"…Se et astantes communiat signo crucis, et aspergat aqua benedicta, et genibus flexis, aliis respondentibus, dicat Litanias ordinarias usque ad Preces exclusive."

The last thing I saw was Elyse, kneeling on the ground with a bruise on her cheek. She looked as defeated as I felt.

Then I was thrown away.

It was like being shot from a cannon. The world flew by at warp speed, a blur of color and earth, heat and cold. I was surrounded by a rumble that felt like God was either laughing or yelling at me, and then almost as quickly as it had started, it was over. Everything moved back into place, and I found myself out over the ocean. Waves rolled around me. A storm roiled in the distance. There was no land in sight.

There was nothing.

What I felt in that moment was despair. Deep and dark, it stretched into the pit of every emotion I had left in my disembodied soul and mashed it all together. I let out a non-verbal scream, a primal roar of defeat that echoed in silence into the water below, and the air above. I had been stupid, careless, reckless, overconfident. I had underestimated the Nicht Creidim, and how far Joe would go to get his hands on the Box. I had made a mistake in trying to join with Brian. Now it had cost me everything.

I was motionless. I wept with whatever faculties I held to weep. Time passed. It began to snow. The waves gained strength. The clouds darkened.

The storm tore the world around me while I suffered through my guilt and regret. It churned still as I forced myself to calm, and came to accept that there was nothing else for me to do.

I pushed myself towards what I hoped was east.

CHAPTER TWENTY-FIVE

Landon

WE STARTED WALKING, THROUGH THE old subway tunnel and down the loop. We could have had Avriel air lift us back to the surface, but it just seemed safer in the enclosed space. I had no doubts that Ross would think of more monsters to conjure up and send after us. According to Clara, he was regaining his power, and biding his time.

She had also said that his death had allowed him to become stronger, like changing the locks on a door, or upgrading a computer. It was the balance, I knew. We were getting stronger, too.

I stayed next to Charis, while Clara and Avriel took point a few yards away. It was nice to have a little more time with her, even if was to walk in the dim light of the subway tunnel without saying much at all.

"It's great to have some calm time to walk with you, but I'd feel better if we had a plan," she said, echoing my own thoughts and breaking the silence.

We were walking a fairly long, straight stretch of track, headed uptown. Not because we had a destination in mind, but because that's where the path had led us. We were wandering right now, twisting in the wind, waiting.

I hated it as much as she did.

"You're right." I reached back and put my hand on the pistol, feeling the splintered wood of the grip. "We need to figure out how to use this thing, and then come up with a way to turn the tables on Ross. A trap of some kind."

"He has a knack for slipping traps."

"Maybe, but we can't play defense forever. Besides, I don't think we need to hold him, we just need to lead him to a predetermined point. An ambush."

"That's easy to say. I don't think it will be so easy to do."

"I don't know. He seems pretty intense when he gets close enough. If he thinks he has a clear shot at us, or Clara, he might get a little reckless to take it. I mean, that's how we dropped him in the first place."

"You want to put Clara out on the end of the stick?"

The repulsion in her voice surprised me. "Charis... she's not... real."

"She's as real as we are, in this place," she replied. "And she's ours. Yours and mine. As long as we're trapped here, this is as close to a family as we're ever going to have."

"With one major difference. If she dies, she'll come back again. Just like we do."

She stopped walking and put her arm out to stop me, letting Avriel and Clara get further ahead. "She still feels it, Landon. Just like we do. It still hurts." Her whispers were fierce and intense.

I put my hand on her shoulder and squeezed. "She doesn't remember it, though. She isn't like us. She doesn't have a soul."

She swatted my hand away. "You don't get it, do you? She has a soul. Our soul. Yours and mine. A piece of each. She isn't a carrot, she's our child."

She started moving again, leaving me standing there, watching her back. I didn't hurry to catch up. A few minutes of breathing room might help her cool her head, and I needed time to come to terms with our difference in opinion.

I was still in the rear when Avriel dropped back next to me. His weathered face looked a little younger, and he seemed renewed for having a purpose.

"You look troubled."

Said the angel who I had betrayed, and then failed. His suffering was still on my hands, and I felt the guilt of it burning through my soul. "Avriel. I know this won't make any sense to you, but I'm sorry."

He gazed at me and nodded. "Penitence is the path to God's grace. I believe you."

They weren't comforting words, but they still found a place in me to warm. "To be honest, I'm worried about Charis." I watched her up in front with Clara. They were talking and smiling. Was she wrong? Or was I?

"You've made a lot of difficult choices. I can see that on your face and in your eyes. I'm afraid that won't end just yet."

"What do you mean by that? Is there something you aren't telling me?" The fact that he was even here was proof enough there was more going on than any of us had been let in on.

"I…" He paused. It was an uncomfortable pause, as if he was trying to decide what to say.

I reached forward and grabbed him by the neck, focusing my power to give me the strength to lift him off the ground.

"I'm sick of games," I shouted.

Avriel was calm, even as Charis and Clara noticed what was happening. They both started walking towards us. Clara froze.

"Mom!"

The tunnel changed around us, shaking and twisting, bricks and mortar and dust churning up into the air. By the time I let go of Avriel, Charis and Clara were gone, a wall of stone dividing us.

"What the hell?" I ripped at the stone with my power, Ross' power, desperate to get to the other side. "You're supposed to protect us."

"Landon!"

I heard Charis' voice. I doubled my efforts.

"Clara…. Abaddon… Save her."

I didn't want to save her. She would come back, she always did. What was Charis thinking? I threw my body into the stone, hearing it crack beneath my shoulder. I rammed it again, and again. On the fourth try, I fell through.

Two tunnels. In one direction was Ross, holding Charis with her arms locked behind her, dragging her away. I could feel their power reverberating against one another, like the static charge of a lightning storm. She was fighting, but we could only stop him together.

In the other direction, the dark mass of the demon that I knew too well. I couldn't see Clara through his veil of nothing, but I knew she had to be there. How had they taken us by surprise? Why hadn't Avriel warned me? How had Clara missed it?

"Go and get her," I yelled at him. "I'll go for Charis."

The angel didn't move. "I can't."

"What do you mean you can't?"

He looked like he wanted to die. "I'm not strong enough. I can't win."

Damn it. "You knew this was going to happen? The hard choice? It isn't hard." I turned to run after Ross. It would be better if we died together, than for me to lose her.

He took hold of my shoulder, his fingers digging in hard enough to draw blood. "No. I said that because of who you are. What you are. There are no easy choices for any who must walk the line between good and evil. It's a pattern that will repeat, again and again for all of your existence. The sooner you are able to come to terms with this truth, the more powerful you will become."

I looked from him, to Ross, to Abaddon. I could just make out Charis' face in the spectral light of old bulbs. She was resolute. She was willing to die so that Clara could live. No, so that we could both live. Ross needed both of us to restart the game. Charis was the carrot.

Avriel was right, this time at least. He wouldn't kill Charis because that would take away my incentive to follow. I threw the seraph's hand off me and chased down the demon.

Power fed strength into my legs, and I raced towards Abaddon with abandon, ready to tear him apart. I felt it when his cloak of despair folded around me. I felt my body weaken and my resolve begin to crack. It wasn't enough. Not now.

Then Clara was there, held tight in his arms. I grabbed on and twisted, hearing him scream as black blood ran from the broken limb and Clara fell free. She rolled on the ground, where Avriel scooped her up.

"That hurt," the demon said in his echoing voice. "You're stronger than the seraph."

I pulled more power into me, focusing on rejecting the pestilence and plague of his energy. I was reckless with anger and hatred, my fists pummeling into anything that looked like flesh.

Abaddon laughed. He let me hit him a few times, and then a black hand took hold of my wrist and threw me backwards. "Not yet, child," he said. His entire entity began to soak into a crack in the tunnel wall. By the time I got back to my feet, he was gone.

"Damn it!" I shouted, as loud as I could. The rage poured out of me, so hard that a burst of power exploded away, sending a shiver through the entire world.

"Dad?"

I looked at Clara. Her face was bruised, her clothes scraped and torn. So many emotions churned inside of me, but the maelstrom died at the sight of her. I fell to my knees, overtaken by an instant exhaustion.

She put her arms around me, enveloping me in the warmth of her shared spirit. "We'll get her back. She's part of me, too."

"I don't understand," I said. "How could he do this? Why didn't you see him coming?"

Clara's eyes dimmed. "Abaddon. He hid him somehow. I thought he was further away."

"He can't be the real Abaddon. He's a shade, like Avriel. How can he be so strong?"

"Avriel destroyed the monsters," she replied. "Both shades are strong."

"I've been here for longer than I know," Avriel said. "Most of the power in this place is his and yours, but I know how to use what I have better than any of you." He pointed at the wall. "Except for him."

I fought against the feelings of despair that threatened to conquer me. I had lost Charis, and Abaddon had escaped. "What are we going to do?" I looked at Clara. "As long as you're here it means Charis is alive, doesn't it?"

She shook her head in the wrong direction. "No. You both need to die for him to change everything again. The good news is that for as much as killing her would weaken you, it would also weaken me. Ross doesn't want that to happen now."

I didn't understand. "Why not?"

"The balance. As much as he hates it, he can't break it without me. Not anymore."

"If he wanted to kill you-"

"He can't just kill me. As long as you and mother are alive, I'll only return. The two of you are like turbines. I'm a battery. He needs you both alive, but he also needs time to discharge the power you've collected. If he just kills me outright it will go back out into wild until I return. He can't simply claim it, because it's been tainted with the power of your connection."

I looked into her eyes, sparkling like gems despite the dim lighting. "He wanted me to chase him so that Abaddon could escape with you. He would have hid you from me, the same as he hid Ross."

She smiled. "Yes. If you had gone after him, he would have let her go and made his escape."

"Not if I had caught up."

"He would have let you kill him again. When he came back, he would know where Abaddon was hiding me and you wouldn't."

It made sense. It almost made too much sense. "How do you know all of this?" I asked.

"I don't. You do, when you take away all of the anger, and the guilt, and the joy. When you dive below the pain and look past the hope. Where your power, his power, is pure. That's where you can feel him, and begin to understand him. The Beast is a powerful entity, but he isn't without sentience or consciousness. He wasn't always the Beast. He wasn't always a harbinger of destruction."

She held out her hand and helped me to my feet.

"Once, many years ago, he was much like you."

CHAPTER TWENTY-SIX

Rebecca

OBI WAS WAITING FOR ME the day I knocked on the door to room number 341 at the Hotel Andra. I hadn't thought there would be anyone in the room at all, but I had been able to hear the television from outside the door. It was twenty-seven days after I had been exorcised by the Nicht Creidim. I had spent twenty-six of them as a disembodied spirit, a lost soul floating across the ocean at a speed barely faster than a walk.

He wasn't the Obi I had expected.

The door opened. He was standing there in a pair of striped silk pajamas, his head newly shaved, with a month's growth of beard framing his jaw. His eyes looked lighter than they had the last time I'd seen him, as if he were happy.

"Can I help you?" he asked.

I wasn't surprised he didn't recognize me. I was wearing the skin of a homeless woman, a vagrant I'd found sleeping in the park near the waterfront. She was dirty and matted, dressed in soiled rags, and her teeth were killing me.

"Obi? It's me, Rebecca."

He regarded me without recognition. "Did you say Rebecca?"

I nodded. "Yes."

Either he was fast, or I was rusty. His hand shot out from his side and tightened around my wrist. "I have a message for you," he said, smiling. "Sacerdos ab Ordinario-"

I still had a hand free. I brought it around and smashed him in the jaw, stopping him from going any further with the exorcism. I should have guessed by the fact that he was even here that I was walking right into a trap. Joe had gotten the Deceiver, and he'd used it to mess with Obi's head.

Obi stumbled backwards before recovering, getting his hand up to block my second swing. His face twisted into a scowl, and he used his bare foot to kick me in the gut. "Sacerdos ab Ordinario..." He started the rite again.

"Shut up," I wheezed. I pulled away, and he held my arms tight, just like I wanted him to. I shifted towards him, and he couldn't compensate in time. My head drove into his nose, and I felt it crumble beneath my host's skull. He let go of me, dizzy from the attack, and teetered back to the dresser where the Eagle was resting.

I jumped forward and took hold of his arm, straining to tug him away. He was too strong, and my shell was too weak.

I let him go and backed out of the room. I used the break to look around, to confirm that my pack was gone, the Box with it. I didn't need to be here, and Obi was useless to me like this. Where the hell was Max? Had he been caught by Joe, or had he escaped? I felt a moment's despair, but twenty-six days as a free-floating spirit had given me plenty of time to strengthen my resolve. As long as I was trapped in this world I was determined to either free Landon, or avenge his loss.

I pulled the door closed behind me and abandoned the bag lady. She looked around for a minute, confused, and then started wandering down the hall. I pushed myself from room to room, passing by an older man in a sweatsuit, a couple having sex, and a rich old lady with a poodle. The fourth try was the winner; a young man with blonde hair, dressed in a sharp three piece suit. He looked like a salesman, or a maybe a high-class drug dealer.

I took him with ease, discovering he was a marketing executive with a wife and a two year old daughter, that he loved baseball, and he was allergic to peanuts. Knowing he had a child made me hesitate to keep him, but I was in a hurry, and his meat suit was perfect for where I was headed next. I would drop him off unharmed once I was done with him.

I wasn't sure what my next move would be, but I knew I needed help, and there was only one person I could think of who might be available. I spent a few minutes getting a better feel for my new host, and then headed out of the Hotel, tracing my steps back towards the underground village where I had last seen Joe and Elyse. I walked past the alley and noticed the door I had entered was clearly visible now, though it had been chained four times over. I stifled the anger I felt at the memory, and kept walking. This time I wanted to go up.

"Can I help you, sir?"

The lobby of Madalytics was all silver, blue, and glass, with a semi-circular receptionist desk pressed against the back wall off the elevator and a massive flatscreen touting all kinds of data metrics behind the receptionist's head.

He was a scrawny man in his early twenties, with six or seven piercings in each ear, spiked blue hair, and a winning smile. It was a look, but it suited him. I glanced up at the cameras covering the area, and then returned his smile.

"I'm here to see Mr. Rutherford," I said. "I'm a college buddy. He told me I could stop by whenever I was in town."

Hearing I wasn't a customer, his formalities dropped. "Oh, cool. Yeah, sure. I think Brian's in a meeting right now, but I'll send him a message."

I closed my eyes and thanked God he was still in town and still alive. I could only guess the Nicht Creidim had more pressing concerns now than dealing with an angelic changeling.

The receptionist's phone buzzed a few seconds later, and he looked down on it, and then at me. "What was your name again?" he asked.

"Rebecca."

He raised his eyebrow at that, and then typed something into the phone. When it buzzed again, his eyes widened. I narrowed mine, prepared to have to either fight my way in, or run away.

"I'll show you to his office. He'll be with you in a minute." He put a little 'be right back' placard onto the desk and stepped out from behind it, leading me through a solid wood door to the left. The offices were open and organized, with rows of people sitting behind rows of computers, in various stages of work and loafing. Neon arrows guided employees to the 'Spa' and the 'Nap Room', as well as 'Stuffy Stuff: Jacket Required'.

We were ignored on our trek past the workers and into a hallway, through a section of spaces that contained a gym, a ping-pong table, and a masseuse. Brian's office was all the way in the back, a huge expanse in the corner decked out much like the subterranean bar had been. I recognized the juke box.

Brian showed up before the receptionist left. He was cautious in his entrance and expression, unsure of what to expect. When he was confronted with a man, he gave the hint of a smile.

"Thanks, Pete," he said to the guy with blue hair. Pete left, and Brian walked right up to me. "Is it really you? I thought you were dead."

"Spirits are hard to kill," I replied. For all I knew, I was impossible to fully destroy in this state. Not that it mattered. Throwing me hundreds of miles away was more than effective enough to put me out of play. "I know Joe got the Deceiver. He used it on my friend and took something from us, something he can use to do a lot of damage to the world." I looked into his eyes. "Something that will either change all of mankind the way you've been changed, or kill it."

Brian was still for a moment, and then shrugged. "I don't know how I can help you with that. I told you, I'm not a fighter, and I don't even have the sword anymore. That man, Joe, he killed all of them. I only escaped because of you." He walked over to his desk, and opened one of the drawers. He placed the ward stone down in front of me. "He didn't even bother taking this. I've spent so much time staring at it, waiting for it to turn, waiting for them to come back for me."

"You'd rather live in fear than fight back?" I asked.

"I don't want to fight."

"I know, it's a choice between crappy and crappy, but I need your help. I need to stop him."

He stared at me. "I can't."

"Do you think God made you an angel so you could just tuck your wings in and hide when things didn't go your way? Do you think you were made unique to hang out in a dungeon and drink beer?" I walked up to the desk and picked up the ward stone. "If you do, you don't need this." I threw it to the ground, breaking it into two pieces. "I'm going to kill you myself."

He was afraid, that much was clear, but he was afraid of the wrong thing. Most of the changelings were demons. If Joe had his way, he would be even more screwed than he already was.

His face was flushing, and I thought he might either start crying, or yell back at me. Instead, he closed his eyes, reached up, and pulled off his shirt. His wings unfolded in freedom, and he lifted a few inches off the ground.

"Okay," he said. "You're right. The Lord didn't make me this way to run a software company. What do you want me to do?"

I smiled, leaned over the desk, and kissed him on the cheek, causing an embarrassed blush. There were two things I needed. To find out what happened to Max, and to get a new partner, even if it was an unwilling one.

"You have a lot of nerds out there, don't you?" I asked. "I need to get my hands on surveillance recordings for the Hotel Andra from the day we met, and the week after."

"Easy enough. Most of the hotels downtown use the same ISP, and they stream their surveillance to offsite data centers for security." He lowered himself to the ground, tucked his wings, and sat down at his desk. His hands were a blur along the keyboard. "I just sent an e-mail. We should have results in a couple of hours."

"I knew you were the right person to come to."

He glanced over at me. "I'm not certain I won't regret this, but hiding hasn't helped much."

"Next request. Can any of your employees do anything with cell phones? I need to find someone's number, and all I can give you is a starting location from a month ago."

He lowered himself back to the ground. "I've got a guy working remote in Australia that can probably do it. I'll send him an e-mail."

He typed it out and sent it off. A few seconds later he pointed at the screen. "My contact at RainierNet is better than I expected." He swiveled the screen so I could see. "Login credentials for the remote surveillance service the Hotel Andra uses."

"Let's see what we can see."

He copied and pasted his way into the remote interface, and entered the date range I had requested. The hotel had a camera in the lobby and a few in the hallways on each floor. It was a lot of video to look through.

"Start with the lobby. Just keep going until Joe turns up," I said.

He started pulling it up, but a notification popped up on the screen. He tabbed back to his e-mail, and then pushed the keyboard over to me. "Put in the address and the date. No promises, but he'll do his best."

I entered the data and he sent the reply back, then returned to the videos. He scrubbed through the lobby on the day we'd lost the Deceiver, turning up nothing until one o'clock in the morning. It wasn't Joe that walked into the hotel lobby.

It was Elyse.

"He got her too," I said. "She was on my side." The camera angle was wide enough to show her going into the elevator. "Can you find the third floor cameras, around the same time?"

He complied, searching for the right clips. "Rebecca, can I ask you something?"

"What?"

"How did you get lost?"

"What do you mean?"

He looked at me. "In my Source, you said you were lost. I could see it in your eyes, you didn't just mean there. You're lost right now too. You must be, to be a spirit."

He wasn't wrong, but the question made me uncomfortable. "It's complicated."

He laughed. "I would imagine it would have to be. Still, maybe when we have more time you can tell me about it? People tell me I'm a good listener."

There was a part of me that wanted to spill the whole thing right then and there. To confide in someone and unleash the torrent of mixed emotions I was holding onto. "Maybe." I winked at him.

He half-smiled and returned his attention to the screen. "Here you go," he said.

Elyse was walking down the hallway. She stopped at Room 341 and knocked. The door opened. Obi. He said something, she said something. He looked back into the room, and then left, closing the door behind him. He followed Elyse to the elevator at a run.

"Is that your friend? What did she tell him?"

"That's Obi, yeah. I don't know what she said. Maybe that I was in trouble?" I had no idea, but it gotten him moving in a hurry.

Brian was ahead of me, seeking out the lobby camera. He found it fast, and we watched Elyse and Obi leave together. Two minutes later Obi came back in, with Joe right behind him.

"What are you hoping to find?" Brian asked.

"I was with two people. Joe got to Obi, but my friend Max is missing. I needed to know if he was killed, or if he got away."

We found the third floor video. We watched Obi and Joe go in, and then Joe come back out with my pack. He glanced up at the camera just before the elevator doors closed.

"It looks like he got away."

It did look that way, but I remembered what Max had said. Deceit and trickery. Was there any way to know if Max had planned for this to happen? I couldn't rule it out. At least I knew he was still out there, somewhere.

The e-mail notification popped up again. Brian switched over to it.

"There's your number," he said.

"Do you have a cell I can borrow?" I asked.

He reached into his pocket and pulled it out. I dialed the number, trying to calm my nerves as I did. I was sure this was probably a bad idea, but I was out of alternatives.

It rang three times before it was picked up.

"Hello?"

It was the voice I had been hoping for, and dreading.

"Hello, Sarah? This is Rebecca Solen."

CHAPTER TWENTY-SEVEN

Rebecca

"I SHOULD HAVE KNOWN IT was you, back at the beach house," Sarah said.

"You don't sound surprised to hear from me," I replied. It made me more than a little uncomfortable.

"I'm not. I knew you were out there, somewhere."

"How?"

I heard the rush of air against her cell's microphone, and then a new voice solved the puzzle.

"Ah, hello my sugared dumpling. I've been waiting for your call."

"What the hell is going on, Max? You left Obi here as an exorcist, and me to walk right into the Nicht Creidim's trap."

He sighed. "It couldn't be helped, dearest. If you had followed the plan, I wouldn't have needed to improvise."

As much as I didn't like it, he was right. "Okay, but I thought the idea was to keep Sarah out of this. She can't be trusted."

Max started laughing. "No doubt. But then, you are the one who called her, are you not? I knew that you would, once you realized you were low on options. Before you ask, I was lucky to get out through the window when Joe came a-calling. He has the Deceiver, Truth, the Damned, and Avriel's Box. Do you have any idea what that means?"

"He's winning?"

The laughter stopped. "Yes. A mortal is winning. Kicking our asses, actually. You're just lucky he has no idea the extent of what he possesses. I know what Joe's plan is for the Box. All he would need is to get his hands on the Destroyer and he would be able to make it happen. I'm not happy about any of this, but seeing as how we're in dire straits, the best thing we could do is add an element of uncertainty to the endeavor. You knew that the moment you started dialing."

He meant Sarah. There was no guarantee she could have all of that power thrown in her face without breaking bad again, with our without her consent.

"The Destroyer?" I asked. It was the one blade left unaccounted for. "Do you know where it is?"

"Yes. Shanghai, China. We can't risk making a move for it until we've gotten the other swords back. I need you to collect Obi-wan and get a flight to Japan. We'll meet you here."

I glanced up at Brian, who was listening to the conversation as best he could. "How am I going to get Obi? Finding a mortal body that's stronger than his won't exactly be easy."

"My apologies, apple tart, but you created this, which makes him your responsibility. I trust you'll find a way to fix it. Be here by this time tomorrow, for all of our sakes."

He hung up.

"Bad news?" Brian asked. He surprised me with the sincerity of his concern.

I kept my eyes on him while my mind ran. I couldn't take Obi on my own, but maybe I didn't have to.

"Are you still in on helping me?"

He hesitated, then nodded. "By necessity, not choice."

"I'll take it however I can get it. I need you to help me kidnap my friend, and I need a private jet that can fly us to Japan."

"At least you aren't asking for anything big."

"Brian, I-"

He put his finger to my host's lips to cut me off. "I'm kidding." He waved his hands around his office. "I have all of this because of the grace of God. If He brought me this so that I would be able to help you when you needed aid, so be it."

It was a nice thought, but I knew that wasn't how it worked. There was no such thing as fate. Who he was, that was God's gift. What he had done with that gift was all his own. Just like what I had done as Reyka Solen was all my own. Blaming Lucifer would be a cop-out, not an absolution.

"Give me the phone," he said. I handed it to him, and he began typing on it. "I'm sending Pete a message to charter a flight to Japan. Which airport?"

"Osaka."

He nodded and kept typing. "Done. Let me grab a fresh shirt, and we'll go and get your friend."

"You really are an angel," I said.

He smirked. "Not completely. I keep picturing you as that sexy raven I saw in my soul. Not all of my thoughts are pure."

"At least you admit it. You're still human too."

"I guess so."

"Do you have a car?"

"No, do I need one?"

We were going to need some way to get Obi to the plane without being noticed. "It would help."

"I'll have Pete send a car over to the hotel." He sent him a text before he had finished talking.

I led him from his office, out to the lobby. Pete was on the phone, making final arrangements for the flight. He asked the person on the other end to hold when he saw us. "The plane will be ready at SeaTac in two hours. Are you sure though, Brian? This is going to cost, and the investors aren't going to like it."

"I know. There's nothing I can do about it. If I don't make this trip, there is no Madalytics."

"Good luck then, bro," he said, and then he resumed the call.

"How did you come up with that name, anyway?" I asked him, once we were on the elevator.

"It's based on Mary Magdalene. It was meant to be a spit in the face for my dad, without it looking too religious and scaring away the venture capitalists."

It made me laugh. "Clever."

We walked the half-mile talking about his company, about his religion, and what was most fascinating to me: his decision to go against everything his father had stood for. There was something about that story that gave me strength and hope for the final step of my own redemption. It was my fault that Joe had taken the Box and the swords, but maybe it was meant to be? Maybe fate didn't exist, but where was the line between it and faith?

"So, what's the plan?" he asked as we stepped off the elevator on the third floor of the hotel. "I take it this friend of yours is strong like a bull?"

"More like a mammoth. He's... enhanced. He's stronger than a regular human, which is why I can't hold him like this." I didn't have time to explain about Landon, or the Beast. "He's also a former United States Marine."

"Is this supposed to be giving me confidence?"

"You're an angel, or at least part-angel. You should be able to Calm him." At least, I was hoping he could. Maybe all he had gotten were the wings.

"How do I do that?"

"You're asking me? Just tell him to relax."

We walked down the hallway, and I knocked softly on the door. I could still hear the television on the other side.

Obi answered it again, his nose wrapped in white gauze. He wasn't alone. Two Nicht Creidim flanked him from behind.

"Crap," Brian said.

"So much for calm." I shot past Obi and planted the flat of my palm into one of his keepers, hearing the bones of his nose crumble and knocking him backwards. Obi turned and tried to hit me, but I ducked underneath the blow and caught him in the lungs with a solid side-kick. Brian threw his arms around him before he could come at me again.

"Sacerdos ab Ordinario…"

The second Nicht Creidim started the exorcism. I saw Obi's gun was still on the dresser, and I lunged across the room towards it. I heard Brian behind me, speaking into Obi's ear, telling him that he needed to relax and find his center.

I felt a hand grab my ankle and send me teetering forward, still too far from the Eagle. I let go of my host and threw myself towards the exorcist, covering the distance of the small room in seconds while the marketing executive's head got twisted against the bottom of the dresser and hit the floor with a solid thud. I went in and latched on, taking in the pain of the man's memories and exulting over it. He was a trained thug, a standard grunt, with nothing special in his past that made him anything more than fodder. The first thing I did was shut him up.

"He should have given you an Eye," I said. He might have seen me coming, and kept me from getting in.

I looked over to Brian and Obi. The angel had gone down to his knees, holding Obi's head in his lap. I guess he could Calm after all.

The first Nicht Creidim got to his feet, one hand on his nose. He tried to defend himself from me, but I had a fighter's body now, and I pushed aside his punches and returned them with force and speed. I put him back on the ground, leaving him unconscious next to the executive. I leaned down to check my former host's pulse, and cursed to find he was dead.

"I'm sorry," I said.

Maybe I shouldn't have taken him.

I went to the dresser and grabbed the Eagle. "Good work," I said to Brian.

"I didn't think that would work. Remind me never to piss you off."

I bent down and grabbed Obi's legs. "I hope the car is outside."

We carried him down the hallway towards the elevator, but I redirected Brian to the stairs. "Can you make it?" I asked.

"As long as we hurry," he replied.

The stairs emptied out into the lobby. The clerk at the front desk tried to get our attention, but we ignored him as we made our way outside. Pete hadn't let us down. A limo was waiting at the curb. I put Obi's legs down to open the back door, and then we maneuvered him in.

"What the hell is going on?" the driver asked.

"I'm Brian Rutherford, and I'm rich. If you want a nice tip, and I mean nice, you'll stop asking questions and drive."

That was all it took to get us moving. I watched the street behind us through the back of the limo. I didn't see anyone following. After a few blocks, I turned around and slumped into the seat.

"We did it," Brian said, with a huge smile on his face. "That was incredible."

"You did it. I couldn't have put Obi out like this."

He looked at the Marine, resting comfortably across the seat. "Maybe what happened to me isn't as bad as I was thinking."

"I don't want to burst your bubble, Brian, but it's worse than you were thinking."

He ran his hand over his bald head and sighed. "I appreciate your honesty. It just feels good to help someone. After what happened in the underground... I feel responsible."

"You're going to help me stop it. All of it. That's something you can feel good about."

We rode in silence for a while, until Brian got on his cell to ask

Pete about the flight. "Plane will be ready before we get there."

I hadn't been too worried about it, but I still felt a sense of relief at the news. "Great. Can I borrow the phone?"

He tossed it over to me. I dialed Sarah's number.

"Rebecca," she said. "What's your situation?"

Businesslike. Cold. I shouldn't have expected anything else. "We have Obi, and a jet chartered for a direct flight. We'll be there in sixteen hours or so."

"We?"

I glanced over at Brian. "I picked up a stray millionaire. You'd like him, he has wings."

Brian's face turned red, and he looked down towards his feet. It was cute how innocent he was.

"A human with wings?"

She didn't know about the changelings? "Long story. Tell Max we'll be there on schedule."

"I will."

She hung up.

"Who was that?" Brian asked.

"I'll tell you on the plane. It'll take a few hours to explain everything."

"I'm not sure I want to know."

"I'm sure you don't, but I need to tell you anyway. All I ask is that you hear me out, the whole thing, before you pass judgement on anybody."

"The only true judge is God."

CHAPTER TWENTY-EIGHT

Landon

"What do you mean, like me?" I asked.

"It is the reason you can absorb his power. You and mother both. The universe demands balance, it depends on it, as you know. The Beast was tasked with keeping that balance."

"For the entire universe?" I was shocked. I had barely managed to keep the balance on earth in check.

"Not this universe, but yes. It's hard to picture, but it was so."

"What happened?"

"He failed."

I laughed. "You mean he decided to side with chaos."

"No. I mean, he failed. He tried to stop it and couldn't. Everything he knew burned. I can feel the flames in his energy, the death of an untold number of planets and peoples in its ripples."

I had no idea. I don't know if anyone did. "Malize told me he came to this universe to hide. That he asked God for safe haven."

"He came in goodwill. The torment of his guilt drove him mad. Now it's all he is."

Could I expect the same to happen to me if I failed? I'd underestimated the costs when I'd agreed to come back from Purgatory and be a champion for mankind and the balance. Had I trapped myself in the one true hell? I took a deep breath and blew it out.

"No matter where he came from, he's a problem now," I said. "We need a plan to get Charis back."

"You can't," Clara said. "He'll know you're coming."

"So what? So he kills me again? So he kills Charis? At least we'll be back together. I'm getting her back." There was no point to any of this if it meant leaving her with Ross, to be tortured for all of eternity.

"Dad-"

"No. I don't want to hear it." I drew the revolver and held it up in front of me. "You talk about balance... what the hell am I supposed to do with this? If I understand what you're saying, it takes all three of us to capture half of his power, right? And now we have enough of it that he wants the part that you have, and he knows how to get it. What is he going to do with it, Clara? Break the balance? Then what?"

She didn't show any emotion. She just stood and looked at me, which only made me more upset.

"I see three possibilities. One, we keep the balance. Two, he breaks it. Three, we break it. What's the difference between two and three? How would us defying the universal law lead to any better outcome than him? He has Charis, and none of this makes any damn sense."

"Whoever breaks the balance has control," she said, in a tone barely above a whisper, like it was a secret she didn't want me to hear.

"Control of what?"

"Everything."

"In here? That doesn't amount to much."

"The Box is locked. Whoever has control can unlock it."

"So Ross can get out?"

"Yes."

"Or we can get out."

"Yes, except…" Her voice trailed off.

"Except what?"

She looked at the ground. "You can't break the balance before we've reached parity with him. It's impossible."

I felt like I was standing naked in the arctic. Every part of me shivered. "So, you want to stall until our power is totally equal, even if that means leaving your mother there to suffer?" I caught myself after I said it. Her mother? She wasn't real.

"I don't want to. We have to. It's the only way."

"To win? I don't accept that. We're going to get her." I looked at her, feeling the chill of the coldness that washed through me. "If he's going to capture you, I'll kill you myself."

She didn't flinch. She just nodded.

"Charis is part of you," I said. "Unless she's with Abaddon, you can sense her. Where is she?"

"Dad, I-"

I knelt down and grabbed her shoulders. "Where is she, Clara?"

"I'll take you," she said. "But you're going to die, and we'll never get another chance at this."

"He doesn't have to die," Avriel said, stepping up to us. "There may be another way."

We both looked at him.

"Abaddon," he said. "Convince the demon to help you. He can cloak you in his power and allow you to attack the Beast before he knows you're there. It may be enough to save Charis, and get you the time you need to overcome him once and for all."

"Abaddon?" I laughed weakly. "No offense, but you do know Abaddon hates me."

"No. Abaddon hates *me*. That doesn't mean you can't bargain with him."

"I think he's already struck a deal with Ross."

"He's a demon. Make him a better one."

"Even if he wants me to hand you over?"

"If that is what it takes, then so be it."

I stared at him while I thought. The last thing I wanted to do was hand Avriel over to Abaddon again. I had enough guilt on my conscience from the first time I'd done it. "I can't. We'll find another way."

"Landon," Avriel said. "I am here for a reason. Abaddon is here for a reason. Can you be sure of what that reason is?"

I couldn't be sure of anything.

"I'm not making any promises," I said. "If we can't sense him, how do we find him?"

"I have an idea where he may be. The place is always the same, but the landscape has been remade since you arrived. Before, I called it the Grave. I could always find the demon there, kneeling before a headstone. We would talk then, before we would fight. He would tell me of his lost love."

He smirked at my surprise.

"Abaddon was a human before Lucifer changed him. I didn't know that either until we were trapped together. He killed his wife, and in time came to regret the decision."

"But he still delighted in torturing you." My mind flashed back to the image of him up on the cross, and the screams of agony that followed my betrayal. Next, I thought of Charis. I was kidding myself to think that I wouldn't hand him over without hesitation if it was the only way to get her back.

"He was always a killer, and I'm not his wife."

"Right. So, where was the Grave?"

"It was on an island. I would fly across, and he would be there."

"That isn't very helpful," I said. "We're on an island right now."

Avriel shrugged. "I'm sorry, but that was how I knew it. It wasn't a large island, and it was home to only the single headstone. It rested right in the center, a block of white marble carved in the visage of a weeping angel."

A statue of a woman alone in the center of an island? "You're telling me he's waiting at the Statue of Liberty?"

Avriel shrugged again. "I don't know that place."

I did, too well. It was where I had learned the truth about what I had agreed to do. Everything was coming full circle, and I didn't like it.

"Okay. We need to get to Liberty Island. Where are we right now?"

The shifting walls had gotten me turned around. I had a sense of where we were in space, but not geography. As much as this place looked and felt like Manhattan, there was no way to be sure that it would stay that way.

"The Chambers Street station should be right up ahead," Clara said.

"Perfect."

I started running. Clara and Avriel had no trouble keeping pace, and we covered the distance in no time. We reached Chambers Street within a few minutes. The station was deserted, the same as the rest of the city.

"Which way to Charis?" I asked.

Clara pointed north. "That way."

The Statue was south. I hated to move further from Charis, but there was no choice. "Okay, let's go."

If I remembered right, it was about a mile from the World Trade complex to the Battery Park ferry, and the Chambers Street subway had only dropped us off a couple of blocks from where the Freedom Tower was rising into a sky painted with purple and black clouds, crackling with blue energy.

"Ross isn't going to like us not moving towards him," I said as we started running down Church Street.

"No, he isn't," Avriel said, pointing towards the sky. A single figure, slender and pale floated in contrast against the clouds.

"An angel?" I asked. I knew it couldn't be so.

The figure swooped down, landing on the roof of the building ahead. Trinity Church.

My eyes followed, and when they reached ground level I drew back. The once empty city had found its populace. People, cars, dogs, and even pigeons now moved through the streets in a smooth flow, headed from one place to another. There were horns honking, voices on cell phones, laughter and shouting. I tried to find the angel again in the sudden rush.

She was gone.

"What's happening?" I asked.

"Just as gathering his power makes us stronger, it also binds us closer together. As we know him better, he knows us better. He's using your memories," Clara said. "Or mother's."

I saw it now. Standing in front of a small storefront was a large man in a white apron, a smile on his face as he waited for patrons to enter his butcher shop. I'd seen that man plenty of times before, walking from the apartment in Harlem to the park where I would play. He was out of place here.

"Stay alert, Landon," Avriel said. "He's doing this to distract you."

I knew it, but still found it distracting. I blinked a couple of times and starting moving again. The traffic didn't break around us like it did in the real world. It made travel slow.

She was waiting for us outside of the church. Now that she was close, I could see what Ross had done.

"Landon." Josette opened her arms wide to me, her round face filled with a cheshire grin.

She was everything that was good in the world, my symbol of the best of both human and Divine. He was using her likeness to get to me, and he was succeeding.

"Not her," I said, feeling my fury building. "Anyone else, but not her."

The attack came from behind us, a flash of cloth and a glint of iron. She was the bait, not the ambush. I was barely able to turn and get my arm up in time, and I cried out in pain as the sword dug down to the bone.

He wrenched it out and stepped back, leaving us standing face to face. I knew the attacker. Charis' lover, Joseph. He drew back the blade and readied himself while blood ran down my arm and dripped on the pavement.

"A poor excuse for a replacement in her bed," he said, spitting at my feet. "You don't deserve her."

Behind me, I heard the sound of steel against steel.

"Avriel the Just," Josette said, laughing. "Just what?"

Even if I could have looked, I didn't want to. Josette deserved to be remembered in the way she lived and died; with dignity and grace.

"I don't have time for this," I said. I could feel the blood pumping through me, my anger at full-tilt. The crowd was a distraction. Josette was a distraction. Joseph was a distraction.

I was angry, but not stupid.

I pulled the gun from my waist. I didn't shoot it. I didn't need to. I threw myself towards Joseph, holding the pistol against my palm to use it as a shield. He smiled and quick stepped towards me, bringing his body perpendicular and his blade through with an amazing grace.

Ross was using Charis' memories, but I had them, too. I knew the move was coming and I ducked under it with only centimeters to spare. In one smooth motion I turned and tossed the revolver into the air, and then launched it forward. Not at Joseph, at Clara.

Until the last moment it looked like it would hit her, but I wasn't aiming for her. When that last moment came, a streak of mottled brown fur wrapped Clara up in a pair of massive paws, and bent its legs to spring away. One moment wasn't enough time, and the iron smashed into its head at mach four, the force of the crack echoing like a massive thunderclap, and the head snapping with such force that the neck was severed from the spine. The fake Ulnyx dropped

Clara while I focused, pulling the gun back to me, using it like Mjolnir and flinging it towards Joseph. He tried to sneak in on me again, but he couldn't. I knew everything he would do because Charis had spent hours training with him. The gun broke his sword hand to pieces.

I could still hear Avriel squaring off against Josette, their blades skittering and cracking against one another. I still didn't want to look, and I knew she was the one false face that I couldn't bring myself to harm. "Avriel, end it," I said. I used my power to break her blade apart. I felt sick when I heard his weapon sink into her.

"Are you okay?" I asked Clara. She was looking down on the Great Were. It was clear she had aged again, her baby fat receded and her dangerously delicate beauty rising to the surface. I could see parts of me in her eyes and face, but her appearance was more Charis.

"We need to move faster," she said.

We couldn't move faster through these crowds. Wasn't that the point? I returned the gun to my pants and wrapped my good arm around Clara's waist. I had been able to use Ross' power to fly in Purgatory. What was keeping me from doing the same here?

"Dad, don't. You're going to weaken yourself."

"I have to." I pulled in the power, focusing on bending this universe to my will. Ripples of energy cracked the world around me, and I launched into the air.

Lady Liberty was easy to spot from altitude, and I only wasted a single heartbeat to ensure the archangel had followed my lead. I took a deep breath to steel myself against the demon's innate power, and then spun in the sky and rocketed towards the Statue.

I could see him before I landed, the dark tendrils of his power trailing out around him like the train of a massive cloak. He was there as Avriel had said, on his knees at the base of the pedestal. I came to ground a thousand feet back, out of the reach of his dark essence. Avriel landed next to me.

"You two wait here," I said. I turned to Avriel. "Do your job, and protect her."

I started walking towards the demon, trying to ignore the pain in my arm and the sudden feeling of exhaustion that was pulling on me. Convincing Abaddon to help me was the only option, because there was no way he wouldn't destroy me in my current state.

"Abaddon." I got as close to him as I could before the reach of his energy threatened to cause me to collapse.

The demon didn't move.

"Abaddon."

He bent down in prostration, and then rose to his feet. The swirling despair that surrounded him was sucked in as he turned, until he stood before me as only a man. His hair was short and white, his skin dark and aged. He wore a heavy wool trench coat above a black tuxedo, leaving him dark and foreboding even without the essence swirling around him. Ruby red eyes pierced the darkness and dove deep into me. When he smiled, his fanged teeth were pleasant instead of predatory.

"Diuscrucis. Have you considered what we discussed, the last time we spoke?"

CHAPTER TWENTY-NINE

Rebecca

"I'M STILL NOT SURE I understand everything," Brian said as we taxied towards a small hanger at Senmon Daiten. "I mean, I get why you're so desperate to get your hands on this Box, but..." He stared out the window at nothing. "There's so much that's happening here, and nobody knows about it."

"You know about it. The question is, what are you going to do?"

He kept looking out the window. "It's a lot to take in, Rebecca. All of this has been a lot to take in, and this is supersonic unbelievable. If I hadn't grown wings, I'd never think it was even possible." He turned his head to look at me, seated across from him in the small jet. "I already said I would help you, before I even understood why. If you're afraid that's changed because of what you were, and what you've done... it hasn't. It's up to God to decide what happens to you, not me."

I'd been waiting for him to pass his judgement on me, despite what he had said. I was surprised to find myself relieved when he proved true to his word. "Thank you, Brian." It was a simple thing, and all I had to offer, but it seemed to be enough.

They were waiting for us inside the hanger. I saw them from the small window over the wing. Max, waving at the aircraft with a huge smile on his face. Sarah, calm and emotionless. Ulnyx, looking like a bodyguard in a black suit and standing with his arms folded across his broad chest.

"He's bigger than I imagined," Brian said.

"You haven't seen him shift yet."

The plane rolled to a stop. The stewardess opened the door and dropped the ladder. I got up and went to the rear seat, where we had bound and gagged Obi. He'd slept most of the trip, but as soon as he'd woken up his efforts to exorcise me had resumed. I was unknotting the nylon rope the stewardess had found in an emergency toolkit when I felt a hand on my shoulder.

"Rebecca. I'll take care of him." I looked up to see Sarah standing there. She had spoken to me without emotion, but I could see the concern for Obi on her face.

Max came up the ladder as I moved aside to let her pass.

"Ah, there you are my tasty raspberry tart. Oh, and in a man now, I see. Hmm... Brother Shane, if I'm not mistaken." He put his arms around me and squeezed.

"How did you know his name?" I asked.

"I know the names of all of my enemies." He let me go and turned to Brian. "And the white knight himself. Your assistance has been invaluable. I'm sorry about your friends, but we'll do our best to make things right."

"Obi." I heard Sarah behind me. "Obi, it's me, Sarah."

He didn't respond.

"Open your eyes."

I didn't see his eyes open, but I heard him begin to speak. She must have taken the tape off his mouth.

"Sarah-" I started to turn, to get her out of the way and put the tape back on.

Max took hold of my wrists. "Wait."

"Obi, shhhh." Sarah put her hand to his mouth and he quieted immediately, following her Command. It seemed even the power of the Deceiver could be overruled. "I want you to remember what happened. I want you to remember the truth."

The glazed look in his eyes vanished. He stared straight ahead for a moment, and then he looked at her.

"Sarah? What are you doing here?" His eyes passed her, falling on Max. "What's going on?"

"The Deceiver," Max said. "The Nicht Creidim used it on you."

"Oh. Crap." He lifted his hand to his forehead. "I didn't do anything stupid, did I?"

"You tried to exorcise me," I said.

I should have expected he would laugh. "They could have convinced me of anything, and that's what they chose? I might have done that willingly."

"They also made you hand over to box."

He stopped laughing. "Right. They would do that, wouldn't they. It looks like we're in an airplane. Where are we?"

"Japan," Sarah said. "Osaka."

"The Nicht Creidim have the Deceiver, the Damned, Truth, and the Box," I said. "We're here to get it all back."

Obi stretched and got to his feet. "So what are we waiting for? You have my Eagle?"

"Up front," I said.

"We aren't here to get it back," Max said.

My head whipped around. "What?"

"You're here to get it back. You and Sarah. You're the only ones who can, but I think you already knew that."

I had considered it. I looked over at her. "You're okay with this?"

"No, but we don't have a choice. I want Landon back too. I'll let you in."

"Wonderful," Max said, clapping his hands together. "Now, if you ladies don't mind, we're on a bit of a tight schedule."

"So what's the plan?" I asked.

"Ditch your current host, and I'll let you hitch a ride. Ulnyx will drive us to the docks. After that, we improvise." Sarah lifted the leg of her pants as she spoke, revealing a cursed and blessed dagger riding on her calf. "I'm not much of a fighter, but I know you are."

"None of the swords will work on you or Sarah. Between her power, and your experience, it should be like a walk in the park."

I was sure it wouldn't be that easy. Joe was guaranteed to have tricks up his sleeve that none of us knew about. "What are you going to do?"

"We'll wait for you here. Once you get back, we'll need to get airborne and go claim the Destroyer." The demon put his hand on Brian's shoulder. "If you wouldn't mind?"

"I'm in," Brian replied. "I'll go talk to the pilot."

"What the heck am I supposed to do?" Obi asked. "You woke me up just to leave me twiddling my thumbs again?"

"We couldn't exactly leave you spouting latin every time you were conscious," Max said. "If you're itching to get involved, you can ride shotgun with the fur ball."

"Not my first choice, but it beats hanging out here."

"Very well. You three better get moving. Be back with the Box in two hours, or I'm afraid the end of the world as we know it will come sooner than we'd like."

Everything was happening so fast. I glanced at Sarah. "Are you ready?"

"As ready as I'll ever be."

I let go of Brother Shane, feeling myself spread away from his soul and exit his body. Max grabbed him before he could collapse, holding him in a tight grip. I didn't want to know what he would do with him.

An instant later, I was trying to wrap myself around Sarah's soul. I could feel the resistance, the energy roiling around me like a massive lightning storm, and I could hear Max telling her to relax. I pushed into the storm even as it rolled, trying to navigate my way through, trying to complete the connection.

When I did, it hurt. Not like the others, where the pain was intense but manageable. It hurt more than any hurt I had ever experienced, or any hurt I could have possibly conceived. It was as if I had been shattered into a million tiny fragments, and each of those shards had been stabbed with a white hot sun. There was nothing to compare it to, and no way to get around it. I was forced to ride through the whirlpool, to hold on while I was pulled through the broken mess that was at the heart of the true diuscrucis. They always went mad eventually, I knew, but to see it, to feel it, to have it run through me... once I had come out the other side, it was all I could do to hold myself together.

How Sarah was managing defied my understanding.

"*Are you with me?*" Sarah asked.

I was with her, but she was still in control. "*Yes. Sarah, I-*"

"*Do you remember our conversation on the beach?*"

"*Yes.*"

"*Let's just leave it at that, okay, Rebecca? I'm trying to forgive you, because I know it's what my mother would want, and what Landon would want. It's not easy, after everything that happened, that you helped to cause.*"

"*I'm sorry.*" I had to say it. She didn't reply.

"We're ready," Sarah said to Max. "Obi, let's go."

He had retrieved his gun and was standing by the ladder. "I'm waiting on you, kiddo," he said.

We followed him out of the airplane and down to where Ulnyx was waiting.

"The other meat," he said with a laugh. "I'm impressed to see you're still alive."

"These are silver bullets, man," Obi replied, tapping the gun at his hip. The Were just kept laughing.

"Ulnyx, we're ready," Sarah said.

"She's in there?"

"Yes."

He stared into our eyes. "I owe you one for saving my ass." He waved towards the back of the hanger. "The car's out back. Well, it's more like a truck. We don't want to be too suspicious."

We followed him out the back door. When he had said truck, he had meant truck. An eighteen wheeler was parked there, a black big-rig with Japanese lettering running along the side, hooked up to a trailer painted with cartoon characters.

"You get the VIP seat in the back," Ulnyx said, pointing to the rear of the trailer. "Meat and I will be in the cab."

"Seriously, man," Obi said. "Stop calling me that."

I could still hear him laughing as we climbed into the empty trailer and pulled down the door.

"*Just you and me,*" I said. "*It would help if I could try your body on, to get used to it before we get there.*"

The floor shifted below us as the truck roared to life. A moment later I could feel us start moving.

"*Okay. I'll give you a few minutes.*"

Give me? Before I could ask what she meant, I found myself in her skin. I stumbled forward, getting my bearings, and then straightened up. Sarah was young, and she had kept herself in good shape. She wasn't Elyse, but she was much closer to my size than Brother Shane had been. I crouched down and grabbed one of the daggers from her calf. In one quick motion, I hurled it forward, smiling when it stuck into the wall of the trailer. I'd been too long without a decent host, and I'd missed it.

"*That's enough,*" Sarah said. I was kicked out without warning. It left me disoriented and angry.

"*What the hell?*" I was the spirit. I was supposed to be in control.

"*Not here,*" Sarah said, leaving me to wonder if she could sense my thoughts. "*I decide when you get to come out and play.*"

It was possible to join with her, but not without complications. At least I hadn't tried to take her back at the beach house.

"Your soul is a mess," I said. Just thinking about what I had experienced made me feel cold.

"Tell me about it."

The truck started vibrating and shifting as we got away from the airport and out onto the highway. Sarah and I sat in silence, and in time I began to count the rivets that held the trailer together.

"Rebecca?" Sarah whispered my name out loud, as if she was trying to say it without spitting, or cursing.

"Yes?"

"Max told me what happened to you. He told me that you've changed. Is it true?"

I remembered the look in Obi's eyes at the train station. I remembered his words. *"I'm not sure. I'm trying to."*

"Do you feel God?"

The question took me by surprise. *"I believe in His redemption. I believe in His forgiveness."*

"You don't believe you deserve it."

It was a one, two punch.

"I don't know how to win without creating chaos around me." I don't know why I was telling her that. Maybe it was the strangeness of my bond to her, the incompleteness. *"On the beach, you said to just do my best. I am, but it's not good enough. Maybe they're right? Maybe I am what I am, and that's all I can ever be."*

She'd opened the floodgates, and every doubt I'd had too much time to think about while I was floating back to shore was surfacing.

"Or maybe you need to stop listening to the chatter, and pay attention to your most honest self."

"I have. I want to go to Heaven, and I'm willing to do whatever I have to in order to get there. I want to help Landon, but I also want to help myself. It doesn't sound very selfless, does it?"

Sarah laughed out loud. "No, but then I don't know of a single being that isn't motivated at all by what they want for themselves."

"*What about you?*"

"What about me?"

"*What do you want?*"

"To live up to the memory of my mother, most of all. She was a strong person, and a stronger angel. She didn't sacrifice her beliefs for anything. You've seen my soul, Rebecca. I don't know if I can fight the turmoil inside forever, but I hope if the time comes that I can't, I'll have the grace to do the right thing before I hurt anyone."

There were a few minutes of silence while I thought about what she had said.

"*Landon was pretty selfless, to throw himself into the middle of the Divine for the sake of everyone else,*" I said at last.

"I think if you ask him, he won't tell you it was selfless."

"*I hope I get to ask him.*"

"Me too."

CHAPTER THIRTY

Rebecca

WE SPOTTED THE FIRST NICHT Creidim laying prone on top of a warehouse two blocks from their main facility. Ulnyx had pounced on him from behind, removed his head, and then thrown the sniper rifle he'd been toting down to Sarah and me. We'd left the truck a few blocks back, and hadn't intended for the him or Obi to leave the vehicle behind, but he'd smelled the cleaning agents they used on their guns at a distance and decided we would need backup until we got a little closer.

I was grateful for the Were's sense of smell when Obi took out a second sniper inside the opposite building.

I knew from Elyse that the sentries wore remotely tracked heart monitors. They knew the moment their people died, and in this case their response was to start blaring an exorcism through hidden loudspeakers.

"We need to shut that up," I said, expecting to start being peeled away, and tightening my grip on Sarah's soul.

"I'm in control, remember? I don't want you to go." It felt as though her soul reached out and took hold of me, steadying my force inside of her. The loudspeakers continued, but I remained planted.

"That crap is hurting my ears," Ulnyx said, leaping down from the building and landing at our side. He had his hands pressed against his head.

"Why don't you go shut it up?" Sarah asked.

"It doesn't look like I'll have a chance." He pointed forward with a massive claw. We looked just in time to see a black clothed figure disappear behind a building. "They're pretty well-armed. We'll clear a path for you." He raised his nose to the air, and looked to the building where we'd last seen Obi. "Hey, meat," he shouted. "You see that?"

The response was a loud boom from the high-powered rifle.

"I smell blood," the Were said.

"*Sarah, warn him about Wolfsbane.*" Joe had taken the pack, which meant he'd recovered the knife.

"Ulnyx, be careful. Rebecca says they have something called Wolfsbane."

He growled at that, but launched forward. Another rifle shot sounded out past the din of the exorcism.

"You're up Rebecca," Sarah said. "I'm a sitting duck out here."

I was in control of her faculties a moment later.

"*Don't get me shot.*"

"I'll do my best." I ducked in a shady corner of a warehouse and kept my ears open. The noise levels rose with an explosion of gunfire, howling, and screaming. I took that as my queue to start moving forward.

I ran a block and peered around the corner. A black-clothed body lay on the ground, a pool of blood around him, running from a single gunshot wound to the head. I thanked Obi silently and raced across the expanse without drawing any fire. The next block was just as clear, and I kept moving until I was right on top of the continuing sounds of battle.

I found Ulnyx pinned down behind a cement truck, his body running with blood from a dozen wounds. Six Nicht Creidim kept up concerted fire from the corner of a warehouse. Of course the

Were could smell us, and he looked over and waved us on. We snuck across the space without drawing attention.

"*We should help him,*" Sarah said.

"*Not our mission,*" I replied. "*He volunteered for this.*"

Our target was only a block away. The roll-up door was down, and I was sure they were just waiting for someone to come and try to open it. Had they identified Sarah already? Did they know I was with her? The Eye didn't work through cameras.

We reached our last hiding spot, and I stared at the door. "*That's the only way in,*" I said. "*You can bet Joe's got an ambush all set for us.*"

"*We don't have a choice,*" Sarah said. "*You're supposed to be good.*"

I took the daggers from her leg. "What if they shoot you before the door opens?"

A bullet answered my question, a loud blast that couldn't have come from more than a dozen feet away and up. A body fell from a far window.

I ran as fast as I could. To the normal observer, the door didn't look like it could be opened from the outside. Elyse had known how to get in, and I had retained that information. I just had to hope Joe didn't know spirits could take memories from their hosts.

I crouched at the door, slamming my fist on the ground at its base. A small, seamless panel opened up, revealing a keypad underneath. I was about to type in the code when I had a better idea.

"Let me go. I'll clear the inside. The code is 947468," I said. "Remember it. 947468. Wait twenty seconds and then put it in."

Her response was to throw me from her at a speed that surprised me. I flowed through the heavily runed steel and concrete, and into the room. There were four Nicht Creidim there, with golden Eyes tattooed to their foreheads. They all looked towards me, able to see whatever it was I actually looked like. One of them started chanting.

A stupid idea, I realized too late. I should have guessed they would be more prepared for me, but I had hoped they would have thought the loudspeakers had done the trick. Joe wasn't taking any chances.

Then the door started rolling up, which took all of us by surprise. The exorcist kept going for another couple of seconds, until a hand appeared under the rising door, a dark hand holding a cannon. The bullet tore into his stomach and shut him up forever.

Sarah came in next, rolling under the small space. I urged myself toward her while she threw herself at one of the defenders, her knife work decent but not good enough to keep herself alive for very long. She didn't need a knife though, she just needed to keep them off-balance.

"Stop," she Commanded. Two of them froze immediately. The other squinted his eyes, fought off the power, and charged.

I grabbed onto her soul. It hurt again, but not as much as the first time. I could feel the power of it, the energy churning and twisting and reveling in the control. It was less painful, but it was more frightening. Using the power to Command was accepting the demonic side of her, the chaos and the evil that threatened to unravel her.

I didn't need to ask for the wheel. Her eyes became my eyes, and I brought a dagger up just in time to push back against an incoming attack, their weapon skidding off my own. He backed away and pulled a gun instead, but Obi had gained enough clearance to get in. His shot came first and left us with no one to fight.

"It's not safe for you here," I said to him.

"You're welcome," he replied. "You're lucky I guessed what you were going to try to do. Jumping from that window wasn't fun."

"What do you see?" I asked, looking around. I knew we were in a warehouse. I could see it through the haze of energy that was left by the Deceiver.

"A warehouse," he said. "Nothing out of the ordinary."

He'd changed something, I could see that much. I figured out what just in time.

I threw myself at Obi, catching him in the chest and throwing him out of the building just in time to save his life. There were shooters clinging to the scaffolding, hiding behind boxes and taking aim. Joe had disguised them, made them invisible, which meant I was the only one who could see them.

I was laying on top of him, looking down at his surprised and angry face. "Snipers. Joe's hiding them. Thank you for your help, but you can't help me anymore. You need to stay out here." I put my hand on the Eagle. "I need to borrow this."

I pulled it from his grasp, rolled off and charged back in. I kept moving at a random pace and in alternating directions towards the elevator I knew was there. Bullets ricocheted off the stone floor and scaffolding around me, one coming close enough that I felt it burn through a wisp of Sarah's short hair. I returned fire, conserving bullets and taking shots only when I could see them hanging out of the corners. With this much movement my aim was crap, but it was enough to keep them on their toes.

We reached the elevator. I hit the button and then dove back under the cover of a few crates. The gunfire stopped, but I could hear clanging as they moved around, trying to shift into a better position to kill me before I could get into the underground. I had no doubt that it would be just as hairy down there, but at least there wasn't enough space for long-range combat.

The elevator reached the top and the doors slid open. It was empty. I took a deep breath. "*If anything happens, I'm sorry,*" I said to Sarah. I couldn't be sure the snipers wouldn't hit us. There was only one place to go.

I started running, and then dove and twisted, landing hard on my ass and sliding the last few feet into the elevator while shooting randomly into the warehouse. I heard the shots echo through the open expanse, and I waited to feel the burning sting of a bullet ending Sarah's life. Pings sounded around me, four of them, and then the doors slid closed. Three more pings told me they had kept shooting, but even the elevator was fortified.

"*We made it*," Sarah said.

"*So far so good. Your turn. If there's anyone waiting at the elevator, you need to stop them.*"

I went from actor to observer. The energy swirling around Sarah's soul was exhilarating and terrifying. She was letting go of the facade of control she worked so hard to maintain. She was walking into potential death, and her will was responding to prevent it.

The Nicht Creidim stronghold was deep underground, so the ride was long. It felt a million times longer. By the time we stopped descending, Sarah was burning with cold fire. I was a moth held tight against it, unable to flee and mesmerized by its beauty.

We crouched in the forward corner of the elevator while the door slid open. I could sense the power of the Deceiver, and see into the illusion. A single large room, with no other way in or out. Two Nicht Creidim held their weapons ready to fire as soon as we appeared.

"Kill him," Sarah said, the energy of her soul discharging like a solar flare. She hadn't targeted either of them, so they both followed the Command. Two gunshots, two thuds.

Sarah smiled.

"Where do we go?" she asked.

"You can't see it. Let me drive."

"Tell me where." Her voice was empty, emotionless.

"Sarah. Let me in. Landon needs us."

It broke her out of it. I was back in control. I scooped up one of the guns on my way down the hallway. I knew there was a lab down here, and I tried to remember how to get there.

I made a left, and then a right, and then ran down a long hallway.

In time I realized that I knew where I was heading. The lab was near where they stored the artifacts. I had to pass Elyse's room to get there.

Was she still alive? I was fairly sure Joe wouldn't have killed her, despite what he had done to her sister. She was his favorite, his pride and joy, and in a twist of irony he had too much respect for her stubbornly strong will to put her down with such disregard.

I stopped at her door and considered opening it. I don't know why I was so concerned about her. I was wasting time checking and putting Sarah at greater risk. It was stupid, and foolish.

I did it anyway.

Her room was just as it had been the first time I'd visited. It was peaceful, serene, with soft music trickling from the walls. It was such a stark contrast to the chaos I had come through that it made me shiver. She was there in yoga pants and a sports bra, whirling and kicking and grunting, sweat running from her pores. When she saw me, she stopped and stared.

He hadn't killed her, but he had disfigured her. The Eye had been removed, cut away so that all that remained was a mess of scar tissue, a red splotch of mangled flesh that screamed out for attention and stole so much from the beauty of her heritage.

"Sarah?" She was breathing hard, and I saw her eyes flick over to where a wooden sword rested on her mat.

I didn't waste time on pleasantries. "Rebecca," I said. "Are you still in?"

She licked her lips, and smiled. "Did you kill Joe yet?"

I shook my head.

"Good. I owe that son of a bitch."

She walked over to the edge of the mat and lifted it up, pulling the black stone from under it.

"I hid this from him, after he captured me. First in my mouth and then... in other places. He beat me more than once asking what had happened to it." Her devious look almost made me blush. The stone was replaced with the obsidian spatha. "Let's go."

We went back into the hallway. It was still clear. We moved at a brisk walk while listening for incoming enemies.

"I didn't think you could bond with Sarah," she said.

"It's complicated," I replied.

We kept moving, but there was nothing. No resistance. Had Joe not expected that anyone would get this far? After all, I was supposed to be exorcised, and who else could have gotten past the warehouse and the elevator?

We were nearing the armory when we heard the first boot steps. They were running, coming on fast and in large numbers. There were too many to fight in the open like this.

"Here," Elyse said. She grabbed Sarah's hand and pushed on a panel on the wall, opening the door to another apartment. "This used to be Rae's."

She swung me inside and closed the door, jamming the end of the blade into the seam so it wouldn't seal completely. We both put our faces to the crack and watched two dozen of them run by.

"We'll wait a minute, and then take them by surprise. Joe sent his youngest... how many have you killed?"

"Personally? None, but I didn't come alone. A dozen, give or take."

She looked shocked and confused. "I don't understand that. He wouldn't have sent those children after you unless he had no other choice. He'd know they'd be running into their death."

We waited and listened. At first, it was quiet, and then the soldiers returned. Each of them was armed with a blessed sword. Ulnyx? Or had Max decided to get involved? Whichever it was, they passed us by and headed back the way they'd come.

"We need to hurry," Elyse said, opening the door again. We ran hard down the corridor, past the armory and down another long hall. We nearly fell over when the entire complex shook.

"What the hell is going on?" I asked.

"The lab is just around the corner. Let's get the Box and get out of here."

We reached another steel door, painted in runes. Elyse put her hand to the biometric lock. The door started to open.

"Just like Joe to be so arrogant," she said.

The walls shook again, and I could swear I heard screaming from somewhere inside the compound.

We ducked under the door before it finished opening, and moved into the lab. It was a large room, filled with standing tables, desks, computers, and a lot of large off-white devices whose purposes I couldn't fathom. To each side was a column of thick glass where even more equipment had been assembled to run different tests. In the center of the room on the right, seemingly floating in mid-air, was Avriel's Box.

"There you are," I said.

"Here I am." Joe stepped out from the room on the left, Deceiver in one hand and Truth in the other. He looked haggard and worn. "I underestimated you. I didn't think you'd come up with a combo that could get past my defenses."

"I'm resourceful like that," I said.

"If you mean the way cockroaches are resourceful, then I guess you're right." He waved Truth towards the Box. "I suppose you came for that?"

"And the swords. Where is the Damned?"

"That one isn't very useful to me. I put it in the stone, where the Redeemer used to be." He shrugged his shoulders. "I figured the swords had something to do with the Box, seeing as how you were collecting them. I had my best people on it. They couldn't work it out, so I sent a team out to capture that Hell reject, Alichino. They haven't gotten back yet, but it doesn't matter now."

The room shook again, as if to emphasize his defeated point.

"What's happening?" I asked.

He took the blades and turned them in his hands, offering me the hilts. "Take the swords. Take the Box. It won't save you. It won't save any of us. We've survived by being smart, by staying out of the spotlight. I thought I could kill all of the Divine with that thing. I thought I could save humanity from you. I thought I was being smart, but I wasn't."

"What are you talking about?" I was getting angry.

Joe's laugh was weak. "I drew too much attention." The building shook again. "I knew you were going to come, Rebecca. I knew I could handle you. We tried touching the Deceiver to the Box this morning. We were afraid to before, but we were getting desperate. The power..." The door to the lab had closed behind us, but now it began to groan. "The power is unbelievable. Just from one of the blades. With all six..." His eyes narrowed. "I don't know what you're going to do with all six, but whoever gets them and puts them to the Box will have the power to change the entire universe. I believe that."

I was starting to feel warm. I turned my head to the door, and saw that the center was beginning to glow with heat. What the hell was happening?

"It has to be better in your hands than in his," Joe said. "I'm an old man. I can't win this fight. Take the swords."

Elyse pocketed the obsidian blade, reached out, and took them. Joe smiled.

"You're the pride of the family," he said. "I love you."

He knew what she was going to do. He didn't even flinch when she stabbed him.

"I love you too, father," she said.

The door behind us was getting too hot for comfort. I grabbed Elyse's elbow and pulled her away, towards the back of the room.

Whatever was melting the steel was powerful enough to convince Joe to surrender.

Whatever was melting the steel was ignoring the runes.

Whatever was melting the steel wanted the Box, and we were

the only thing standing in its way.

We were pressed against the rear of the room. The center of the door had liquified, and now ran away in a fit of smoke that obscured our view.

"*Time for you to leave,*" Sarah said. I was thrown from her body and into Elyse's. She didn't resist me. She knew I was a better fighter.

The smoke started to dissipate. A figure stepped through. It all began to make sense.

Izak.

CHAPTER THIRTY-ONE

Landon

"THE LAST TIME WE SPOKE?" I raised my eyebrows. The last time we had spoken had been only hours before I'd gone into the Box. How could this shade of the demon know about that?

"On the top of the mountain, at the temple," he said. "Ah, I see you're surprised. The universe is filled with things you don't understand. I have lived for over a thousand years, and even I am still in awe of it at times."

"So, you know what's happening outside of this place?" I asked, turning my head and glancing back at Avriel.

He laughed. "Not in so much detail. The senses are clouded. I hold the memories of thought and word. I remember our battle." He closed his eyes and took a deep breath. "It has been so long since I've felt a touch, even one made in violence. I was mortal once, did you know that?"

I nodded. "Avriel told me that you two speak sometimes."

"Yes. I despise that seraph with every spark of fire that burns in my heart and soul, and yet even in that hate I find myself overwhelmed with loneliness. For all the power given to me by Lucifer, his trap is that he damned me to a hell all the same."

I could't imagine being him. For as difficult and painful as the mantle of diuscrucis had been, at least I could love and be loved.

At least not everything I drew near was destined to die.

"You asked me where I saw myself in ten thousand years," I said. "You asked me why I was working so hard to save mankind." I hadn't given it much thought. I had been too busy acting on instinct, following my gut and my heart into the rabbit hole. "I can't help but think about the people I've known. The sacrifices they've made. Josette spent seven hundred years fighting for the goodness of God's creations. You've spent over a thousand years fighting to tear them down."

"And for what, child?" Abaddon asked. "What have I achieved? What did she achieve?"

"Nothing." It had to be that way. It was my job to make it so. That wasn't the point. I looked up at the Statue behind him. "That never stopped her. It never would have stopped you."

"It is what I was made to do. Yet, I have become tired of it."

"Have you?" I asked. "If you remember then tell me, why did you run?"

He recoiled as though I had used the revolver on him.

"What?"

"Why did you run? I had the Deliverer to your neck. It could have been over for you, but you took off."

His face darkened. I realized I needed to be more careful. I wanted him to help me, and pissing him off wasn't the way to do it. He turned his back to me, and fell to his knees once more.

"Where do we go when we die, diuscrucis?" he said. "Heaven, Hell, Purgatory. These are places, destinations. A continuation of the path we travel from the moment our soul catches its first spark of life. You and I have made that journey, but tell me, child, what comes after?"

I took a few steps towards him. He didn't react. "I don't know," I said.

His laughter was deep and full of sorrow. "You don't know... Neither do I. For one as old as I am, the idea of the unknown is more frightening than the idea of being trapped." He raised his hand to his lips, kissed it, and waved it out towards the Statue. Then he rose and faced me again. "You should appreciate the sentiment. It is a balance... between my hatred of being, and my fear of not being. The Beast promises to end all of that. Here, and out there. All I need to do is help to set him free. You weren't supposed to follow me." He looked back at Clara. She was still standing with Avriel, her hands on her hips and her expression impatient.

"I won't let you touch her," I said.

"Do you really think you can stop me? You aren't even armed."

"I have the Beast's power. I don't need a weapon." It was a bit of a bluff. I had no idea how to fight him with it.

"You don't know how to use it against me. Oh, you've done well so far, but this is a large step to take."

His essence began to ooze out around him, a semi-solid mess of darkness that formed an intricate pattern at his back.

"Wait. I don't want to fight you. That isn't why I came."

He seemed surprised. "No? Then why bring the seraph?"

"I know you can hide yourself from Ross. I know you can hide others."

He laughed again, a deep booming sound of wisdom and years. "What can you offer me, diuscrucis?"

I swallowed the growing lump in my throat. I had nothing to bargain with.

"Well?" His power continued to spread, moving out to the sides to slowly encircle me, but leaving me a clear path and a clear head.

"An end," I said, the idea coming to me in desperation. "A true end. You can't trust Ross to do as he says. You can't trust him not to enslave you when this is over. You've said I have your respect - I ask you to trust in my word. If you help me against him, I'll put an end to your existence. I'll find a way."

My heart pounded while he considered. Every second of silence only made me feel more vulnerable. Finally, he nodded.

"Here is our deal, diuscrucis. I will guide you to the Beast, but you must walk my path, and it is on you and yours to survive. It is not an easy path, and I will not help you. If you aren't strong enough to walk it you will never be strong enough to defeat him, or end me. When you defeat him you will have the power to end me here, and I know you will do it. How you will keep your promise out there... not with a blade, for I will not go willingly despite my desire. Do you understand?"

I'd made so many promises I wasn't sure I could keep. What was one more? "I understand."

"Promise in blood."

He took three steps towards me, a dagger appearing in his hand. He cut his palm and offered me the blade.

I took it from him, the coldness of it seeping deep into me. I made a quick stroke, and he clasped his hand in mine.

"It has been too long," he said, holding my hand tight while our blood mixed. I felt the immensity of the bargain clamp down on me. It filled me with a cold dread at what I might one day be forced to do.

I had to pull my hand away. For all of the demon's strength and power, he was so alone that he didn't want to let go.

"It is done," Abaddon said. "Gather your child and her keeper, and we will go."

I walked away from him, back to where Clara and Avriel were waiting.

"Well?" she asked. "I saw you shake his hand, that has to be a good thing?" She looked older again; almost the age I had been when age had stopped having meaning.

"I don't know if it's a good thing, but he'll take us. He said we have to walk his path, and it won't be easy." I looked at Avriel. "Do you know what that means?"

"No."

"He also said he remembers everything that happened to him once he was out," I said, staring into the angel's eyes. "Why didn't you tell me?"

Avriel stared back at me, his lips moving in silence before his mind caught up to them. "What is there to say? I know what you did to me out there. I also know I forgave you. Is this a guilt that you desire to carry with you for the rest of your existence?"

"But... the Beast?" He had destroyed the angel as completely as anything could be destroyed.

"I am a shadow of the seraph known as Avriel. I felt the loss as sharply as anything can be felt here. When you have control of this place, you can finish what he started and let me be at peace forever."

"Do you think that after this, there is peace?" It was in stark contrast to what Abaddon must believe to be so afraid of it.

He nodded. "I believe it. What comes next is as much a matter of faith as what comes before."

"I'm sorry," I said.

"It is over. I was left here to protect your child and to help you defeat the Beast. That is my purpose now. It is all that I desire. If you want to feel the forgiveness that you will not claim otherwise, let me do as I have been willed."

I bit my lower lip and nodded. "Abaddon is waiting for us."

Avriel's eyes narrowed when he looked out to where he stood wrapped in darkness. "Don't forget he is a demon. He can't be trusted."

"I'm counting on you to keep a close eye on him," I said. "You know him better than anyone."

A sword materialized in the angel's hand. "As you say."

The three of us walked over to where he was standing. We were halfway to him when Clara put her hand in mine and squeezed it. "It'll be okay, dad. There's nothing this one can do that we can't handle."

She was comforting me? It worked. I squeezed her hand back. "You better believe it."

His expression was flat, though I could see the spark of fire in his eyes when they passed over Avriel. "A truce for now, seraph," he whispered.

Avriel nodded his agreement.

Abaddon took a step closer to me. "The path I take is beyond the reach of the Beast's power. Understand that you will have only what you carry in, and nothing more." His eyes shifted to Clara. "I know you wouldn't want to harm your child."

I took a deep breath, focusing and pulling in power from the air around us. If Clara was a battery, that meant I could use the power she was holding if I needed to, but it would come at a cost. We wouldn't have the luxury of waiting for her to recharge once we were in Ross' presence.

I felt the energy rush in and fill my soul, creating a throbbing pressure at the base of my spine. Unarmed, with no idea what we were walking into and only a gut full of power to fight it... I wasn't certain this wouldn't be the true test of strength.

"I'm ready," I said, looking over at Clara. She squeezed my hand again, and I returned the gesture.

"Then follow," Abaddon replied. He turned, swinging his dark essence behind him like a cloak and letting it wash over us for just an instant. It was an intentional move, a warning. He was powerful enough out here. Where we were going, he was the ultimate force.

"Can you fight him inside, if you need to?" I asked Avriel in a whisper.

"I will do my best, but I expect that I will lose. All I can do is buy you time to flee."

They weren't the words of encouragement I was looking for, but they would have to do.

We walked behind him, through the doors into the pedestal, and then up the stairs and around back. When Abaddon pushed open the door to the janitor's closet, I lost my breath.

I should have guessed that his secret path would be hidden here. I fought against the memories and emotions as he swung open the hidden door and climbed down ahead of us. Was Ross the one making things this way? Was he using what he was learning against me, to try to put me on shaky ground? I remembered that he couldn't know where we were now that we were under Abaddon's wing.

We reached the base of the ladder and Abaddon led us forward. The hallway here was unlike the one under the real Statue. It was pitch black save for a few dim sconces of purple hued flame that lined the walls, tracing the route forward into a doorway of nothingness.

"Remember, child," Abaddon said, turning back to look at me. "I will not help you once we pass through. I am only a guide, and an observer."

"Yeah, I got it," I replied, trying to calm the beating of my heart. I felt Clara take my hand again.

"Let's make them regret ever messing with us."

I couldn't help but smile. I was really starting to feel a bond with her.

Together, we stepped into the void.

CHAPTER THIRTY-TWO

Rebecca

"REBECCA, GET THE BOX," SARAH said. "Now!"

I was frozen in shock while the demon walked towards us. His eyes were washed in hellfire, his body glowing along the scarred runes dug into his skin. He'd trimmed his beard and slicked back his white hair. Even more surprising, his damaged hand was whole.

"Izak, no!" Sarah moved to intercept him.

I broke out of my trance and headed towards the airlock that separated us from the Box. A line of hellfire rose up in my path.

"Izak!"

Sarah stood right in front of him, looking up at him with tears in her eyes. He met her gaze, and his face twisted in pain.

The Deceiver. I gripped the hilt tight, feeling the warmth of the power through my hand. It was a simple illusion, but I hoped it would be enough. I ran for the door again.

I could feel the heat from the other side of the room. I'd flipped his perception of it, and he had attacked the wrong place. I fell into the clean room, stumbling towards the Box.

"Izak, don't let him control you. Izak!" Sarah pounded her fists against his chest, but he didn't react to her at all. He clenched his new hand and closed his eyes. When he opened them, he looked right at me.

I don't know how he defeated the power of the Deceiver, and I didn't have time to care. I rolled away from the blast of hellfire that flowed from his other hand, passing easily through the glass and striking the air above me. I felt it hot against Elyse's scarred head, and I scrambled on my elbows towards the Box. Even if I reached it, I had no idea how I would get past the fiend.

"Izak!" Sarah backed away from him. "Stop, now!"

I felt the wave of power. I went to my knees and looked through the melted glass. Izak stood there, looking at Sarah.

"You can fight," she said. "Don't let him own you."

I stood and approached the Box, feeling a sense of relief at its proximity. I put down Truth and took it in my hand, and then jammed it under the tight waistband of the yoga pants. It was uncomfortable against the skin, sending waves of heat and cold through Elyse's body.

Sarah was stroking Izak's face, her small hand gentle on his rough skin. He was branded, a puppet to Gervais. That meant the archfiend had to be nearby.

Without warning, his hand came up, and smacked Sarah's away. His mouth curled into a snarl and his muscles rippled in confusion. He shoved her back, throwing her across the room.

I didn't have time to think. I leaped towards him, through the open space the hellfire had made, bringing the swords to bear and coming down on him with a fierce double-strike.

He took two steps back and raised his hands, summoning a sword of hellfire and using it to deflect Truth. He caught the Deceiver on the forearm, the runes flaring and deflecting the demonic blade.

His return blows were blurs, and it was all I could do to get Truth up in time to block the sword and protect me from the heat of the fire. I caught it edge on edge and twisted, turning beneath the momentum and stepping back beside him. He smiled and drove forward, flaring the hellfire and leaving me on the defensive.

The lab wasn't a wide open space to fight in. I ducked and dodged around tables and computers, staying close enough that he had to use his sword but far enough back that he couldn't hit me. It was clear within a few seconds that he was a superior fighter, and it would take pure luck to get out of here with the Box.

Then I tripped on a wire. It caught my foot and sent me stumbling backwards. I dropped Deceiver to put my hand against a wall and keep my balance, and got Truth up only inches from my face. It protected me from the heat of the hellfire, and the demon and I grappled together. He was taller than me, but my face was close enough to his to see his expression clearly. He didn't want to fight, but he had to.

Which made him as much of an enemy as anyone else. More than anyone else. He had put enough fear into Joe that he'd given up without a fight. Looking into his sorrowful eyes, I knew he was the biggest thing standing between Landon's freedom and his complete slavery. If Gervais got his hands on the Box and the archfiend knew what to do with it…

My anger flared, and I shoved against him with as much force as Elyse's small frame could muster. It was enough to slip the lock. I leaped sideways and rolled across a desk, feeling the heat of his blade behind me and hearing the spark and sizzle as it tore through the furniture. I hit the ground already moving laterally, digging into the sports bra and finding the black stone. We were so close, Izak and me. I pressed my palm tight against the stone to summon the black blade in the same motion I threw the rock at him.

He didn't see it as a threat. He didn't even try to block it. It changed in midair, replaced with the long stick of alloy that could kill both demon and angel alike. It went right past his defenses, hissing and sparking when it struck the skin and buried itself deep inside. The runes of power covering his arms flickered and faded. He stopped moving and looked down at the protruding expanse.

Then he looked at me.

I'd expected to see anger, and relief. I hadn't thought his sad expression could get any sadder.

The sword hissed in his chest and the smell of frankincense was overwhelming. He should have fallen. He should have died.

He didn't.

He reached up with his new hand and took hold of the hilt. He was slow and deliberate while he pulled it out of his chest, his eyes locked to mine. If I hadn't been so surprised, I might have been smart enough to run while I could. Then again, I doubt I would have gotten far.

He held the blade up. I watched his wound vanish beneath the stench of dead flesh. It was only then that I realized what was happening, and what Izak had truly become. His hand was whole again, but it wasn't *his* hand. I couldn't be sure, but it wouldn't have surprised me if it had once belonged to Gervais. That was how he was controlling him. That was how he had healed.

My revelation was short-lived. The spatha whistled through the air towards my head. I backed up just in time, feeling the coldness of it nick Elyse's cheek and send a line of blood into the air. I got Truth up to block the second thrust, and felt the flare of tattoos trying to fight off hellfire that got too close. It would have incinerated my arm, but instead it only burned.

The dance started again, only I had been losing before, and now I was down to a single blade. I ducked and twisted, thrusted and parried, turned and leaped and kicked. I used everything I knew, and every muscle Elyse had worked to perfection.

In the end, it wasn't enough.

In the end, there was only one thing left for me to do. There was only one thing I could do. It was the path of least resistance, and it made me question everything Sarah had said and everything I wished I could be.

In the end, I had to be the demon, and think only of the win. It didn't matter if the cause was good, or even if Elyse would have understood and done the same thing. In my heart I knew it was wrong and I did it anyway. It had worked the first time after all, but I could have saved her the first time.

I knocked aside the hellfire sword and leaned forward, into the path of the second blade. I prepared to be run through, ready to use the moment that Izak dropped his guard to remove his hand.

I hadn't expected Sarah to screw it up.

The Deceiver knocked against the spatha, pushing it out of the path of my body. She put her weight against Izak, shoving him to the side and succeeding in bringing him off his feet. He crashed into a table and onto the ground, his hand raised and shooting more of the flames towards her. The Deceiver protected her from the heat, and she rushed him and brought it down at his chest.

He knocked it away with one hand while bringing the spatha up with the other, stabbing Sarah in the gut and catching her in his arms as she fell. For just an instant his eyes changed, and he let out a weak wail of torment that would plant its memory forever in my soul. His hand fell away from his body, and he burst into tears.

There was no time to waste. I was on him in two steps. I found the Deceiver laying next to them and I scooped it up and brought it down, severing his arm at the elbow. He grunted in pain and looked down at the wound. The hand landed on the ground and began to scream.

"Izak, we need to get her to the armory. Let's go." The Nicht Creidim had one of the amulets. If she were still alive, it might save her.

He didn't hesitate. He got to his feet, still holding her in his good arm and ignoring the damage to the other. The sword was still buried in her stomach and blood was running down her legs, but her eyes were open and holding a measure of life.

He paused on the way out, putting his foot to the hand and igniting it in hellfire. The screams continued until it had finished burning away.

I picked up Truth and we raced out of the lab, down the hallway to the armory. The walls around us were singed and burned, the remains of Izak's inception. I put Elyse's hand to the lock and cursed at the slowness of the door mechanism. Once inside, I found the small shelf where the amulet had been kept and prayed to God that it was there.

It was. I cracked the crystal open in my hand and pushed Sarah's head back so I could pour the blood into her mouth. If Elyse was right, her wound would heal. I could only hope Elyse had been right.

I pulled the spatha from her stomach while Izak rocked her in his arm, the tears flowing down his face. I pressed my hands against the wound, willing the warmth of the flow beneath them to decrease and subside. It didn't matter what I wanted, only how the power of the blood would act on her mortal self.

Her eyes opened more, and she took a deep gasping breath. The wound grew hot beneath my fingers, forcing me to let go. She gulped in more air, and then turned her head to the demon.

"Izak. Are you okay?"

Izak smiled and nodded his head, then lowered her down and kissed her on the cheek.

"Are you okay?" I asked.

"You saved my life," she said.

"I owed you one."

CHAPTER THIRTY-THREE

Rebecca

"IT LOOKS LIKE THE GANG'S all here," Obi said.

"Not the whole gang," Ulnyx replied, looking at the Box.

We had retrieved the Damned from the stone in the ruins of the Nicht Creidim stronghold, and taken it, Truth, the Deceiver, and the Box out of the area; which had been decimated by Izak's attack. The entire dock was on fire, the cement and steel scorched and melted, and on emerging from what was left of the warehouse I had made the assumption that Obi and the Were couldn't have survived.

They had proven me wrong.

According to them, Ulnyx had benefitted from Izak's first pass, when he had killed the soldiers who were pinning him down. Free to move, he'd followed behind the demon, and bounded past him to grab Obi before he was noticed. Izak had been focused on retrieving the Box, and had ignored the two of them. Or, more likely, he had bypassed them and spared their lives because they weren't standing between him and his orders.

They were waiting on the outskirts of the damage, hidden in a dark corner and keeping an eye out for either us or Izak. When we'd exited together, Obi had stolen the closest vehicle he could find and brought it into the war zone. We'd gone full-speed back to the airport, and now we were standing in the hanger outside the plane, waiting for the techs to finish refueling.

"I can only imagine how Gervais is going to react when Izak doesn't come back," Sarah said. She was holding tight to the fiend's good arm. As soon as we had gotten clear of the docks, he'd used his own hellfire to cauterize the wound and begun treating it as though he had never had the damaged arm to begin with.

"He's going to be rightfully angry," Max said, emerging from the plane with Brian trailing behind him. He was holding towels coated in a wet gel; an anti-burn ointment to treat the blistered skin my brush with Izak had left Elyse with.

"This is going to hurt," Brian said when he reached me. He took the towels and wrapped them around my forearm. "The towels were dipped in holy water. Max says it will help you heal faster."

The pain of the wound had been excruciating, but I had refused to show it. Now I smiled at the icy hot relief given by the wrap. The holy water couldn't mend mortal skin, but it would negate the nature of the wound.

"We need to collect the remaining blades and make our way to Paris," Max said. "As I had feared, Gervais was alerted to the swords' relevance to the Box when Joe put the two together. He sent Izak here for the mother load, but he'll have other servants searching for the Destroyer. Izak, do you know if he knew its whereabouts?"

Izak shrugged with his good arm, pointed at me, and then moved his fingers as though he were typing.

"No," I said. "If Joe had found it, he didn't tell Elyse." But why would he?

"You understood that?" Obi asked. He had warmed to me just a little, after Sarah had recounted what had happened. On one hand, I was grateful to have proven something to him. On the other, I knew what I had been about to do. If he had known, his opinion would surely have gone the other direction.

"Excellent." Max said. "I was hoping that would be the case. We can still come out on top, but we're going to have to get the timing right. I believe divide and conquer will be appropriate here."

"What do you mean?" I asked.

"We booked a flight plan for Paris," Brian said.

I was still confused. "I thought the Destroyer was in Shanghai?"

Max smiled and clapped is hands. "It is, my hot buttered rum. In the hands of a seraph named Lu, though he may not quite remember he has it." He pulled a folded piece of paper from a pocket, and tossed it to me. "His address is on the paper."

"Great, you gave me a piece of paper. Unless it can transport me a thousand miles west, how am I supposed to get there?"

Max put up his hand. "If you'll step outside with Brian and myself," he said, motioning towards the front of the hanger.

I followed behind him, with Brian at my side.

"You look amazing in that body," he whispered. "Much better than that salesman you showed up at my office in."

"Impure thoughts?" I asked. I tried not to smile, but failed.

"A few," he replied. "It's the tattoos."

Max opened the smaller door inset into the larger hanger doors, and then waved us through with a flourished bow. "Right this way, my friends, right this way." We shuffled past him and onto the tarmac. He closed the door behind him, and put up his hand again before I could say anything. "All will be revealed, cupcake. Give me just one moment."

He reached into his pocket, removing a small gold cross from it. I could see the Templar script etched into the back. Max closed his eyes and began to murmur. A moment later he changed, his body growing and transforming into his true reaper form.

"Max?" I had no idea what he was doing, but they had hidden the plane for a reason, and now he was making himself as obvious as any Divine could.

He turned his head back. "A moment, Rebecca. Please."

"Did he tell you what this was about?" I asked Brian.

He shook his head. "He just said he wanted me to be out here because it would help smooth things over. I don't know what that means."

I couldn't even begin to guess, but I didn't have to. Max stopped talking. A breeze began to blow along the runway. Something fell from the sky - a white streak of light that touched down right in front of him.

"You?" the newcomer asked, his gold-edged wings folding back behind him.

"Adam," Max said. "It's a pleasure."

The seraph glowered, and a blade appeared in his hand. He had brought the Deliverer. "If you were calling me for a fight, have at it."

Max chuckled. "Do you think I'd have gone to the trouble of summoning you just to box your ears? We need your help."

"We?" Adam glanced past Max, to where Brian and I were standing. His eyes stayed on his mortal counterpart. "What kind of angel are you?"

Brian's face flushed. He already looked unnerved by Adam's presence. "I... uh... I..."

"He's a changeling," I said. "A mortal angel."

The Deliverer vanished, and Adam strode over to him and put his hand onto his back. "How?"

"You don't know?" I asked.

He turned to me. "I've been busy trying to fix the damage the Beast did when he possessed one of the most populated cities on the planet." His attention returned to Max. "A Nicht Creidim, Max? You expect me to take you seriously?"

The reaper put his hand on Adam's shoulder. "Don't underestimate her. She's full of surprises." His eyes fell on mine for a short second. "I expect you to help us solve a problem. A mortal has turned into an angel. Think on that for a second or two, and maybe you'll make the correct connection."

"Mortals changing into demons," he said.

Max clapped his hands. "Bingo, old chap. Now, how many angels do you think have been created?"

He shrugged.

"I can count them on one hand." He pointed at Brian. "Do you want to guess how many demons?"

"They aren't all bad," Brian said, before Adam could answer. "Most of the ones I met are just as confused about this whole thing as I am."

"Yet, my boy," Max said. "Their genetics and their personalities mark them. But then, the seraph have been forbidden from dallying with mortals for how long? Oh yes, since God created them." He smirked at Adam. "By the way, Brian, your father wasn't your father, if you know what I mean."

Brian turned white.

"Get to the point," Adam said.

"I told you, we need your help. Landon put the Beast in the Box, but he didn't capture all of his energy. It's leaking out into the world at large, and the consequences are disastrous."

Adam was still while he considered. "We're stretched thin to breaking as it is."

"He isn't telling you everything," I said. "For one, people who aren't being turned into angels and demons are getting sick and dying. For another, Gervais is after the Box. You can imagine what he wants with it."

Adam's face paled. "I've heard stories about Gervais. I was hoping they weren't true." He held up the Deliverer. "They say this thing is about as useful as a toothpick against him."

"Maybe slightly more useful," Max said. "It is longer, after all. Anyway, we do have one ace up our sleeve. Izak is back in the fold."

"At least you have some good news." His eyes were hard, and his jaw clenched. "Tell me what you need. I knew our situation was fragile, but it seems everything I'm fighting for will be for nothing if I don't at least listen to you."

Max punched him playfully in the shoulder. "That's my boy! I have some more good news. We have the Box, and I have a plan to rid ourselves of the Beast once and for all. The first part is simple: I need you to take Rebecca here to Shanghai. Are you familiar with Master Lu?"

Adam shook his head.

"I'm not surprised. He's been here for quite a bit longer than you have. He owns a large estate outside of the city. It's more of a Buddhist monastery, really. Anywho, be careful. His followers are quite zealous."

"Zealous how?" I asked.

"Lu is a bit of a recluse, but I don't blame him considering what he has been charged to do. He won't see you, despite our feathered friend's credentials as the First Inquisitor. You'll have to... shall I say... make him? Defend yourselves if needed, and subdue your opponents, but don't kill them. He won't talk to you if you kill them."

"What is this Master Lu supposed to do for us?" Adam asked.

"The Destroyer," I replied. "The Sword of Gehenna."

His eyes widened. "You know where it is?"

"I know where all of them are," Max said. "Three of the six are in the hanger behind us. You have one, Gervais has one. Can you see where I'm going with this?"

"Why do you need them all?"

Max's smile was devious. "It's a long story, but why do you think they were all created, and then stolen away?"

Adam didn't respond. His eyes came back around to me. "I've never tried to carry a mortal," he said. "I don't know if she'll survive."

"We'll be fine," I said. I lifted my shirt just below the chest to show him some of the lines of tattoos covering Elyse's body. "She has protection, and I'm not mortal."

I could feel Brian's eyes on Elyse's firm abs, but Adam didn't even notice. His eyes traced the runes, deciphering them. "We?"

Max circled around and put his arm across my shoulders. "I said full of surprises, did I not? Adam, meet Rebecca Solen. She was stabbed in the heart with the Redeemer, and now-"

"You're a spirit," Adam finished. "I also know who you were... before." I expected him to be condemning, but instead he just looked sad. "It will take a large measure of penitence to earn your way to His grace."

I felt the same sadness in my soul, but I fought to hold it back. Regret wouldn't help me. "I know," I replied.

Max stepped forward, pulling me along until I was only a few inches in front of the angel. "Satisfied?" he asked.

"Yes," Adam replied.

A soft shove, and I was against his muscled chest. Strong arms wrapped around me, and I looked up at him. His expression was kind and nurturing. Of course he knew how the Redeemer worked, and what it had done. At least there was one person who could see me as I was today, despite my past betrayals.

"Meet up with us in Paris," Max said. "Try to be discreet when you arrive. We don't want to attract attention too soon."

"Hold on tight," Adam said. I put my arms around his torso, locking them just below his wings. They flared out behind him. "This will only take a minute."

"How do you know my father wasn't my father?" I heard Brian asking Max as we launched into the sky.

CHAPTER THIRTY-FOUR

Landon

THE BLACK DOORWAY STOOD IN the center of a vast sea of ruin. It was attached to a slagged metal frame, a remnant of a structure whose shell and girders hinted at its past magnificence. Destruction surrounded us. Massive buildings, taller than anything I had ever seen, twisted and bent and broken. Roads that stretched on to the horizon cracked and torn apart.

Bodies laying everywhere.

It was a scene right out of any number of dystopian sci-fi flicks. It was the end of the world brought to life.

"How far do we have to go?" I asked.

Abaddon was standing in front of us, looking out over the wasteland.

"Abaddon?"

He turned around and looked at me, raising his eyebrows. He smiled and pointed out the way forward. That was all the help he was going to give.

"Where are we?" Avriel asked. I could see his body shivering at the sight of all the dead. They were almost everywhere; men, women, and children. They lay crushed under chunks of metal, run through by glass, or simply ripped apart, their bodies in pieces amongst the stone and steel.

"It looks like Mumbai," I said. "Or what it would have looked like if we hadn't stopped Ross."

Except the landscape didn't match the Indian city. It was somewhere else, or more likely it was nowhere; a representation of a city, not an actual city. It was Abaddon's creation; his road, his rules. I stopped gawking and hurried to keep up with him.

We picked our way through broken stone and mangled streets. We passed hundreds of corpses. The smell of spilled blood hung heavy in the air, mingling with burned flesh and offal. It was disturbing to look at, and I could feel my stomach churning with increasing urgency for every step we took.

Still, it hardly seemed dangerous.

There was nothing alive here. No people, no animals. Not even a single blade of grass. It was cement, and mortar, and iron.

The demon continued in front of us, marching through it all with his power flowing out around him, the lord in his finery. His head moved back and forth over the wreckage, as though he expected something to move out there.

Nothing did.

"I don't get it," I said to Clara. She continued to keep a grip on my hand, while Avriel stayed right behind making consistent turns and twists, keeping a vigilant eye on our surroundings. "Abaddon made it sound like we'd be lucky to make it through here in one piece."

"I don't know," she replied. "I have no sense of anything here. It's like we're in the Box, but not in the Box."

We kept walking. I don't know how much time passed, but it felt like hours. Regardless of how far we had gone the landscape never changed. More buildings, more bodies, and after a while we all became numb to it. I stopped smelling the death, and soon enough stopped noticing it at all.

Then, I heard crying.

It was the first sign that there was anything out here besides us.

A soft, deep whimper that rose through the rubble and found its way to our ears. It was hard to pinpoint at first, and I motioned for Clara and Avriel to stop so their footsteps wouldn't cloud my hearing. Only Abaddon continued ahead, oblivious to my intent.

"Get him to stop," I said to the angel. The sobbing was louder now, somewhere off to the left, amidst what looked like a burned out department store.

Avriel's eyes landed on Abaddon. "I'll do my best, but I cannot make him do anything here."

His wings spread and he hopped forwards, a giant leap that brought him down before the demon. Abaddon tried to keep walking, but Avriel moved into his path. After a few repeated attempts to go around, he stopped and looked back at me. A smile creased the corner of his mouth.

"A trick?" Clara asked.

It made sense that it would be. We had no idea if the demon was playing it straight, or if this whole thing was a setup. He didn't need to go to such lengths. If he'd wanted to take me on, he could have done it the moment we'd entered this place. There was no reason for him to walk us for hours. It wasn't as though we would tire, starve, or die of thirst here. I could hear the crying, and I wanted, no, needed to find the source. I couldn't picture anyone or anything being left alone out here, even if they turned out to be a figment of my imagination or a random construct of Abaddon's will.

"This way," I said, following the sound off into the destruction with Clara trailing right behind me. I found the power I had conserved, making sure I could call on it if there was a need.

I picked my way over the frame of a door, reduced to nothing more than a hunk of slagged metal, and wound my way through some fallen stone. Chest high shelves were visible throughout the space, though most had been toppled, some had been trashed, and all were empty. A portion of the roof had collapsed near the back, and a beam of sunlight was angling in to land on the corpse of a woman. She looked peaceful there, wearing a long silver dress and bathed in light, wisps of long brown hair pushed over a long face.

What made me cautious was that I didn't see any wounds, or any blood. What had killed her?

I moved more slowly, crouching down so that I wouldn't be visible if there was anyone or anything else in here with us. Clara followed my lead, and together we wound our way through the aisles, the sound of sobbing growing louder as we moved further inside.

Then it stopped.

Of course it did. Whoever was there, they had heard us coming. I stopped moving, and listened.

Footsteps.

They were slow and careful, just like ours. One set, a single person walking perpendicular to our position. I stayed crouched and looked back at Clara. She raised her palms to the sky, suggesting we go up and over the obstacles. I nodded and gestured for her to wait.

I was careful in pulling on the power. I needed just enough to stay airborne for a few seconds, to find the target and come back down in front of them. I didn't want to waste energy I might need. I bent my legs slightly and focused, pushing off and bouncing towards the ceiling. I put my hand up to steady myself when I reached it, and scanned the space for the target.

A person, a man, it seemed. He was on his knees, leaning over the woman in the silver dress, his right arm out and touching her face. I pushed off from the ceiling and angled myself towards him, landing behind him with little more than a soft swish of air.

He turned his head.

I was looking at myself.

I stumbled backwards, confused. He stood up and watched me, hands at his sides and tears wetting his cheeks. I balanced myself, trying to swallow my surprise. He didn't just look like me. He was me. My eyes fell back to the dead woman on the floor. I didn't recognize her.

"Who are you?" he asked. "How did you survive?"

"I... I don't know what you're talking about?"

"The cataclysm. It isn't possible." He drew what looked like a cross over her forehead and stood up.

I glanced back, looking for Clara. She was still hiding amidst the shelves. "What happened here?"

His eyes narrowed. "Did the council send you?"

A gust of wind crossed between us, scattering some of the dust like ashes.

"Council? No. The demon, Abaddon, brought me here. I don't know where I am."

"Abaddon?" He was more confused. "I can tell you aren't lying, but how can that be? I have never heard of any Abaddon. Not on the council, not anywhere." He laughed. "And to bring you here? Here of all the places in the universe? I take it he is no friend of yours." He continued laughing, long after he stopped talking. There was something about the laugh, something very familiar.

"Where is here?" I asked again.

"It doesn't matter," he replied. "One world of many that are dying, thanks to the guile of Erastus and my own fool heart." He looked back at the woman. "Thirty thousand years. I should have known better. Love them, adore them, but never put them first."

I stared at the body, feeling my heart begin to race. Thirty thousand years? I looked at him again. I wasn't stupid, but I was still in the dark.

"What happened?"

He shook his head. "The whole story would take a lifetime. It is enough to say I made the wrong choice, and now the balance I have spent an eternity fighting to maintain has been broken. This world is burning because of my mistake, as are all of the inhabited worlds." The tears dropped from his eyes, falling to the ground at the feet of his love. "An eternity," he repeated. "For nothing."

Clara had told me that Ross was once like me, although I never expected that he would look like me. Somehow, Abaddon had arranged for me to see him at the moment of his failure. To what end? To make his point about the futility of fighting to keep the balance, and show me that no matter how many eons passed I was ultimately doomed to follow in Ross' footsteps? Maybe he wanted me to give up and let Ross loose, so his own end could come more swiftly than I could manage it. Maybe he simply delighted in watching my reaction. Or maybe...

"Clara," I shouted. "Clara."

She didn't respond to my calls.

I focused, gathering my power for another leap. Not for height, but to get out of this place and back to the demon. He had done a fine job distracting me, and I had fallen for his betrayal like a complete chump.

"Erus." A new voice, and then a new person appeared, materializing from nowhere halfway between Ross and me. I knew him in an instant.

"Malize?"

He didn't respond to me. His hand rose, and Ross was blasted back into the rubble. His face reddened, and he strained against invisible bonds.

"The council has found you guilty of treason," Malize said. "You're to be brought before them to face your punishment."

This wasn't right. Malize was an angel, a creation of God. I had to find Abaddon.

"I will not," Erus said. The wind gathered around us, throwing rubble everywhere. I focused, dropping to the ground and creating a vortex of my own, defending myself from the incoming storm. Malize pulled his cloak tight around himself, using it to deflect the stones. The action freed Erus from his tether. He saw me hunkered down below the onslaught, and the maelstrom paused. "Get out of here," he said. "Die a death that is more dignified than this."

A gust of wind caught me and pushed me back away, even as Malize let go of his cloak and drew a golden blade from his hip. Erus turned to him and snarled, changing into something wholly inhuman. He slammed into the angel, throwing him backwards with such force that they both crashed through the mangled shelving, through the stone and steel and out into the distance. I heard a crack echo, and felt the heat of flames.

I needed to find Clara. I ran back the way I had come, past where I had left her hunched and in hiding. I left the remains of the building, and looked out across the destruction to where I had last seen Abaddon and Avriel.

They were both gone.

Anger filled me, and I focused, steeling my muscles and launching forward. Even as I did, a dozen monsters appeared from within the broken frames of the buildings. They were duplicates of the creatures we had fought earlier. The demons Abaddon had sent for Avriel.

They tried to circle me, but I threw myself at the nearest one, pushing aside its grip with enhanced strength. I hit it hard in the jaw with a fist and sent it tumbling backwards into a wall. Twisting in the air, I landed facing the others. They were coming on strong, heavy legs shaking the ground below me. I could sense my own power diminishing, certain that I didn't have the reserves to take them on. I had known trusting in Abaddon was a risk, but I hadn't expected him to break a promise in blood.

I found a stone and picked it up, holding it in front of me like a shield. It was heavy in my grip, and I didn't dare waste the energy I had to make it easier to carry. Instead, I crouched and waited, ready to use my own power in bursts to swing the stone in an effort to break them. I wasn't about to give up, to let Abaddon win, or let Ross win, or abandon Clara and Charis. What he had tried to show me hadn't wounded my spirit, it had only made it stronger. If I was destined to fail, then one day I would fail. One day, I might regret my decision to love, my decision to connect, and my decision to hold onto the things that made me most human. One day, I might find myself faced with the death of everything I believed in, and everything I had hope for.

One day... but not today.

CHAPTER THIRTY-FIVE

Rebecca

WE LANDED ON THE OUTSKIRTS of Shanghai less than a minute later, in a small, empty field of grass. The flight had been both terrifying and exhilarating, putting an extreme amount of pressure on Elyse's mortal body, while also providing a sense of freedom that was undeniable.

"Where to?" Adam asked, releasing me from his grip.

I pulled the address from my pocket. "I don't suppose you have GPS?"

Adam smiled. "Not quite, but I do have perception of where the other seraph are. I think it's safe to assume this Master Lu would be one of the strongest signatures."

"Makes sense, but then why would Max have even bothered giving me an address? He'd planned on having me take the Adam express."

"Good point." The seraph reached out and took the paper from me. "Xincunxiang." He shook his head. "I can sense something there, but its weak. Weaker than any angel I've ever met. Weaker than most Touched."

"Sounds like the perfect disguise."

He nodded and held out his hand. I took it, and he pulled me back into his embrace. "We aren't far. This one will be quick."

It didn't seem as much like flying as it did teleporting. One second we were in the field, the next we were standing at a set of large timber gates. They had carvings of dragons on the face, and had been lacquered over in blue about a hundred years ago, leaving them faded and chipped today. A small canvas banner hung from the sides of the gate.

"The House of Life," Adam said.

"Why did you land on the outside?" I asked.

"Max said they wouldn't take kindly to aggression, and I'm not sure the monks inside know that their master is a seraph. I'm not even sure he knows he's a seraph."

"How is that possible anyway... a buddhist angel?"

"Buddha wasn't a god, and didn't call himself one. You can believe in the one true God, and still seek to be enlightened."

A small bundle materialized in his hands, and he shed the toga for a more modern t-shirt and jeans combo. I tried not to stare while he was stripped down, but the seraph's sex appeal was undeniable. He seemed oblivious, and as soon as he was dressed he stepped up to the doors and pulled a handle attached to the left dragon's nose, bouncing it off the door a few times with a solid thump. I hadn't even realized it was a knocker.

We didn't wait long for the doors to swing open. A small boy in gray robes smiled at us and waved us in. Adam bowed to him, so I followed suit, and then we entered the complex.

It was a simple place, a large green yard in the fore, with gardens sectioned off further back. To the right was a long, low house where I could see other monks entering and departing, and to the left was an open pagoda structure under which others sat prostrate and still on woven mats. I could see that the compound stretched further out behind the buildings, but the layout was obscured from view.

"Welcome. Namaste," the boy said. He was speaking Chinese, but I found I could understand him. Normally I was only able to handle whatever languages my host knew. It had to be Adam's doing. "Did you come to enroll?"

"Enroll?" I asked.

"To join the House of Life," he said. His voice was soft and peaceful.

"Perhaps," Adam said. "We'd like to speak to Master Lu. It's very important."

The boy smiled wider and bowed his head. "My apologies, traveler, but Master Lu is in a deep meditative state. It would be very unwise to wake him."

"I understand," Adam replied. "Perhaps there is another we can speak to? Someone must be in charge of the House while Master Lu is meditating?"

The boy bowed and waved his hand again. "Yes. Please, follow me." He started walking towards the building to the right, talking as he did. "Back there are the gardens, where we grow all of the vegetables, and you can see our outer sanctum." He pointed at the building as we circled around it. "This is the longhouse, where we sleep. There are ninety-three brothers and sisters in the House right now, but I'm the youngest. I was born here."

He led us past the longhouse, and now we could see another grass field, with a much larger structure behind it. It was simple despite its size, made of wood and needing a paint job as badly as the gates had.

"The inner sanctum, and administration," he said. "We work with local farmers, mending clothes and the like in trade for rice and occasional transportation to the village. It is a simple life, but such simplicity breeds self-mastery and understanding."

A group of three monks exited the building and walked past us as we entered, two women and a man, all with gray robes and shaved heads. They gave short nods in our direction. Even their steps seemed peaceful to me.

"Everyone here is Touched," Adam whispered beside me. "He's

blessed them all. That must be why his power is so diminished."

"How are we going to get them to let us see Lu?" I asked.

He shrugged.

"Sister Xiang is overseeing the Master's affairs while he is occupied," the boy said. He stopped and removed his shoes, and then pointed at our feet. "It is a sign of respect to leave your feet bare, but then comes the true test. Only those with pure hearts may enter."

Adam slipped off his sandals, and I reached down and pulled off the hard-soled slippers Elyse had been wearing. Our guide waved us on, and we passed under the entrance to the building - an archway with seraphim scripture carved into the wooden frame. I felt a bit of pressure as we passed beneath. A pure heart had nothing to do with it. The building was warded against demons.

The inside of the structure was as worn and simple as the outside. Wooden beams crisscrossed one another on the ceiling, holding up wooden planks that composed the upper levels. The walls were made of rice paper, grimy with their years, but still covered in beautiful depictions of mountains, flowers, and oceans. Simple sliding doors separated one room from another, and the sounds of talking, cooking, and praying could be heard echoing along the corridors.

"This is the door to the inner sanctum," the boy said, tapping on a slightly more ornate, hinged wooden door. It bore the same dragon on its face as the gates. He pulled it open just a crack so we could see inside. "There is Master Lu."

I could feel my jaw go slack when I saw him. A diminutive man with long white hair occupied the center of the room. He was tied at the wrists and hung from an ornate crossbeam that bore a vague resemblance to a cross. The beam and Master Lu rested in the center of a small pyre which engulfed him to the knees, though he appeared unharmed. He wore nothing but a loincloth, and his head lolled to the right.

"Is he-"

"Dead?" the boy asked. "No. He is in a deep meditative state. He does this to show us what we can accomplish by unlocking the true power of our souls. The flames cannot harm him." He pulled the door closed. "If you decide to stay, maybe one day you'll be able to sleep in the flames. I hope to try it for the first time next year. If I do, I will be the youngest ever." He looked down at the floor. "Master Lu would tell me not to be so proud. That is why he is the Master, and I am just a student." He looked at us and smiled. "Come, Sister Xiang is right over here."

He led us across from the inner sanctum, to an open room with a small flat table in the center. A woman knelt there, scribbling on top of a stack of papers.

"Sister Xiang, we have visitors," he said.

The woman looked up. She was a tiny thing, even smaller than Elyse, with a round face and brown splotches along her otherwise fair skin. Her robe was brown instead of gray, and it blended with her tone so that it looked more like a part of her body instead of cloth. She rose and bowed to us. There was a soft shimmer around her, like the air couldn't quite stay still in her presence. It followed her motion as her head dipped and rose again, leaving me staring.

"Welcome. I am honored to meet you both. My name is Xiang. I am the keeper of the House of Life while Master Lu is sleeping in the flames."

Our eyes met, and I felt a strange chill run through me. I looked over at Adam to see if he had noticed something strange about Sister Xiang, but I expected he couldn't.

She was a spirit.

"The honor is ours," I said, fighting to stifle my surprise and returning the bow. "My name is Elyse, and this is my brother, Adam."

Adam bowed his head. "We've come to speak with Master Lu about a matter of some urgency," he said.

Xiang smiled. "I have learned over the years that impatience is a cancer on our souls. Geishan, would you honor us by fetching some tea?"

The boy bowed and ran from the doorway.

As soon as he was gone, I pulled the black stone from my pocket and summoned the spatha. Adam's gaze flipped towards me in shock, but Xiang's only reaction was to let the smile fade from her lips.

"Re... I mean, Elyse, what are you doing?" Adam asked.

"Who are you really?" I said. I had no way to know that she wasn't the spirit of Sister Xiang, surviving in the small woman's body, but I doubted it. If you could take any mortal host you wanted, why would you choose someone with obvious abnormalities?

Adam put his attention back on Xiang, sizing her up. He surprised me by trusting enough to follow my lead.

"Another poltergeist?" she said. "I had thought there was a chance someone would come around asking for the crumpled old chicken, but I hadn't anticipated one of my kind." She reached under her robes, extracting a pair of sai. She planted them into the table in front of her. It was beneath her standing reach, but I was sure she wouldn't have done it if she didn't know she could grab them.

"Adam, you need to try to wake Lu," I said. "I'll take care of this one."

I felt his hesitation for only a breath, and then he backed out of the room.

Xiang laughed. "Don't you think I've tried to wake him?" she asked. "I've been trying for almost two weeks. I even stabbed the little bastard in the heart, but I couldn't get any cursed weapons in here to really give him grief."

"Adam has something you don't," I said.

"What's that?"

"He's family." I lunged as if to attack. She didn't move.

"I'm four thousand years old, Elyse. I'm not going to fall for cheap tricks."

"It was worth a shot." I took a step backward and moved into a guard posture. "Whose side are you on, anyway?"

"I'm, shall we say, a free spirit," she replied. "For now, my lot is cast with the Parisian archfiend."

Hadn't she said she arrived two weeks ago? Max had made it sound like Gervais had only learned about the swords when Joe had tried to use one on the Box, but that had only been this morning. Something was off somewhere, and the one thing I knew for sure about Max was that he was an accomplished liar. The question was, why?

She must have seen the confusion in my face, because she dove forward, grabbing the sai in mid-roll and coming up in a billow of her robes. I barely managed to move my face in time to keep the thrown blade from skewering my eye. Even so, it grazed the side of my temple and left a sharp sting in its wake.

The other sai was still in her hand, and she stayed low and went for my calf. I danced back away, avoiding the stroke, but she spun neatly on her toes and swept her leg through my path. I let the collision knock me over, falling to my back.

She didn't press the attack. It was a more subtle trick, but she knew it all the same, settling herself on her feet in front of me and drawing another sai from her robes.

"How many of those things do you have?" I asked as I got back up. I used the back of the towel on my arm to wipe the blood away from my face.

"Enough," she said. "Your form is clumsy."

"What did he promise you? Money? Power?"

"I could take those things for myself, as you well know. This world is a playground for us, an endless stage of existence. We can be any mortal we want, we can do anything we want. Even the other Divine hardly know we exist at all."

"Then why?" It was a strange time to be having the conversation, but I really wanted to know. Was there something to my situation that I had missed?

"He won't let you in, Elyse."

"Who?"

Her eyes flicked upwards. "You know who. I was a mortal once, and later a fiend. I was stabbed in the heart with a sword, a special sword that brought me into this life and gave me a new purpose. It was a gift that I believed had saved me. Redemption." She spat the word as though it was a curse. "For nearly a thousand years I moved from mortal to mortal, seeking to make amends for the evils I had done. I became a midwife, and saved hundreds of mothers and children from certain death. I became a scientist, and worked to cure disease. I even became a missionary, spreading His word across the world, in hopes of earning His forgiveness."

A sad smile spread across her face, and she shook her head. "One day, I went to a sanctuary in Turkey. I approached the angels there and told them my story. They brought me inside, and bade me to step into the light of Heaven." Tears began to roll from her eyes, two tiny slivers of moisture that dripped and vanished into the robes.

"What happened?" I asked. I could feel my heart was racing.

"Nothing."

"Nothing?"

"They told me that if I was truly redeemed, He would have lifted me up into His arms. They said my penitence was not complete."

The words made me cold. A thousand years of good, and she had been denied? What did that mean for me, the vampire who had freed the Beast?

"So you decided to be evil again?"

"Don't be foolish. I decided that I was done existing to the whims of hidden masters. I'm not good or evil. I'm only what they've made me, and what I've chosen to be. Today I serve Gervais, because he's promised me retribution. To help bring the end of God? That leaves a thrill in my soul." She lifted a hand and wiped away the tears with the back of her index finger, her face turning to stone. "You'd be wise to save yourself the heartache, and follow my lead instead."

Her words made sense. I knew they did. How could He truly forgive me for loosing the Beast on the world? There was no level of sorry that could cover it, and no amount of piety to bring back the lives of the thousands who had already died because of my actions. I lowered the spatha, aiming the point at the ground and keeping my eyes on Xiang. She was still, waiting for me to see her reason.

What was I? A vampire? A demon? An angel-in-waiting? My mind raced and whirled. At the center of the storm there was one word that stayed focused, a small bubble of energy that held the secret of my own truth. Sarah had understood, because she had needed the same kind of clarity. Maybe Xiang understood too, but she had chosen a different path. God's greatest gift was also His greatest weakness. I was free.

"That isn't who I choose to be," I said, raising the blade again. "Maybe He'll never call me into His warmth, but I have no right to demand that He does. Neither do you."

She shrugged. "Have it your way. You still can't defeat me, and Adam will never be able to wake Master Lu." She lunged forward again, faster than I could follow, leading with her left arm and using it to hook my own blade and pull it out of the way so the second sai could get through. It jabbed into my abdomen, digging through muscle before being stopped by bone.

"You must have been in a hurry to find a mortal body," I said through the pain. I reached down and grabbed her arm before she could bring it back, squeezing her wrist to make her drop the blade stuck in my side, and then twisting until it broke. I still didn't let go, instead pulling her towards me and slamming my forehead into her nose. Elyse was a warrior. Sister Xiang was a capsule. The spirit's mind may have been willing, but its host wasn't able.

I could have killed her then, by stabbing her through the heart a second time. I didn't need to. The body fell limp in front of me, the shimmer in the air fading. My true enemy had fled.

I lowered the woman gently, wincing at the pain from the sai in my gut. I held my breath while I removed it and tossed it onto the floor. I needed to go find Adam.

I stumbled out of the room, almost knocking into Geishon on the way by. He looked at me with fear in his eyes, and then turned his head towards Sister Xiang.

"She's alive," I said. "We were attacked." I showed him my own wound. "She needs help."

"Give me your hand," he said.

"What?" I didn't have time for this. I could see the door into the inner sanctum was hanging slightly open, but it seemed still inside.

"Give me your hand." He reached out and took it. I watched as his eyes began to glow in a faint white light, and I felt a warmth flow through my body. The pain in my stomach began to fade, as did the stinging of my arm.

"What did you do?" I asked as he let go of me. The wounds were healed.

"Master Lu says we must always give succor to those of pure heart. Your wounds were made with evil intent, and so they have been healed. That is the power of the House of Life." He smiled mischievously. "Well, one of them."

"Sister Xiang," I said. "It wasn't her fault. She was possessed. She needs healing."

"Don't be afraid, Elyse. The pure of heart will always be healed. Where is your brother?"

"Inside. I'm sorry, but he needed to wake Master Lu."

"He did wake Master Lu," a soft, old voice said. The ancient seraph ambled through the door, with Adam right behind him.

"Master Lu, my apologies," Geishon said. "I told them not to wake you."

"Be at peace, my son. You have done well. You have all done well." He took my hand and patted it. "Let go of the fear in your heart and follow the path you know is right."

My heart started pounding again, and in that moment I felt enough joy to bring tears to my eyes.

"I've got something for you," Adam said, bringing the Destroyer from behind his back. "It turns out Master Lu is not as confused as Max would have us believe."

"Be wary of that one," Lu said. "I don't know what game he is playing, and it may be that he has the best of intentions. A creature like Samael cannot help themselves but to lie and cheat, even when the truth would be the straightest path."

Enough lies had been revealed in the last five minutes that I didn't need the angel to tell me that. Max was up to something, and the shaky trust I'd been reserving for him was eroding fast.

"Do you know Max, Master Lu?" I asked.

"Samael gave me the sword for safe keeping many years ago. I was never sure of his purpose, and that is why I devoted myself to meditative practice. I needed to know that when he came seeking the blade again I could give it to him with a clear conscience. And so you have come, and so I have released it from my protection. The meditation allows me to see the world as it is, my child, not how each of us would like it to be, or believe it to be." He brought my hand up to his lips and kissed it. "Go now, and be at peace. Even if you lose, you will still win."

I didn't completely understand, but I didn't need to. I felt a strange peace settle over me. "We will. Thank you, Master Lu."

Adam and I headed for the door, while Lu knelt down and whispered to Geishon. I looked back and saw the boy scamper into the room with Sister Xiang. Lu saw me look, and he bowed his head to me.

"You didn't kill the spirit?" Adam asked.

"I don't know how to kill a spirit," I replied. "She ran away, and there aren't any clean mortals she can take for a dozen miles at least. How did you wake him?"

He laughed. "I didn't. He opened his eyes as soon as I approached him and asked me to take him down. The weakness... it's a gimmick. I don't completely understand his purpose here, but it isn't my place to question the Lord's will."

We passed beneath the scripted doorway and out onto the lawn. "Let's get ourselves to Paris," I said. "I'll wait while you change." I set my eyes on him and smiled.

"I don't need to use the wings to fly," he replied, reaching out and gathering me in his arms. "It's one of the perks of being an Inquisitor. They can really get in the way when you're trying to be discreet."

"Adam?"

He had looked up towards the sky, about to take off. Now he stopped. "What is it?"

"The Inquisitors were formed to find the swords. Well, we've found them. What are you going to do after this?"

His breath tickled my ear when he spoke. "Assuming there is an 'after this'? Our main purpose was to track down the swords, but our secondary mission is to find whatever lost relics and artifacts we can. I suppose we'll put a greater focus on that."

"So you're counter to the Nicht Creidim?"

"In a way. We've clashed with them a number of times over the centuries, but the Nicht Creidim are the enemy of all the Divine. Present company excluded, I guess."

"This is a temporary truce," I said. "It will end when Landon is free and the Beast is destroyed once and for all." I had no idea what Elyse planned to do after that. Her father was dead, and her home was ash.

He chuckled. "I'd be interested to see how your host is received by her people, after she gave aid to the Divine."

"The Beast is everyone's problem, as are the changelings. Can they be that steadfast in their rules that they won't be able to see how she's helping them?"

Adam lost his humored edge. "Trust me, Rebecca. I know from experience how blind we can be in service to our beliefs."

Before I could say anything else, we were launching into the sky.

CHAPTER THIRTY-SIX

Rebecca

ADAM AND I WERE WAITING on the runway when Brian's jet arrived. It touched down without fanfare and taxied over to a spot on the tarmac not far from where we stood. We walked towards it, arriving at the base of the ladder at the same time Max's face appeared in the doorway.

"Ah, there you are, peppermint patty. I take it you retrieved the blade?"

Adam turned his hand, and the Destroyer appeared in it.

Max clapped his hands together. "I knew I could count on the two of you." He started climbing down the stairs, with Ulnyx, Obi, Sarah, Izak, and Brian behind him. "We have much to do, and not a lot of time."

"The van should be here soon," Brian said, looking down at his phone.

"Well done, my good man." Max reached us and put his arms around me. "So, how is Master Lu? I see your burns have been healed."

I wasn't sure how much I should tell him. The angel's warning was still fresh in my mind. His heart might be in the right place, but I had been on the deceitful side before. If he was as good at it as he claimed, we'd never see it coming. "Old," I replied. "His stand-in, Sister Xiang, gave us the sword. She also healed the burns."

He pulled back and looked at me, testing me for my honesty. "Interesting."

"Is Izak safe to be this close to Gervais?" I asked, looking at the demon past Max's shoulder. The fiend was sticking close to Sarah, his demeanor suggesting the loss of half his arm was nothing more than an inconvenience.

"Yes, yes. I carved a ward over the brand. They're easy enough to deal with if you can get close enough to the branded, and if you know what you're doing."

"So, what's the plan, man?" Obi asked.

"Good question. Sarah, the Box, if you please. Adam, I'm afraid we'll need the Deliverer and the Destroyer now."

Both weapons reappeared in his hands. "Now? We still only have five."

"I'm afraid so. All of the swords need to make it to the Beast's prison. Any one of us can carry them, but they all need to make it. Do you understand?"

Adam nodded slowly and held them out. Ulnyx stepped forward. He was holding a long duffel.

"Just toss them in here," he said, unzipping it.

I watched him surrender the weapons. Max was taking away our best protection. I looked at him for a reaction, but there was none.

Sarah had pulled the Box from a canvas bag, and now she handed it to the reaper. "Now what?" she asked.

"We just brought Avriel's Box to Paris," Max said. "By my calculations, we have between three and ten minutes before all hell breaks loose."

We all stared at the reaper.

"That's why we're here, isn't it. In any case, it will spare you the anxiety of anticipation. Don't think, just act."

"We're still forty miles from Gervais' chateau, Max," I said.

"What the hell are you thinking?" I looked out over the horizon, and felt a chill. Ulnyx was looking that way too, and he started to shift.

"You thought we were going to do this at Gervais' house? Now that would be suicide. Trust me, pudding, and retrieve that dark sword of yours."

The problem was, I didn't trust him. He always seemed to be one step ahead of everyone, and Lu's warning had only cemented it.

"Ulnyx, you'll need your hands free. Rebecca can take the blades."

"Just what I wanted to hear," the Were said. He had finished shifting, and used his claws to slip the bag off his massive frame.

He heaved the duffel at me like it was made of paper. I let it clatter onto the ground, and then scooped it up by the handle and slung it across my back. I shook a couple of times to make sure it was somewhat secure, and then grabbed the black stone and summoned the spatha. It was weird to be holding such a relatively simple blade when I had an arsenal hanging over my ass.

"What am I supposed to do?" Brian asked. His face had turned white and he was shaking.

"Just stay behind me," Sarah said. She held her hands at her sides, her expression fierce. There was no fear there, only a smoldering anger that surfaced whenever her father was involved.

He didn't keep us waiting long.

He came from the air, falling from the sky in a streak of darkness, hitting the ground with a loud smack, and rising to his feet unharmed. A wave of demons landed behind him; fallen angels and winged devils carrying vampires, weres, and fiends. There were at least a hundred of them, a number that would have been challenging but doable for the force we'd assembled.

Except, these weren't typical demons.

None of them were alive.

They were damaged in different ways. Some had nasty gashes across the face, others scars along their leathery skin. All of them had a dullness in their eyes, and they moved with such uniform precision that it was obvious their ultimate freedom had been taken from them. They were zombies, much like what the Beast had launched at Landon in Mumbai, only augmented by their Divine size and strength.

"You see, the power of the swords won't help us here," Max whispered to me.

"This is crazy," I said.

"Trust me," he repeated.

The fate of the world may have been resting in the palm of his hand, and the self-proclaimed God of Lies was asking for trust. I tried to stay calm, but I was starting to feel like I imagined Brian did.

"Do you like them?" Gervais asked. He didn't look much different now than he had before, beyond the flatness of eyes that bore no reflection, no pupils, no living energy. His curly mop of black hair twisted down over them, and his simple beige cotton tunic and pants made him look like he should be vacationing in the Caribbean. "The perfect demons. Completely under my control." He glanced over at Izak, whose own eyes were alight in fury. "Free again, I see. Enjoy it for the few remaining minutes it will last. It is good to see you again, daughter." He leered at Sarah, and then turned to Max. "I'll take that."

Max looked back at me, pausing for only the barest instant.

He tossed the Box to Gervais.

"Max?" I meant for it to come out as a shout, in anger and pain at the betrayal. It left my mouth as little more than a whisper.

"My apologies, pumpkin pie," he said. Then he punched me in the mouth.

The blow caught me off-guard, and sent me reeling. I could feel the weight of the duffel slipped from me as I stumbled, grabbed by the reaper in one quick motion. There were shouts of confused anger behind me, and all hell *did* break loose.

An angry snarl sounded behind me and Ulnyx leaped forward at Gervais, his huge claws spread wide to scissor his head from his body. It was a rash move, an emotional outburst, and a stupid thing to do. Gervais didn't flinch, didn't move. He just put his hands up and caught the Were's wrists on their way in, a black energy pouring from him. The oil-like power coated Ulnyx, and when it vanished there was nothing but ash. It floated into the archfiend, catching in his hair but leaving him otherwise unharmed.

Gervais looked back at Sarah and smirked. Max had shifted into his reaper from, and he lifted the archfiend away even as a gout of hellfire fell where he had been standing.

"Trust me, my ass," I shouted after him. It was all I had time to do, because his undead demons rushed in at us.

Adam found his way to the front of the horde, a new blade in his hand. It was a standard-issue seraphim sword, but blessed or cursed, it didn't matter. The only thing that would stop them was the cruel cutting edge. We put ours to good use, digging in and getting washed over by the wave, flailing claws and teeth against metal. I heard Sarah try to Command the ones that moved past me, but I doubted it would have much of an effect.

Blasts of heat sent tingles up my spine as Izak joined the fight, his hellfire seeming to be our best weapon against them. I twisted and swung, decapitating a vampire and finding myself facing him. I could see him standing his ground ahead of half a dozen burning effigies, alight in the deadly flames that could reduce Brian and Sarah to ash in seconds. Even on fire, as long as they could move they would keep coming, and Izak lashed out with his good arm to keep them back, only to find more coming his way. They knew who the real threat was, and they focused on it with all of their intensity.

I cursed Max again and jerked away from the tip of a sword,

grabbing the wrist that held it and lopping it off with a backhanded cut. There was no cry of pain. In fact, the attacking demons made no sound at all. It was the quietest battle I'd ever heard.

Sarah screamed, and I saw one of the fiends had gotten his hands on her. Izak was too far away. We were all too far away. He brought his other hand up to her throat, wrapping it there and holding tight. For an instant, there was fear, and then it was gone. Something inside her broke. I could almost feel it, even in the middle of the scrum. Her lips curled into a snarl, and she brought her own hands up. The tips had extended into claws of her own, and she succeeded where Ulnyx had failed, bringing them together through the demon's neck and severing his head. The hands didn't let go.

I heard Obi then, his voice loud and angry. He didn't have the Eagle, but he did have a long dagger that he was using with reckless efficiency, tearing through flesh and clearing a path to Sarah. He got to her and grabbed the headless form, forcing it to release her and then throwing it to the ground, where a line of hellfire burned it.

"This is bad," Adam said, coming to stand next to me. He had a deep gash on his free arm, the bone protruding through it. "Their touch isn't killing me at least, but it isn't healing either."

"We're dead either way."

"You're not."

In the moment, I had forgotten about that. The demons could kill Elyse, but they couldn't actually hurt me. I could get away. I could find a new host and chase after Max and Gervais. I could try to stop them, and if I failed I could find another host and try to stop them again, until there were no more people left in France, or until they succeeded in taking the power of the Box for themselves.

I shook my head. "I can't stop them alone."

"We can't stop them at all."

"Just keep swinging that sword of yours, Adam. Maybe we'll get a miracle. Let's fall back to the others."

We started retreating as we fought back-to-back, trying to get closer to where Izak, Obi, and Sarah were standing their ground in front of the jet, with Brian hunched down behind them. We had put at least two dozen of the demons out of the fight, but it was hardly enough to slow them down. Even worse, Izak had been forced to stop washing them in flames, since it had only made them more effective weapons.

"Welcome to the cool kids club," Obi said as we joined them. He was drenched in sweat but otherwise unharmed. "It just so happens we have a few new openings."

A patched and mottled were snapped its jaws at my face, and I leaned back while Obi stabbed it in the neck and used the dagger as a handle, flexing his arms and throwing it to the side. It knocked over a vampire and they both stumbled, but only for a second.

"The plane," Brian said in a weak voice. "We need to get in the plane."

"The plane will help you, signore, but not if you go in it," Dante said. He appeared out of nowhere right next to Brian. He grabbed the fake angel and vanished.

"Dante?" Obi asked. He reappeared, wrapped his arms around Sarah, and disappeared again.

"Grab onto one another," Dante said when he popped into existence the next time. He put his hand on Izak's shoulder and faded away.

"I don't know what the hell is happening, but getting out of the middle of this crap is fine with me," Obi said. He backed up so that he was pressed up against Adam and I. Together, the three of us pushed back against the horde, their numbers working against them while they all tried to grab us at once. When Dante appeared again, he was so close I had to banish the spatha to keep myself from stabbing him.

"Time to go," he said, pointing to the distance. A lone figure was standing there, bathed in hellfire. Vilya.

He grabbed my wrist and I felt like I was falling through a black hole. Then I was back in the real, standing outside a hanger well away from the demons. Obi and Adam were still pressed against me. I regained my senses just in time to feel the rumble and see the earth split below the plane. A geyser of molten earth and flame burst up into the jet. I could feel the heat of it from across the distance, even more so when it exploded, catching all of the demons in a massive burst made more powerful by the Demon Queen's power.

Not all of them were incinerated, but the ones that weren't found themselves on fire, turning in circles in an effort to find us, their eyes burned away in the heat. Vilya walked right into them, sword in hand, decapitating them and knocking them away. Once there weren't any left standing, she started coming in our direction.

"I don't understand," I said. "She's a servant of the Beast."

"Not quite, Signora Solen," Dante said. He looked on me with an odd mix of respect and disdain. "Consider your source."

"Max?" Obi asked. "I'm going to rip that guy's head off."

Dante smiled. "Don't be so quick to judge. He is a liar, it is true, but he plays that card quite well."

"What are you talking about?" Sarah asked, her voice hoarse, her face a dark mask of conflict. She flexed her hands, which had reverted back to normal, and leaned on Izak like she was about to collapse. "They killed Ulnyx."

"I'm sorry about the Were. It was an unfortunate miscalculation," Dante said. "We should have accounted for his temper."

"Miscalculation?" I asked. What would Landon think about that?

"We need to move," Vilya said, having run the rest of the distance to reach us. "The rift is inside." She moved through us to a hanger door that I hadn't had a chance to notice yet, shoving it open and waving us in.

"It was all a trick," Dante said. "To separate Gervais from his army. Max planned the whole thing, and only Vilya and I knew about it. Now we need to get to the chateau before the archfiend has a chance to begin his work."

"A trick?" I said. "A freaking trick!" Master Lu must have been in on it too, or at least known about it. He had planted the seeds of doubt in my mind and made my reaction to the betrayal all the more believable.

I followed the others inside, to where Vilya was finishing opening a hell rift.

"What the heck is that?" Brian asked, shying away from it.

"It's okay," Adam said. He was holding his broken arm across his chest, and using his other hand to put pressure on the still bleeding wound. "Just wait here. It's clear you aren't cut out for this."

"No," Dante said. "He needs to come." He put his hands on Brian's shoulders. "It is no accident that you are here, signore. Please, help us to save this realm from destruction." Brian still looked frightened, but he nodded. Dante smiled. "Grazie."

The rift lit up, and Vilya stepped through. Izak, Sarah, and Obi followed.

"It's like Star Trek," I said. "There's nothing to worry about."

He reached out for my hand, and I took it. Rifts weren't that much like Star Trek - a first-timer was guaranteed to come out the other end disoriented. I only hoped he wouldn't faint.

I led him through, and we came out the other side in the sewers below Paris, in the room where I had left Avriel to be tortured by Abaddon. Izak was waiting there alone, and he waved for us to follow.

"Are you okay?" I asked Brian. He leaned over and vomited in response.

"Keep moving," Dante said, appearing away from the rift. "I shall meet you inside the chateau." He vanished.

I pulled Brian along while we ran after Izak, making our way through a tunnel covered in burn marks, soot, and ash. I could see there had been runes lining the walls once, but they had been mangled and broken by whatever heat had made its way along the length.

We caught up to them at another rift, which Vilya had just finished activating. "This leads to the chateau," she said. "I think we've killed most of Gervais' creatures, but I wouldn't put it past him to have left a few behind. I'll go first. Izak, protect our rear."

He nodded and turned his attention to Sarah, who was hanging even more heavily from his arm.

"Leave her here," I said. "She can't help like that."

"No," Vilya replied. "She has to come, I'm sorry."

"It's okay. I'm okay." Sarah looked up at me, her eyes heavy and filled with tears. Her free hand was balled into a tight fist. "I have to do this."

Vilya vanished into the rift. Brian groaned as we approached it, but didn't slow.

"I'll never go to another trekkie convention," he said.

We stepped through.

CHAPTER THIRTY-SEVEN

Landon

THE CREATURES MOVED IN WITHOUT fear, as though they knew I wasn't strong enough to repel them. I held the stone at chest height, muscles straining to maintain it. Finally, three of them came within reach, and with a howl I focused and brought the stone up, leaping and cracking it into a skull that was ten feet over my head, using my other hand to grab the beaten monster's shoulder and vault over it, while the other two tried to change direction. It brought me down closer to the others, but the maneuver confused them, and their size made for poor agility.

I swung the rock around, cracking it into a kneecap, ducking and rolling backwards away from a gigantic foot. The demons howled and screeched around me, shoving each other aside to make room. I brought the stone up over my head to block an attack, tensing my arms and feeling my feet sinking into the ground in an effort to deflect the force. I threw the rock upwards, smashing another skull, leaping up behind it and catching it on the way down.

If there hadn't been so many of them, it might have been impressive.

Instead, my strength was fading, and one more blow against my shield from a heavy claw left me on my back a dozen feet away. I dropped the now too-heavy stone and tried to scramble to my feet, feeling a level of exhaustion set in and starting to accept that I was going to lose.

The demons approached, their howling louder, their teeth chattering in anticipation.

Abaddon stepped in front of them.

His essence billowed out around him, casting forward like a net and wrapping around the creatures. Their glorious howls turned to hopeless moans, and their knees buckled beneath the power. I watched while he fed, the tendrils of his energy forcing their way into the monsters, finding their souls and drinking them dry. I could barely see him amidst the shadow of his power, but I was sure I heard him sigh.

Then it was over. The creatures were gone, their bodies gray and falling to ash. Abaddon turned to face me, his cloak shrinking out of my path.

"Hurry, child. We must hurry." He held out his hand to help me to my feet.

I grabbed it and let him pull me up. "I thought-"

"I betrayed you? In other circumstances, perhaps, but we had a promise in blood, and my word is the only precious thing that remains to me." His red eyes filled with dark flames. "He found a way to use your child against you and I both."

"The Beast?"

He shook his head. "No. Not the Beast. There is another entity here, one that I do not recognize, and did not see. She tried to warn you, to show you his true purpose."

"Malize?"

"I do not know that name."

My blood ran cold. Malize had come to collect Ross after the universe had been broken, and now Abaddon was suggesting he was somehow here, in the Box, and he had taken control of Clara. Was it Malize, or a shade of Malize? Or was it some nascent energy that had been embedded in the Templar script that powered it? Either way, I wasn't sure what to make of it. He had passed himself off as an archangel to Charis and me, but Clara's warning was suggesting something far more sinister. Was he a benevolent being in search of justice, or an agent of whatever had caused the destruction, seeking its final end? He had brought me this far, aided us in our fight against Ross. He had delivered Avriel to us, and provided the gun that was still resting in the small of my back. He was supposed to be an angel of God.

He had also sent the first round of monsters to attack us, and now he had taken Clara. Her power, our connection... had it ever truly been ours?

What the hell was he really?

"Diuscrucis, come."

I looked at Abaddon and felt my heart sinking. Charis was a Templar, a secret society of Divine that had been founded by the archangel. Did she know the truth of him?

"Diuscrucis." Abaddon's hand touched my face, and I felt the coldness of the despair. It was enough of a shock that it drew me out of my daze.

"Where is Clara?" I asked.

"She and the seraph have taken the path."

"Then we need to follow. Which way?"

Abaddon motioned off to a pile of rubble, and a ruined street beyond it. "There."

We both ran.

My power was gone, spent. My energy was almost the same. I staggered behind Abaddon, fighting to keep up with nothing more than sheer will. If I was going to do anything to help anyone, I needed to get out of this place, whatever this place was.

We reached the road beyond the rubble. Abaddon stopped.

"It has been altered."

"What do you mean altered? Isn't this your path, your route?"

"Yes. It was, until I brought you here." He kneeled down and put his fingers to the ground. "He is trying to keep you away."

I heard motion from our left. Another of the creatures moved out from behind the blown out wall of what used to be an apartment building. Three more followed behind it.

"I can't fight them," I said. "My power is gone."

He turned his head in their direction. His power snaked away from him, tendrils running along the ground. The creatures never saw it until it had pooled below their feet. "He would never expect me to help you, child. He has no concept of my promise, or my respect." The idea seemed to make him angry. The creatures bellowed and turned to dust under his strength.

"Great. Which way?"

He lifted his fingers to his lips, and pointed back the way we had come. "That way."

I followed behind him again, every step leaving me burning with pain. It felt like we ran forever, along burned and blasted roads.

Erus stepped out in front of us.

His face was burned, his right eye gone. His clothes were torn and singed. I don't know how he was still standing with so much damage. He saw us coming and began to scream.

"For all I have sacrificed. For all I have endured. This is how it ends."

Abaddon lashed out with his power, and threw him away from us. I gave him only a quick look as we passed him by; crying in the dirt, a pitiful, broken wreck.

"We are near," he said. He stopped again and put his fingers to the ground.

"What are you doing?"

"Tracing the power. I have taken this path. I have claimed it with all of the essence that remains to me in this place. It is but a single thread, but it is my domain. He cannot hide from me here, not completely."

He grabbed my arm and leaped. We launched high into the air, a hundred feet, two hundred, approaching a tall building that once had been coated in thousands of panes of glass, but now was just a metal framework. We came down on the roof, landing without a sound. He let me go.

Avriel was standing there. Clara was gone.

"You're supposed to be helping me," I said.

"No, diuscrucis. I was charged with protecting the girl." He held his blade in his hand, and he was blocking the small steel door into the stairwell. I had a feeling it didn't lead down into the skeletal remains of the building.

"Let him pass," Abaddon said. "I made a promise in blood, and you have interfered." A sword grew from his darkness, a scimitar of black despair.

"I cannot. I delivered the girl to him. Now my purpose is to prevent him from fulfilling his duty." The archangel's eyes caught on mine. "All you need do is wait, Landon. He means you and Charis no harm. You will be rewarded for what you have done."

No harm? Clara had shown me who he was for a reason, and it wasn't so that I would put my faith in him.

"Let me pass," I said. I didn't have a sword. I could barely stand up.

It didn't matter.

I walked towards the seraph, my eyes fixed on his. I reached behind me and pulled out the gun. It was still the same, plain thing it had always been. Why had Malize sent me to find this thing, if I wasn't supposed to use it?

Avriel attacked before I could aim, shooting forward and bringing his sword down in a smooth stroke towards my head. I slipped aside, Josette's training and muscle memory kicking in through my subconscious. I reached out and grabbed the angel's wrist, meaning to throw him over my shoulder.

I just wasn't strong enough.

I pulled against him, but it wasn't even enough for him to lose his balance. He wrenched back, throwing me towards the end of the rooftop. Somehow I managed to hold onto the pistol and come to a stop before I plunged over.

Abaddon picked up my slack. He came at Avriel in a flurry of motion, his tendrils of power whipping out around him in an effort to distract the demon. They had danced this dance an infinite number of times, and the angel didn't fall for any of it. He stayed focused on the dark sword, and they came together in a furious clash of energy. I pulled myself to my feet and held up the gun, trying to get a clear shot. The motion was just too quick.

They pounded at one another, the hate and anger obvious from both. I could feel the temperature drop around me, and my breath caught when the first wave of hopelessness crashed against my soul. I knew the same power was hitting Avriel, but which of us would break first?

It wasn't going to be me. I got on my hands and knees, and then on my stomach. I inched towards the doorway, sliding along the rooftop, using my arms to propel me and trying desperately not to attract their attention. They circled one another at a dizzying rate, their weapons smacking and crashing, each hit a sizzle of energy that ionized the air around them.

Still I crawled, my mind focused only on Clara and Charis. What was Malize going to do to them? What was Malize going to do to us all?

A sword landed in front of my face.

"You will not pass," Avriel shouted. His need to stop me was without logic. Abaddon tackled him, and they both vanished from the rooftop.

I reached up and grabbed the hilt of the sword, using it to pull myself to my feet. Then I removed it from the stone, feeling the lightness and balance. The door was only a few feet away. I stumbled forward and grabbed the handle, turning it and throwing it open.

I stepped through.

CHAPTER THIRTY-EIGHT

Rebecca

WE CAME OUT OF THE other side of the rift and into the small room Gervais had set aside for it. Vilya was already at the door, holding her hand out to keep us quiet and surveying the hallway.

"It's clear," she said. "Follow me."

We filed out into the hallway, a long corridor that ended in a set of stairs. Brian was a new shade of white at my side, clutching his stomach and trying to hold back another round of puking. He knew we couldn't afford to make a sound, and he made a valiant effort to keep quiet.

We reached the stairs and made our way down, into the lower levels where the archfiend kept his laboratory, as well as his prisons. We moved with a slow haste past the barred cells where corpses of demons remained imprisoned, awaiting their return from the end. They were damaged but well-preserved; Gervais must have been doing something to them to keep them in a more usable state. With every footstep I expected them to rise up and cry out in alarm, or try to rip their way through the runed bars, but they remained still.

I heard Sarah gasp when we passed the final row of cells, having reached the one unique prison where her mother had once been held captive. I glanced back and saw her clenching her hands and teeth, with Izak rubbing her back and gently pushing her forward. There was no time for memories.

We'd reached the archfiend's torture rooms when we heard the murmurs of his voice, speaking to Max from the room beyond. There had been a solid door there once, but now it was missing, the hinges bent and mangled like it had been ripped away. I knew Landon must have done it. I had left Gervais there for him to find, and he hadn't let me down.

"I'm telling you, my Lord, it won't work. Even in your state you can't collect that much power without being burned away by it."

"You promised me you could assist with that, Samael. You swore." Gervais' voice was flat, emotionless. Even his anger came across as a dead thing.

"I can, but I need more time. Malize-"

"There is no more time. Fulfill your obligation."

"Malize hid the ring even from me. He must have known not to trust me too far. I know I can find it given time, but this was to be expected. You can't rely on a trickster like me and not face a certain amount of adversity."

We crossed the room, using their voices to help disguise the sound of our footsteps. I didn't know how the archfiend hadn't sensed our presence, but I had a feeling Max had something to do with it.

"Adversity?" Gervais chuckled. "I'm minutes from becoming a god, and you want to speak to me of adversity? Where is the ring, Samael?" Max cried out, and I heard a thump. The archfiend must have thrown him into a wall. "Never mind. I'll take my chances that you're either wrong, or lying to me."

Vilya waved us to either side of the doorway. I came to rest against the wall right behind her, with Brian still tailing close to me.

"Izak and I will distract him," she said over her shoulder. "Dante will get the Box. You need to grab the swords. Max will lead you through the portal to the Beast's prison."

"What do we do then?"

"We must sink the blades into the Box at the same time. When the door opens, the Beast's power will be drawn into it. We are hoping it will draw in Gervais' stolen power as well."

"Hoping?" I didn't like the sound of that.

"My Lord, you can't," Max said. "If you fail, you will destroy everything."

"I'll destroy everything anyway," he replied. "Once I am a god, why would I settle for just these worlds? The entire universe will be for the taking."

Vilya motioned to Izak, an intricate pattern that I didn't understand. The demon nodded, stepped out into the doorway, and coughed.

There were no words spoken. There was no sound. At first, a stillness sat in the air that threatened to choke off all of reality. Then I felt the coldness of Gervais' power. I heard a crash, and Izak and Vilya rushed ahead. I trailed right behind them, waving for the others to follow.

Max had used the surprise to ambush the archfiend, slamming him hard in the head and throwing him across the small room. He was still on the ground when I entered, getting to his feet and looking amused.

"The deceiver has double-crossed me? Well done, Samael."

Max hadn't waited to see his reaction. He was crossing the floor to the southern wall, where I could see an intricate patchwork of Templar script had been etched. Had he learned the language, or had someone written it for him?

"Go ahead and open it, Samael," Gervais said. "I'll be along soon." His eyes fell on Izak, and he leaped forward, moving so fast I couldn't follow him. A slick of darkness trailed behind, and then snapped forward when he reached the demon. Izak fell sideways, avoiding the dark energy, and Vilya moved in behind the archfiend, slamming into him and sending him ahead. He hit the wall with enough force to dent the metal, rolled over, and got back to his feet.

"Signora, the swords." Dante appeared out of nowhere. The Box and the blades were resting on a small cart in the center of the room. He grabbed the cube and started backing away.

"No," Gervais said, rising to his feet. He put out his hand, and arcs of black energy launched towards the poet. They fell away when Izak tackled him.

"Follow Dante," I said to those behind me. I couldn't waste any more time watching. I dashed forward, coming to a quick stop at the cart. I grabbed the duffel and swung it over my shoulder, returning it to my back.

Dante was nearly across the room, and Max was already there, chanting in a deep voice with his hand pressed to the etched metal wall. The runes were glowing in a golden hue, casting an eerie light that began to fill the room. Adam was leading the others to the same spot.

"I'm done with you, Izak," Gervais shouted, loud enough to overcome Max's incantation, and loud enough to get our attention. He held the demon by the neck with one hand, and had pinned his good arm with the other. Anger and pain swam across the fiend's face. "I tried to make you part of this. What demon doesn't dream of standing in the shadow of such power? Yet you continue to abandon me, first for my sister, and then for my daughter."

"Let him go," Sarah said. Her voice was weary, her face ashen.

Gervais spun to face her, still holding Izak. "Let him go?" He laughed. "Make me."

Vilya was a bolt of lightning, shooting towards Gervais. She had a blade in hand, and she leaped towards him, rotating her torso and bringing it down on the archfiend with all of her strength. He didn't move. He didn't react. He continued staring at Sarah, challenging her, daring her to attack him. The blade struck him at the base of his neck, and disintegrated into nothing.

She had put all of her energy into the blow, and she lost her balance, stumbling away and falling to the floor. The corrosion continued down the hilt of the sword and onto her hand. She held it up to her face, panic in her eyes, and watched her skin and bone begin to waste away.

"You can't hurt me, Vilya," he said, his voice still flat. "None of you can hurt me. All of your tricks, Samael. All of your lies. They're for nothing."

Max finished his work and fell silent. The light from the door was intense now, bathing everything in its glow. The script had faded away to nothing, as had the wall. All that remained was a glowing portal that led to the Beast's prison.

"Let's go," he said.

Dante was the first to go through.

"What about Izak?" Obi asked. "And Vilya?"

"They're dead," the reaper replied. "They knew it was going to end this way. They understood the need." He stepped through.

"I'm not leaving him," Sarah said. Her head stayed fixed on her father, as though she could see him through her eyeless sockets. Her flesh was gaining color, and she continued to flex her hands. "Even if you kill him, I'm going to kill you."

"A pleasant thought I'm sure," Gervais said. "Come and get him."

"Obi, take Brian and go," I said. I took the duffel from my back. "Adam, take the swords. I'll get Sarah."

None of them looked happy, but they knew they had no choice. Gervais would kill us all. Adam took the swords and vanished into the light, with Obi and Brian right behind.

Vilya had stopped screaming. The decay had done its work, reducing her to a layer of dust on the cold floor.

"Well, my dear?" Gervais said.

"Sarah, don't," I said. "We can't beat him this way. We have to go through the portal and use the Box."

She didn't react. I don't know if she even heard me. Her breathing had slowed, and she looked calm and peaceful. It was more frightening than when she had looked angry. She started walking towards Gervais.

"Sarah!" I grabbed her arm. Pain lanced through every nerve of my body, my muscles spasming and freezing and forcing me to let go. She didn't even seem to notice. "Sarah!"

I had no idea how to stop her. I couldn't touch her, couldn't reason with her. She kept walking towards Izak, and I saw lines of blood along the back of her shirt. With each step she took the blood thickened, until it burst in a flurry of cloth and flesh, and a pair of red and gold feathered wings sprouted from her back. They weren't plush and light like a seraph's, but ridged and serrated, menacing and dark.

Gervais laughed.

"I knew it," he said. "I knew I could coax you to change. I knew I could turn you, and bring out your true power. I knew I could break you." He shifted his grip, and pulled Izak's head from his neck. He held it out to her, letting the body fall away. "Thousands of years and all of that power. Wasted on the weakness of love."

Still Sarah was silent. She was getting close to the archfiend now, and her wings had extended fully from her back, stretching wide behind her and obscuring my view. Izak was dead, Vilya was dead. How was I going to stop Sarah from joining them?

"Sarah," I cried, one last time. I couldn't stop her. I couldn't touch her, and I couldn't touch Gervais. All I could do was watch her die.

They stood face to face, father and daughter. They regarded one another without emotion.

"I knew it was there," he said. "We will rule the universe, daughter. You and I."

"No," Sarah replied. "You'll die."

There was no battle. There was no struggle. Her wings folded down and in, spreading and changing as they moved. Two tips caught the archfiend's wrists. Two tips caught his ankles, and another caught his head. The feathers dug into the skin like spears, spreading him and lifting him up off the ground. His eyes widened in surprise, and he tried to move, to touch her with his power, but there was nowhere he could reach. He was pinned tight.

I could barely see through the wings to Gervais' face. Sarah brought her hands up to it, and cupped his chin beneath clawed fingers. "Thank you, father," she said. "I could never have stopped you without you." She turned around and started walking towards me, while I stood there in shock.

"Sarah?"

"Let's finish this, Rebecca," she said, walking past me.

"Rebecca?" Gervais asked. All the defiance had drained from him.

She held him aloft in her wings, and carried him through the portal.

I followed right behind.

CHAPTER THIRTY-NINE

Rebecca

THERE WAS SILENCE WHEN SARAH and I came through, into the prison where I had been killed. It hadn't changed much since I had been there last, except the blue glow that had once filled the room was nearly gone. Only a slight flow had been left behind, unable to be collected without the blood of the true diuscrucis. The white star still floated near the top of the prison, and it cast a soft light on us.

Then I noticed it out of the corner of my eye. It was sitting exactly where it had fallen those long months ago. The Holy Grail. I felt the sting of memories, and the guilt of what I had helped to start. Now I would help to finish it.

"Holy crap," Obi said, breaking the silence. "That is seriously unreal."

"Sarah?" Adam said.

"I brought him," she said. "Where is the Redeemer?"

"Here." A new voice. A small black and white demon scampered out from behind Dante's legs, dragging the final Canaan Blade behind him.

"Alichino?" I said. "Where did you come from?"

"Alichino was helping Gervais to unlock the power of the Box," Max said. "It seems his allegiance changes as easily as the wind."

The demon snickered. "Always bet on the winning team. That's what I always say."

"At least we can thank him for creating the portal."

"We must hurry," Dante said. "I can't remain here for long."

Max held the Box in his hands. "Adam, take the Destroyer. Obi, the Deceiver. Sarah, the Redeemer, Brian, Truth. Alichino, you will take the Damned, and Rebecca, the Deliverer."

Adam leaned over the duffel, taking out the swords and handing them to each of us.

"An angel, a demon, a diuscrucis. A mortal, a spirit, a changeling."

He lifted the Box into the air, and let it go. A beam of light shone down from the white star, capturing it and holding it in place at chest level.

"Six swords. Six sides. Six creations. We must all use the blades at the same time."

Adam rose into the air, to place the Destroyer into the top of the box. Alichino positioned himself below it, and the rest of us each took a side. I felt my heart begin to race, the end of my journey and Landon's freedom so near. We each held our blades ready.

The Box sat in front of us, its lines pulsing with blue power, its energy radiating around it. Max stood behind me, but he didn't give the word.

He was waiting for something.

I saw it when he did. A single thread of white in the sea of blue. It raced around the Box, following the scripture that had been carved into its sides.

"Now," Max said.

I stabbed.

The swords sunk into the Box, much further than they should have been able to without coming out the other side. At the same time, the white light intensified. The Deliverer grew too hot to hold, and I let go and backed away at the same time as the others. We all watched as the light from the star continued to expand, growing larger and larger until the Box was swallowed by it.

Gervais began to scream.

Sarah had held him up above her, still trapped in the wings, but now she shifted and lowered him towards the light. It stretched out a thin tendril and wrapped around his leg, spiraling up and encircling him while his screams became louder and more pained.

"Sarah, don't do this," he said. "Sarah, I'm your father. All I wanted was for us to be a family, to rule together."

"All I want is for you to die," she replied. "You've hurt enough people. You've killed enough of my friends. Mother may have forgiven you. I never will."

The power was draining from him, feeding back into the white light and through it to the Box. His entire body began to compress on top of itself, losing the energy that was holding it together and keeping him in his existence. Sarah released her hold on him, dropping him to the ground. His eyes shifted wildly, looking at each of us as he shook and screamed.

Then he was gone.

"Max, where is Landon?" I asked. I turned my head, looking for the reaper. "Max?"

He was gone, too.

"Where the hell did he go?" I said. There was nowhere to go. We'd all been watching Gervais, and he had disappeared. Then I looked at the light again. It was definitely big enough, and it did look a bit like a door. "Damn it. He did it again."

"Did what, signora?" Dante asked.

"What do you think? The swords don't open a way out of the Box. They open a way in." I looked into the white light, and took a deep breath. I knew in that moment that this was why I was here. This is what I had been redeemed for. This was His task for me, His test. I released Elyse from my hold.

"*Take care of yourself,*" I said to her.

"Rebecca, what are you doing?" she asked.

"Saving him."

I pushed away from her, letting myself move into the light. I could feel the energy of it, the power surrounding me. I didn't know what Max's intentions were, but I wasn't about to let him have free reign to do whatever it was he wanted to do. If I had to, I would stop him.

A final burst of light greeted me, and then I was through. Everything was dark.

I opened my eyes and blinked a few times, trying to clear them. I took a breath. Another. I looked down to see that I was whole once more. It was my form, my body. I took my hair and moved it in front of my eyes so I could see it. I licked my lips to feel the fullness of them. I winked my eye.

Max vanished around a corner in front of me.

I knew where I was. I had been here often enough to recognize it. The Museum of Natural History in New York.

I started running.

CHAPTER FORTY

Landon

I KNEW WHERE I WAS as soon as I stepped into it. The Museum of
Natural History. The place where it had all began. It was fitting
that it would end here too.

I was right outside the chalice exhibit, where the Holy Grail had
once rested, and the place where I had died. I could hear voices
coming from the far end of the room, though I wasn't close enough
to see the speakers yet.

"How did you find me?" Ross asked.

"We always knew where you went, Erus. We couldn't reach you
because He gave you asylum. When you repaid Him with your
treachery, He allowed me to come to this realm to collect you. I
underestimated the damage to your soul."

Ross laughed at that. "Does He even know who you are? What
you are?"

"He knows what you are. That is enough."

"I'm what you made me," he shouted. "What you forced me to
be. This is your fault."

"Then why was it your guilt that drove you mad? You were safe
here, Erus. He had given you the sanctuary you begged for. Why
did you destroy it?"

I shouldered Avriel's sword and started walking. After a few steps, I realized that something was wrong. I was back on the normal path of the Box, but the power hadn't returned. Why had Malize prevented me from coming through, if he knew I was powerless anyway? What was it that he didn't want me to see or do?

I decided to be more subtle than I had originally planned. Instead of walking right in on them, I ducked behind one of the display cases and inched my way forward one obstruction at a time. The one benefit to having no power was that they probably couldn't sense my presence.

"Why did I destroy it? It is what you taught me, Malus. You and your council. Destruction is the only thing that eases the pain. It's also the only pleasure that remains, when nothing ever ends. It's the only challenge left to us."

When we had fought Ross outside the Great Pyramid, he had recognized Malize. He had said his name. Only, now I heard Malus. I was sure of it. Why had he sold us a different name? Had anything he'd told us been true? He wasn't a demon, so I couldn't spot his lies. I had trusted him because Charis had trusted him. We had both made a mistake.

"To us, Erus? No. To me. Catching up to you has almost been fun. A masterpiece of controlled chaos."

I peeked my head up from behind a large, jewel-encrusted cup. I could see them now, near the front of the room. Ross standing face to face with Malus. Charis was bound and unconscious, sitting up against the pedestal where the Grail had sat, her head slumped to her chest. Malus was definitely Malize, and he absolutely wasn't a good guy. The boyish angel was in the same robes I had seen on the path.

He had his arm around Clara.

She was clay-faced, motionless in his grasp. Whatever force was giving her life, it had been put on hold. Could she even hear what they were saying?

"So, now here we are. I knew you were somewhere behind the Box, but I hadn't expected you to make a personal appearance. I've been trying to overcome these two meat sacks so I could bust out of here before someone delivered it to you. They're more resilient than they look."

He kicked Charis in the ribs for emphasis, which almost brought me out of my hiding place.

"It took me a long time to prepare this trap," Malize said. "Almost as long as it took me to break you. There were so many pieces, so many possibilities. In the beginning, I thought to just collect you and take you home, so we could both delight in your torture, and repay you for your years of service. Only your power has grown in your madness, hasn't it? My first prison was only barely enough to hold you, and nowhere near good enough to transport you."

"How many of His seraph did I destroy, Malus?" His eyes gleamed with satisfaction.

"Millions. He was furious enough to allow me free reign. That was when I decided the prison wasn't enough. That taking you home wasn't enough."

I moved forward again. I didn't like any of the directions this conversation was going in. I focused, trying to find the power, but there was none. I had to stop them both somehow, and I had nothing but a sword and a gun with a single bullet. A bullet that I was pretty certain couldn't harm either of them.

"There is so little left to us," Malize said. "So little that can consume the years, and bring us feeling. So few places left that we haven't conquered. He is more powerful than you and I, and yet He refuses to get involved. I will make Him get involved. I will make Him fight."

"I can help you," Ross said, a smile growing on his face. "We may not have enough power to defeat him on our own, but together? Together we can not only take His realms, but destroy

Him completely."

Malize regarded him for a moment. "How far you have fallen, Erus. How sad and pathetic you have become. At least when you were fighting for the balance, there was something there to respect. Now, I don't even pity you."

He put out his hand and Ross collapsed into a heap on the floor. He didn't move again.

My brain raced ahead at a million miles per hour as I tried to remember everything that Malize had said to us. The story about his origins, his creation, his tag-team with Lucifer in the war against Ross. He was the forgotten for a reason, and now I knew why. Did God even remember where he had come from?

Malize leaned down over Ross and put his hand on his forehead. He closed his eyes as the connection began to glow.

I stood crouched behind the chalice, unsure of what to do. Avriel had said we would be rewarded, but what kind of reward could we expect? Malize meant to absorb Ross' power, and then take up his own banner against God and our worlds. He had trapped Charis and I in here because he wanted all of it, every last drop that we held in our souls. He knew the way in, and I was sure he knew the way back out.

I looked over at Charis, eyes still closed but her expression more peaceful now that Ross was dead. How could she have known what Malize was? How could anyone? Few enough could remember him a minute after they left his presence. I looked at Clara, silent and frozen in time. He wanted the power that was trapped in the Box. She had called herself a battery. All of the energy Charis and I had collected by surviving here and absorbing it was held in her visage. More than that, she had said there was a bond between our power and Ross', because it came from the same place. He had no chance against Malize with only half of the power, and he had cut me off from my share.

Divide and conquer.

Now I knew why he wanted to keep me away. I held the gun in my hand, and took a deep breath. I wasn't sure if my idea would work, but there was a sense to it, a logic that snapped into place in my mind.

I heard a groan. Charis. Her eyes fluttered open, and widened with recognition of her supposed mentor.

I didn't know what he would do if he saw she was awake. My time was up.

I stood up. Malize was too busy with Ross to notice. I raised the pistol, extended my arm, and took aim.

CHAPTER FORTY-ONE
Rebecca

MAX MOVED THROUGH THE MUSEUM at high speed, making it obvious he knew exactly where he wanted to go. I ditched my shoes and chased behind him, treading as light on my bare feet as I could, hoping that he wouldn't hear me. I didn't want to just jump him, because I couldn't be sure he wasn't trying to help.

So I followed.

We raced past dioramas, through the huge hall full of dinosaur bones, and down the stairwell into the main entrance hall. All the while I remained at least fifty feet behind him, weaving and ducking behind anything I could find. I thought I saw him look back twice, but he didn't react. Either he knew I was there and he was fine with it, or I was imagining things.

At last I heard voices. One I recognized, the other I didn't. I knew the Beast for what he was. I knew him better than most. The other speaker wasn't Landon or Charis. How many people were actually in here?

Max slowed to a stop, and I dropped to my knees and slid at an angle, coming to rest behind a pillar. I peeked out a couple of seconds later and saw him standing to the left side of the archway into the room beyond, listening.

I stayed low and made my way forward, dancing from column to column in near silence, doing everything I could to avoid detection. I didn't have any weapons, but I was me again. I held out a hand and watched my fingers grow into sharp talons. I opened my mouth and felt my fangs with my tongue. I was all the weapons I needed.

I still couldn't see what was happening, but I got within a dozen feet of Max without being noticed. Just as I reached the spot, I felt a wave of coldness flow through me, a strange feeling of an immense but silent shockwave of energy. Max had felt it too, and now he was back on the move.

I slipped to the wall where he had just been standing, and ducked my head in. Landon! I could see him now, crouched near the front of the room, behind a display case with a large golden chalice in it, a look of indecision crossing his face. I followed his eyes to a woman I didn't recognize, standing still as a statue, to a man hunched over the Beast, and then to Charis. I snapped back to Max. He was sneaking towards Landon, and now I saw he had a dagger in his hand.

There was no time to try to figure out what was happening. It was obvious Max was here to help the stranger. I swung myself around the archway and into the room, hugging the wall and trying to remain silent. Everything I had gone through over the last five months had come down to this place and this time. I needed to stop Max, but the timing had to be perfect. Otherwise I would mess everything up, instead of helping to fix it.

Max was only a dozen feet away from Landon, and I was almost the same distance from him. I watched Landon rise to his feet, a gun in his hand. A gun? He raised it and held it out, aiming it forwards.

My hands became claws, my senses sharpened.

Max stepped up behind Landon, pulling back his arm to strike.

I lunged forward, covering the remaining distance in one long leap. I came down right behind him with silent grace, digging my left hand into his back, and grabbing his right arm with my right hand. I used my momentum to pull him sideways and throw him away, stopping him from his assassination. Without looking, he locked his arm against my grip and pulled me with him as he tumbled.

I heard a gunshot.

CHAPTER FORTY-TWO

Landon

I HEARD THE COMMOTION BEHIND me, the sound of two bodies crashing into the display of chalices against the wall. I fought every instinct to turn and look. I held my breath, and pulled the trigger.

Clara's head snapped to the left as the bullet pierced her skull and travelled through to the other side. I heard Charis cry out in shock. Malize's head whipped towards me while her body tumbled to the floor.

I felt it instantly. The power unconfined, released from the battery in one tremendous burst. I focused, pulling it into me, gathering it as quickly as it exploded away, taking hold of every line and tendril and dragging it inward towards my soul with a desperation beyond desperation. I traced it through her, to the energy of a dying Beast. Malize had been trying to take it, but he had been resisting.

He didn't resist me.

"*I still hate you, kid,*" I heard in my mind. "*But I hate him more.*"

Malize was on his feet. He stretched a hand out towards me, and I felt the push of his power. I caught it, met it, and turned it around, drawing from a well that seemed infinitely deep. He stumbled back, and then recovered with a smile.

"I had hoped to keep you out of this," he said.

"You knew this might happen," I replied, throwing the gun towards him.

"Balance."

He launched towards me, his entire body changing as he approached.

I focused, casting the power out at his growing mass of dark strength. He fell straight down, once more in human form. He looked up at me.

"I've destroyed one of you already, and you're using the same power. You can't beat me." He swiped his hand to the left, and one of the pedestals flew towards me from the side. I should have been thrown across the room, but I planted my feet and hardened myself. It crumbled against me.

"Do you know why he could't beat you?" I asked. I brought the sword to bear, stepping in towards him and bringing it down. He caught it in his hand and snapped it in half.

"Why?" His face was right next to mine, our eyes locked.

"He didn't have a good enough reason to live."

I focused, pushing against him. The power sent a shockwave through the air that shattered the glass of every display case in the room. Malize flew backwards, slamming into the rear wall and dropping to the ground. I didn't hesitate to chase after him.

He was on his feet again before I could get there. His eyes flared with white energy, and he threw his hands out towards me. I couldn't overpower it this time, and I found myself on my back.

"Erus wanted to be a god. I *am* a god where I come from, Landon. When I'm done with you, I'll be a god here as well."

I rolled away from the blast of power that drove a deep hole into the marble floor, spinning fast enough for the momentum to bring me to my feet. I could feel my power growing even now, the spigot opened fully. I skipped towards him, catching his waist with my arms and powering ahead. We blasted through the wall of the Museum together, and out into the street. Except there was no street, just cold, empty ground. The entire world was burning in blue flame, dark clouds, lightning and wind. Malize used my shock to slam my back, knocking me down.

"The Box can't handle this much power," he said, hovering above me. "You'll destroy your world In your effort to stop me."

I had no choice. I shot up at him, my own energy dancing from my fingertips. It lanced out, catching him off-guard. He screamed in pain and recovered, firing back with his own power.

We circled like that, rising up and up into the Box's atmosphere, into the heavy clouds filled with our warring energy. I strained against the force of his power, and he strained against the force of mine. We traded blows, we ebbed and flowed like the tide. We were evenly matched. Balanced. All of Ross' power versus all of his.

The world around us began to shake.

"You'll kill us all, Landon," Malize said. "Submit, and I'll spare your life, and Charis'. Of all of your kind, I always intended to keep her safe."

I felt like I was burning alive, the power coursing through me reaching its upper limits. I was on fire. I was drenched in ice. I was drowning and suffocating and overwhelmed. I couldn't lose, not like this. We both knew it.

I also couldn't win.

It was a simple decision, made in the height of my pain and in the desperation of distant hope. I let it go. I let all of it go. I dropped my guard, and his power dug into me, lacing me with pain and forcing every part of my soul to cry out in horror. He stopped attacking, and followed me down as I went into free-fall, riding from the heights towards the welcoming ground below.

I closed my eyes and thought of Josette, her plain face and soft smile, her bright and shining heart of pure goodness.

I thought of Ulnyx, my antagonistic conscience, putting the truth before me and pummeling me with it like a blunt instrument.

I thought of Dante, sending me off from my demise to protect the world from dangers we had all underestimated.

I thought of Sarah, of her strength and resolve, and the battle I hoped she would always win.

I thought of Obi, the truest friend I had ever had.

Last, I thought of Charis. I had never truly loved before. I hadn't even known what it meant. She had opened my eyes to everything, in more ways than I could count.

There was one other person, one who I had almost forgotten about. I didn't really know what to make of her, or what to feel or think. She was an afterthought, a piece of my existence I had believed settled.

She was the reason I was going to win.

I hit the ground hard, but I didn't even feel it. Every part of me was already in so much pain, there was nothing left to add. I looked up at Malize, who landed softly at my side and knelt down beside me.

He reached out towards my forehead. "We can only be what we are, Landon."

"I can't believe you fell for that," Rebecca said from behind him.

It was the slightest distraction, but it was what I had been waiting for. I reached up and grabbed Malize's head, twisting it and breaking his neck.

CHAPTER FORTY-THREE

Landon

HIS BODY FELL ON TOP of me, his eyes still open. I could see the power swimming in them. I could almost hear it calling out to me. Rebecca came and knelt at my side, but I ignored her. I lifted my hand and put it to Malize's forehead.

I touched his power.

I took it in.

"Landon, are you okay?" Rebecca asked. Her voice was far away, and growing more distant.

The entire universe of the Box opened up to me as I connected Ross' power to Malize's. I drew it in, and in doing so was revived. I didn't so much stand up as drift to my feet, and then further upward. I floated into the air once more, into the roiling clouds of wayward energy, into the hurricane of unstable power. I held my arms out and commanded it still, and it responded.

I could see everything now. Every line of power that held the Box together, every calculation, every note. I had sensed Rebecca below me right before I had fallen, and had guessed right that Malize was too concerned with me to notice. Now I could feel Charis, the dying energy of the demon Samael, and even those who were gathered in a ring around this place. Malize's energy reached into the Box from the clandestine white star at the top of the prison, the astral glow that I had seen but not understood. It connected this universe to that one, and was the secret sauce to his ingress. Take Ross' power, mix it with his own, and carry both out of the Box and into our world. The truth of it was staggering.

The same option was available to me.

The power of a god, or maybe even two. Enough to challenge God, if that was what I desired. It was certainly enough to keep both sides at rest for all of eternity, and I would never need to lift more than a finger to do it.

I looked down to where Rebecca was standing, gazing up at me. I re-ordered the world. I took away the clouds, I took away the emptiness. I put us in Dante's garden, where the roses shifted in the breeze and a trickling brook poured serenity into a small pond. I lowered myself to the ground, walked past Rebecca and into the mansion, to where Charis was waiting for me.

She was kneeling over Clara, cradling her head in her lap.

"What did you do?" she asked me.

"What do you mean? It's over. We won."

"You killed her."

"Ch…" I started to argue, but we'd had this fight already. "I know. I'm sorry. It was the only way."

Her anger lessened. Not her pain, but her anger. "Malize?"

"Gone. The Beast is gone. I can get us out of here. I can do anything, now. I have their power. All of it." It was strange to say. I couldn't even fathom the depths of what I had under my control.

"Can you bring her back?"

I could, in this place. Maybe I could have even made her real out there. What kind of thing would she be? What kind of life would she live?

"No."

She leaned down and kissed Clara's forehead, and then stood. "Where will she go?"

"She'll always be part of us." I put my arms around her, holding her tight while she sobbed into my shoulder. I don't know how much time passed, but eventually she pulled away and wiped her eyes.

"I love you."

"I love you, too."

We kissed. A simple kiss, basic and plain, a sharing of affection and understanding. I hated that it had to end. I hated the understanding that it gave me.

"Charis... I can't."

"You have to."

"Why?"

"I'm tired, Landon. Finished. I gave everything I had to being a Templar, to protecting the world from the Beast. Only, it wasn't just the Beast, was it? Everything I was fighting for was a lie."

"You mean Malize? Without him, Ross would have destroyed everything a long time ago. He told me he wanted to make God fight, but He does fight. He fights with the free will He gave His creations. He allows us to make our own decisions, and forge our own destiny. Malize knew he might lose. Hell, he gave me everything I needed to defeat him. He had to maintain the balance if he wanted to stay hidden until the last moment."

As I said it, I wasn't so sure. Maybe Malize had intended to lose. Maybe, like Abaddon, he had lived beyond his desire, but couldn't bring himself to make his own end.

"I'm glad you stopped him, Landon. I'm proud of you. I just..." She didn't know what to say, but she didn't need to say it. I saw it in her eyes. I heard it in Abaddon's voice, and in Erus'. For a few eternal life was a gift. For most, it was a curse.

"You'll still have me," I said. It was a weak attempt to change her mind, but it was all I had.

"You don't have to go back," she replied. "It can end for you, too. The fighting, the loss, the hurt. You've done your part. You saved the world."

Maybe if I hadn't seen what Clara had shown me. The death, the destruction. Maybe if I had been more selfish, or more experienced, or more tired. Maybe if my judgement weren't clouded by the power of a god, or my eyes opened with the clarity of one.

"I do," I said. "Someone has to."

She looked down. "I'm sorry."

I picked her chin up with my hand. "Don't be. You saved the world, Charis. You brought me here. You taught me, you trusted me, you loved me. I know what I'm going back to is anything but peaceful, but every day when the sun rises, I'll know it was because of you and I. I'll know that six billion people get their shot at their hundred years, and then another six billion people after that. I'll help them with you in my heart, and in my soul."

I kissed her forehead. I held my lips there and exerted my will on her.

"Rest now. You've earned it."

"I love you," she said again.

It was the last thing I heard. Her body turned to energy, and the energy swirled around me. First, she would be with Clara here in the Box. Then, she would be free.

I watched her dissipate into the air. Right before she did, I captured a single point of light, and I breathed it in. I pushed it down into my soul, and I trapped it there for all of eternity. I couldn't stand to have our connection completely broken.

She would have agreed.

I stood there for hours, still and silent. I let the tears fall, because I was going to miss her. I let my heart soar, because I was happy she was free. Eventually, Rebecca came into the mansion. She didn't speak to me. She just stood there and waited, her own tears joining at my pain. I never would have expected that.

"It's time to go," I said to her at last.

"Landon, I…"

"I forgive you."

I focused, and a new doorway appeared in the center of the room. The door was mottled wood, and I remembered it from a dream. It was a symbol of struggle, and of hope. I pushed it open.

"Go now, Rebecca."

"Aren't you coming?" she asked.

"Yes, but I have one more thing I need to do first. Tell Sarah I'm proud of her. Tell Dante I'll be in touch. Tell Obi, Adam and Elyse that they have my infinite thanks."

"I don't understand."

"You don't need to." I pointed towards the door.

She walked over to it and paused.

"Landon, I..."

I held up my hand, and she stopped. "Be good, Rebecca."

She smiled, winked at me, and stepped through.

I took a deep breath. I could feel the power coursing through me, the energy sizzling at every tip of my being. I had observed what the thirst for it had done on every level. I had witnessed the death, the pain, the destruction. I had seen it in Josette, in Sarah, in Ulnyx, in Gervais and Abaddon, Ross and Malize. I was a diuscrucis. One part demon, one part angel, one part human. That meant I was all parts fallible and corruptible.

Such power didn't belong in my hands.

I held it in my soul for a brief moment. I kept a grip on just enough, and I let the rest go. I pushed it all out into the Box, a Box that I knew couldn't hold it. It didn't need to.

I walked over to the door, took one last look back, and fixed the world.

CHAPTER FORTY-FOUR

Rebecca: Epilogue

"ARE YOU READY?"

I PURSED my lips and stared into the white light in front of me. Master Lu was standing on my right, dressed in the plain gray robes of the House of Life.

"As ready as I'll ever be."

It had been nearly a month since we had freed Landon from the Box. At least, I could only assume he had been freed. The last I had seen of him was right before stepping through the doorway back to the Beast's prison, and rejoining those who had been waiting on the outside. I had waited for him there with the others, only to have it all vanish in a flash of light. The Box, the star, even the prison itself. We had found ourselves back in Gervais' chateau, left to wonder what exactly had happened.

It had only been his words to me, words I shared with the others, which brought us any comfort. They weren't the words of someone who was gone for good. They were the words of someone who needed a break and time to heal their battle scars, who would overcome their grief and loss and return stronger and more resolved than ever.

We'd gone our separate ways then. Dante had returned to Purgatory, bringing a reluctant Alichino with him. Adam had gone back to Heaven to report on the fate of the swords that his Inquisitors had been hunting for so long. Elyse had expressed her need to return to Japan, to a family estate that she could only hope had avoided Gervais' attentions, where she planned to regroup and come to some kind of closure on the death of her father and her status in the Nicht Creidim.

Obi was going to return to New York, but Sarah had wanted to stay, and so he had stayed, naming himself her guardian in Landon's absence. She wanted time to mourn the loss of her friend and mentor, and to deal with the power her father had unlocked with her fury. The chateau was probably hers anyway. I couldn't imagine that any Divine would lay claim to it any time soon, especially if word got out about what she had done to the archfiend.

I had remained a spirit from the moment I had used Elyse to pass along Landon's message until I had been drawn back across the world to the small monastery in China, run by one of the oldest angels on Earth. The world was safe from the Beast and the one called Malus. Landon was free. I had accomplished my mission. I had earned my redemption.

Master Lu had known I was coming. I don't know how, but he knew. He had a volunteer waiting for me, a new initiate to the House who he had yet to gift with the Touch. She was no more than twelve, and her memories were so simple and so pure. After all I had been through and witnessed, it was hard to keep myself from weeping at the beauty of them. I was sure she would make a good monk.

I stared into the white light and shuddered. I was nervous, excited, and afraid. I remembered what the other spirit had said to me. I knew there was a possibility my road to Heaven would end here, at least for now. Still, I was hopeful. I hadn't saved a kitten from a tree, after all.

"Step into the light, child," Master Lu said. "Bare your soul to the Heavenly Host, and allow them to make their judgement."

I held my breath, trying to calm my pounding heart. There was no sense in delaying.

Be good.

It was the last thing Landon had said to me. I had my flaws, but for better or worse, Heaven or not, that was what I was going to do.

Be good.

My host's feet carried me forward until I was inside the light, surrounded by it so that I saw nothing but a field of bright emptiness. I wasn't sure what was supposed to happen, but I felt a warmth surround me for a fleeting instant and then retreat.

I stepped out of the light.

Master Lu was smiling at me. A comforting, gentle smile.

Be good.

CHAPTER FORTY-FIVE

Landon: Epilogue

I WATCHED THE WAVES ROLL across the beach. It was early morning on a clear day. A crisp breeze was blowing from the north. The sun would be coming up soon.

I hadn't missed a single sunrise in the three months since I had gotten out of the Box. Even when it was cloudy or raining I would come out here, I would look in the direction I knew it to be, and I would smile. It wasn't just because it meant humanity got one more day, it was also because I knew Charis was out there somewhere, and in a sense so was Clara.

I had made myself a new body, a replica of what I had lost, but no longer a thing of the Divine. I had taken the Box, and I had brought it with me to this remote place, unseen by those gathered in the Beast's prison. I had left the doorway open, and I had pushed it up into the stars, where the energy would leak out and become a smaller part of the thread that wove this universe to all of the other universes. Then I had stretched out in the sand below those stars and cried myself to sleep.

I had done the same every day for eighty-one days, alone with my thoughts, my grief, and my joy. I had seen the potentials of my future in the despair of the Beast, but in the end I rejected them. I wasn't him, and he wasn't me. I was free to choose, and my choice was to stick with the hope and the unbreakable spirit that made every single member of mankind capable of rising up to do great things. My plan wasn't so much to be their protector, as it was to help them learn to protect themselves. The Nicht Creidim weren't right, but they weren't completely wrong either. There had to be a balance there, somewhere.

In the end, if I taught them, and I helped them, then the loss of one diuscrucis would never be enough to break the world. It would never be enough to break the will and the spirit.

The game was over. We had won.

A new game would start soon.

I was ready.

Author's Note:

There was some confusion after the release of Broken that it was the end of the Divine Series. I want to make sure I avoid making the same mistake twice. This IS the end of what I've been self-referring to as 'the Beast Cycle'. It IS NOT the end of the Divine novels.

Landon's adventures will continue.

I can't say thank you enough to everyone who has gone on this ride with me. I appreciate your continued patronage and support, and I hope to be able to keep entertaining you for years to come.

Join the Mailing List!

"No," you cry. "I will not submit myself to even more inbox spam. I have quite enough garbage coming in from people and places that I care a lot more about than you."

"But," I reply, "if you sign up for my mailing list, you'll know when my next book is out. Don't you want to know when my next book is out?"

"Eh... I'll find it on Amazon."

"True enough, but you see, a mailing list is very valuable to an author, especially a meager self-published soul such as myself. I don't have a marketing team, and I don't have exposure in brick and mortar stores around the world to help improve my readership. All I have is you, my potential fans. How about a bribe?"

"Hmm... Keep talking."

"Picture this... giveaways, a chance at FREE books. There is a 10% chance* you could save at least three dollars per year!"

Silence.

"Where'd you go?" I ask. "Well, I'll just leave this here, in case you change your mind."

http://mrforbes.com/mailinglist

* For illustration only. Not an actual mathematical probability.

Thank You!

It is readers like you, who take a chance on self-published works that is what makes the very existence of such works possible. Thank you so very much for spending your hard-earned money, time, and energy on this work. It is my sincerest hope that you have enjoyed reading!

Independent authors could not continue to thrive without your support. If you have enjoyed this, or any other independently published work, please consider taking a moment to leave a review at the source of your purchase. Reviews have an immense impact on the overall commercial success of a given work, and your voice can help shape the future of the people whose efforts you have enjoyed.

Thank you again!

About the Author

I grew up with books. When I was eleven, I used to ride my bicycle three miles to the nearest bookstore to check the shelves for any new science fiction or fantasy titles they may have added in the last week, and eagerly put down almost all of my paper route money for the pleasure of escaping to a different place.

It's hard to be an avid reader without wanting to create worlds of your own, and so that's what I then set out to do. Too many years later, it's a dream come true to be published, and have people read and enjoy my work.

Mailing List:

http://bit.ly/XRbZ5n

Website:

http://www.mrforbes.com

Facebook:

http://www.facebook.com/mrforbes.author

Goodreads:

http://www.goodreads.com/author/show/6912725.M_R_Forbes

Twitter:

http://www.twitter.com/mrforbes

Printed in Great Britain
by Amazon